Rumi, known in Iran and Central Asia as Mowlana Jalaloddin Balkhi, was born in 1207 in the province of Balkh, now the border region between Afghanistan and Tajikistan. His family emigrated when he was still a child, shortly before Genghis Khan and his Mongol army arrived in Balkh. They settled permanently in Konya, central Anatolia, which was formerly part of the Eastern Roman Empire (Rum). Rumi was probably introduced to Sufism originally through his father, Baha Valad, a popular preacher who also taught Sufi piety to a group of disciples. However, the turning-point in Rumi's life came in 1244, when he met in Konya a mysterious wandering Sufi called Shamsoddin of Tabriz. Shams, as he is most often referred to by Rumi, taught him the profoundest levels of Sufism, transforming him from a pious religious scholar to an ecstatic mystic. Rumi expressed his new vision of reality in volumes of mystical poetry. His enormous collection of lyrical poetry is considered one of the best that has ever been produced, while his poem in rhyming couplets, the *Masnavi*, is so revered as the most consummate expression of Sufi mysticism that it is commonly referred to as 'the Qur'an in Persian'.

When Rumi died, on 17 December 1273, shortly after having completed his work on the *Masnavi*, his passing was deeply mourned by the citizens of Konya, including the Christian and Jewish communities. His disciples formed the Mevlevi Sufi order, which was named after Rumi, whom they referred to as 'Our Lord' (Turkish 'Mevlana', Persian 'Mowlana'). They are better known in Europe and North America as the Whirling Dervishes, because of the distinctive dance that they now perform as one of their central rituals. Rumi's death is commemorated annually in Konya, attracting pilgrims from all corners of the globe and every religion. The popularity of his poetry has risen so much in the last couple of decades that the Christian Science Monitor identified Rumi as the most published poet in America in 1997. The popularity of Rumi's poetry in English translation has spread to Europe more recently, and UNESCO designated the commemoration of the eight hundredth anniversary of Rumi's birth in 2007 as an event of major international importance.

Jawid Mojaddedi, a native of Afghanistan, is Professor of Religion at Rutgers University. He was a 2014–15 National Endowment for the Arts Literature Translation Fellow. Dr Mojaddedi's translation, *The Masnavi: Book One* (Oxford, 2004), was awarded the Lois Roth Prize by the American Institute of Iranian Studies. His previous books include *Beyond Dogma: Rumi's Teachings on Friendship with God and Early Sufi Theories* (Oxford, 2012) and *The Biographical Tradition in Sufism* (Richmond, 2001).

OXFORD WORLD'S CLASSICS

*For over 100 years Oxford World's Classics have brought
readers closer to the world's great literature. Now with over 700
titles—from the 4,000-year-old myths of Mesopotamia to the
twentieth century's greatest novels—the series makes available
lesser-known as well as celebrated writing.*

*The pocket-sized hardbacks of the early years contained
introductions by Virginia Woolf, T. S. Eliot, Graham Greene,
and other literary figures which enriched the experience of reading.
Today the series is recognized for its fine scholarship and
reliability in texts that span world literature, drama and poetry,
religion, philosophy, and politics. Each edition includes perceptive
commentary and essential background information to meet the
changing needs of readers.*

OXFORD WORLD'S CLASSICS

JALAL AL-DIN RUMI

The Masnavi

BOOK FOUR

Translated with an Introduction and Notes by
JAWID MOJADDEDI

OXFORD
UNIVERSITY PRESS

OXFORD
UNIVERSITY PRESS

Great Clarendon Street, Oxford, OX2 6DP,
United Kingdom

Oxford University Press is a department of the University of Oxford.
It furthers the University's objective of excellence in research, scholarship,
and education by publishing worldwide. Oxford is a registered trade mark of
Oxford University Press in the UK and in certain other countries

First published as an Oxford World's Classics paperback 2017

Impression: 8

Published in the United States of America by Oxford University Press
198 Madison Avenue, New York, NY 10016, United States of America

British Library Cataloguing in Publication Data
Data available

Library of Congress Control Number: 2017931341

ISBN 978-0-19-878343-5

Printed and bound in Great Britain by
Clays Ltd, Elcograf S.p.A.

This volume is dedicated to the memory of
Paul E. Weber
(d. 25 February 2016)

ACKNOWLEDGEMENTS

I SHOULD like to express my gratitude to my family, my friends, and all of the teachers I have studied under. Time spent with Dr Alireza Nurbakhsh and the late Paul E. Weber served as an inspiring reminder of the living reality of what Rumi points to in his thirteenth-century poem. I am indebted to the National Endowment for the Arts for awarding me a literature translation fellowship in 2014–15, during which time most of this translation was completed. I alone am responsible for any flaws.

CONTENTS

THE MASNAVI
BOOK FOUR

INTRODUCTION

Rumi and Sufism

RUMI has long been recognized within the Sufi tradition as one of the most important Sufis to have lived. He not only produced the finest Sufi poetry in Persian, but was also the master of disciples who later named their order after him. Moreover, by virtue of the intense devotion he expressed towards his own master, Shams-e Tabriz, Rumi has become the archetypal Sufi disciple. From that perspective, the unprecedented level of interest in Rumi's poetry over the last couple of decades in North America and Europe does not come as a total surprise.

Rumi lived some 300 years after the first writings of Muslim mystics were produced. A distinct mystical path called 'Sufism' became clearly identifiable in the ninth century and was systematized from the late tenth and eleventh centuries. The authors of these works, who were mostly from north-eastern Persia, traced the origins of the Sufi tradition back to the Prophet Mohammad, while at the same time acknowledging the existence of comparable forms of mysticism before his mission. They mapped out a mystical path, by which the Sufi ascends towards the ultimate goal of union with God and knowledge of reality. More than two centuries before the time of the eminent Sufi theosopher Ebn 'Arabi (d. 1240), Sufis began to describe their experience of annihilation in God and the realization that only God truly exists. The illusion of one's own independent existence began to be regarded as the main obstacle to achieving this realization, so that early Sufis like Abu Yazid Bestami (d. 874) are frequently quoted as belittling the value of the asceticism of some of their contemporaries on the grounds that it merely increased attention to themselves. An increasing number of Sufis began to regard love of God as the means of overcoming the root problem of one's own sense of being, rather than piety and asceticism. The most influential of these men was al-Hallaj, who was the most prolific Sufi poet of his time and was executed for heresy in 922.[1]

The Sufi practice discussed the most in the early manuals of Sufism

---

[1] Translations of representative samples of the key texts of early Sufism are available in M. Sells, *Early Islamic Mysticism* (Mahwah, 1996).

is that of listening to music (*sama*'; see Glossary). Listening, while immersed in the remembrance of God and unaware of oneself, to love poetry and the mystical poetry that Sufis themselves had begun to write, often with musical accompaniment, induced ecstasy in worshippers. The discussions in Sufi manuals of spontaneous movements by Sufis in ecstasy while listening to music, and the efforts made to distinguish this from ordinary dance, suggest that this practice had already started to cause a great deal of controversy. Most of the Sufi orders that were eventually formed developed the practice of surrendering to spontaneous movements while listening to music, but the whirling ceremony in white costumes of the followers of Rumi is a unique phenomenon.[2] Although it is traditionally traced back to Rumi's own propensity for spinning around in ecstasy, the elaborate ceremony in the form in which it has become famous today was established only centuries later.

The characteristics of the Sufi mystic who has completed the path to enlightenment is one of the most recurrent topics in Sufi writings of the tenth and eleventh centuries. Students of Sufism at that time would tend to associate with several such individuals rather than form an exclusive bond with one master. By the twelfth century, however, the master–disciple relationship became increasingly emphasized, as the first Sufi orders began to be formed. It was also during this century that the relationship between love of God and His manifestation in creation became a focus of interest, especially among Sufis of Persian origin, such as Ahmad Ghazali (d. 1126) and Ruzbehan Baqli (d. 1209), both of whom drew inspiration from the aforementioned al-Hallaj. The former's more famous brother Abu Hamed was responsible for integrating Sufism with mainstream Sunni Islam, as a practical form of Muslim piety that can provide irrefutable knowledge of religious truths through direct mystical experience.[3]

In this way, by the thirteenth century diverse forms of Sufism had developed and become increasingly popular. Rumi was introduced to Sufism by his father, Baha Valad, who followed a more conservative

---

[2] Concerning the contrast between the Mevlevi *sama*' and other forms of Sufi *sama*', see J. During, 'What is Sufi Music?', in L. Lewisohn, ed., *The Legacy of Medieval Persian Sufism* (London, 1992), 277–87.

[3] The chapter of Abu Hamed Ghazali's autobiography which describes his experience on the Sufi path is available in translation in N. Calder, J. Mojaddedi, and A. Rippin, eds. and trs., *Classical Islam: A Sourcebook of Religious Literature* (London, 2012), 299–302.

tradition of Muslim piety, but his life was transformed when he encountered the profound mystic Shams-e Tabriz. Although many of the followers of the tradition of his father considered Shams to be totally unworthy of Rumi's time and attention, Rumi considered Shams to be the most complete manifestation of God. He expressed his complete love and devotion for his master Shams, with whom he spent only about two years in total, through thousands of ecstatic lyrical poems. Towards the end of his life he presented the fruit of his experience of Sufism in the form of the *Masnavi*, which has been judged by many commentators, both within the Sufi tradition and outside it, to be the greatest mystical poem ever written.

Rumi and His Times

The century in which Rumi lived was one of the most tumultous in the history of the Middle East and Central Asia. When he was about 10 years old the region was invaded by the Mongols, who, under the leadership of Genghis Khan, left death and destruction in their wake. Arriving through Central Asia and north-eastern Persia, the Mongols soon took over almost the entire region, conquering Baghdad in 1258. The collapse of the once glorious Abbasid caliphate, the symbolic capital of the entire Muslim world, at the hands of an infidel army was felt throughout the region as a tremendous shock. Soon afterwards, there was a sign that the map of the region would continue to change, when the Mongols suffered a major defeat in Syria, at Ayn Jalut in 1260. Rumi's life was directly affected by the military and political developments of the time, beginning with his family's emigration from north-eastern Persia just a couple of years before the Mongols arrived to conquer that region. Although they eventually relocated to Konya (ancient Iconium) in central Anatolia, Rumi witnessed the spread of Mongol authority across that region too when he was still a young man.

In spite of the upheaval and destruction across the region during this century, there were many outstanding Sufi authors among Rumi's contemporaries. The most important Sufi theosopher ever to have lived, Ebn 'Arabi (d. 1240), produced his highly influential works during the first half of the century. His student and foremost interpreter, Sadroddin Qunyavi (d. 1273), settled in Konya some fifteen years after his master's death and became associated with Rumi. This could have been one channel through which Rumi gained familiarity with Ebn 'Arabi's theosophical system, although his poetry does not clearly suggest the direct influence of the latter's works.

The lives of two of the most revered Sufi poets also overlapped with Rumi's life: the most celebrated Arab Sufi poet, Ebn al-Fared (d. 1235), whose poetry holds a position of supreme importance comparable with that of Rumi in the Persian canon; and Faridoddin 'Attar (d. *c.*1220), who was Rumi's direct predecessor in the composition of Persian mystical *masnavis* (see below), including the highly popular work which has been translated as *The Conference of the Birds*.[4] It is perhaps not surprising that the Sufi poet Jami (d. 1492) should want to link Rumi with 'Attar directly by claiming that they met when Rumi's family migrated from Balkh; 'Attar is said to have recognized his future successor in the composition of works in the mystical *masnavi* genre during that visit, when Rumi was still a young boy. Soon afterwards 'Attar was killed by the Mongols during their conquest of Nishapur.

As the Mongols advanced westwards, Anatolia became an increasingly attractive destination for the inhabitants of central parts of the Middle East who wished to flee. A number of important Sufis and influential scholars chose this option, including Hajji Bektash (d. *c.*1272), the eponym of the Bektashi order which went on to become one of the most influential Sufi orders in Anatolia in subsequent centuries, and Najmoddin Razi (d. 1256), whose teacher, Najmoddin Kobra (d. 1221), the eponym of the Kobravi order, had been killed during the Mongol invasion of Transoxiana.

Many works have been written about Rumi's life in Konya, since shortly after his death, but contradictions in these sources, and the hagiographic nature of most of the material compiled, mean that a number of important details remain uncertain. Nonetheless, the general outline of the life of Rumi seems to be presented relatively consistently in the sources, and remains helpful for putting the *Masnavi* into context.

Rumi was born in September 1207 in the province of Balkh, in what is now the border region between Afghanistan and Tajikistan. His father, Baha Valad, was a preacher and religious scholar who also

---

[4] See e.g. F. Attar, *The Conference of the Birds*, ed. and tr. A. Darbandi and D. Davis (Harmondsworth, 1983).

led a group of Sufi disciples. When Rumi was about 10 years old his family emigrated to Anatolia, having already relocated a few years earlier to Samarqand in Transoxiana. This emigration seems to have been motivated primarily by the approach of Genghis Khan's Mongol army, although rivalries between Baha Valad and various religious scholars in the region may have also played a part. Instead of directly moving westwards, Rumi's family first made the pilgrimage to Mecca, and it was only a few years after arriving in Anatolia that they decided to settle permanently in Konya. By this time, Rumi had already married (1224) and seen the birth of his son and eventual successor in Sufism, SoltanValad (1226).

In Konya, Baha Valad found the opportunity, under the patronage of the Seljuk ruler Alaoddin Kay Qobad I (r. 1219–36), to continue his work as a preacher and to teach students in a religious school. He had been grooming Rumi to be his successor, but died only a couple of years after settling in Konya, in 1231. Although the original reasons for his arrival remain unclear, it seems that one of Baha Valad's students, called Borhanoddin Mohaqqeq, arrived in Konya from northeastern Persia soon afterwards to take over the management of his school. He also took responsibility for overseeing the continuation of Rumi's education and training. Within a few years, Borhanoddin had sent Rumi to Aleppo and Damascus to continue his education in the religious sciences. It is possible that during his stay in Damascus Rumi may have heard the lectures of Ebn 'Arabi, who was living there at the time. Rumi returned to Konya in around 1237 as a highly accomplished young scholar, and took over leadership of Baha Valad's school from Borhanoddin.

After his return to Konya, Rumi's reputation as an authority on religious matters became firmly established there, and he reached the peak of his career as a scholar, achieving what his father seems to have hoped for him. In November 1244, after seven years of excelling as a religious teacher, Rumi experienced a challenging encounter that would prove to be the most significant event of his life. As one would expect, an event as important as this has generated many competing accounts. However, most versions at least share the same basic elements. According to one popular and relatively simple account, Rumi is asked about his books by an uneducated-looking stranger, and responds by snapping back dismissively, 'They are something that you do not understand!' The books then suddenly catch fire, so Rumi asks the stranger to explain what has happened. His reply is: 'Something you do not understand.'

Rumi was immediately drawn to this mysterious figure, who turned out to be a wandering mystic called Shamsoddin from Tabriz (known popularly as Shams, or Shams-e Tabriz) in north-western Persia. The two began to spend endless hours together in retreat. What was shared by the pair during this time remains a mystery that can only be guessed from the volumes of poetry that it inspired.

What is reported consistently about the period of approximately a year and a half that Rumi spent with Shams is that it provoked intense jealousy and resentment among his disciples, who also feared that their highly respected master was risking his reputation by mixing with someone so unworthy in their eyes. These disciples eventually drove Shams away, but, on hearing reports of sightings of him in Syria, Rumi sent his own son, Soltan Valad, to ask him to come back. Although Shams did return a year later, in 1247, he soon disappeared forever. According to tradition, Shams was killed by Rumi's disciples after they had seen that driving him away had failed to separate him permanently from their master.

Although he was already a respected religious authority in Konya and had trained in a tradition of Sufi piety under his father, whom he succeeded as master, Rumi frequently affirms that he was led by Shams to a far loftier level of Sufi mysticism. His poetry, for instance, emphasizes the importance of love in transcending attachments to the world, and dismisses concerns for worldly reputation, literal-mindedness, and intellectualism. From dry scholarship and popular piety, Rumi turned his attention to mystical poetry, and he became known for his propensity to fall into an ecstatic trance and whirl around himself in public. The fact that Rumi's writings are replete with biting criticisms of religious scholars and intellectuals should be seen as a sign of his own background which he had turned away from: he draws upon their kind of scholarship subversively again and again even as he tears it apart, showing that he had already mastered it in the past. Rumi innovatively named his own collection of ghazals, or lyrical poems, as 'the Collection of Shams' (*Divan-e Shams*) rather than as his own collection, and also included Shams's name at the end of many of his individual ghazals, where by convention the poet would identify himself. This can be seen as Rumi's acknowledgement of the all-important inspiration that Shams had provided for him.

After the final disappearance of Shams, Rumi remained in Konya and continued to direct his father's school. However, he chose to appoint as deputy, with the responsibility to manage many of the affairs of the school in his place, a goldsmith called Salahoddin. Like Shams, he was disliked by many of Rumi's disciples, who considered him uneducated. A colourful story about the first encounter between the two describes Rumi as falling into ecstasy and whirling, on hearing the rhythmic beating of Salahoddin at work in his market stall. After Salahoddin's death in 1258, Rumi appointed Hosamoddin Chalabi in his place. When Hosamoddin became a disciple of Rumi he was already the head of a local order for the training of young men in chivalry. He brought with him his own disciples, the wealth of his order, and the expertise he had acquired in running such an institution. However, his most important contribution was serving as Rumi's scribe and putting the *Masnavi* into writing as Rumi recited it aloud. Rumi praises Hosamoddin profusely in the introduction of the *Masnavi*, which on occasion he even calls 'the Hosam book', indicating the vital importance of Hosamoddin's role in this work (see, for example, the first page of the poem in Book Four).

In addition to Rumi's poetry, three prose works have also survived: collections of his letters, sermons, and teaching sessions. These reveal much about aspects of his life that have been neglected by most biographers. His letters testify to his influence among the local political rulers and his efforts to secure positions of importance for his disciples through letters of recommendation. This contradicts the popular image of Rumi withdrawing from public life after the disappearance of Shams. It would be more accurate to say that he entrusted everyday matters, including the training of disciples, to his deputies, but he still represented the order in external matters. His collection of seven sermons attests to the fact that he was highly esteemed by the local Muslim population. It reveals that he delivered sermons at the main congregational mosque on important occasions, and that he used such opportunities to give Sufi teachings, albeit within the rigid constraints of a formal sermon. Rumi's most important prose work, however, is the written record of his teaching sessions, which was compiled after his death by his students as seventy-one discourses. This work, called 'In it is what is in it'—probably on account of its diverse and unclassified contents—provides intimate glimpses of Rumi as a Sufi master. The content of this work is comparable with his didactic poem the *Masnavi*, in that it contains many of the same teachings.

Rumi died on 17 December 1273, probably very soon after the completion of the *Masnavi*. Tradition tells us that physicians could not identify the illness from which he was suffering, and that his death was mourned not only by his disciples but also by the large and diverse community in Konya, including Christians and Jews, who converged as his body was carried through the city. Many of the non-Muslims had not only admired him as outsiders, but had also attended his teaching sessions. The 'Green Dome', where his mausoleum is found today, was constructed soon after Rumi's death. It has become probably the most popular site of pilgrimage in the world to be visited regularly by members of every major religion.

Hosamoddin Chalabi served as the leader of Rumi's school for the first twelve years after Rumi's death, and was succeeded by Soltan Valad. Rumi's disciples named their school 'the Mevlevi order' after him, for they used to refer to him by the title 'Mevlana' (in Arabic 'Mowlana', meaning 'Our Lord'). It became widespread and influential especially under the Ottoman empire and remains an active Sufi order in Turkey as well as in many other countries across the world. The Mevlevis are better known in the West as 'the Whirling Dervishes' because of the distinctive dance that they perform to music as the central ritual of the order.

The Masnavi *Form*

Rumi chose a plain, descriptive name for his poem, 'masnavi' being the name of the rhyming couplet verse form. Each half-line, or hemistich, of a *masnavi* poem follows the same metre, in common with other forms of classical Persian poetry. The metre of Rumi's *Masnavi* is the *ramal* metre in apocopated form ($- \breve{\ } - - / - \breve{\ } - - / - \breve{\ } -$), a highly popular metre which was also used by 'Attar for his *Conference of the Birds*. What distinguishes the *masnavi* form from other Persian verse forms is the rhyme, which changes in successive couplets according to the pattern *aa bb cc dd* etc. Thus, in contrast to the other verse forms, which require a restrictive monorhyme, the *masnavi* form enables poets to compose long works consisting of thousands of verses.

The *masnavi* form satisfied the need felt by Persians to compose narrative and didactic poems, of which there was already before the

Islamic period a long and rich tradition. By Rumi's time a number of Sufis had already made use of the *masnavi* form to compose mystical poems, the most celebrated among which are Sana'i's (d. 1138) *Hadiqato'l-haqiqat*, or *Garden of Truth*, and 'Attar's *Manteqo't-tayr*, or *Conference of the Birds*. According to tradition, it was the popularity of these works amongst Rumi's disciples that prompted Hosamoddin, Rumi's deputy, to ask him to compose his own mystical *masnavi* for their benefit.

Hosamoddin served as Rumi's scribe in a process of text production that is traditionally described as being similar to the way in which the Qur'an was produced. However, while tradition tells us that the Sufi poet Rumi recited the *Masnavi* orally when he felt inspired to do so, with Hosamoddin always ready to record those recitations in writing for him as well as to assist him in revising and editing the final poem, the illiterate Prophet Mohammad is said to have recited aloud divine revelation in piecemeal fashion, in exactly the form that God's words were revealed to him through the Angel Gabriel. Those companions of the Prophet who were present on such occasions would write down the revelations and memorize them, and these written and mental records eventually formed the basis of the compilation of the Qur'an many years after the Prophet's death.

The process of producing the *Masnavi* was probably started in around 1262, although tradition relates that Rumi had already composed the first eighteen couplets by the time Hosamoddin made his request; we are told that Rumi responded by pulling a sheet of paper out of his turban with the first part of the prologue of Book One, 'The Song of the Reed', already written on it. References to their system of production can be found in the text of the *Masnavi* itself (e.g. I, v. 2947). They seem to have worked on the *Masnavi* during the evenings in particular, and in one instance Rumi begs forgiveness for having kept Hosamoddin up for an entire night with it (I, v. 1817). After Hosamoddin had written down Rumi's recitations, they were read back to him to be checked and corrected.

Rumi's *Masnavi* belongs to the group of works written in this verse form that do not have a frame narrative. In this way, it contrasts with the more cohesively structured *Conference of the Birds*, which is already well known in translation. It is also much longer; the *Conference* is roughly the same length as just one of the six component books of the *Masnavi*. Each of the six books consists of about 4,000 verses and has its own prose introduction and prologue. There are no epilogues.

The component narratives, homilies, commentaries on citations, prayers, and lyrical flights which make up the body of each book of the *Masnavi* are often demarcated by their own headings. The text of longer narratives tends to be broken up into sections by further such headings. Sometimes these headings are positioned inappropriately, such as in the middle of continuous speech, which might be interpreted as a sign that they may have been inserted only after the text had been prepared (e.g. vv. 1528 and 1642 in this volume). Occasionally the headings are actually longer than the passage that they represent, and serve to explain and contextualize what follows. It is as if, on rereading the text, further explanation was felt necessary in the form of an expanded heading.

The frequency of breaks in the flow of narratives, which is a distinctive characteristic of the *Masnavi*, reveals that Rumi has earned a reputation as an excellent storyteller despite being primarily concerned with conveying his teachings in homily form as frequently as possible to his Sufi disciples. The *Masnavi* leaves the impression that he was brimming with ideas, images, and intense feelings which would overflow when prompted by the subtlest of associations. In this way, free from the constraints of a frame narrative, Rumi has been able to produce a work that is far richer in content and more multivocal than any other example of the mystical *masnavi* genre. That this has been achieved often at the expense of preserving continuity in the narratives seems to corroborate Rumi's opinion on the relative importance of the teachings in his poetry over its aesthetic value, as reported in his discourses.[5] If it were not for the fact that his digressive 'overflowings' are expressed in simple language and with imagery that was immediately accessible to his contemporary readers, all the time held together by the consistent metre and rhyme of the *masnavi* form, they would have constituted an undesirable impediment to understanding the poem. Where this leads Rumi to interweave narratives and to alternate between different speakers and his own commentaries, the text can still be difficult to follow, and, for most contemporary readers, the relevance of citations and allusions to the Qur'an and the traditions of the Prophet will not be immediately obvious without reference to

---

[5] Rumi expresses his frustration about having to return to the narrative after a break also towards the start of Book Two (Rumi, *The Masnavi: Book Two*, tr. J. Mojaddedi (Oxford, 2007), vv. 194–202).

the explanatory notes that have been provided in this edition. None the less, it should be evident, not least from the lengthy sequences of metaphors that Rumi often provides to reinforce a single point, that he has striven to communicate his message as effectively as possible rather than to write obscurely and force the reader to struggle to understand him.

Rumi made painstaking efforts to convey his teachings as clearly and effectively as possible, using simple language, the *masnavi* verse form, entertaining stories, and the most vivid and accessible imagery possible. The aim of the present translation is to render Rumi's *Masnavi* into a relatively simple and attractive form which, with the benefit of metre and rhyme, may enable as many readers as possible to read the whole book with pleasure and to find it rewarding.

Book Four of the Masnavi

The current volume is a translation of the fourth book of the *Masnavi*, and follows Books One, Two, and Three, also published in Oxford World's Classics.

As mentioned in the introduction to Book Three, the major preoccupation of each book of the *Masnavi* is indicated in its exordium and prose introduction. For instance, that of Book Three is pointed out at the very start of the Prose Introduction with which it begins. Rumi comments: 'Pieces of wisdom are the armies of God by which He strengthens the spirits of seekers, and keeps their knowledge away from the tarnish of ignorance' (III, p. 3). Book Three as a whole correspondingly presents Rumi's epistemology by classifying different levels of knowledge, from the limited amount possessed by fools who are controlled by their lusts and the rational knowledge of the well-educated to the all-consuming mystical knowledge of the Sufi adept, or 'Friend of God' (*wali*), and it does so largely by means of teaching-stories that involve nourishment. Book Two similarly begins with an exordium that stresses the importance of choosing one's companions carefully, and then expands on this teaching through its stories, while Book One, as mentioned earlier, begins with the famous 'Song of the Reed' about the origins of Man with God and then culminates in the story about Ali ebn Abi Taleb succeeding in making the return journey to Him.

Book Three is joined with Book Four through its final story, 'The Union of the lover who was not true', which begins in Book Three and finishes in Book Four, and also shares a common general preoccupation with epistemology. However, in Book Four, the focus is the divinely revealed knowledge of the Prophets and Friends of God, which is compared in its exordium with the light of the sun.

In Book Four, Rumi's main aim is to highlight the superiority of divinely revealed knowledge over the highest of other forms of knowledge, namely the rational knowledge of the philosophers. For instance, he specifically compares the former favourably with the knowledge of the most celebrated Islamic philosopher, Avicenna (v. 507), and also includes a whole section on 'the difference between philosophers and mystics'. More specifically, he clarifies there that philosophers say 'Man is the microcosm' while mystics say 'Man is the macrocosm', and that this is because the knowledge of philosophers is restricted to the form of Man, while that of mystics penetrates to the inner being of Man (vv. 522–38).

Rumi argues that divinely revealed knowledge is also actually the source of the intellect's knowledge with the example about how burying corpses was learnt by Cain after observing a crow which had received knowledge about burial by inspiration from God (*elham*; v. 1308). Moreover, divinely revealed knowledge sees for certain the outcomes ahead rather than only what is immediately perceptible in the material world (vv. 1619–20). Regarding such matters the intellect must rely on mere conjecture (vv. 3221–42). Rumi's universal tendency can be seen in his implication that the potential for mystical perception is inside humans like forgotten butter in buttermilk, and can be rediscovered through being shaken by a Prophet or mystic (vv. 3031–51). With such knowledge, the Unseen world can be discovered and translated through the material world (vv. 3052–73). The latter is in fact a representation of the former, which comes prior in the causal chain (vv. 3678–97).

The main theme can also be detected in Rumi's choice of stories. It should be no surprise that Solomon features prominently in this book, and that the story of Moses and Pharaoh contrasts Moses' prophetic knowledge with the intellect of Pharaoh and his vizier Haman. This book also includes two of the longest stories about Rumi's favourite early Sufi, Bayazid Bastami, whom he mentions much more frequently in his oeuvre than any other. The first of these concerns his knowledge about the future, which Rumi compares with that of the Prophet Mohammad, even going as far as to say that Bayazid's knowledge comes from the same source as that of Mohammad, the Preserved Tablet in heaven (v. 1852; see 'Tablet' in the Glossary). Ebrahim ebn-e Adham, the second most frequently mentioned Sufi in the *Masnavi*, is also the subject of a story here (vv. 727 ff.). It discusses the Sufi practice of *sama'*, a recurrent topic in this book, with a stress on the conviction that music is a powerful medium for divine communication.

It has been common to identify the story about the old harpist in Book One as one that may be autobiographical, because of Rumi's undeniable sensitivity to music. However, it should not be forgotten that he was an accomplished religious scholar before his transformation into an uncompromising mystic, which is reflected even in the stories about his life-changing first conversation with Shams-e Tabrizi. This important point may help explain why even in Book One it is the story about the limitations of intellectual knowledge ('The Bedouin and his wife') which is by far the longest, while in Book Four Rumi devotes more than 3,800 verses to his central preoccupation about the overwhelming superiority of divinely revealed knowledge over the intellectual knowledge he had once prized so much.

NOTE ON THE TRANSLATION

RUMI put his teachings into the *masnavi* verse form in order that, with the benefit of metre and rhyme, his disciples might enjoy reading them. I have therefore decided to translate Rumi's *Masnavi* into verse, in accordance with the aim of the original work. I have chosen to use rhyming iambic pentameters, since this is the closest corresponding form of English verse to the Persian *masnavi* form of rhyming couplets. These are numbered and referred to as verses in the Explanatory Notes and Introduction.

Book Four of the *Masnavi* consists of over 3,800 couplets, the continuity of which is broken up only by section headings. For the sake of clarity, in this translation further breaks have been added to those created by the section headings. In order for the Contents pages to fulfil their function effectively, alternative headings have been employed there, albeit at corresponding points to the major section headings in the text, which refer in many instances to merely the first few subsequent verses rather than representing the section as a whole.

Although the *Masnavi* is a Persian poem, it contains a substantial amount of Arabic text. This invariably takes the form of citations from Arabic sources and common religious formulae, but the sources for some of these passages are either unknown or oral. Italics have been used to indicate Arabic text, except in the section headings, which are fully italicized. Many Arabic terms and religious formulae have become part of the Persian language, and have therefore not been highlighted in this way. Capitalization has been used when reference is made to God. This includes, in addition to the pronouns and titles commonly used in English, the ninety-nine names of God of the Islamic tradition, as well as certain philosophical terms.

Most of the sources of the *Masnavi* are not widely available in English, if at all, and so references have been provided in the notes only for citations of the Qur'an. Verse numbering varies in the most widely available translations of the Qur'an, some of which do not in fact number individual verses, but since this variation is very slight (a maximum of a few verses) the reader should still be able to find the relevant passages without difficulty. The notes also identify those passages in the translation which represent the sayings and deeds of the Prophet Mohammad (*hadith*) when this is not already self-evident in the text (e.g. by 'the Prophet said'). It should be pointed out that citations in the original *Masnavi* are very often variants of the original sources, including the Qur'an, rather than exact renderings, due to the constraints of the metre that is used. The same applies in this verse translation.

This translation corresponds exactly to the text of the fourth volume of the edition prepared by Mohammad Estelami (6 vols. and index, Tehran, 2nd edn., 1990). This is by far the best critical edition that has been prepared, since it offers a complete apparatus criticus, indicating the variant readings in all the early manuscripts more comprehensively and transparently than any other edition. Although R. A. Nicholson's edition of the Persian text is more widely available, due to the fact that it is published in Europe, its shortcomings for today are widely recognized and outweigh the advantage of having his exactly corresponding prose translation and commentary to refer to.

As far as possible, the English equivalents of technical terms have been provided, in preference to giving the original in transliteration and relying on explanatory notes. Where it is provided, the transliteration of names and terms has been simplified to such a degree that diacritics are rarely used. It is designed simply to help the reader use Persian pronunciation, especially where this would affect the metre and rhyme.

SELECT BIBLIOGRAPHY

General Background

J. T. P. De Bruijn, *Persian Sufi Poetry: An Introduction to the Mystical Use of Classical Poems* (Richmond, 1997).

C. W. Ernst, *The Shambhala Guide to Sufism* (Boston, 1997).

L. Lewisohn, ed., *Classical Persian Sufism: From its Origins to Rumi* (London, 1993).

J. W. Morris, 'Situating Islamic Mysticism: Between Written Traditions and Popular Spirituality', in R. Herrera, ed., *Mystics of the Book: Themes, Topics and Typologies* (New York, 1993), 293–334.

J. Nurbakhsh, *The Path: Sufi Practices* (London, 2002; 2nd printing, with revisions, New York, 2006).

O. Safi, 'On the Path of Love towards the Divine: A Journey with Muslim Mystics', *Sufi*, 78 (2009–10), 24–7.

Reference

Encyclopaedia Iranica, ed. E. Yarshater (New York, 1985–); also available online at www.iranicaonline.com.

Encyclopaedia of Islam, ed. H. A. R. Gibb et al., 12 vols. (Leiden, 1960–2003).

J. Nurbakhsh, *Sufi Symbolism*, 16 vols. (London and New York, 1980–2003).

On Rumi

W. C. Chittick, ed., *The Sufi Path of Love: The Spiritual Teachings of Rumi* (Albany, NY, 1983).

F. Keshavarz, *Reading Mystical Lyric: The Case of Jalal al-Din Rumi* (Columbia, SC, 1998).

F. D. Lewis, *Rumi, Past and Present, East and West: The Life, Teachings and Poetry of Jalal al-Din Rumi* (Oxford, 2000).

J. Mojaddedi, *Beyond Dogma: Rumi's Teachings on Friendship with God and Early Sufi Theories* (Oxford, 2012).

Rumi, *Mystical Poems of Rumi, 1 and 2*, tr. A. J. Arberry (New York, 1979).

Rumi, *Signs of the Unseen: The Discourses of Jalaluddin Rumi*, tr. W. M. Thackston, Jr. (Boston, 1994).

N. Virani, '"I am the nightingale of the Merciful": Rumi's Use of the Qur'an and Hadith', *Comparative Studies of South Asia, Africa and the Middle East*, 22/2 (2002), 100–11.

Editions of the Masnavi

Masnavi, ed. M. Estelami, 7 vols. (2nd edn., Tehran, 1990). Vols. i–vi each contain the editor's commentary in the form of endnotes; vol. vii is the Index.

Masnavi, ed. T. Sobhani (Tehran, 1994).

Masnavi-ye ma'navi, ed. A.-K. Sorush, 2 vols. (Tehran, 1996).

The Mathnawi of Jalalu'ddin Rumi, ed. and tr. R. A. Nicholson, E. J. W. Gibb. Memorial, NS, 8 vols. (London, 1925–40). This set consists of the Persian text (vols. i–iii), a full translation in prose (vols. iv–vi), and commentary on Books One to Six (vols. vii–viii).

Interpretation of the Masnavi

W. C. Chittick, 'Rumi and *wahdat al-wujud*', in A. Banani, R. Hovannisian, and G. Sabagh, eds., *Poetry and Mysticism in Islam: The Heritage of Rumi* (Cambridge, 1994), 70–111.

H. Dabashi, 'Rumi and the Problems of Theodicy: Moral Imagination and Narrative Discourse in a Story of the *Masnavi*', in A. Banani, R. Hovannisian, and G. Sabagh, eds., *Poetry and Mysticism in Islam: The Heritage of Rumi* (Cambridge, 1994), 112–35.

R. Davis, 'Narrative and Doctrine in the First Story of Rumi's *Mathnawi*', in G. R. Hawting, J. A. Mojaddedi, and A. Samely, eds., *Studies in Islamic and Middle Eastern Texts and Traditions in Memory of Norman Calder* (Oxford, 2000), 93–104.

A. Karamustafa, 'Speaker, Voice and Audience in the Koran and the *Mathnawi*', *Sufi*, 79 (2010), 36–45.

M. Mills, 'Folk Tradition in the *Masnavi* and the *Masnavi* in Folk Tradition', in A. Banani, R. Hovannisian, and G. Sabagh, eds., *Poetry and Mysticism in Islam: The Heritage of Rumi* (Cambridge, 1994), 136–77

J. Mojaddedi, 'Rumi', in A. Rippin and J. Mojaddedi, eds., *The Wiley Blackwell Companion to the Qur'an* (2nd Edition, Oxford, 2017), 362–72.

J. Mojaddedi, 'The Ebb and Flow of "the Ocean Inside a Jug": The Structure of Rūmī's *Mathnawī* Reconsidered', *Journal of Sufi Studies*, 3/2 (2014), 105–31.

J. R. Perry, '*Monty Python* and the *Mathnavi*: The Parrot in Indian, Persian and English Humor', *Iranian Studies*, 36/1 (2003), 63–73.

J. Renard, *All the King's Falcons: Rumi on Prophets and Revelation* (Albany, NY, 1994).

O. Safi, 'Did the Two Oceans Meet? Historical Connections and Disconnections between Ibn 'Arabi and Rumi', *Journal of Muhyiddin Ibn 'Arabi Society*, 26 (1999), 55–88.

Further Reading in Oxford World's Classics

The Masnavi, Book One, tr. and ed. Jawid Mojaddedi.
The Masnavi, Book Two, tr. and ed. Jawid Mojaddedi.
The Masnavi, Book Three, tr. and ed. Jawid Mojaddedi.
The Qur'an, tr. M. A. S. Abdel Haleem.

A CHRONOLOGY OF RUMI

1207	Rumi's birth in Balkh, north-eastern Persia
c.1216	Rumi's family emigrate from Persia to Anatolia
1219	Alaoddin Kay Qobad ascends Seljuk throne in Anatolia
1220	Death of Faridoddin 'Attar
1221	The Mongol army conquers Balkh
c.1222	Rumi's family settle temporarily in Karaman, Anatolia
1224	Rumi marries Gowhar Khatun
1226	Birth of Soltan Valad, Rumi's son and eventual successor
c.1229	Rumi's family relocate to Konya, Anatolia
1231	Death of Baha Valad, Rumi's father
1232	Borhanoddin Termezi arrives in Konya
c.1233	Rumi begins his studies in Syria
1235	Death of Ebn al-Farez in Egypt
1237	Rumi returns to Konya as leader of Baha Valad's School Ghiyasoddin Kay Khosrow II ascends Seljuk throne in Anatolia
1240	Death of Ebn 'Arabi in Damascus
1243	The Mongols extend their empire to Anatolia
1244	Rumi meets Shams-e Tabriz in Konya for the first time
1246	Shams leaves Konya
1247	Shams returns to Konya
c.1247–8	Shams disappears Salahoddin the Goldsmith begins tenure as Rumi's deputy
1258	Death of Salahoddin Hosamoddin Chalabi begins tenure as Rumi's deputy The Mongols conquer Baghdad, the Abbasid capital
1260	The Mongols are defeated in Syria by the Mamluks
c.1262	The *Masnavi* is started
c.1264	The *Masnavi* is resumed after a pause on account of the death of Hosamoddin's wife
1273	(17 December) Death of Rumi in Konya

THE MASNAVI

BOOK FOUR

Prose Introduction

The fourth departure to the best of abodes and the most glorious of benefits. The hearts of mystics, through studying it, will be given joy like the joy of the meadows and the sound of the clouds, and the intimacy of eyes with the pleasantness of sleep. In it there is the exhilaration of spirits and the cure for bodies. It is such that the pure of heart crave it and love it, and spiritual wayfarers seek it and yearn for it. It is delight for eyes and joy for souls and the best of fruits to gather, and the most glorious of wishes and desires. It takes the afflicted to the doctor and it guides the lover to his beloved.

Praise be to God for the most magnificent of gifts and the most precious of wishes. It is the renewer of the pledge of love and makes easy the problem faced by people in difficulty. Perusing it will increase sorrow for those who are far from the truth, while increasing the happiness and gratitude of the fortunate ones. Its bosom holds fineries that even the bosoms of singing girls do not hold, as a reward for the people endowed with both knowledge and action, for it is like a full moon that has risen and good luck that has returned; it increases the hope of the hopeful and augments the devotion of the practitioners. It raises expectations after depression and increases hope after despair. Like a sun shining between clouds, it is light to our companions and a treasure to our successors, *And we ask God to help us to thank Him, for thanksgiving is a means of binding what is at hand and for hunting more of it, and only what He wishes happens.*

> I had been roused from sleep to love's sensations,
> Preoccupied by cool, sweet exhalations,
>
> When a dove in a thicket close to me
> Began to sing with sobs so beautifully;
>
> If I had sobbed before her with such passion
> For So'ad, then my spirit, through contrition,
>
> Would have been healed, but hers predate my own:
> 'Preceders have more excellence' it's known.

May God have mercy on those who came prior and those who come later and those who fulfil their vows and those who seek to do so, with His grace and generosity and many benefits and favours, for He is the best petitioned one and the noblest object of hope:

'*God is the best protector and He is the most merciful of those who show mercy*'* and the best of friends and the best of heirs and the best successor, and the provider to worshippers who sow and till, and God bless Mohammad and his noble family, and all the Prophets and Messengers. O Lord of the two worlds, Amen.

Exordium

O Light of God, Hosamoddin, tonight
    The Masnavi outshines moons through your light.
Men's hopes lie in your lofty aspiration,
    Which draws this poem, but to which location?
You've tied *The Masnavi*'s neck, and held tight;
    You drag it in directions out of sight.
The Masnavi runs there; the dragger's hidden,
    Unseen by people who lack proper vision.
Because you are *The Masnavi*'s real source,   5
    If it extends, that's due to you of course.
Since it's your wish, God wants that too, no doubt—
    God grants each single wish of the devout.
You have been someone who *belongs to God*—
    Now '*God is for Him*'* comes as your reward.
The Masnavi gives thanks for you and raises
    Its hands up for thanksgiving and your praises.
God saw its lips and hands had your thanks' trace
    And granted favour, increase, and His grace.
Since those who thank are promised gain, it's clear   10
    Those who prostrate are blessed by drawing near:
'*Prostrate and draw near!*'* God said, didn't He?
    This leads to spiritual proximity.
It's due to this that He'll bestow His favour
    Not for the clamour caused by such behaviour.
We're happy like the vineyards here with you—

Since you decree, draw us as you can do.
Draw to the Hajj this caravan through distance,
    Esteemed prince of 'Joy is the key to patience'.
Hajj is a visit only to the building—
    Hajj to the building's Lord is more fulfilling.
I called you 'Sword of Truth' and 'Light'—you are
    The sun; both epithets are of that star.
The sword and light are one if you can see:
    The sun's sword is from light most certainly.
The moon sends moonbeams while the sun shines light—
    Find this in the Qur'an now and recite.*
The sun was called 'the light' in the Qur'an
    While 'beam' stands for the moon in there, good man.
The sun is praised more, so its light must be
    Ranked higher than the moon's light obviously:
In moonlight, many couldn't see the way,
    But saw it when the sunlight shone by day.
Sunlight shows what is bartered, and that made
    The daytime the appropriate time to trade—
Then real from counterfeit is plain to see
    And traders saved from fraud and trickery.
The sunlight therefore shines on earth as aid,
    '*A mercy to the worlds*'* for all who trade.
The forger hates it as a wretched pain;
    It makes his forgeries valueless and vain.
The false coin loathes the traders with a passion
    And curs true Sufis in a similar fashion.
The Prophets have to deal with enemies,
    Then angels shout out, '*O Lord, help them, please!*
Preserve the lamp's flame that shines light forever
    From puffs to blow it out from every robber.'
The light's foes are the thief and counterfeiter—
    Deliver us from these two foes, O Saviour!
Shine light down on this fourth book we've begun,
    Since the fourth heaven sends the rising sun.
The same way from the fourth shine bright light down,
    So it may reach each country and each town.
If men say 'It's a tale', then they're tales too;
    If they see it as gold, they're just as true.

15

20

25

30

The Nile was made of blood to each Egyptian,
    Pure water, though, to Moses's saved nation.*

Here now appears a sight of these words' foe—
    He's falling headfirst to hell's flames below:
O Light of Truth, you saw that one's condition—   35
    God showed the outcome for his every action.
Your eyes see the unseen and they possess,
    Like it, a mastery—may they not see less!
If you complete the story that we view
    As our state's essence, that act would be true.
For 'somebodies', leave 'nobodies' of earth—
    Complete it for those who have actual worth.
This tale was left unfinished in Book Three;
    Now it's the fourth book, finish it for me!

*Conclusion of the story about that lover who fled
the nightwatchman into an unfamiliar orchard,
and, through sheer joy at finding his beloved there,
prayed for blessings for the nightwatchman, saying:
'It may be that you hate something, but it is
better for you.'*

We were relating how that person fled   40
    From the nightwatchman, and then found instead
Inside the orchard, she who'd won his heart,
    For whom he'd pined much during years apart.
Her shadow wasn't seen—he'd only heard
    About her like a legendary bird,
Apart from once, when it occurred by fate,
    And seeing her made his heart palpitate.
After that, though he tried relentlessly,
    That harsh one gave no opportunity.
Neither his wealth nor begging could succeed—   45
    She was indifferent and lacked any need.
On lovers' lips God smeared well at the start

A taste of their desired aim or sought art.
When they begin to hunt their goal, each day
   He sets new snares for them along the way.
After He hurls them to continue searching,
   He'll say, 'Bring payment first ahead of entering!'
They follow still that scent and alternate
   Between deep love and being disconsolate.
Each one hopes for a fruitful end in store,   50
   That on that day they'll open up the door.
Again, it's shut to that door-worshipper,
   But he grows ardent, hopeful, thirstier.

That youth stepped in the orchard happily
   And came upon his treasure suddenly.
Thus, the nightwatchman was a means God made
   To drive him to the orchard unafraid:
He saw his sweetheart with a bright lamp look
   In search of a lost ring beside a brook;
Savouring the moment, he then started praying   55
   To God, and prayed for that nightwatchman, saying:
'I caused him loss by my flight and departure,
   So scatter on him much more gold and silver.
Relieve him of his toil and let him be
   As happy as I am now she's near me.
In this world and the next, bless him with peace,
   And from his toil please give this man release,
O God, although it is the watchman's nature
   To always wish for people harm and bother.'
If they hear of a new fine from their king   60
   On subjects, they enjoy their suffering;
And if the king's kind mercy is reported,
   That his old plan to fine them is aborted,
Nightwatchmen's souls mourn his decision badly—
   They have so many negative traits sadly.
He prayed for that nightwatchman—it was due
   To him that comfort came within his view;
He was his cure, though poison to another,
   Because that man had joined him with his lover.

Absolute evil's nowhere to be seen;
   Evil is relative—that's what I mean.
In this world there's no poison and no meat
   That's not one's fetter and another's feet:
The feet to one, a fetter to another;
   The meat to one, yet poison for his brother.
Snake poison gives the snake some benefit,
   But men will meet their death because of it.
The sea's a field for creatures of the water,
   But for terrestrials it is death and torture.
Experienced men, consider carefully   70
   The thousand ways of relativity:
Zayd* might be like a devil to one person,
   But to another he is like a sultan.
One will call Zayd a saint, another will
   Say Zayd's an infidel whom we should kill.
Zayd is one essence, yet he is protection
   To one, while to the next he is affliction.
If you want him as sugar-like to you,
   Then look at him now through his lover's view—
Don't look with your own eyes! No, you must try   75
   To look with the beloved's seeker's eye.
Close your own eyes from that one who's so lovely;
   Borrow eyes from his lovers to see sharply!
Borrow from Him directly eyes and vision,
   Then look at Him with His eyes for precision.
You'll not feel weary then, nor satiated.
   '*God shall belong to Him*,' Mohammad stated,
'I'll be his eye, his hands and heart, so he
   Can flee unfortunate things successfully.'
Things normally disapproved can in the end   80
   Become approved when leading to the Friend.

Story about that preacher who began every homily with a prayer on
behalf of oppressors, unbelievers, and the hard-hearted.

A preacher prayed for highway robbers when
   Upon the pulpit, which astonished men.
He raised his hands, 'My Lord and my Possessor,

Forgive the fraud, the bad man, the oppressor,
　And all who mock the people who act well,
　　And those with doubting hearts, each infidel.'
He wouldn't pray for pure and godly people,
　Only for those whom most considered evil.
They told him, 'This is not the normal way;　　　　85
　One shouldn't pray for those who go astray.'
He answered, 'Goodness is all I've received
　At their hands. This is why I'm not deceived:
They did so much wrong, so much tyranny,
　That from bad ways to good they prompted me.
Whenever worldly things stole my attention,
　I suffered beatings from those men I mention.
I then sought refuge from foes up above—
　Those wolves thus drove me to the path of love.
Since they have caused my self-reform, I should　　90
　Pray for their sakes much more than for the good.'

God's slave cries out to Him because of pain;
　His suffering makes him desperately complain.
God answers, 'Pain and suffering in the end
　Have made you beg Me and find ways to mend
Your flaws—complain instead about My grace
　That drives you far from Me and out of place.'
Every foe is your medicine—it's true
　He's the elixir, benefiting you,
Because you flee them, then in your withdrawal　　95
　You seek assistance from the Lord's bestowal.
In truth, your friends are your real foes, since they
　Distract you from God's Presence far away.
The porcupine's behaviour is so similar:
　When it is beaten hard, it then grows bigger.
It will expand the more men cudgel it,
　Becoming fatter every time it's hit.
The faithful's soul is similar, you know:
　It grows expansive with each powerful blow.
That is why suffering and debasement both　　　　100
　Were tasted more by Prophets—for their growth:

It's so their souls grow stronger than the rest,
    For others have not been through such a test.
People will rub harsh liquid into hide,
    To make it soft and fine, a source of pride.
If that harsh liquid isn't rubbed this way,
    The hide becomes unclean and rots away.
Consider Man an untanned hide, since he
    Becomes both stiff and foul so easily.
Rub in much liquid, though it's harsh and bitter,   105
    Then see the hide turn pliant, clean, and firmer.
But if you cannot, try to be content
    With suffering you wish God had never sent.
Suffering for the Beloved cleans your soul;
    His knowledge is beyond your mind's control.
When one sees sweetness, suffering then tastes sweet;
    When one sees good health, medicine tastes sweet.
In death, one sees one's own victorious end;
    One then would say, '*Kill me, O trusty friend!*'*

That nightwatchman brought someone benefit;   110
    He was rejected still for doing it.
Faith's mercy was cut off from him—the spite
    Of Satan had enveloped him that night.
He was a factory's store of spite and anger;
    Such spite's the root of unbelief and error.

Jesus was asked 'What is the hardest thing to face in existence?'

Jesus was asked by a clear-headed man once:
    'What is the hardest hurdle in existence?'
Jesus told him, 'God's rage, and it is clear—
    Even hell trembles at it out of fear.'
The man asked, 'What can grant security   115
    From it?' 'Quit your own rage immediately!'

The watchman had become a mine of rage,
    His rage surpassing wild beasts' at that stage.

How could he hope for mercy from the Lord
   When he had not turned back from what's abhorred?
Although the world can't just discard their kind,
   Such talk can make you leave the path behind—
The world can't do without your urine either,
   But that is not the purest *gushing water.**

The lover intends to take advantage and the beloved screams at him.

She was alone when that most simple lover   120
   Attempted suddenly to kiss and hug her.
That beauty screamed at him and left him shaken:
   'You mind your manners! Do not be so brazen!'
He said, 'But we're alone with no one near;
   I am a thirsty man and water's here.
Apart from wind there's nothing else here stirring—
   Who's present? Who's to stop this from occurring?'
She said, 'You crazy man, a fool today
   As ever, heedless of what sages say.
You saw the wind stir, so you now should know   125
   The wind's own mover's here and makes it blow.
The fan, or rather God's control of it,
   Makes the wind move whenever He deems fit.
That portion which is under our direction
   Will not blow till you start its operation—
The movement of this wind, you simple man,
   Depends upon you and upon the fan.'

Breath from one's lips is under the control
   Likewise of your own body and your soul:
Sometimes you turn breath into eulogy,   130
   Sometimes into most biting mockery.
The different winds' states you should tell apart,
   For brains see the whole picture from one part:
In spring, God makes wind gentle, but remember
   How He transforms that same wind in December.
He sent the Sarsar* wind to Aad; with ease
   For Hud* He made it a sweet-perfumed breeze.

He makes one wind like Simoom,* poisonous,
　　But also makes a breeze enliven us.
He put the wind-like breath in you and me,   135
　　So we can know winds by analogy.
Speech comes from breath and can be harsh or sweet,
　　Poison to some, while to some others meat.
The fan does not just give a pleasant breeze;
　　It's also meant to drive off flies and fleas.
Why should the fan for God's Divine Decree
　　Never send people trials and misery?
The air that any single fan blows out
　　Will either benefit or harm, no doubt.
Why shouldn't harsh winds, when appropriate,   140
　　Bring gentleness instead and benefit?
From your few wheat grains try and understand
　　That all will look like what is in your hand.
How could the circling winds above, good man,
　　Bow as they do without their Driver's fan?
Is it not true that when it's time to winnow
　　The farmhands pray that God will make the wind blow,
So that the chaff's kept separate from the grain,
　　So some go to the barn, the rest remain.
And when the wind is subject to delay,   145
　　You see them beg God as they turn to pray.
When labour pains continue without cease,
　　Loud screams for air will beg for a release.
If those who seek wind don't know God's its source,
　　Why then do they entreat Him with such force?
Men on a boat will likewise hope winds blow
　　And ask their Lord to send them some below.
When you have toothache it's the same again—
　　You beg with passion to be spared the pain.
Soldiers beg God, 'Make us victorious,   150
　　You who can grant all wishes now for us!'
And talismans are sought out as a favour
　　To help reduce contraction pains in labour.
Everyone therefore knows with certainty,
　　That none but God sends wind originally.
It's certain to the rare men who can tell

That what moves has one moving it as well.
If you can't see Him with your own eyes' vision,
   Perceive Him then through His effects' impression:
The soul's what moves the body—though you don't see,   155
   Perceive it through the movement of your body.

The lover said, 'I'm rude. That's probably true.
   But wise in genuinely seeking you.'
She said, 'Your manners are as seen, I know.
   As for the rest, you know the truth, you foe.'

Story about the Sufi who found his wife with another man.

A Sufi went home earlier than before.
   His wife was in, behind the only door,
Having sex with the cobbler secretly,
   Her body tempted in there carnally.
The Sufi then knocked loudly and the pair   160
   Felt stranded, with no route away from there.
The Sufi hadn't come back from his store
   So early in the afternoon before.
He came at a most strange time by intention
   On this day, due to an inspired suspicion.
His wife was counting on the fact that he
   Had never come home early previously.
Her reasoning turned out wrong by fate that day—
   God can conceal or He can make you pay.
When you've done wrong, be scared you'll suffer woe,   165
   Because that is the seed that God will grow.
He will conceal it for a while, His aim
   Being that you soon feel some regret and shame.
When Omar ruled as caliph, he once brought
   To his police a thief whom they had sought.
The thief screamed, 'Mercy, Caliph! My defence
   Is that this was my very first offence.'
Omar said, 'God forbid that God's decree
   Should punish first offenders mercilessly.'
He hides it many times to show His kindness   170

And then He punishes to show His justice,
So both these attributes are in plain view,
  One giving hope, the other warning you.

The wife had also done this frequently,
  So it seemed trivial, done so easily.
Her weak intelligence did not then dream
  The jug might not return whole from the stream.
Fate made her now behave as desperately
  As hypocrites when death comes suddenly:
No refuge, hope, or way out from this hole   175
  When Azrael comes reaching for one's soul.
The wife trapped in the bedroom felt that way,
  Paralysed with her partner in dismay.
The Sufi whispered to himself, 'You two—
  I'll wait before I take revenge on you.
For now, though, I'll pretend I've no idea,
  So no one else hears of commotion here.
God will make sure you pay the penalty
  The way an illness strikes one, gradually.'
The sick man wastes away, like ice, each moment,   180
  But keeps imagining: 'I feel improvement.'
Like the hyena caught when hunters shout
  'Where is it?' from afar, to lure it out.
That woman had no other place to hide,
  No exit door below, above, outside;
No oven even that could hide her lover,
  Nor any large sack that could serve as cover,
Just like the plain on Resurrection Day:
  No hill, no ditch, no place to hide away.
God has described the Last Assembly's place: 185
  *'There's no unevenness found in that space.'**

The wife hides the lover under her chador and gives an excuse, for
'The wiles of you women are tremendous.'**

She quickly threw her chador on the man,
  Disguising him as much as someone can.

Under the chador it was still so clear,
  Like a sore thumb, that he was hiding here.
The Sufi said, amazed, 'What's up? Tell me.
  I've not seen her before here—who is she?'
His wife said, 'She's a lady from the town;
  A rich and noble lady of renown.
I'd locked the door, so strangers can't come in   190
  Unawares quickly, leading thus to sin.'
The Sufi said, 'How can we help this one?
  I don't expect to be paid in return.'
She said, 'She wants now to become related.
  She's decent, and by God she's highly rated.
She wished to see our girl and run the rule
  Over her, but today she is at school.
She's said, "No matter what she's like, I will
  With heart and soul make her my son's bride still."
Her son, who's out of town, is strong and clever;   195
  He's independent and a high achiever.'
The Sufi said, 'We're poor and have low standing;
  Her family's rich, respected, deemed outstanding—
How can our daughter be her rich son's bride,
  Ivory one side, twigs the other side.
In marriage, partners ought to match each other
  Or joy won't last as marriage will then suffer.'

*The wife says, 'She is not attached to possessions; her wish is
modesty and uprightness.'*

She said, 'I gave such answers. She replied:
  "I don't seek property. I'm satisfied.
Of wealth and property we're very bored,   200
  Unlike the common, greedy men who hoard.
We're seeking purity and modesty—
  In both worlds these ensure prosperity."'
The Sufi cited poverty again,
  So it should not be overlooked, and then
His wife said, 'I've been telling her throughout
  How poor we are, so she would have no doubt.
She has a mountain-like conviction; she

Will not be put off by our poverty.
"My wish is chastity," is her retort,   205
    "You are sincere with values; you're my sort." '
The Sufi said, 'This woman's obviously
    Seen all that we can claim as property:
A cramped home that has room for just one person,
    Where even one small needle can't stay hidden.
She has seen self-restraint and modesty
    With your fine virtues and chaste purity;
She knows this better than we fathom it—
    The front, the back, the head, the arse of it!
Yeah right, she can see virtue, and apparent   210
    As well is that our daughter has no servant.
A daughter's modesty is clear as day,
    So fathers need not brag in any way.'

I've told this story so that you won't boast
    As much when your offence becomes exposed.
You make pretentious claims continually;
    It is your creed and practice obviously.
You've cheated like this wife, yet you still dare
    To lie and with pretence set your own snare.
You feel ashamed before some low-life babblers   215
    But not before God—who would you say matters?

The Reason why God is called 'the Hearing One' and 'the Seeing One'.

God called Himself '*the Seeing One*' to be
    A strong deterrent to you constantly.
He called Himself '*the Hearing One*' so that
    You'll close your lips to any odious chat.
He called Himself '*the Knowing One*', my dear,
    So you won't nurse corrupt thoughts out of fear.
These names do not define God all the same—
    'Kaafoor' can sometimes be a mere slave's name.*
God's names come from His attributes, so they   220

Aren't rootless like the first cause in some way;
Otherwise it would be false mockery,
   Like calling someone blind 'one who can see',
Or using 'shy' for someone who is shameless,
   Or calling 'beautiful' one who is hideous.
A girl's name can be 'Hajji' or 'God's warrior',
   But this tells of her lineage, not about her.
If you apply to her such titles though
   She lacks credentials, that's an empty show;
It would be madness and a joke that way—   225
   God is so far *from what wrongdoers say.*

'I always knew', the sought one clarified,*
   'That, though you're handsome, you are bad inside.
I also knew full well before our meeting
   You're bent on being wicked through disputing.
When my eyes redden due to a disease
   I know it's you, though I can't see with ease;
You saw me as a lamb without a shepherd,
   None watching over me to say I mattered.
When lovers moan in pain and in dejection   230
   It's due to looking in the wrong direction—
They viewed as shepherdless their sought gazelle,
   And thought their captive up for grabs as well,
Until an arrow from God's glance had flown
   To say, "I am their Guard. They're not alone."
How can I be less than a goat or sheep
   To lack protection? I am in the keep
Of someone who is fit for sovereignty—
   He knows about the winds that blow on me.
Whether it should blow hot or cold out there   235
   That Knowing One is never unaware.
The self is deaf and blind to God, and I
   Can easily tell you're blind with my heart's eye.
I didn't ask about you for eight years
   Since I saw idiocy up to your ears!
Someone peers down a bath-stove and falls through—
   Why should I have to ask him "How are you?" '

Comparison of this world to a bath-stove and piety to a public bathhouse.

Lust for this world is like the bath-stove: it
   Is what lets piety's bathhouses be lit,
But it cannot pollute the pure man's share   240
   While he is in the bath and clean in there.
The rich are carriers of mere dung—they take
   It to the bath-stove men for their fuel's sake.
God has filled them with lust and greed inside,
   So that the baths are hot and well supplied.
Leave the stove and dive in the baths, my friend—
   You must leave it to reach them in the end.
Anyone in the stove-room's like a slave
   To patient men who know how to behave.
One in the bathhouse, on his lovely face,   245
   Displays for all a special sign's clear trace;
The stokers have their own mark, which is found
   On clothing, soot, and smoke that's all around.
If you can't see, then use your sense of smell
   Which is the best tool for the blind to tell.
If you can't smell, then make them talk to you,
   Then trace old clues in discourse that is new.
A stoker who possesses gold will say:
   'I've filled with grime some twenty bowls today.'
Fire in this world and your greed are the same: 250
   Men's mouths are opened by each tongue-shaped flame.
Gold here is worthless dung to wisdom's eyes,
   Though, like dung, it will cause the flames to rise.
The sunshine, which emits heat, also can
   Turn moist grime into fuel for fire, good man.
The sun can also make stone seem like gold
   To some men's eyes, raising greed twentyfold.
One says, 'I've gathered wealth.' (What does he own?)
   'I've brought so much grime.' (Now his meaning's known.)
Though sounding like the butt of a good joke,   255
   One hears such boasts at stoves from men who stoke.
They say, 'You filled just six bowls—look at me:

I've filled up twenty times that easily.'
Those born in stove-rooms don't know what is pure—
They say that musk smells worse than foul manure.

The story about the tanner who fainted and fell sick from the scent
of musk and perfume in the bazaar of the perfumers.

At the perfume bazaar one busy day,
    A tanner fainted and lay in the way:
The scent of perfume reached his nose, then he
    Felt giddy and collapsed immediately.
Still like a corpse, this man lay unaware   260
    In front of passers-by who would walk there.
A crowd of people rushed near suddenly,
    Praying, '*God's strength!*',* each with a remedy.
One felt his heart to check he wasn't dead,
    Another sprinkled rose water instead,
Unaware it was due to the sweet smell
    Of such rose water that the victim fell.
Another rubbed his head and hands, then after
    An equally concerned man brought a plaster.
Another brought some sweetened aloes wood.   265
    Another stripped him then for his own good.
Another checked his pulse in case of death.
    Another stooped down low to smell his breath
In case he had consumed hashish. These men
    Could not wake that poor victim up again,
So they rushed to inform his family:
    'So-and-so fell and suffers tragically.
He's lying face down, but no one's aware
    Of why or how he had his seizure there.'
That tanner had a brother who was clever   270
    And very wily, so he hurried over,
Bringing some dog shit with him in his sleeve.
    The crowd gave passage when they heard him grieve.
'I know what made my brother faint down here,
    And when one knows the cause, the cure is clear.
It's difficult for those who aren't sure,
    Through trial and error's way, to find the cure.

It's easy when you know the cause—that key
    Is what ends ignorance immediately.'
He then thought, 'Awful dog shit's smell remains   275
    So concentrated in his brain and veins—
He's used that for his tanning every day,
    Trying to earn a living in this way.
Galen once said, "Give sick men what they will
    Remember from before they'd fallen ill—
When doing something different is to blame,
    Seek cures in what's familiar and the same."
He's just like a dung beetle, so don't doubt
    Rose water's scent will knock dung beetles out.
His remedy is dog shit, as its smell   280
    Is what he is accustomed to as well.'
'*The wicked women for the wicked men*'*—
    Remind yourself of its intent again.
Well-meaning helpers would most likely see
    Rose water as a better remedy,
But lovely things don't suit the wicked, friend.
    It's not appropriate; it can't heal or mend.

'*We see you as bad luck,*'* rejecters said
    When from God's message's fine scent they'd strayed.
'Your words mean misery and painfulness.   285
    Your sermon doesn't augur well for us.
Do not reprove us; do not waste your breath—
    Do that in public, we'll stone you to death!
We've thrived so long on trivial things and playing;
    We've not experienced this approach you're saying.
Our nourishment is bragging, lies, and jest.
    Your speech makes us feel nauseous now at best.
You're multiplying many times our pains;
    You've drugged us and your opium harms our brains.'

The tanner's brother treats him with the smell of shit.

The brother kept on pushing men away,   290
    So none could see his treatment on that day.

As if to whisper secrets, he leaned close,
  Then put the hidden stuff up to his nose.
He'd smeared the dog shit on his palm to ease
  And cure the sick man's brain's infirmities.
That man began to stir a short while later.
  They said, 'What spells his brother said, the saviour!
He whispered spells and blew inside his ear.
  His spells revived a dead man—it was clear.'

Corrupt men always have an inclination   295
  Towards flirtation, winks, and fornication.
If prudent counsel's musk won't make them well,
  They have to learn to like a noxious smell.
God called the polytheists unclean, for they
  Were dung originally, and some men say:
'The worm that has been born in dung won't ever
  Transform its nature to sweet-smelling amber.'
From God's light's sprinkling if one's kept apart
  He'll stay shell-like, all body with no heart.
If God had given him a share, a bird   300
  Could have been conjured easily from a turd.
And not a low, domestic fowl, but one
  Known as the bird of wisdom, my dear son.

His sweetheart said,* 'If you lack light as well,
  You bring your nose to shit, so it can smell.
From being apart your face is yellowy;
  Unripened fruit are what hang from your tree.
Although the pot was blackened by the flame,
  Bad meat would not turn tender all the same:
I've made you boil in separation now   305
  For eight years, but you're still false anyhow.
Your young grape is as bad as stones for sickness,
  Unripe, sour, while the rest are sweet sultanas.'

*That lover begs forgiveness for his sin and his beloved perceives
that as well.*

'I did the test', the lover said, 'to see
    If you're a flirt or modest genuinely.
I knew of course before the actual test,
    However seeing for yourself is best.
You're sunshine and you're famous, so what harm
    For me to test you? Why feel such alarm?
You are I, and I test myself each day   310
    With loss and profit that should come my way.
Prophets were tested once by enemies,
    So miracles would bring them to their knees.
With light I've tested my own eye—you are
    The one from whom the evil eye stays far.
The world's a ruin, you're the gold within—
    Don't be annoyed I've already looked in.
I acted foolishly then, heaven knows,
    So I could boast forever to my foes,
So when my tongue named you, my eyes could then   315
    Give proofs of what I'd seen to other men.
If I've robbed you of honour, I'm not proud—
    Come here, moon, take this sword then use my shroud:
By your hand only cut apart my body,
    As I belong to your hands and yours only.
You talk again of separation—cease!
    Do what you wish to, but don't do that please.'
Eternal speech's way is open now,
    But time's run out, and so we can't see how.
We've talked of husks, the kernel's hidden though.   320
    If we persist it won't be always so.

*The beloved rejects the apology of her lover, and rubs his duplicity
in his face.*

That man's beloved answered him to say:
    'On your side it is night, on mine it's day.
Why bring here to be judged your shady plot

To those who see what's true from what is not?'
Whatever schemes you try to hide away
   Are manifest to us as clear as day.
For you we hide them to give you protection,
   So why persist, blasé, with your transgression?
Learn from your ancestor: Adam descended   325
   Down to the trial hall when he had offended.
He saw the Knower of all mysteries
   Then stood and begged forgiveness without cease.
He sat contrite on dirt eventually,
   Yet didn't try evading destiny.
He said, '*We've sinned, Lord*,'* not another sound
   On seeing guards were standing all around.
He viewed the guards soul-like, invisible;
   Their maces reached as high as possible.
'Be ant-like when near Solomon,' they said,   330
   'Or else this mace will break in two your head!'
Stand where you see the truth and far from lies;
   For men the best of guardians are your eyes.
Others' advice gives blind men purity,
   But when alone they're soiled repeatedly.
Human, you don't lack vision now, but when
   Destiny turns eyes blind, you'll lack it then
It's only very seldom, isn't it,
   For one who sees to fall inside a pit?
But for the blind this isn't very rare—   335
   It's in the blind man's nature to fall there.
He falls in filth, not knowing what it was:
   'Do I smell or is something else the cause?'
If someone sprays some musk on him, of course
   He'll think he is himself its sweet smell's source.
O man with vision, your eyes therefore function
   As guarding parents giving you protection,
Especially the heart's eye, for that pair
   Which see just sensually cannot compare.

'The highwaymen were lurking where I walked;   340
   They tied my tongue in knots in case I talked.

A horse with chained legs can't trust easily—
    This is a heavy chain, so pardon me!'
O heart, these words are broken up and stuttering—
    They're pearls, God's jealousy the mill that's crushing.
Though pearls be ground to tiny bits, they can
    Be used for eyes as tutty still, good man.
For being broken, pearl, don't start lamenting;
    When ground up you will be illuminating.
Speech must be broken up at first, before   345
    God, who is needless, fixes it once more.
Though wheat is broken up and ground for bread,
    'Look here! A perfect loaf!' will soon be said.
'Since your crime's also been exposed, O lover,
    You too, get broken! Don't try painting over.
Adam's elect descendants all admit:
    "*We have done wrong!*"* as they acknowledge it.
Make your plea and don't argue or debate
    Like Satan, that hard-nosed, cursed reprobate.
If you think he succeeded through that action   350
    Then try and be contentious and as stubborn.
Abu Jahl asked for proof a miracle
    From our great Prophet—he was terrible—
Abu Bakr though did not insist; instead
    "This face speaks naught but truth," is what he said.
So how can someone like you ever be
    Fit to test someone loved as much as me.'

A denier tells Ali, 'If you are sure of God's protection, throw yourself from the top of this building,' and Ali answers him.

A man who did not worship God one day
    Turned his head to the great Ali to say,
While standing on a high roof, 'O wise person,   355
    Are you now conscious of your God's protection?'
'Yes, He's the guard, though He is self-sufficient;
    Ever since I was born He's been consistent.'
'Then throw yourself down from this roof for me—

Rely on God's protection totally!
Your certainty will be displayed this way;
  This proof for your faith will be clear as day.'
'Be quiet and begone!' that man was told,
  'So that your life's not pawned for being so bold.
How should a slave be fit to test out God?   360
  Does this not strike you as the least bit odd?
How can slaves out of curiosity
  Possess the gall to test God, fool? Tell me!
Only God has the right, and He'll prepare
  More tests for slaves each moment, so beware!
It's to expose us to ourselves, revealing
  The real belief within we've been concealing.
Did Adam tell God, "I have tested you
  With all my sins and flaws in order to
Witness, dear King, the clemency You'll show."   365
  Who could attempt this ever? Do you know?
Your intellect is so confused this time
  That your excuse is much worse than your crime.
Who do you think you are to ever try
  To test the one who raised up the whole sky?
You even can't tell good from bad—first test
  Yourself before you try to test the rest.
Once you have tested first yourself, no longer
  Will you desire to ever test another.
On learning you're a sugar grain, you'll see   370
  The sugar house is where you're meant to be.
No need to test God to know you belong—
  God won't send sugar somewhere plainly wrong.
The One who has all knowledge will not send
  His chief to be a doorman, my good friend.
Intelligent men won't throw jewels in
  A toilet bowl with urine still within.
A knowing sage won't send his wheat away
  Into a barn that's used to store just hay.'

If a disciple tests his master, he   375
  Is asinine, as everyone will see.

If you test out the sacred things, then you,
  Doubting man, will yourself be tested too.
Your impudence and ignorance at most
  Will be then shown, but he won't be exposed.
If a dust mote should ever try to weigh
  A mountain, its scale pans will break away,
For he weighs with his own mind, and a man
  Of God can't ever fit a measuring-pan—
Intellect's scales can't bear his weight, so he   380
  Smashes them into bits dramatically.
To test him is presuming you've more power
  Than such a king, above whom none can tower.
What power do pictures have to think they can
  Test their own painter—they're drawn by that man!
If they're aware of tests, is it not true
  That these tests are what the same artist drew?
What are these pictures worth? It's no doubt less
  Than pictures that his knowledge can possess.
When the temptation comes to test, bad luck   385
  Has visited you and your neck's been struck.
On feeling this temptation, do not wait
  But turn to pray to God and then prostrate.
Soak your prostration spot with tears and pray:
  'God, free me from this doubting mind today!'
That moment when you seek to test is not good;
  Your faith's prayer-house is then filled up with brushwood.

Story about 'The Furthest Place of Worship in Jerusalem'* and carob brushwood, and David's resolution before the time of Solomon to build that house of worship.

When David's firm resolve to build from rock
  The Furthest Worship-House took a big knock,
God said to him, 'Announce across the land   390
  You've given up—it won't be by your hand.
It's not in Our decree that you erect

This worship-house, though you're of the elect.'
David said, 'Knower of the mysteries,
    Explain my sin for You to tell me "Cease!"'
'Without sin, you've spilled blood and now you pay
    The price for the oppressed's blood in this way,
For countless people have been stupefied
    By your voice and have consequently died!
Much blood was spilled by your voice when you'd sing—   395
    It moves the soul and pleases everything.'
David said, 'I was overwhelmed by You,
    Drunken with hands tied, what could I then do?
Is it not true that when they are repentant
    Overwhelmed ones are deemed as non-existent?'
'This overwhelmed one is in fact negated
    Relatively to Me,' the Lord then stated.
'The one who's left himself behind is best
    Among all humans, and the loftiest,
Next to God's attributes annihilated,   400
    Though it's subsistence if the truth is stated.
Spirits are under His control; you'll see
    Appearances are subject equally.'
God said, 'One overwhelmed in Our grace will
    Not be compelled, possessing a free will.'
The end of his free will is also clear:
    It will be lost completely over here.
One with free will has no delight within him
    Unless he's fully rid of egotism.
The world can offer food that most would treasure,   405
    His joy will come though from being rid of pleasure.
Such pleasures won't affect him when he's tried
    Spiritual pleasures and grown satisfied.

Explanation of 'the Believers are brothers'* and 'the
truly learned are like one soul', especially the unity
between David, Solomon, and the other Prophets, for if
you reject one of them, your faith in no Prophet will be
perfect—this is a sign of the unity, that if you destroy
one house among a thousand, all of them will be
destroyed, and not a single wall will be left standing, for
'We do not distinguish between any of them'* and 'An
allusion suffices the intelligent'. This is much more than
an allusion.

'Although it won't be built by you,' God said,
    'Your son will soon erect that house instead.
His work is your work, great king of the sages—
    Believers have bonds outside time and ages.'
They're numerous and yet their faith is one,
    Many bodies, although in soul they're one.
Beasts' intellects and souls are lower than   410
    The different kinds that are possessed by Man,
And yet beyond men's souls there is the soul
    Of God's Friends with divine breath for their role.
Animal souls lack union, so don't seek
    It from a spirit that is much too weak.
If one eats food, the other won't be sated;
    If one bears loads, the other won't be weighted.
One's happy with the other one's demise,
    Then, jealous of what they own, quickly dies.
The souls of dogs and wolves are all divided,   415
    The souls of lions of God, though, are united.
I used the plural 'souls', since one is many
    When soul is in relation to the body,
Just as the sunlight seems to multiply
    In separate courtyards to the human eye.
All of the rays are really one—it's proved
    When separating walls are all removed,
For if they're gone, Mohammad told us all:
    'Believers then are like a single soul.'

This discourse raises problems now, my son,   420
     Since it is only a comparison.
There is a world of differences between
     A lion and a brave man whom you've seen;
When one compares the two though, you would say
     They are as one in gambling life away,
Because that brave man does resemble it,
     But doesn't match exactly every bit—
No form exactly matches with another
     In this world, as you quickly will discover.
I'll raise an inexact match nonetheless   425
     To spare your mind confusion and distress:
A lamp is lit in every house at night,
     So one can see in darkness through its light.
Light is the soul, lamp body, and the latter
     Requires a wick and other kinds of matter;
The lamps with six wicks, for six bodies, need
     As their foundation both to sleep and feed.
They can't survive when lacking food and sleep,
     And neither with them both, but this gets deep:
They cannot last without a wick and oil,   430
     But with them they still aren't reliable—
Their light's a cause and will expire, my friend.
     How can they last when daylight brings their end?
And human senses cannot last, since they
     Are naught next to the light of Judgement Day.
The senses' light and souls of fathers here
     Don't die like grass or fully disappear:
Like stars and moonbeams which still shine at night,
     They are effaced by day in sunshine's light,
The way the flea's sting disappears the moment   435
     A snake has bitten you—that bite's more potent.
A naked man jumped in a lake to flee
     The danger posed by a big bumble bee;
The bee just hovered over him and when
     He raised his head above, it stung him then.
The lake is *zekr*, the bee in this example
     Is your remembrance of some other people;

Inside *zekr*'s waters hold your breath, be strong,
   Leave thoughts and the temptation to do wrong.
You'll then acquire pure water's nature, so   440
   You will be filled with it from head to toe.
That nasty bee flees water, and now you,
   Just like the water, terrify it too.
If you wish, leave the water now you can—
   Boast water's nature too within, good man.
Those who have fled this world aren't naught; I've said
   They're steeped now in God's attributes instead.
You could explain this by comparison
   With stars and their relation to the sun.
If you want a Qur'anic verse, then read   445
   '*They'll be brought to Our presence*'*—so take heed!
There's no negation when *brought to Our presence*;
   With certainty observe the soul's subsistence.
Souls blocked from this subsistence just feel torture;
   Souls which attain are free from any barrier.

I've shown this lamp of sensual perception;
   It is for animals—don't seek its union.
Unite your soul with those of mystic searchers
   Travelling the path instead—their souls are nurturers.
Your hundred lamps, whether or not they burn,   450
   Are separate from each other, not as one.
That's why men go to war with one another,
   Though Prophets never fight against a brother.
The Prophets' light comes from the sun, but sensual
   Light we possess comes from a smoking candle.
The latter dies, the former in the morning
   Shines bright again—one's snuffed, one keeps on burning.
The animal soul stays alive through food,
   Dies with what's bad in it as well as good.
If such a lamp goes finally out one night,   455
   Why should the neighbour's house as well lose light?
The neighbour's house stays bright, so you can see
   The houses' sensual lamps shine separately.
The animal soul is intended here,

Not the divine soul. Let this be quite clear.
When the new moon splits darkness suddenly
  At night, light fills each window equally.
Light in a hundred homes is one. To test,
  Watch if one's light does not fade with the rest.
So long as the bright sun is shining light,   460
  It is a guest at every home in sight.
And when the soul's sun sets, without a doubt
  The light in all its houses will go out.
They're not the same—it's an analogy:
  It guides you, but it robs your enemy.
That vile one's like a spider and he'll spin
  A veil of webs that stinks although it's thin.
With his own web he blocked the light by day;
  He made his seeing eyes turn blind this way.
Steer with a horse's neck and you'll succeed,   465
  But rub its leg and you'll be kicked. Take heed!
Don't ride a wild one with no bridle on.
  Heed intellect and faith, then journey on.
Don't view the rest as weak and as inferior.
  Destroy the self with patience on this venture!

Remainder of the story about the building of the Furthest Place of Worship in Jerusalem.

When Solomon began the new construction—
  Pure like the Kaaba, Mina-like perfection*—
In it much splendour could be easily found,
  Not bland like other buildings seen around.
Each rock cut for that building audibly   470
  Said right from the beginning, '*Please take me!*'
Just as with Adam's body, light shone out
  From all of the cement. And then, without
Someone to carry them, rocks would arrive,
  And all the doors and windows came alive.
God says the wall of paradise is not
  Ugly and lifeless like the walls we've got;
Just like the body's wall, they are aware—
  The house is living, for the king's in there.

Pure water, trees, and fruit—yes, all of them   475
    Have conversations with those in that realm,
Since paradise was not made from material
    But actions and intentions in its people.
This building is from lifeless clay and water;
    That building lives through dutiful surrender.
The first looks like its source with imperfections,
    The second like its source—knowledge and actions.
Throne, palace, crown, and robes give their replies
    To questions from those up in paradise;
The rug will fold itself and then each room   480
    Inside the house is swept without a broom.
Behold the heart's house—grief makes it untidy;
    Without a broom repentance makes it tidy.
His throne moved by itself across the floor;
    Minstrels emerged from knockers on the door.
The everlasting realm is in the heart—
    Since my tongue can't explain it all, why start?

Solomon went to that house every dawn
    To guide the worshippers who'd also gone.
He counselled using song as well as speech;   485
    By action, such as bowing down, he'd teach.
Counsel through action is much more effective,
    Reaching souls though their hearing be defective;
Leadership's false airs too become much less,
    And so such counsel will have more success.

Story about the beginning of the caliphate of Osman and his sermon
explaining how the counsellor who practises what he preaches is
better than the one who just talks.

When he became the caliph, Osman sat
    Upon the pulpit's top step, knowing that
Mohammad's pulpit had three steps and on
    His turn Bu Bakr sat on the second one,
Then Omar chose the third on his accession   490
    Out of respect for custom and religion—

When Osman's turn came he went all the way
   Up to the top on his blessed, fortunate day.
A fault-finder protested, 'You should stop!
   Those two did not take that seat at the top,
So how come you've gone higher than that pair
   When you rank lower and cannot compare?'
'If I select the third step,' Osman said,
   'They'll reckon I'm like Omar then instead.
If on the second, then you will exclaim: 495
   "That's Abu Bakr's! He thinks he's the same."
The top step is Mohammad's—no one can
   Imagine that I'm similar to that man.'
Instead then of a sermon while sat there,
   He sat in silence till the time for prayer.
No one dared say, 'Recite or go away
   From our mosque!' as the hours passed on that day.
Deep awe filled all those gathered in that place
   And God's light filled completely all the space.
The seeing saw His Light fill all those spaces;   500
   The blind could feel its warmth upon their faces—
Through warmth alone the blind could realize
   A never-setting sun shone on their eyes.
This warmth can open eyes, so they can view
   The essence of all hearable things too.
Its heat induces new states of contraction;
   Its radiance gives hearts freedom and expansion.
When the blind one is warmed by lasting light
   From joy he says, 'I can see. I have sight!'

You're drunk Bo 'l-Hasan,* but a word of caution: 505
   There's still a long way till that total vision.
The blind one's portion from the sun can be
   A hundred times this! *God knows best for me.*
Great Avicenna lacked the power to write
   Descriptions of the one who's seen that light.
Though many times as strong, whose tongue's description
   Could draw the veil that covers its perception?
If it should touch the veil, then understand

God's sword will cut off that poor person's hand.
What's a mere hand? He'll chop his head off, brothers.   510
     That stupid head which chops off heads of others.
I've said this hypothetically, since speech
     Cannot extend as far as that its reach.
With testicles my aunt would be my uncle—
     That's hypothetical; it isn't factual.
The tongue's far from the eye of certainty.
     A thousand years? No, more than that for me.
But don't despair, for if God wills, at night
     Immediately the sky will shine down light.
His power each moment chooses to bestow   515
     On stars their influence over mines below.
The sky's stars end the darkness—higher than these,
     God's star is rooted in His qualities.
Seeker of help, the distant sky is near
     To earth through its effects—this should be clear:
Saturn looks so remote from earth, for instance,
     Yet it exerts its influence through the distance.
He folds it like a shade on its return—
     What is a shadow's length next to the sun?
And from pure star-like souls comes succour to   520
     The stars up in the heavens over you.
These stars' forms keep our forms in their control,
     But they must all obey the human soul.

*In explanation of why philosophers say 'Man is the microcosm',
while mystics themselves say, 'Man is the macrocosm'. It is because
the knowledge of philosophers is restricted to the form of Man, while
that of mystics penetrates to the truth of the essence of Man.*

Therefore, in form, you are the microcosm,
     While inwardly you are the macrocosm.
The branches look like they're the ripe fruit's source,
     But they exist for that fruit's sake of course,
Which makes that first. With no prior wish for fruit
     Why would the gardener ever plant the root?
That tree was born from fruit thus inwardly,   525

Though outwardly the fruit comes from the tree.
'Adam and other prophets now stand after
    Myself, Mohammad, and my mission's banner.'
That's also why that virtuous one insisted:
    'We're last yet also first'—that isn't twisted.
'In form I come from Adam, but in essence
    I'm my forefather's father—that's not nonsense,
Since angels bowed to him obediently
    And he rose up to heaven thanks to me.
This forefather was really born from me,   530
    And likewise from the fruit emerged its tree.
Thought leads to action, which is consequential,
    Especially the thought that is eternal.
To sum up, it increasingly is clear
    The caravan from heaven heads down here
In one breath, for it's not a lengthy journey—
    Deserts can't be too vast for the Almighty.
Every moment the heart goes to the Kaaba;
    The body, through the heart, too gains much favour.
Near and far are for bodies in this realm;   535
    They've naught to do with God's transcending them.
Once God transforms the body, then its motion
    Is not in lengths for measured calculation.
There's still much hope—step forward and keep walking,
    Young man, just like a lover, and *quit talking*!
Although you close your eyes without a care,
    You are not still—the ship transports you there.

*Explanation of the hadith: My community is like Noah's
ark—whoever joins me will be saved and whoever stays behind
will drown.*

That's why the Prophet said what now seems clearer:
    'I'm like the ark of Noah for our era,
With my companions in huge storms of rain—   540
    If you hold onto us, there's grace to gain.'
When you are with the master far away
    From ugliness, on his ark night and day,
Protected by a soul that is life-giving,

Asleep on his ark, you are then still travelling.
Don't cut links with the prophet of your day—
    Do not rely on your own skills this way!.
Even if lion-like, without a guide
    You are astray and base, though puffed with pride.
Fly only with the master's wings, so you   545
    Might see the master's armies in plain view.
Your wings will be the waves of his own kindness;
    Later you're borne by flames of his own harshness.
Do not imagine they're a contradiction—
    Through their effects observe how they're in union:
Now he will make you fertile like the land,
    Then he'll inflate you hugely. Understand,
He leaves the mystic's body to lie fallow,
    So roses grow on it, as in a meadow.
But only he sees it—let it be known   550
    That heaven gives scent to the pure alone.
Remove denial of him now from your brain—
    His garden's basil will come as your gain,
And you'll perceive His perfume sent from heaven
    The way Mohammad smelt that scent from Yemen.*
If you line up now in ascension's queue,
    Like Boraq, non-existence soon draws you,
Not physically as if your aim's the moon,
    But how a cane can change to sugar soon;
Not how the vapour rises in ascent,   555
    But how the foetus turns intelligent.
Non-existence's steed takes you through the distance,
    If you're effaced, up to the real existence.
Its hooves brush past the mountains and the seas,
    Leaving behind the sensual world with ease.
Alight the ark and ride the way souls flow
    Towards their True Beloved from below.
Without limbs soar to the eternal realm,
    As souls flee non-existence, just like them.

If listeners' ears were not asleep, you may   560
    Have torn the veil of reasoning away.

Rain pearls, O heavens, on His speech for me.
    Feel small, world, when in His proximity.
Your pearls will multiply if you comply,
    And you'll gain speech and sight, too, from on high.
You'd rain them for your own sake after all,
    Since this would multiply your capital.

Story about Belqis, the Queen of Sheba, sending a gift
to Solomon.

Belqis's gift was forty mules, which bore
    As gifts some gold bricks taken from her store.
On reaching Solomon, all could behold   565
    A marvellous realm carpeted with gold.
Her messengers rode on deep in that realm
    Until the gold no longer dazzled them.
'Let's take our gold back and retrace our route,'
    They said, 'Our task with gold will not bear fruit.
The ground itself is gold in this strange country—
    Bringing gold here as gifts is utter folly.'
(You who bring intellects to God with pride,
    It's worth less than the mud beneath your stride.)
When their gift's worthlessness was very clear,   570
    They were drawn back, embarrassed to be here.
'Whether or not it has worth in this land,
    It's not our call—we're bound by her command.
We have to take it, whether mud or gold;
    The order means we'll do as we've been told.'
'If they say, "Take it back!"' the leader said,
    'We will obey the new command instead.'
Solomon smiled when it was brought in view:
    'When did I ask for mouldy bread from you?
I don't say, "Bring a gift obediently!"   575
    But "Show you're worthy of a gift from me."
For I've got gifts from the Unseen, which you
    Would want if you knew them, but you've no clue.
The gold-producing star's your deity—
    Worship the one who made that star you see!
You pray towards the sun up in the sky,

Devaluing the soul which should rank high.
The sun heats for us at God's order, dunce—
    Calling that "God" is foolish ignorance.
And if the sun's eclipsed, what use is it?   580
    Can you remove the blackness over it?
Won't you then bring to God's court your sad plight,
    Begging: "Remove the blackness. Send us light!"
If you are killed at night, where's your sun then
    To cry to it and beg it saves your men?
Disasters usually happen late at night
    And that is when your god is not in sight.
If you bow properly to God, you'll be
    Rid of stars, welcome in His company.
When you come close we will share a discussion   585
    To see the sun at midnight with new vision:
Pure spirit is its actual rising place;
    Night and day have no difference in that space.
Day is what starts at sunrise usually—
    When this sun shines though, night fades permanently.
An atom cannot stand before the sun.
    Your sun stand next to God? That can't be done.
Your sun which dazzles eyes by its bright glare,
    Leaving men all perplexed—you'll see it there,
Next to God's Throne's Light, atom-like, my friends,   590
    Compared with Boundless Light that never ends.
You'll see it vulnerable and small in size
    When God bestows the power to your eyes.'
God's light, like alchemy, can from afar
    Send sparks through vapour to create a star.
The rare elixir can with half a beam
    Create this sun from darkness while men dream.
The marvellous alchemist, with just one action,
    Attached so many qualities to Saturn.
The other stars and spiritual essences   595
    Must similarly be compared with this.
Physical eyes are subject to the sun—
    Seek a divine eye, a superior one,
So sparkling rays of sunlight will appear
    Abased before its vision when drawn near,

Since light is fire, while this is much more bright;
  Fire seems so dark compared with such pure light.

The miracles and light possessed by Abdollah Maghrebi.

Abdollah Maghrebi said, 'With my sight
  For sixty years I never saw dark night.
For sixty years my eyes did not see darkness,   600
  Neither by night nor day, and not in sickness.'
Sufis confirmed, 'His words are true, for we
  Would follow him at night-time carefully
To wastelands full of thorns and ditches, where
  He shone like the full moon's most radiant glare.
Without the need to turn around he'd say:
  "Watch out for that ditch. Veer the other way!"
Later he would advise, "Head right instead
  Because a thorn bush lies where you will tread."
We'd kiss his feet at daybreak and they would   605
  Seem like a bride's unweathered, soft feet should.
No trace of dirt on them that we could notice,
  Nor scratch, nor bruise—they were completely flawless.'
God had made Maghrebi a 'Mashreqi':
  He made the sunset sunrise-bright, you see.*
This sun of suns' light rides so high by day;
  This man protects all people, come what may.
How should that glorious light not be protection
  When it brings countless suns before one's vision?
Through his light you keep safely walking on   610
  Near dragons and each deadly scorpion.
That holy light proceeds ahead and can
  Tear totally apart each highwayman.
He won't see Prophets put to shame—recite:
  '*In front of them what travels is the light.*'*
That light increases at the Resurrection,
  But ask God for a sample at this junction,
Since He bestows it on the clouds and mist.
  God knows best what to say. Do not resist!

*Solomon told the messengers of Belqis to go back to her with the gifts
that they had brought and invited Belqis to his faith and the
rejection of sun-worship.*

'Go back, embarrassed messengers! This gold   615
    Stays yours. Bring me a heart. Do what you're told.
And add this gold of mine to yours, then stuff
    It up your mule's rear end! I've had enough.
Gold rings are for mules' genitals. For lovers
    Gold is a face turned yellow from love's tortures.
That face becomes the object of God's gaze,
    While gold mines will receive just solar rays.
Is it appropriate for comparison—
    The Lord's attention and that of the sun?
Turn your souls to a shield preventing me   620
    From seizing you, though captive already.'
Birds lured by bait are on the roof up there;
    With wings outstretched they're trapped still in the snare.
Each pinned its heart and soul both on the bait,
    Though not yet in the trap, but it's too late:
Glancing towards the bait is actually
    Binding its feet with knots unwittingly.
The bait says, 'Though you glance to snatch a view,
    I've snatched stability and calm from you.
When that glance pulls you to me, be aware   625
    That I'm not heedless of you drooling there.'

*Story about the pharmacist whose weight was clay soap and how a
customer who ate such clay stole some of it secretly while sugar was
being weighed.*

A man who would have cravings to eat clay
    Bought sugar from the pharmacist one day.
The pharmacist was a most cunning man,
    Using clay weights, not stone, with a clear plan.
He said, 'My weights are made of clay, and so,
    If you desire some sugar, you should know.'

The customer replied, 'My need is desperate,
   So use whatever you think most appropriate.'
He then thought to himself, 'If truth be told,   630
   For one who eats clay they're worth more than gold.'
Just like the broker who once told his son:
   'I've found a bride for you, a lovely one.
She's very pretty, but that ravisher
   Is daughter of the town's confectioner.'
The son said, 'That to me is even better—
   His daughter must be curvier and sweeter.'

The buyer said, 'If you have only clay
   For weights, that's better—I crave clay all day.'
The pharmacist placed clay inside one pan   635
   Instead of stone weights, then that clever man
Placed sugar in the other the same way
   Up to the weight of that first piece of clay.
He took his time to find a pick to use,
   Leaving the customer there as a ruse—
That one gazed at the clay and stealthily
   He stole some, acting so predictably.
He feared, 'He'd better not look round at me
   To check up on me for security.'
The pharmacist saw, but stayed occupied.   640
   'Steal more, sick man, till you are satisfied.
If you desire to steal clay, go ahead—
   You'll just be stealing from yourself instead.
You're frightened of me, but from foolishness.
   I'd be more sad if you were eating less.
Though I am busy, I'm not such a donkey
   To let you pilfer this fine sugar from me.
Once you see how much sugar you have bought,
   Matching the clay that's left, you'll see I'm not
The fool—you are.' The bird likes watching bait,   645
   But bait is robbing it—to see, just wait.
While coveting your brother's meat, your eye
   Is feeding off your own kebab supply.
Such staring is a poisonous arrow—cease

Or else your lust will grow, restraint decrease.
Worldly wealth snares the birds here that are feeble;
   Wealth from beyond snares those birds that are noble,
For it makes mighty birds fall captive there
   Within that realm, which is the deepest snare.

Solomon said, 'I don't crave your dominion,   650
   But rather I will save you now from ruin,
For in your kingdom you are now the bondsmen;
   True rulers are the ones who flee destruction.'
O prisoner of this world, ridiculously
   You've called yourself its ruler—can't you see?
The world's slave with soul captive, for how long
   Will you claim lordship, as if you are strong?

Solomon shows kindness and gentleness to the envoys,
drives away annoyance and harshness from their hearts,
and explains to them the reason he did not accept
the gift.

'Envoys, I'll send you as my envoys now,
   And my refusal's better anyhow.
Relate to Belqis wonders you have seen   655
   About the gold-filled fields where you have been,
So she learns we don't covet gold at all—
   We get ours from the One who makes it all.
The One who, at His mere wish, the whole planet
   Would turn to gold with precious pearls laid on it.
(You who choose gold, it is for this same reason
   God turns earth silver for the Resurrection.)*
We don't need gold; we are so skilful we
   Turn earthly beings to gold with alchemy.
How could we beg more gold from you, we who   660
   Can make an alchemist of all of you.
Abandon even your own realm, my sons—
   Beyond these there are more dominions.
You call a mere stone "throne" and deem it more

Your seat of honour, while outside the door.
You don't rule your own beard—your power's that feeble.
    You can't claim mastery over good and evil.
Your beard turns white regardless of your wishes.
    You with strange hopes should feel embarrassed by this.
He owns the kingdoms; He'll give hundreds to   665
    Those who bow down and wipe all else from view.
Prostration to the Lord tastes sweeter than
    Two hundred worldly fortunes to each man.
"I don't want kingdoms," then you will exclaim,
    "Keeping prostration's kingdom is my aim." '

Worldly kings have an evil attitude;
    They've no clue of the wine of certitude,
Or they'd, like Ebn-e Adham, lose their wits
    And start to smash their kingdom into bits.
But God wished to maintain this world, so He   670
    Placed seals on mouths and eyes deliberately,
So thrones and crowns would taste sweet and they'd say:
    'We'll tax landowners and then have our way.'
Should taxes raise gold-filled dunes of much worth,
    Inheritance like this must stay on earth:
Kingship and gold can't travel with your soul—
    Give gold away, acquire true vision's kohl
To see this world's a well, and then grip fast
    The rope as Joseph did once in the past,
So when you get out from it finally,   675
    Your soul says: '*Goodness—this youth is for me!*'*
Inside the well you see the wrong way round,
    Labelling 'gold' some stones upon the ground.
Children in folly, when they wish to play,
    Claim crockery is gold in the same way.
Mystics are alchemists, so to their vision
    Gold mines are worthless and have no attraction.

How a dervish saw in a dream a group of shaikhs and begged for a daily portion of lawful food without having to earn it and while unable to worship, and how they instructed him and how the bitter and sour fruit of the mountain became sweet to him through their grace.

A dervish once said, 'In my dream last night
    I saw some Khezr-like Sufis. What a sight!
I asked them, "Where can I obtain, for free,   680
    Lawful food that will not be bad for me?"
They led me to the mountains and they shook
    The fruit down from the trees, and I partook.
"God made the fruit taste sweet to you," they said,
    "Through our grace and arrival for your aid.
Eat what is pure and lawful now without
    A headache or the need to rush about."
This food gave me amazing speech that day
    Which stunned minds who'd now relish things I'd say.
I asked, "O Lord, is this a strange temptation?   685
    Give something to me that from most stays hidden."
That speech left me; I gained a happy heart.
    Like pomegranates I could split apart
From mystic savour: I said, "On that side,
    If there is just this joy I feel inside,
I wouldn't ask for more grace or more gains;
    I'd shun the houris and the sugar canes.
From former earnings, as most people do,
    I've saved in my shirtsleeve a coin or two." '

He resolves: 'I will give this gold to that firewood-carrier since I've gained sustenance from the miracles of the shaikhs,' but the firewood-carrier is upset with his thought and intention.

'A poor man with some brushwood passed that way,   690
    Weary and worn out by his work that day.
So I thought, "Since I have become now free
    From earning my own living, thankfully,

Fruit tasting sweet to me which others hate
　　And sustenance arriving on my plate,
Since I don't need to fill my stomach, I
　　Will give these coins to that man passing by,
So that hard-working man enjoys a day
　　With the provisions for which they will pay."
He read my thoughts since he had the perception　　695
　　That God's light gives to certain people's vision.
To him, the secret thoughts would all appear
　　Just like the lamp's glass—bright and crystal clear.
From him, no thoughts were hidden; he could reign
　　As ruler of what people's hearts contain.
Under his breath he muttered to what I
　　Had thought about in this form of reply:
"You think about the kings in such a way?
　　If they don't give, how will you eat each day?"
I didn't understand, but my heart shook,　　700
　　Affected sharply by this man's rebuke.
Then, with the grandeur of a lion, he
　　Put down his load and walked across to me.
The way he put the wood down was so powerful
　　That all my limbs began right then to tremble.
He said, "O Lord, if You have an elite
　　Whose prayers are always answered and whose feet
Are blessed, let Your grace now with alchemy
　　Transform this wood to gold immediately."
I watched the brushwood turn to gold, amazed.　　705
　　It was as if a massive fire had blazed.
I lost my wits for quite a while and when
　　I came back to myself through fervour, then
He said, "God, should those great ones be discreet
　　And fame be shunned by this reserved elite,
Then turn the gold to brushwood now once more
　　Without delay, just as it was before."
To brushwood all the gold at once transformed—
　　I got drunk witnessing what was performed.
He picked the wood up and walked rapidly　　710
　　Towards the town and far away from me.
I wished to follow him with every question

I had that puzzled me, and then to listen,
But awe of him had shackled both my feet:
  The vulgar can't get close to God's elite,
But if one does approach, give this instruction:
  "Bow down, for this is due to their attraction." '

Consider as a godsend then their guidance,
  If God's friends should admit you near their presence.
Don't be like one who nears, then suddenly   715
  Falls off the path for nothing, flimsily.
When out of kindness they let him nearby,
  He will complain, 'It's just an ox's thigh.'
Liar, it's not an ox's thigh! It has
  Appeared to you as one, for you're an ass.
This is a royal gift. It is pure grace
  With no ulterior aim or other face.

Solomon urges the envoys to hasten Belqis's emigration for the sake of faith.

King Solomon in battle had no peer,
  And he attracted Belqis's troops near,
Saying, 'Come back soon for God's Bounty's ocean,   720
  Has surged and now, dear men, its waves have risen;
The surges of these waves each moment are
  Scattering more waves to you from afar.
Welcome, you righteous ones and wait no more,
  For paradise has opened now its door.'
He added then, 'Head off, dear messengers,
  To Belqis and her faithful followers,
To say, "Come here as fast as possible
  For *God invites to peace.** This is for all."
Come, seeker of felicity! Don't wait   725
  For grace is opening up right now its gate.
And you who're not a seeker, hurry too—
  This friend will help you find the urge in you.'

The reason for Ebrahim Ebn-e Adham's migration and relinquishing the kingdom of Khorasan.

Like Ebn-e Adham, break up rapidly
  This kingdom, and thus gain eternity!
One night while he was sleeping on his throne
  Guards on his rooftop made their presence known.
By having guards, this king's aim wasn't to
  Ward off all rogues and burglars, for he knew
That the just man is always free from harm   730
  And in his heart he feels secure and calm.
Justice is thus protector of delight,
  Not guards who beat their sticks throughout the night.
His aim in listening to these lute sounds rather
  Was to hear God's speech to His ardent lover:
The clarion's blasts and banging on the drum
  Evoke the trumpet of that world to some.
Theosophers say, 'These tunes reach our ears
  Directly from the turning of the spheres,
And all the songs men sing and lutes they play   735
  Are the spheres' turning sounds which come our way.'
The faithful say, 'It's heaven's influence
  That makes harsh noises beautiful at once.
We were all parts of Adam, and back then
  We heard those tunes which now we hear again.
Now inside earthly forms, we're doubting it,
  But we still can remember them a bit.'

It's mixed now with the dust of earthly grief—
  How can that music give the same relief?
Pure water mixed with urine and pollution   740
  Becomes an acrid and most foul solution.
Our bodies hold some water, too, no doubt,
  Though it be urine, which can put flames out.
When made unclean, water won't lose its power
  To put grief's flames out even if they tower.
Sama' is food for God's true devotees,

For it induces union's ecstasies.*
Music can strengthen mental images
   Which change to forms through music's influences.
Music intensifies the fire of love,   745
   Like flames in one who dropped nuts from above:

*Story about the thirsty man who, from the top of a walnut tree,
would throw down walnuts into a stream within a hollow below
without himself going to the water, so that he could hear the sound
of splashing as the walnuts fell, and how the sound of the splashing
made him as happy as sweet* sama' *does.*

Water filled hollows near a walnut tree,
   From which one thirsty threw down nuts with glee.
The walnuts rained down from the treetop where
   He'd climbed up—he heard splashes form down there.
A knowledgeable man said, 'Stop it! Cease!
   The walnuts only make your thirst increase.
The harder walnuts are thrown down that way,
   The further that they will be borne away.
When you come down from there it will be clear.   750
   The stream will then have borne them far from here.'
The thrower said, 'These nuts aren't my objectives.
   Observe beyond appearance new perspectives.
The splashing sound is what I want to hear,
   And I want surface ripples to appear.'
In this world what do thirsty men desire?
   To circle pools forever and not tire:
To circle streams, their water and its sound,
   Just like the Kaaba pilgrims circle round.
Hosamoddin, Truth's Light, this *Masnavi*   755
   Makes you my actual aim so similarly.
In both its roots and branches, altogether
   It's yours and you've accepted it, my brother.
By kings, both good and bad things are accepted;
   When they accept, it is no more rejected.
If you have planted it, now water it.
   If you've released it, then untangle it.
My aim's your mystery with this composition.

My aim's your sweet voice with this recitation.
Your voice is God's voice to my loving heart;   760
   God won't force lovers to remain apart.

Beyond analogy there is a union
   Between God and the soul of every human.
'Human', I said, not 'ghoul'—fit for this role
   Are just souls that can tell another soul.
If that's a human, where's humanity?
   You just see its rear-end unfortunately.
You've read ' *You did not throw when you just threw,* '*
   But you're mere body, separate with no clue.
Like Belqis, throw the kingdom's body out   765
   For Solomon's sake—leave behind all doubt.
I say, ' *God's strength!* '* not for myself, but due
   To thoughts in the suspicious person who
Hears what I say and inwardly imagines
   Some reasons for denial and suspicions.
By ' *God's strength!* ' 'I am helpless' is my aim
   Since your heart's filled with oppositional blame.
My words stick in my throat, and so I'll stay
   Silent—you say what you would like to say.
The reed-flute was once played by a reed-player   770
   When suddenly a fart boomed from his chair.
The reed-player turned to his backside and said:
   'If you can play it better, go ahead.'
While on the mystic path, please realize
   You must bear what's ill-mannered to your eyes.
If you see someone who complains forever:
   'So-and-so has bad traits and a bad temper,'
Count that complainant as himself ill-mannered
   For he speaks ill of someone else bad-tempered.
Good men are unassuming and forbearing   775
   Of every brother's temper and shortcoming.
The shaikh's complaint, though, comes from God's command,
   Not finding fault, desire, or rage that's fanned.
That's not complaint, but to reform your soul
   Like that of prophets carrying out that role.

The Lord commanded their intolerance;
　　If not their kindness would bear insolence.
Forbearance killed their low selves long ago;
　　God ordered the intolerance they show.
Solomon, show God's clemency to crows   780
　　And falcons both, all birds, both friends and foes.
Your clemency won scores like Belqis there—
　　'Guide my folk! They don't understand,'* your prayer.

Solomon sends a threat to Belqis, saying: 'Don't think of persisting in polytheism. Don't delay!'

'Come, Belqis, or it will turn out so badly.
　　You'll face a huge revolt from your own army.
Your chamberlain will break your gate apart.
　　Your soul will then become your foe at heart.
All atoms are God's army—you will see
　　When you investigate this carefully.'

You've seen how wind spilled all the Aad folk's blood,   785
　　And what mere water managed with the Flood,
And how waves struck at Pharaoh with such hate,
　　And what the earth displayed through Korah's fate,
And what mere birds did to that elephant,*
　　And how the gnat ate Nimrod's skull, how stunned
Men were when Prophet David hurled one stone
　　That toppled a huge foe all on its own,
While on the foes of Lot stones once rained down,
　　Driving them in black water's depths to drown.
And then there's rational help I could relate   790
　　Prophets received from what's inanimate.
But then *The Masnavi* would stretch too long
　　For forty camels: their backs aren't that strong.
Against the infidels hands testify
　　As God's troops, for on that day they can't lie.
Your learning leads you to oppose God—here
　　You are among His army, so feel fear:
Each limb of yours is from His troops—though they

Obey you now, they're being false today.
If He tells your eyes, 'Give him pain!' then you　　795
　　Will feel severe eye pain without ado.
If He tells your teeth, 'Make him ill!' you'll feel
　　Your teeth soon make you suffer pain so real.
Open your textbook's chapter on disease;
　　Read what the bodily troops can do with ease.
He is the soul of everything in sight—
　　How can His enmity be something light?

'Leave demons and the jinn alone instead—
　　They rout foes' troops for me!' Solomon said.
Relinquish, Belqis, first your monarchy,　　　800
　　Then find me—you'll then gain all sovereignty.
And when you reach me you will then find out
　　Without me you were just a form sketched out.'

Even a sultan's sketch upon a wall
　　Is just a form without a soul at all.
And its adornment is for others' gain;
　　Its eyes and mouth are open, but in vain.
You've wasted your life on what doesn't matter
　　And you can't tell yourself now from another.
You stop at every form you see, to say:　　　805
　　'I am this.' No, by God, you're not. No way!
If you withdraw from people for one moment,
　　You fill with grief, anxiety, and torment.
When you are That One, you can't be just body.
　　You're drunk then through yourself and truly lovely.
You're your own hunting bird, prey, and the snare;
　　You're your own rooftop, rug, and special chair.
An essence is completely independent;
　　From them all accidents emerge, dependent.
If born of Adam, sit now like that first king　　　810
　　And see within yourself all of your offspring.
What's in the jar that's not found in the river?
　　What's in the house that's not in cities ever?

The world's the jar, the heart's the river clearly;
    The world's one room, the heart a marvellous city.

*Solomon declares, 'My effort concerning our faith is purely on
God's command. There isn't the slightest self-interest in me
concerning you, your beauty, and your kingdom. You'll see for
yourself when your inner eye is opened with the Light of God.'*

'Come, for I am a Prophet with a call.
    Like death, I slay lust; I've fled its control.
I rule lust, if there is some still in place,
    Not captive to lust for an idol's face.
My roots are steeped in smashing them—I am   815
    Like idol-smashing Prophet Abraham.
If I go to an idol's temple, it
    Prostrates to worship me, not I to it.'

The Prophet and Bu Jahl in one instance
    Both stood in one, but their acts had much difference:
Bu Jahl bowed to the idols on display;
    They bowed before Mohammad straight away.
The world of lust's an idol temple where
    Both infidels and Prophets live, but there
Lust is the slave for every holy one—   820
    Unlike mere alloy, pure gold doesn't burn.
The holy are pure gold, the infidel
    Is false coin—both are in the crucible.
The latter turns black once it enters here;
    The former's goldenness is made more clear.
Pure gold will gladly throw its limbs in there;
    Its veins smile in the fire without a care.
Our body veils us from the people's vision;
    Hidden beneath mere straw, we are an ocean.
Don't look at faith's king as mere bodily clay—   825
    That's what accursed Satan did that day.*
How can one smear the lofty sun with just
    A handful of your mud? If you pour dust
And ashes now on top of shining light,

It will still rise through them before your sight.
What's straw to cover water? What's mere clay
    To cover up a single solar ray?
Rise Belqis and her kind like Ebn-e Adham,
    Scatter the smoke of this most transient kingdom!

Remainder of the Story of Ebrahim Ebn-e Adham.

That man of good repute while on his throne   830
    Heard banging on his roof one night alone:
Loud footsteps from the roof of his great palace.
    He thought, 'Who has the gall now to attempt this?'
He shouted through the window, 'Who's up there?
    Is it a ghost, since humans wouldn't dare?'
A wondrous group brought their heads to his sight:
    'We're going all around to search tonight.'
'What are you seeking?' 'Camels,' they replied.
    'Camels on roofs? Why have you even tried?'
They snapped back, 'Why seek God while you still sit   835
    On a grand throne? That's mad too, isn't it?'
He wasn't seen again. That was it. Closed.
    He vanished from all people like a ghost,
While from the people his true nature then
    Was veiled—just cloak and beard were seen by men.
On leaving everybody's vision, he
    Became just like the phoenix, legendary:
The soul of every bird that's risen to
    Mount Qaf draws from all praises that are due.

Once this light from the East had reached her nation,   840
    Belqis and all her men made a commotion.
All the dead spirits took wing suddenly:
    They peeked out of the body's grave to see
And gave each other good news, 'Now a call
    Is coming from the sky above us all.'
That call makes faiths grow that before were lean
    And the heart's branch and leaf transform to green.
Like Resurrection's blast, Solomon's breath

Freed all the corpses from the grave of death.
   After this, may felicity reach you,   845
      Solomon. It has passed. *God knows what's true.*

*The remainder of the story about the People of Sheba and the
advice and guidance Solomon gave to them, for each one something
appropriate for him and his difficulties with faith and the heart, and
how Solomon hunted each kind of intellectual bird with the whistle
and bait appropriate for it.*

I'll speak with force about the Sheba nation:
   When His fine breeze came to the tulip garden
People attained their union on that day;
   Children went to their source then straight away.
Secret love's group among groups is like kindness
   Surrounded by the censure caused by sickness.
Bodies give spirits what they have of baseness;
   Spirits give bodies what they have of greatness.
O lovers, this sought draught of love's for you.   850
   You will endure—Eternity's yours, too.
Forgetful ones, arise and love. This is
   Joseph's scent, so inhale it and feel bliss.*
You know bird-speech, so share with us the song
   Of every single bird that comes along.
God sent you to the birds and so He taught
   The song of every bird, which you had sought.
Tell the determinist bird of that notion;
   Speak patience to the bird whose wings are broken.
Maintain the patient bird both safe and cheerful.   855
   Describe Qaf to the Anqa—it's not fearful.
And warn the pigeon of the hawk, then talk
   About peace and forbearance to the hawk.
As for the bat that is deprived of sight,
   Help it become familiar with the light.
Teach peace now to the partridge, that warmonger,
   And show dawn's indications to the rooster.
From hoopoe to the eagle similarly
   Please show the way. *God knows best, doesn't he?*

Belqis becomes liberated from the kingdom and drunk with longing
for belief, and the attention of her aspiration becomes severed from
all of creation at the moment of her migration, except for from her
throne.

Solomon whistled to the birds of Sheba   860
   And captured all of them at once, all eager,
Except those not possessing any heart,
   Or soul, or thought, deaf and dumb from the start.
I'm wrong for if the deaf one should submit
   To God's speech, He'll give hearing then to it.
Belqis resolved with heart and soul at last,
   Regretting time she'd wasted in the past.
She gave her wealth and kingdom up the same
   As lovers who shun honour and good name.
The slaves she'd had, and all the fine handmaidens   865
   Now seemed in her eyes like some rotten onions.
Palaces, orchards, rivers all around
   Now seemed like trash heaps due to love she'd found.
Love overwhelms and even makes the lovely,
   Through its dismissiveness, appear so ugly.
God's jealousy makes emeralds appear
   Like leeks—negation's meaning is thus clear.
It is '*There is no God but He*'* that can
   Make the full moon appear like a mere pan.
Sheba's queen missed no wealth and no possession   870
   Except for her throne—that's the sole exception.
Solomon realized then what she'd tried
   To hide, since his heart had a route inside—
Someone who hears the voice of ants can hear
   The secret groans of people who aren't near.
One who perceives what '*One ant said*'* can tell
   The ancient heavens' secrets just as well.
From distance he saw that the one now known
   For her submission longed still for her throne.
It would take far too long now to explain   875
   Why she still loved the throne from her past reign.
The writer's pen might be inanimate

Unlike him, but it's his associate,
And every tool belonging to the craftsman
   Is an inanimate friend of that person.

I would have told the reason with precision,
   But fog now clouds your eyes of comprehension.
Transporting that throne to her new abode
   Was not an option for that huge a load.
Too risky to attempt to take apart,   880
   Its parts were joined just like a body part.
Solomon said, 'Although to me it's known
   She'll in the end lose feelings for that throne,
For when the soul shows it has turned so fair
   Through union, then the body can't compare;
And when the pearl is captured from the ocean,
   One then sees foam and twigs with much revulsion;
And when the sparkling sun should raise its head
   Who'd settle then for Scorpio's stars instead?
Despite all this, we have to seek for now   885
   A way to have it moved here anyhow,
So she won't feel deprived when we next meet,
   At peace like children with their yearned-for treat.
For us it's trivial, but to her it's dear—
   Admit the bad to join the good ones here.
That throne will then remind her of her roots,
   As Ayaz used his old cloak and old boots,*
So that flawed one remembers still her past,
   From where she came to where she's reached at last.'

God also keeps before our eyes each day   890
   Our origin of semen, flesh, and clay:
'Where did I bring you from, you whose intentions
   Are so bad that you now raise your objections?
You used to be a lover of that place,
   Denying talk about this present grace.
This grace here is your past denial's rebuttal,
   What you would claim when clay still and not rational.

The proof against it is your transformation,
    But medicine's made you a sicker person!
How could an earthly form start contemplating,   895
    And semen start denying things and hating?
You lacked both heart and soul then, and so you
    Denied reflection and rejection too.
From that inert state your denying began,
    And you were resurrected as a man.'
It is like knocking on a door to hear
    That owner claim, 'The owner isn't here.'
'Isn't' means really 'is' here if you're looking
    For that same person, so you won't stop knocking.
Your past denying serves to make so obvious   900
    That from inert things He can raise what's wondrous.
So much was done until from the terrestrial
    Through '*has there come a time?*'* emerged denial.
Water and clay would say, 'There's no denying!'
    And they'd shout, 'Nor informing!' while informing!
I'd like to show this in a hundred ways
    But brains can't follow subtle speech's ways.

Solomon solves the problem of bringing Belqis's throne from Sheba.

A ghoul claimed, 'I will conjure it right now
    Before you leave this place, if you allow.'
Asaf said, 'Using God's Most Powerful Name,   905
    I'll fetch it here for you if that's your aim.'
The ghoul had mastered sorcery, no doubt,
    But Asaf's speech's breath brought it about:
That very moment Belqis's throne came
    Through Asaf, not the ghoul with his big claim.
Solomon said, 'Praise be to God for this
    And countless other miracles of His.'
Solomon looked then at the throne with glee
    And said, 'You're a fool-catcher, former tree!'
How many fools bow down their heads before   910
    What's carved from stone or wood and nothing more.
Clueless about the soul, the fool detects
    Movement inside him, some most slight effects:

He has perceived while drunk and stupefied
    That stones speak and instruct. His mind has lied,
Playing in wrong locations worship's game
    He deems a real and a stone lion the same.
The lion that's actually real throws him a bone
    Nonetheless from munificence alone,
Saying, 'Although that dog is flawed, my kindness   915
    Gives bone-like gifts to everyone regardless.'

Story about how Halima asked idols for help when she lost Mohammad whom she had been weaning and how the idols trembled and prostrated and bore witness to the magnificence of Mohammad's mission.

I'll tell you of Halima's mystery
    So her tale can reveal your misery.
She parted young Mohammad from her breast,
    Holding him like a flower that's caressed
So he would be untouched by any bother,
    So she might take this king to his grandfather.
While bringing what had been entrusted, fear
    Led her towards the Kaaba, and once near
She heard a voice shout: 'Kaaba's wall, a sun   920
    That is magnificent chose you and shone
Its light on you—there comes to you today
    From that Most Generous Sun ray after ray.
Today a king, who has great fortune too,
    Will bring each kind of trapping here for you.
Today, without doubt, you'll become once more
    The station for exalted souls that soar.
Souls of the holy now will come to you
    From all around, drunken with passion too.'
This shouting made Halima lose her mind;   925
    Nobody was in front, no one behind;
Nothing in any of the six directions
    But all this shouting had no interruptions
Nor pause. She put Mohammad on the ground
    And sought the shouting's source from all around.
She sought it everywhere and then, with pleas,

Cried, 'Where's the king who speaks such mysteries?
For such a loud shout comes from all around,
   So, Lord, please tell me where its source is found.'
She didn't see a soul—inevitably   930
   This made her shake like branches on a tree.
She went back to that child with holy grace,
   But couldn't find Mohammad in his place.
Her heart grew more bewildered than before;
   Her world turned dark through all the grief she bore.
She ran to houses and made a commotion:
   'Who's taken that unique pearl from the ocean?'
The Meccans answered, 'We were not aware
   That you had even left a child back there.'
She wept and moaned so much then, mesmerized,   935
   That others wept because they sympathized.
Beating her breast she wept so movingly
   This made the others weep in sympathy.

Story about the old Bedouin who directed Halima to seek help from the idols.

An old man with a cane approached the screamer
   And asked, 'What's happened now to you, Halima,
That you have stoked a fire inside your heart
   And burned it with laments? How did this start?'
She said, 'I am Mohammad's foster-mother,
   Trusted to take him back to his grandfather.
I made it to the Kaaba, but once there   940
   I heard strange voices sounding in the air,
And when I heard like this that awesome sound,
   I put the boy that moment on the ground,
So I could see whose voice it was, for it
   Was very lovely, fine, and delicate.
I neither found a trace of anyone
   Nor did the sound pause for one breath. Not one.
And when from my heart's turmoil I returned
   I couldn't find the boy there. My heart burned!'
The man said, 'Daughter, don't you suffer grief.   945
   I'll take you to a queen now for relief—

She can tell you that lost child's situation:
   She'll tell you how he is and his location.'
Halima said, 'I'd be your sacrifice,
   Well-spoken man who seems to me so nice.
Come, show me to that queen that has this vision
   Through which she can tell of the child's condition.'
He took her to Ozza: 'This idol's been
   Gifted with knowledge of all that's unseen.
Each person finds his lost one thanks to her   950
   Once he has hurried here as worshipper.'
He then prostrated to Ozza in prayer:
   'Goddess of Arabs, sea of kindness, fair
And generous to us, Ozza, like a saviour,
   Rescuing us from snares with every favour,
For which all Arabs feel a debt to you,
   So they must do what you tell them to do—
Halima has come here in hope of aid
   Beneath your willow branch's soothing shade,
For she has lost a child and feels to blame;   955
   Mohammad is that lost child's lovely name.'
All of the idols bowed and made prostration
   As soon as they had heard Mohammad's mention.
They said, 'What kind of search is this? Begone!
   Mohammad has deposed us. He's the one
By whom we've been reduced to rubble and
   Have been stripped of all value in this land.
The covetous saw in us fantasies
   Before his coming, but they'll all now cease.
They'll vanish now his court has reached this land: 960
   Water rules out ablution using sand.*
Do not stir trouble, old man—leave today!
   Mohammad-envy might burn us away.
For God's sake, go before it is too late,
   So you don't get burned by the fire of fate.
Why play around now with a dragon's tail—
   Do you not know what all this will entail?
This news makes oceans surge up and mines quake
   And all the seven heavens start to shake.'
On hearing this from those stone idols, he   965

Dropped his cane on the floor immediately.
Then, trembling due to all that had been happening,
    The old man's teeth could be heard loudly chattering.
Just like a naked man in freezing winter
    He loudly screamed, 'Disaster!' with a shudder.
Halima saw him in that awful way
    And she lost self-control too straight away,
Saying: 'Old man, although I suffer grief,
    I am bewildered now beyond belief.
The wind one moment is addressing me,   970
    And then the next stone forms are schooling me.
The wind speaks now to me with words and language,
    Stone forms then start to teach me some new knowledge.
My child was snatched by those from the Unseen
    Who live in heaven and whose wings are green.*
Who should I moan about? To whom complain?
    I'm now impassioned, dizzy in my brain.
God's jealousy has closed my lips. I'll say
    This much: My child's lost—that's all I'll convey—
If I say any more and not restrain   975
    Myself, they'll tie me with a madman's chain.'
The old man said, 'Halima, for this grace
    Rejoice and bow in thanks—don't scratch your face.
He won't be lost to you, so don't you fret.
    The world will get lost in him once they've met.
Each moment countless guards of his are found
    In front of him, behind, and all around.
Didn't you see those idols of renown,
    On hearing your child's name, come tumbling down?
This is a wondrous era and so rare—   980
    In my long life I've seen none to compare.'

Since stones wept at the news about his mission,
    What will it do to sinners—just imagine!
You can't blame stone that people worshipped it—
    No one was ever forced to pray to it.
This helpless idol is so terrified—
    Imagine how the guilty will be tried?

*Abd al-Mottaleb, Mohammad's grandfather, learns about Halima
losing Mohammad and searches for him around the city, then weeps
by the door of the Kaaba, prays to God, and finds him.*

Mohammad's grandfather soon heard about
    Halima's public screams and shouting out,
Which were so loud that people miles away   985
    Could hear. Abd al-Mottaleb right away
Perceived what they must mean and he began
    To weep and beat his breast. That frantic man
In grief went to the Kaaba's door to pray:
    'You who know mysteries of both night and day,
I don't see in myself the qualities
    Entitling me to know your mysteries,
Nor any virtue that might give me more
    Chance for acceptance at your fortunate door,
Or that my lowered head should qualify   990
    For fortune to smile down when I should cry.
But I did see in that unique pearl's face,
    O Generous One, the traces of Your grace.
Though from me, he does not resemble me,
    Nor any copper ones—he's alchemy.
The wonders I have seen in him are vast;
    I've not seen them in others in the past.
No one could ever properly convey
    The wonders which Your grace has sent his way.
Since I have seen them all with certain vision,   995
    I know he is a pearl from your deep ocean.
I also hope he will convince you, so
    Please tell me how he's faring, you who know!'

A shout then came out from within the Kaaba:
    'He now will show his face to you, grandfather.
He's fortunate to have received our favours
    And he has angels as protecting saviours.
We make so famous that which is revealed
    Of him, but keep his inner being concealed.

Water and clay was gold originally; 1000
    As goldsmiths we use it for jewellery:
Sometimes a sheath to hold a sword of iron,
    Sometimes a collar for a special lion,
Sometimes balls fixed on top of thrones instead,
    Sometimes the crown that men want on their head.
We love this earth of ours—that's truly meant—
    Since it surrenders and remains content.
Sometimes we manifest a king from it,
    Sometimes we make it crazed by him a bit.
A thousand lovers and beloveds all 1005
    Because of him, while searching, weep and bawl.
This is our work, unnoticed by those who
    Have no deep interest in the work we do,
Though we bestow on earth this fine distinction
    Just as we give food to those fleeing famine.
Earth has the form of dust to normal sight;
    Within it has the attributes of light.
Its form is warring with its inner being,
    Which is a jewel; stone's its low form you're seeing.
Its form says, "We are this and naught besides." 1010
    Its inner being: "Look carefully on all sides."
Its form denies: "There's nothing there inside."
    Its inner being: "We'll show what it's denied."
Its form and inner being war on—the two
    Of course draw succour from what they both do.
We make forms from this sour-faced earth, and we
    Reveal its hidden laughter inwardly:
The earth's in tears with sorrow shown outside;
    A million smiles which none can see still hide.
Revealing secrets is the work we do— 1015
    We bring all hidden matters in plain view.
The thief stays silent to deny of course,
    But law enforcers bring truth out by force.
These earthly forms have stolen all our favour,
    So we make them confess—we make them suffer.
Many great children have been born on earth,
    Mohammad though is of superior worth.
The earth and sky together grew so joyful:

"Such a great king was born from this fine couple!"
Joy made the sky split open so abruptly;   1020
   His liberty turned earth white as a lily.
O fine earth, your exterior and interior
   Are warring and they're striking at each other.
Whoever fights himself for His Lord's pleasure
   Such that his soul opposes scent and colour,
Their darkness fighting with his light, soon finds
   His soul's sun never sets like other kinds.
The sky lets people rest their feet on it
   If they have striven for our benefit.
Your outward form laments because of darkness;   1025
   Your inner being's a garden full of roses.
His aim's like that of Sufis with sour faces
   Who shun those who would douse their light's last traces;
Mystics are like the hedgehogs which conceal
   Their pleasure deep behind sharp spines foes feel:
The orchard's hidden, thorns as clear as day:
   "Enemy thief, stay far away!" they say.
Hedgehog, your spines stop you from being hurt
   And Sufi-like your head hides in your shirt,
So rosy-cheeked ones with a thorn's bad nature   1030
   Will not attain a fraction of your pleasure.
Although your boy is like a child he feeds
   The whole world by providing for their needs.
Through him we made a world alive and we
   Make heavens slaves who serve him dutifully.'
'Where is he now?' Abd al-Mottaleb said,
   'You who know, tell me which way I should head!'

*Abd al-Mottaleb asks where Mohammad is: 'Where can I find
him?' An answer comes from inside the Kaaba to tell him where.*

A voice reached him from deep inside the Kaaba:
   'The child who is well guided and pure, searcher,
Is in a certain valley near a tree.'   1035
   The blessed old man set off immediately,
The Qoraysh* leaders riding by his side,
   Since his forefather was their source of pride.

They all went back to Adam, and today
    They were the champions at the feast and fray.
The lineage was his husk, though it had been
    Filtered through the best rulers they had seen;
His kernel was beyond the husk, and there
    Was naught in this world like it to compare.
None seek the birth of God's light as a proof—   1040
    What need does God's robe have for warp and woof?
The plainest robe of honour He bestows
    Outshines that of the sun with its bright glows.

Remainder of the story about God's mercy calling Belqis.

Rise, Belqis, see God's kingdom with true vision!
    Gather pearls from the shore of God's vast ocean.
Your sisters live in heaven's lofty palace—
    Why do you act a queen for just a carcass?
Of all the fine gifts they've gained, do you know
    What that Great Sultan opted to bestow?
Why bring out drummers to create a scene,   1045
    Proclaiming: 'I'm the grimy bath-stove's queen!'

Parable about Man's satisfaction with this world and his world-desiring covetousness and heedlessness of the fortune of the spiritual ones, who are his kindred and are crying out: 'If only my people would know!'*

A dog saw a blind beggar down an alley
    And tore his cloak by biting him so badly.
We're telling a fine tale we've shared before*
    To stress the moral point in it once more.
'Your friends are in the mountains,' that man said,
    'Right now they're busy hunting there instead.
They hunt up there wild asses they can find,
    So why in alleys do you hurt the blind?'

False shaikh, don't try evasive lies again.   1050
    Your briny water tempted some blind men:

'They're my disciples and I'm brackish water;
   They drink from me then turn blind not long after.'
Make yours sweet from that of the mystic ocean—
   Don't make snares from yours for those who lack vision.
God's lions hunt wild asses—come and see!
   How come you hunt the blind pretentiously?
What's a wild ass? They block all things from sight
   Since they are brave and drunk with God's pure light.
They left then died in sheer bewilderment   1055
   After they witnessed this King go and hunt.
He uses them like dead birds He puts there
   To lure more of their kind towards the snare.
The dead bird has no choice regarding union:
   '*The heart's between two fingers*'* says tradition.
Those lured by that dead bird look up to see
   They are the King's prey in reality.
But those who turn away from it won't ever
   Approach close to the hand of that Great Hunter.
Each says, 'Don't look at me as if I'm dead—   1060
   See how He has preserved me here instead.
Since I was killed by him, I'm not a carcass.
   Just my appearance looks now like I'm lifeless.
My wings produced my movement previously,
   Now it's the Judge who is controlling me.
My body's lost the motion that was transient;
   My motion's now from Him, so it is permanent.
If one moves crookedly in front of me,
   Even a phoenix, I'll kill mercilessly.
If you're alive, do not see me as dead.   1065
   Slave, see me in the Ruler's hand instead.'
Jesus revived the dead with holy grace—
   The palm of his Creator's hand's my place.
Can I stay dead while held in God's own hand?
   Jesus's hand is similar—understand!
I'm Jesus, but whomever my pure breath
   Gives life to always lives and won't taste death.
The corpse revived by Jesus did die later—
   Give your life to this Jesus, live forever!
The staff in my own Moses-like pure hand,   1070

I'm visible, though he's not—understand!
I span the sea for the believers' sake
    Bridge-like, but for vile Pharaoh I'm a snake.
Don't look at just the staff, son, for without
    God's power the staff would not be strong. Don't doubt!
The flood's waves were a staff and they consumed
    Sorcery's followers whose pomp was doomed.
If we should now count all the staffs of God
    We'd tear up Pharaoh's followers' vile fraud,
But leave them there on pastures where they graze   1075
    On sweet, but poisonous grass in their sick ways.
If there weren't Pharaoh and his role as head,
    Where would hell find the fuel with which it's fed?
First fatten it, then kill it as you should,
    O butcher, for in hell the dogs lack food.
If in this world there were no enemy,
    Then people's rage would vanish instantly.
That rage is hell. Enmity is its food
    To live, without which it's killed by the good.
If mercy should remain without wrath here,   1080
    How would a king's perfection be made clear?

Deniers mock the parables we tell
    And explanations of pure men as well.
You also make fun, if that's your desire—
    Corpse, how long now remains till you expire?
Be joyful, lovers, as you beg and pray
    At the same door—it opens up today.
The garlic, herbs, and such each have their plot
    Inside the well-kept garden, do they not?
Each stays inside its bed with its own type   1085
    And then draws moisture so it can grow ripe.
You who are in the saffron bed, be saffron;
    Don't mix with different kinds inside the garden!
Saffron, until you're fully ripe, drink water—
    You'll then become part of the sweetest halva.
Don't ever trespass on the turnip bed,
    For they will not become like you instead.

You're in one bed and they are in another.
   '*God's earth is vast*'* is verified by scripture,
Especially that realm the other side—   1090
   Demons and spirits all get lost inside.
Imaginings and fancies will all end
   In that sea, plain, and mountain there, my friend.
Our plain is like a hair inside the sea
   Compared with His vast plains beyond, trust me.
Still water that is hidden is much fresher
   And sweeter than the obvious flowing river,
Because within itself, like soul and spirit,
   It has a hidden path with feet that move it.

The audience has dozed off, so cut this short,   1095
   Stop sketches on the water of this sort.
Arise, Belqis—this market trade's rate's swift,
   Shun anyone who is a slow spendthrift.
Arise, Belqis, now that you have free will
   Before death takes control, as it soon will.
Death will then pull your ears and give no peace,
   So you will run in pain to the police
Although a thief. How long will you steal ass shoes—
   If you steal, steal a gem the buyer values.
Your sisters gained the everlasting kind,   1100
   Your kingdom though is for the dead and blind.
Happy is she who manages to flee
   This kingdom which death ruins totally.
Arise, Belqis, and view the true faith's realm
   Ruled by its monarchs—try to be like them.
Sitting inside a garden inwardly,
   But one of many comrades outwardly.
The garden goes wherever they should go,
   But it's concealed so most men do not know.
The fruit are pleading: 'Eat me!' desperately.   1105
   Water of Life has come to say: 'Drink me!'
Without wings, fly around the open heavens
   Just like the sun and moon do to your visions.
How will you move? Without feet. You will eat,

Without the need to chew, food that tastes sweet.
Grief won't attack your boat like a huge whale
   And death won't make you hideously pale.
You are king, throne, and army—you're all three.
   Both fortunate and good fortune similarly.
Though fortunate as a king, that fortune parts   1110
   From you and one day finally departs.
Then you'll be empty-handed and alone,
   So fortunate one, be fortune on your own!
Mystic, when you are your own fortune, then
   How can good fortune ever leave again?
How will you lose yourself, O man of wisdom,
   When your identity becomes your kingdom?

*Remainder of the story about Solomon building the Furthest
Worship-House in Jerusalem* by instruction and divine
communication from God, from wisdom which He knows and how
angels, demons, sprites, and humans openly helped.*

Solomon, build God's worship-house today
   For Belqis's troops have begun to pray!
Once he had laid that future mosque's foundation   1115
   Genies and men helped work on its construction,
One group with love, others unwillingly
   Like servants doing duties outwardly.
Men are like demons, chained and dragged as well
   By lust to cultivate then buy and sell.
This chain is of bewilderment and fear—
   Don't view men as unchained and in the clear.
It drags them off to earn and hunt, you see,
   Then to the mine of gold, then to the sea.
It drags them to both good and bad—recite: 1120
   'A cord of palms on her neck'*—that's their plight.
Upon their necks we've placed the cord,* and we
   Make it from every human quality.
Among the clean and the unclean, there's none
   Whose neck is spared reports on what they've done.*
Your lust for bad deeds is fire-like in fervour;
   Only live coals admire the fire's bright colour.

In fire, coal's blackness seems to be concealed,
　　But when the fire dies it is soon revealed.
Your greed turns black coal red—when that greed goes,　1125
　　The wicked coal remains and each then knows.
The coal just looked red briefly due to greed
　　And not because it did a righteous deed.
Greed made your act appear so beautiful;
　　When greed left your act stayed dark, miserable.
Only fools think a fruit is ripe when it
　　Has been embellished by the ghouls a bit.
When their souls try it, in embarrassment
　　Their teeth will fail in this experiment.
Lust made that trap look so good men would drool　1130
　　Over unripe fruit—it's due to greed's ghoul.
Direct your greed to godly deeds, my friend;
　　Once greed has gone they'll stay here till the end.
Good things don't need reflections of some rays
　　From others—though they pass, true goodness stays.
When greed's glow leaves the world's affairs, instead
　　What's left is black coal for what once was red.
Greed can make children play-act, so they will
　　Ride make-believe steeds just to feel a thrill,
But when that feeling gets away from one　1135
　　He'll look back and then laugh at what they'd done:
'What was I doing? Why pretend? What need?'
　　Vinegar can seem honey-like with greed.
What Prophets built had no greed whatsoever—
　　That's why it keeps increasing in its splendour.
Many build worship-houses and yet none
　　Of them was ever called 'The Furthest One'.
The Kaaba's grandeur constantly grows more
　　Due to what Abraham did long before.*
Its bricks are not what make it so superior;　1140
　　It's due to lack of greed within its builder.
Their books are not like other people's pages,
　　Neither their worship-places, homes, or wages,
Nor their chastisement, manners, nor their anger,
　　Nor their analogies, speech, nor their slumber.
Each has a different grandeur that he brings;

Their souls' birds soar up high with different wings.
Thinking about their state makes men's hearts tremble;
　For our own actions theirs serve as example.
Their birds lay golden eggs—make no mistake:　　　　1145
　Their spirits can see midnight at dawn's break.
Whatever heartfelt words that I should say
　In praising them they'd fall short in some way.
So build the Furthest Worship House anew,
　For Solomon has come back. Peace to you!

If sprites and demons try to turn away,
　Angels will then enslave them right away.
If out of fraud the demons should act wrongly,
　The whip, like lightning, strikes their heads most strongly.
Become like Solomon, so demons too　　　　1150
　Carry bricks to build palaces for you.
Be Solomon-like, free from false pretence,
　So jinn and demons show obedience.
Your heart is like your seal, so take good care
　That demons don't entrap it in their snare,
And then, like Solomon, rule over you
　With the seal. Watch out! God's peace be with you!
Heart, Solomon's power never did depart;
　There's one with power still in your head and heart.
Satan seeks to control you the same way,　　　　1155
　But all can't weave fine satin cloth, can they?
They may well move their hands in the same manner,
　But they still are apart and greatly differ.

*Story about a poet receiving a gift from the king, which the vizier
called Abo 'l-Hasan multiplied.*

A poet gave a poem to the ruler
　In hope of a raised rank and robes of honour.
That kind king gave a thousand coins of gold
　With other gifts too precious to be sold.
'This is too small!' the king's vizier then said,
　'Give him ten thousand gold coins now instead.

He passed on wisdom—from a king like you   1160
    Even ten thousand gold coins are too few.'
He talked with his king using sophistry
    Until a sum was reached eventually.
The king then gave ten thousand coins instead
    And robes—Thanks and praise filled the poet's head,
And he enquired, 'Which man deserves the credit
    For showing to the king that I have merit?'
'This kind vizier called Hasan was your helper,
    The one with a good heart and fine behaviour.'
He wrote a poem in his praise and then   1165
    Went on his way back to his home again.
The king's gifts with no lip nor tongue in ways
    That are well hidden sung that ruler's praise.

After a few years that poet returns in the hope of the same reward,
and the king orders a thousand dinars on principle, but his new
vizier, who was also called Hasan, tells the king: 'This is too much
and we have other expenses and our treasury is empty, and I can
satisfy him with one-tenth of that amount.'

After a few years, just like previously
    That poet came in need from poverty.
He thought, 'In want it's best to try once more
    To go to someone whom I've tried before.
I have already tested that court where
    A king was generous, so I'll seek help there.'
'*The meaning of "Allah*"', Sebawayh said,   1170
    '*Is that they take their needs to him instead.*'*
Then: '*We have come to have our needs met and*
    We've found them here with you, as had been planned.'
Countless wise ones in pain will weep before
    That One, Unique God, whom all men adore.
Would any mad buffoon instead attempt this:
    Plead his case to a miser who is helpless?
If the intelligent had not before
    Found answers why then go to Him once more?
All of the fish that swim inside the ocean   1175
    And birds up on the peak of the high mountain,

The hunting lion, wolf, and elephant,
  The massive dragon, serpent, and the ant,
Even the elements: earth, wind, fire, water,
  Find sustenance in Him in spring and winter.
Each moment he's entreated by the sky:
  'God, do not for a moment pass me by!
My pillar of support, in your protection
  Folded inside Your hands* is my position.'
The earth says, 'You who've made me ride this way   1180
  On water, keep me still so I won't sway.'
All have sewn closed their purses and have heeded
  Words from Him on providing what is needed.
Every Prophet has got this guarantee:
  '*Through prayer and patience seek out help from me!*'*
Therefore, ask Him and no one else instead:
  The sea gives water, not the dry stream-bed.
And even if you ask another, He
  Makes that one's hand give to you generously.
He who makes Korah, through gold, turn away—   1185
  Imagine what He gives if you obey!

In search of gifts, that poet once again
  Headed towards that kindest king of men.
His own new poem was the poet's stake
  Brought to the king for sustenance's sake.
Generous ones had already put gold down
  Through kindness, waiting for him to reach town.
To them a poem's valued preciously,
  Especially pearls from the deepest sea.
Men covet food at first—that's their resort,   1190
  For nourishment is what gives life support.
They risk their lives for hope and greed; we see
  Struggles to earn, violence, and trickery.
When a rare one can do without such food
  He loves fame, praising poets who are good,
So they may give fruit to his personal tree,
  Build pulpits to proclaim his dignity,
So that through their words news of all his splendour

And generosity may spread like amber;
God made us in His image: His example   1195
   Is what our qualities take as their model.
Since the Creator wishes thanks and praise,
   Man also has a liking for such ways,
Especially mystics with such excellence
   That fills old empty sacks like wind at once.
The sack gets torn though, if he isn't worthy,
   By falsehood's wind—it can't make things more lovely.
I haven't just made up this parable—
   Don't deem it nonsense if you're curable.
The Prophet said this when he heard the question: 1200
   'Why does he get pumped up by adoration?'

The poet took his poem to the king,
   Deeming his kindness undiminishing—
Kind men die, but their kindness stays the course;
   Happy are those who've ridden on this horse.
Tyrants died, but their cruelty didn't go—
   Fraudulent, lying souls will suffer woe.
'Happy the one who left,' the Prophet said,
   'Whose good works lasted on, though he was dead.'
The kind man died, but not his kindnesses.   1205
   To God, faith and good works aren't valueless.
The stray one dies, but not his disobedience;
   His soul will not be saved by death's experience.
Leave this because the poet is now busy;
   He is in huge debt and so needs gold greatly.
He took his poem to the king once more
   In hope of gifts just like the year before.
The poem, full of perfect pearls, was lovely.
   He thought last year's gifts would be matched exactly.
'One thousand,' ordered that king, true to form,   1210
   Because for him this much had been the norm,
But that most kind vizier of yesteryear
   Had passed away—he was no longer here,
And now in charge instead was someone new
   Who was a miser and lacked pity too.

That one advised, 'King, we've got costs to count
   And for a poet that's a huge amount.
Great one, I'll bring contentment to this poet
   By giving him a fortieth fraction of it.'
'But last time he received', some others said,   1215
   'Ten thousand coins from our kind king instead.
How can one eat straw after tasting sugar?
   How can a former king become a beggar?'
Then the vizier said, 'I'll inflict some pain
   That makes him too crushed to expect more gain,
Then if I give him mud from streets he'll try
   To snatch it like a flower men would buy.
Leave it to me—this is my expertise
   Even if this requestor's hard to please.
He might have strength to fly as high as heaven,   1220
   But when he sees me he is bound to soften.'
The king said, 'It's your call, so go ahead,
   But make him happy for the praise he said.'
'Leave him and others with high hopes to me
   And I'll take full responsibility.'
He made the poet wait then for his pay;
   Winter passed and then came the spring's first day—
The poet aged through waiting still in hope;
   The suffering made him feel he couldn't cope.
'If there's no gold, then treat me terribly   1225
   And I will be your slave once my soul's free:
Waiting has killed me—make me leave at least,
   So that my captive soul can be released.'

Once the vizier gave him the fortieth portion;
   That poet just stood there in deep reflection:
'Then it was more and it came readily—
   This one bloomed late and grew thorns tragically.'
People told him, 'That generous old vizier
   Has passed away and now another's here.
Through him those past gifts were all multiplied;   1230
   Faulting his gifts was never justified.
He's gone and taken all his kindnesses;

In truth, he's not dead but his kindness is.
　　The generous, upright one has gone away;
　　　　The one who flays the poor is here today.
Take this amount he's given and tonight
　　Escape before he tries to pick a fight.
We used a hundred tricks so you would get
　　This much, though you don't know of our work yet.'
He turned to them and asked, 'Friends, tell me where　　1235
　　This cruel man has come from, if you're aware,
And what's the name of this clothes-ripping man?'
　　They told him, 'He is also called Hasan.'
He sighed, 'O Lord, how did these different men
　　Possess the same name? Lord, I sigh again!
From that old Hasan's personally signed decrees
　　Countless viziers tried to be kind and please.
From this Hasan's vile beard we all can make
　　A hundred ropes—how much more can one take?
When a king heeds such ministers, then we　　1240
　　And his great realm are shamed perpetually.'

The resemblance of this base vizier's bad recommendation which
corrupted the king's kindness to that of Pharaoh's vizier, Haman,
which corrupted Pharaoh's receptivity.

Pharaoh turned pliant and at peace when he
　　Heard God's words come from Moses powerfully.
The sweetness of those special words alone
　　Could make milk suddenly gush out of stone.
When he consulted Haman, his vizier,
　　Whose spiteful nature was so very clear:
'You've been a ruler up till now,' he'd say,
　　'Will fraud make you that old tramp's slave today?'
These words of his were like a hurtling mass　　1245
　　Of rocks flung at a building made of glass.
At once he'd ruin and completely raze
　　What Moses's words had built up for days.
Lust can control your brain, and then it later
　　Becomes, while you are travelling, your waylayer:
If holy men give you advice that's sound,

It will, through cunning, fling that on the ground,
Saying: 'Beware, this isn't right at all.
  Do not be moved or lose your self-control.'
Pity the king with such viziers, for hell   1250
  With all its spite will be his home as well.
Happy the king whose own vizier is one
  Like Asaf, the vizier of Solomon.
With such a good vizier sat by his side,
  He gets called '*Light upon light*'* far and wide.
A Solomon-like king and a vizier
  Like Asaf would bring light and perfume near.
Those Pharaoh-like and Haman-like instead
  Find that misfortune fills them up with dread.
Then *darkness upon darkness* is the way—   1255
  No wisdom and no fortune for that day.
In wretches I've seen naught but misery;
  If you've seen more, send greetings please from me.
The king's the soul and the vizier's the brain:
  Corrupt brains drag them like they have a chain.
The angel of the intellect has turned
  Like Harut, from whom many demons learned.
Don't make that intellect vizier—select
  Instead the Universal Intellect.
If you should make lust your vizier, that day   1260
  Your pure soul will no longer want to pray,
For lust is greedy and thinks of the present,
  While intellect thinks of the Day of Judgement.
True intellect can see the end—it knows
  To bear the pain of thorn pricks for the rose
That does not age nor drop off in the fall—
  May it stay from those who can't smell at all!

How the demon sat on Solomon's throne and copied his actions.
Explanation of the difference between the two and how the demon
called himself Solomon, son of David.

Though you have intellect, you must select
  Others you can consult with intellect
As well, because paired intellects spare sorrow   1265

And help you step on heaven's peak tomorrow.
The demon might claim his name's 'Solomon',
   Gain wealth and rule a nation, and so on,
But it just saw King Solomon perform—
   His demonhood was traced still from his form.
Men said, 'This Solomon lacks excellence—
   Between the two there is much difference.
Distinct like sleep and waking, every man
   Can see they're different like those called "Hasan".'
'God gave to Ahriman',* the demon said,   1270
   'A lovely form resembling mine instead:
God gave the demon my form—don't you let
   That one now capture you inside his net.
If he appears and play-acts, please take caution—
   Don't give his outward form alone attention.'
The demon told them this as trickery,
   But good hearts witnessed the reality:
They are discerning; there's no fooling them;
   Their intellect sees every hidden realm.
No falsehood, sorcery, no fraud nor lies   1275
   Can place a veil to cover these ones' eyes.
In answer they then all thought inwardly:
   'You're upside-down. You speak misleadingly.
You'll travel upside-down like this as well;
   O lowest of the low, you'll go to hell.
Though Solomon became deposed too soon,
   His forehead still shines brighter than the moon.
Even if you have seized the signet ring,
   You are a hell—a gloomy, awful thing.'

We won't bow our heads to his pomp and show;   1280
   We wouldn't give a foot too since we know.
And if we do bow down in ignorance,
   A hand will rise up from the ground at once,
Saying, 'Don't bow down to this wayward one!
   Do not prostrate to this ill-fated one!'
I would give you a thrilling explanation
   But for God's jealousy and indignation.

Be satisfied with this amount, and then
 I will explain more when we meet again.
The demon said he's Solomon—the truth   1285
 Is that he masked himself from every youth.
Transcend form, pass beyond names, and then flee
 From name and title to reality.
Enquire about his action and abstention
 Then seek him through these two things by convention.

*Solomon would enter the Furthest Place of Worship in Jerusalem
every day after its completion to worship and guide worshippers
and those in retreat. Medicinal herbs started to grow in the
place of worship.*

When Solomon came early every day
 Inside the Furthest Worship-House to pray,
He saw a new plant there and questioned it:
 'Tell me your name and how you benefit.
What are you called? Which medicine are you?   1290
 Who do you help? Who do you harm? What's true?'
Then every plant would answer Solomon:
 'I give life to this one, death to that one:
Poison to this, sugar to that one though—
 This is my name fate wrote down long ago.'
Knowledge about plants came from Solomon
 Down to physicians we depend upon
Who wrote great books on medicine and then
 Removed pain from the bodies of sick men.
God taught this medicine through revelation;   1295
 Reason and sense can't reach this last dimension.
This lower intellect can't make things new;
 It must receive them. It's reliant, too.
Able to learn new science through education,
 It must be taught by one with revelation,
Which is the source of skills originally
 That intellect acquired eventually.
Have skills been learnt by this lower intellect
 Without a teacher's help? Please now reflect.
Though it can split hairs, it can never master   1300

A skill or craft without a guiding tutor.
If our own intellect were capable,
    You'd know crafts with no teacher's help at all.

How Cain learnt grave-digging from a crow before there was
knowledge about grave-digging and graves in the world.

When first did people's minds begin to know
    Grave-digging, which as trade is ranked so low?
If Cain knew it, then why did he instead
    At first place Abel's body on its head,
Saying: 'Where can I put this out of sight?
    Grimy and blood-smeared, it will here cause fright.'
He saw a crow which in its beak was holding   1305
    Another crow and looked like it was bolting—
It swooped down from the air for this intention:
    To teach grave-digging skills by demonstration.
It scooped up soil first with its talons, so
    It could lay in its grave the other crow.
It buried it, then placed soil over it.
    The crow had knowledge God inspired in it.
'How small my intellect is!' Cain exclaimed,
    'A crow's more skilled than I am. I'm ashamed.'
On Universal Intellect, God said: 1310
    '*The sight did not swerve.*'* Ours looks round instead.
The light of the elect ones is the former;
    The grave-master for corpses is the latter.
The soul that flies towards the crows will be
    The one the crows drag to the cemetery:
Don't run behind the crow-like self—that's backward;
    It leads not to the garden, but the graveyard.
Chase the heart's phoenix, if you must depart
    To Qaf and Furthest Prayer-House of the heart.
Due to your passions, saplings at fast pace   1315
    Blossom in the heart's Furthest Worship-Place.
Give them their due like Solomon before:
    Don't stamp on and reject them. Find out more
Because the various plants make clear to you
    The state of this firm ground that you can't view.

Whether plain reeds or canes that give you sugar,
    Plants serve as every soil's true state's translator.
The heart's soil is where thoughts are planted, so
    All of the secrets of the heart they'll show.
If I find one who draws true speech, I'll yield   1320
    A hundred thousand roses like a field,
But if I find one who's that speech's killer,
    Wise words will flee my heart like a chased burglar.

Things move to their attractor's own direction,
    And true attraction's not like false attraction:
Sometimes your path's correct, sometimes it's wayward;
    The lead's not seen, nor who is pulling forward.
You're a blind steed; your reins are surety—
    Observe the pulling, not your reins. Heed me!
If the reins and attractor come to vision,   1325
    This world won't stay *the area of delusion.*
If infidels could only see that they
    Are chasing dogs in that vile devil's sway,
How could they follow him pathetically?
    They would hold back as well assuredly.
If cows knew of the butcher's ways at all,
    How could they follow him back to his stall,
Or eat the fodder given and then share
    Their milk due to his flattery and hot air?
How could they then digest the fodder after   1330
    They find out the whole purpose of the fodder?
Heedlessness is this world's support. Where's fortune
    When you run here, but get hit hard for certain:
At first told 'Run!' you get struck in the end.
    Donkeys die only in this ruin, friend.
The tasks that you with zeal have taken up
    Have all their flaws that moment covered up.
The reason why you toil hard as you do
    Is that God has concealed its flaws from you.
It is the same with every pleasing thought: 1335
    Its flaws are hidden from you, for if not,
If their appalling flaws were manifest,

Your soul would run *from east to furthest west.**
If the regret you feel once it is done
    Were with you at the start, would you have run?
He hid it from our souls initially,
    So we would do what is our destiny.
Only when destiny made clear its plan,
    Eyes opened and contrition then began.
Contrition is a worldly matter, son—   1340
    Abandon it and worship God, the One.
You will be a repenter, if from habit
    You do this, and with more zeal you'll regret it.
Half of your life will pass in being distracted;
    The other half regretting that you'd acted.
Take leave of contemplation and distraction
    And seek God, mystic states, and lovelier action.
If you don't have the lovelier action, say
    Why you repent an act from yesterday.
Worship, if you do know the path that's good.   1345
    Only then are the bad things understood.
You have to know what's good to know what's bad—
    Through contrast opposites are seen, young lad.
If you became unable to stop thinking,
    You also couldn't stop yourself from sinning—
If so, then why repent it nonetheless?
    Explain whose pulling brings this heedlessness.
Nobody had distinguished over here
    Impotence without power to make it clear.
And similarly you're veiled from ever seeing   1350
    A flaw in each desire that you are feeling.
If the desire's flaw had been shown to you,
    Your soul would have fled from what you pursue.
If He had shown its flaw to you that day
    No one could have then dragged you to its way.
You find another action so abhorrent—
    The reason is its flaw is so apparent.
O Knower of the secret with fine speech,
    Don't hide our bad deeds' flaws from our sight's reach.
And don't show flaws in a good act, lest we   1355
    Lose all our zeal for this itinerary.

It was due to this habit Solomon
    Went to the worship-house on one bright dawn.
On these grounds every day he'd walk about
    And see if new plants had begun to sprout.
The secret of the plants is manifest
    To the pure heart, though hidden from the rest.

*The story about the Sufi who was meditating in the rose garden with
his head resting lowered on his raised knee, and whose friend told
him: 'Lift up your head and take pleasure in the rose garden, the
aromatic herbs, the birds, and the signs of God's grace.'*

A Sufi seeking God's proximity
    Sat with his head supported by his knee.
He grew immersed in matters very deep;   1360
    A meddler fumed that he appeared asleep:
'Why sleep? Look at the vines and trees, the traces
    Of God that can be seen in all such spaces.
Heed God's command: "*Look!*"* and lift up your face
    Towards the origin of all this grace!'
He answered, 'Lustful one, the heart's God's place;
    Outward things are just traces of a trace.
Inside the soul are the real fields and gardens;
    Those outside are like water's mere reflections.
Images on the water that you see   1365
    Are choppy—water has fragility.
Real gardens are inside the heart—it's their
    Loveliness's reflection seen out there.
God wouldn't have called it "realm of delusions"
    If they weren't actually derived reflections;
They are delusory since they all start
    As mere reflections from the mystic's heart.
Deluded ones think this reflection's nice
    In the belief that it is paradise—
Far from the gardens' source I see them run: 1370
    With a mere phantom they are having fun!
They will all finally see correctly when
    Their heedless sleep ends—what use is it then?
Inside the graveyard they'll begin to cry

And till the Resurrection they will sigh.
    It's best to die before your own life ends,
        Meaning one's found the vineyard's scent's source, friend.'

Story about the growing of the carob in a corner of the Furthest Place of Worship in Jerusalem and how Solomon grew upset at this once it started to talk to him and told its name and special property.

A new plant rising like an ear of corn
    Was noticed in a nook by Solomon.
It was a very rare plant, fresh and green,   1375
    And this plant had a brightly dazzling sheen.
It greeted Solomon who then replied,
    While by its beauty he was stupefied:
'What's your name? Speak without a tongue!' he said.
    ' "Carob," this world's best king and greatest head.'
He asked, 'What is your special quality?'
    'I ruin places that have nurtured me.
I'm carob, wrecker of your buildings and
    Destroyer of foundations in the land.'
Solomon quickly understood that now   1380
    The journey would reveal itself somehow:
'While I'm alive this worship-house won't be
    Damaged at all. I know with certainty.
How could men try to damage or deface,
    While I'm alive, this Furthest Worship-Place?
Our worship-place's ruin won't occur
    Till after our deaths. Ponder and concur.
It is the heart; the body's in prostration
    To it. The carob is its bad companion.'

When love for bad companions grows in you,   1385
    Don't talk with them, but flee without ado.
Tear it up from its roots, for if it rises
    It tears you up and all your worship-houses.
Lover, your carob is your own corruption—
    Why, like a child, do you lean to perversion?
Admit you are a sinner. Don't be scared,

So that the Master's teaching will be shared
When you say, 'I don't know and want to learn.'
   Honesty's better than a strong concern
For reputation. Learn from Adam's woe: 1390
   '*Lord, we've done wrong!*'* he uttered long ago.
He neither made excuses nor spoke falsely,
   Nor did he try to raise the flag of trickery,
But Satan quarrelled, 'I once had much fame
   And was revered, but You've put me to shame.
The dye is Yours and You're the dyer too—
   The source of all our sins and flaws is You.'
Recite from '*Since, Lord, You led me astray,*'*
   So you won't be a fatalist today.
Why choose the tree of fatalism still,   1395
   Jumping up there, discarding your free will,
Like Satan and all of his progeny,
   Talking back to the Lord combatively.
How can it be against your will to sin
   When all see you with joy go rushing in?
Under duress does anybody prance?
   While being forced astray would someone dance?
You fought like twenty men just for its sake
   Though counsellors warned you it was a mistake.
You said, 'This is the way exclusively.   1400
   Who'd fault me other than a nobody?'
How can one speak like this and claim duress?
   How can one forced fight for it nonetheless?
You claimed free will for pleasing things you craved,
   But blame fate for your reasoning that's depraved.
Those fortunate and in the know can fathom
   Reasoning is Satan's while love comes from Adam.
Swimming in seas is clever reasoning, friend—
   That swimmer ends up drowning in the end.
Quit swimming, pride, and your hate-fuelled emotion.   1405
   This isn't a small sea; it is the ocean.
The huge, deep ocean with no sanctuary
   Can swallow up those small seas easily.
Love is a ship for the elect ones' voyage;
   It usually saves and rarely causes damage.

Sell cleverness and buy perplexities:
 The former guesses while the latter sees.
Before Mohammad, sacrificially
 Slay your reasoning, say: '*God suffices me!*'
Don't draw your head back from the ark like Canaan   1410
 Whose clever self led him into delusion,
Saying, 'I'll reach the mountain that soars over;
 Why should I feel indebted now to Noah?'
How can you not? There is no doubt you should
 Since even God expresses gratitude.
When God thanks him, how can it not be due
 From our souls to feel very grateful too?
What do you know when envy makes you hateful?
 Even God praises him and feels so grateful.
If only Canaan had not learned to swim,   1415
 He might have then pinned all his hopes on him.
If he were innocent of scheming too,
 He would have sought his mother as boys do.
From God's Friend's hearts he'd have gained revelations
 If he'd had less book knowledge through relations.
Compare a book with such light and discover
 Your soul from its depths blame you for it, brother.
Transmitted knowledge when the Qotb's breath's present
 Is dry ablution while streams are abundant.*
Make yourself simple. Follow the direction.   1420
 Through 'foolishness' like this, you'll gain salvation:
Mohammad said, '*In heaven most are fools*'—
 Among Mankind he is the king who rules.
With cleverness, your pride and airs abound—
 Make yourself foolish, so your heart stays sound.
Not the fool acting wilfully in that fashion,
 But that one who's bewildered due to passion,
Like women cutting their own hands—disgrace
 Comes from their having been shown Joseph's face.*
Sacrifice reasoning out of love today.   1425
 Real intellects are with God anyway:
The wise have sent their intellects up there;
 Just idiots stayed away from Him. Beware!
If through bewilderment your brain selects

To leave your head, each hair grows intellects.
Up there the brain's set free from thinking's burdens
   And stress; brains there just grow lush fields and gardens.

Hear from the field a subtle point—come near
   The garden, for your palm will flourish here.
Abandon on this path all pomp and pride.   1430
   Don't move unless there's movement from your guide.
Only a tail moves when its head is still.
   That movement's like a scorpion's. It is ill,
Venomous, walking crookedly, blind, ugly,
   And he makes ill the ones with a pure body.
If someone's like this in his inner heart
   And disposition, beat his head apart!
Pounding his head will benefit him truly,
   Since his soul then can flee his body's cruelty.
Take from the madman's hand his weapon too,   1435
   So justice will be then content with you,
For he has weapons, but no brain to use—
   Bind his hands to stop damage and abuse.

Explanation that acquisition of knowledge, wealth, and rank by an
ill-natured one becomes the means to disgrace him and is like a
sword that has fallen into the hands of a highwayman.

Teaching bad-natured men a single word
   Is handing to the highwayman a sword.
Better to hand it to a savage than
   To teach a thing to such an awful man.
Give the bad-natured knowledge, rank, and fortune,
   And it will lead to trouble and misfortune.
Believers must fight wars so they can seize   1440
   The spears from hands of wretches such as these.
The madman is his soul, the sword his body—
   Seize the sword from that man who's vile and ugly!
A hundred lions cannot cause more damage
   Than giving a high office to a savage—
His flaws are hidden, but in such a role,

His strengthened snake will soon rush from its hole.
Scorpions and snakes will fill the vast plains when
  The ignorant one is made king again.
If he gains wealth and an esteemed high place,   1445
  He then begins to seek his own disgrace:
Either he stops bestowing gifts through meanness
  Or in the wrong place he becomes too generous.
He places his king in the pawn's next square—
  The gifts from fools are like this, so beware!
When one astray gains power he savours it,
  Thinking it is high rank, though it's a pit.
He acts as guide, but doesn't know the way.
  His ugly soul burns the whole world away.
When children on this path act like a master,   1450
  Their followers will suffer much thereafter.
'Come and I'll show the moon to you!' he'll say,
  Though he has never seen it anyway.
How can you when you've never spied upon
  Even its image on a lake, raw one!
Wretches act now as leaders and from fright
  Wise men have hidden their heads out of sight.

Commentary on 'O you who wrap yourself in your garment'.*

God called Mohammad '*One who wraps about*
  Himself his cloak' for this, and said, 'Come out!
Don't cover your face, don't draw in your head—   1455
  The rest are giddy, but you're wise instead.
Don't hide from the false claimant's opposition;
  You have the candle of bright revelation.
Stay up at night,* your candle burning bright,
  Great prince, the candle's active most at night.
Daytime's night-dark without your radiance there;
  Without your backing, lion falls to hare.
Captain the ship in purity's great ocean,
  For you're a second Noah; you've been chosen.
Every path needs a man with expertise   1460
  Who knows the path, especially on seas.
Look at the waylaid caravan. Arise!

Ghouls captain ships each side you turn your eyes.
Ship-rescuer, you are today's Khezr, so
   Don't choose retreat like Jesus long ago.
You're heaven's candle to this group—don't run
   Towards retreat, cut off from everyone.
Come to the crowd—it's not time for seclusion.
   You are Homa with guidance to Qaf Mountain.
The moon keeps moving steadily in the dark;   1465
   Its orbit won't stop just because dogs bark:
Critics are like dogs next to your full moon—
   They howl against your rank. You stay immune.
They're deaf towards *"Keep silent!"** and through folly
   They bark at the full moon that is so lofty.
Healer of sick men, don't drop on the floor
   The blind's staff, due to deaf men's angry roar.
Didn't you say: "The one who leads the blind
   God will reward a hundred times in kind."
If you should lead a blind man forty paces,   1470
   You will gain guidance and God's pardon's graces.
Lead from this world that's transient all the blind,
   Group after group—don't leave them all behind,
For this is guidance; you're the true guide who
   Can turn the final hour's dirge to joy too.
Leader of the God-fearing, cause those men
   With fancies to seek certainty again.
If someone schemes against you, I will strike
   His neck—proceed with joy the way you like.
Over his blindness I'll place as a cover   1475
   More blindness—he'll think poison then is sugar.
Intellects are lit up by My light, while
   Plots are informed by My plots and My guile.
How can the felt tent of the Turcoman
   Resist the elephant's huge feet, good man?
What is the wind, O Prophet who's most glorious,
   To now withstand My wind that's so ferocious?
Arise and blow the trumpet that scares men
   So thousands of the dead will rise again.
Angel of Death of your age is your function—   1480
   Bring Resurrection prior to Resurrection!

If asked, "What's Resurrection?" you be bold,
  O beauty, show yourself and say, "Behold,
I'm it, enquirer, victim of affliction.
  A hundred worlds rose from this Resurrection." '

If he's not fit for prayer and *zekr* remembrance,
  The answer for that stupid wretch is silence.
And when a prayer does not get a reply,
  Silence is the response from God on high.
It's harvesting time and we are unlucky   1485
  Because the day has almost gone completely.
Time is short and this discourse's sheer strength
  Can make a lifetime seem too short in length.
Throwing spears in a narrow lane lets down
  Spear-throwers who have earned worldwide renown.
Time is short and the people's understanding
  Is shorter still—too short for what I'm offering.
When silence is the answer wretches earn,
  Why do you talk so much? When will you learn?
Due to His kindness and most perfect grace   1490
  Moisture and rain head to each barren place.

*A demonstration showing that 'Choosing not to answer is an answer
itself' in confirmation of the saying 'Silence is the reply to the
wretch'. An explanation of these two sayings is in the story which
will be related.**

There was a king once with a slave whose brain
  Was dead, while he had lust he'd not restrain.
He didn't carry out his job with care;
  Deceptive, he hoped none would notice there.
The king decreed, 'Reduce his salary,
  And, if he fights, sack him immediately!'
His intellect was weak, his lust intense—
  So he reacted badly, lacking sense.
With intellect he would have been more prudent: 1495
  Perceive his error and then be repentant.
A tethered ass should never lose its temper,

For this makes its condition worse than ever.
It thinks, 'It can't get worse than one leg tied,'
But soon its other leg is also tied.

*Explanation of the saying of Mohammad: 'God created the angels
and put intellect in them, and He created the animals and put lust
into them. He created humans and put both intellect and lust in
them, so the human whose intellect prevails over his lust is higher
than the angels, while the one whose lust prevails over his intellect is
lower than animals.'*

Mohammad said that God created three
    Types of created beings originally:
The first have wisdom and munificence—
    They're angels bowing in obedience.
Their nature's free from lust and craving's blight.   1500
    Through love of God they are eternal light.
Another group do not have wisdom: they
    Are animals which get fat eating hay.
They see just hay and stables, unaware
    Of wretchedness and honour to compare.
The third group are the humans, and our masses
    Are all of them half-angels and half-asses.
The latter half leans to what's low and base,
    The former to what's wise and filled with grace.
The first two don't have inner conflict's torments,   1505
    But humans suffer from those two opponents.
Humans are also tried by destiny;
    In form one, they're divided into three:
The first group's totally submerged inside—
    Like Jesus, they have joined the angels' side:
Adam's form, Gabriel's reality—
    They've quit rage, lust, and talking pointlessly,
Through their trials, struggles, and renunciations
    As if they weren't really born of humans.
The second group have joined the ass instead,   1510
    Possessed by lust and with a rage-filled head.
Gabriel's traits had once been shared by these,
    But they proved too small for grand qualities.

If you should lose your soul, you will be dead;
   Lose Gabriel's traits and you're the ass you dread.
Souls lacking Gabriel's qualities are low—
   This talk is true and Sufi greats say so!
They suffer more than animals can ever;
   In this world they do things that are so clever:
In scheming and pretence they are accomplished   1515
   Unlike the animals—they're thus distinguished,
Weaving clothes with fine gold embroidery,
   Fetching pearls from the bottom of the sea,
Astronomy and science on top of these,
   Knowledge of medicine, philosophies,
All of which link to this world that they live in
   And have no power to reach the seventh heaven,
All knowledge useful to construct a stable,
   The life support of every cow and camel.
These giddy ones call them their 'mysteries',   1520
   Since they prolong the life of beasts like these.
Knowledge of God's path and His place is known
   By owners of a mystic heart alone.
In composite form He made in this fashion
   Animals who have knowledge too as ration.
He called this group of people *cattle-like**
   For how can sleep and waking be alike?
Animal spirits know just sleep for they
   Inverted their own senses, but that day
When waking comes and sleep will finally end   1525
   They'll learn all from the Tablet, my dear friend.
Just like the senses of a sleeping person—
   When he awakes he'll notice their inversion.
He is *the lowest of the lows**—forget
   And leave him: *do not love the ones that set,**

Exegesis of the verse: 'As for those in whose hearts is a disease, this
book added to their disgrace' and 'He leads many astray by it*
*while also guiding many by it'.**

Since he had the potential to transcend
   From baseness, but he lost it in the end.*

An animal lacks that kind of potential,
   So it's excused of course from being bestial.
Once he's lost his potential, there's no gain   1530
   For this man—food turns to a donkey's brain.
If he eats healing herbs, they make him sicker
   Like bad drugs causing stiffness and dementia.
There is another sort left in the battle—
   They are half rightly guided and half bestial.
In war all night and day they are immersed,
   The bestial half still battling with the first.

The battle between intellect and the carnal soul is like the
dispute between Majnun and his she-camel: Majnun wants
to go towards Layli, but the camel wants to go back to her foal,
so Majnun says:
My she-camel's desire's behind, mine here:
That I and her are now at odds is clear.

Majnun and his she-camel were this way,
   Pulling to different sides all night and day:
Layli was for Majnun the journey's goal;   1535
   The camel wished to go back to her foal.
If he grew absent-minded for a moment,
   The she-camel would turn round in that instant.
Being so filled with love and passion, he
   Often lost self-awareness helplessly.
Reason is what is watchful all the way;
   Passion for Layli carried that away.
The she-camel was watchful and so cunning
   The moment she felt her own bridle slackening:
She'd know his thoughts then floated far away   1540
   And turned back to her foal without delay.
When he returned to his wits he'd then find,
   From where they were, that she'd gone miles behind.
Majnun remained for years stuck in such ways,
   Still on a journey that should take three days.
He said, 'She-camel, since we are both lovers,
   We're opposites who're not good fellow travellers.
Your love and toggle don't conform with me;

I have to choose some different company.'
This pair will try to take each other out.   1545
    Souls that will not leave bodies will lose out.
For God's Throne every soul still has great thirst;
    The body, like the camel, loves thorns first.
Souls open up their wings and soar so high;
    The body sticks its claws in soil nearby.
'You'll long for home', Majnun said, 'While still with me
    And this will keep my soul so far from Layli.
My life's been wasted by such problems falling,
    Like Moses's men in the desert, wandering.
The path to union was *two steps* away,   1550
    But it's been sixty years due to your sway.
The path is not that long, but I've been tarrying,
    And I have grown so sick of all this travelling.'

Majnun leapt from the camel in the air:
    'This grief has burned me. How much more is there?'
The massive desert seemed small to his eye;
    He flung himself on rocky ground nearby:
He flung himself so fiercely on those stones
    That this brave lover broke a lot of bones.
And when he flung himself, by destiny,   1555
    As a result his leg broke instantly.
'In spite of that,' he said while tying it,
    'I'll roll like balls that Layli's bat might hit.'
That's why Sana'i curses anybody
    Who rides on and does not dismount his body.
Can love for God be less than love for Layli?
    It's better to become the Lord's ball surely?
Roll like a ball sincerely just like that
    Across the curve of His love's polo bat,
Because from now on it's through God's attraction,   1560
    Though camel-riding brought us to this junction.
And this new kind of travelling is astounding,
    Beyond a human being's understanding.
And this pull is distinct from any other;
    It is what makes Mohammad so superior.

That young man writes a complaint to the king about the reduction
of his wages.

Stop this, resume that young man's tale and bring
    Details about his letter to the king.
He sent a letter to that nice king, writing
    With anger, hatred, self-conceit, and fighting.
The body is a letter—look inside   1565
    Before you send it to him. Step aside
And open it so you can read it all
    And judge if for a king it's suitable.
If you decide it isn't really fit
    For kings, write it again, correcting it.
Opening the body's letter isn't easy
    Otherwise all could read its secret clearly.
Opening the body is so hard, I'd say
    It's only for the brave—it's not child's play.
We're all contented with the contents page,   1570
    Steeped in desire and greed, a trap and cage
For ordinary men who then imagine
    The actual contents must match with precision.
Open more pages—don't remove your sight
    From these words here: *God knows best what is right.*
The contents page is what the tongue declares—
    You need to see inside how it compares,
Whether or not it actually fits,
    So that your acts aren't those of hypocrites.
If carrying a heavy sack, begin   1575
    By checking first of all what is within,
To know which sweet and bitter things it's holding,
    Then take it if it's really worth transporting.
If not, then empty it of rocks and spare
    Yourself the fruitless toil that none should bear,
Keeping inside the sack just those good things
    That should be taken to the righteous kings.

Story about the jurist with a big turban and that man who snatched
it. The jurist shouted: 'Unravel it first to see what you have
snatched before you take it away!'

A mullah had collected rags and wound
    Them in his turban's small cloth, round and round,
So it would look impressively enormous   1580
    When he went to the madrasa vainglorious.
He had cut strips from clothing, so his turban
    Could be embellished by this secret burden.
It looked so heavenly from the outside,
    Though it was false and hideous inside.
Foul animal skin strips and old, plain cotton
    Were buried secretly inside that turban.
At dawn he went down to the seminary,
    So he might profit from this trickery.
In a dark lane a clothing thief was waiting   1585
    To use the skills in which he'd had his training.
He snatched the turban from the mullah's head
    And then as fast as possible he fled.
The mullah shouted, 'Young man, won't you listen—
    Open it first before you take that turban.
As you rush like the birds up in the air,
    Unwrap what you have snatched away with care.
Unravel it and rub it with your hand,
    Then if you want it, I won't reprimand.'
When that escaping thief unravelled it   1590
    Thousands of tiny rags fell out of it.
One short old strip was all that was remaining
    Of that huge turban that he had been craving.
He threw that last piece down immediately:
    'You've put me out of work through trickery!'

The world's advice to worldly people through mystical communication
and its display of faithlessness to those who desire it to be faithful.

The mullah said, 'I fooled you, that is true,
    But I had warned you of the matter too.'

The world, though finally blooming, similarly
   Cried out about its infidelity.
Existence and corruption are a pairing: 1595
   The fraud's the first, the latter is the warning:
Existence says, 'Come here, for I am lovely,'
   Corruption, though, says, 'Go, I'm nothing really.'
You who are stunned by spring's exceptional splendour,
   Observe the autumn's cold and sickly pallor.
You saw the lovely sun rise—don't forget
   The sun's death later at its time to set.
You saw up in the sky the full moon's rays—
   Notice its grief too in its waning phase.
A child was loved by men due to his beauty— 1600
   Once he had aged, those same men thought him ugly.
Though a slim body makes you now its prey,
   It sags like cotton on a later day.
You love devouring those fine delicacies—
   Look at the drains filled with their excess grease.
'Where is your loveliness?' they ask the waste,
   'Your beauty, scent, and most delicious taste?'
'That was bait; I'm the snare,' the food will say,
   'The bait is hidden now you've turned to prey.'
Fingers that were the envy of craft masters 1605
   Often end up just trembling due to tremors.
The soul-like, drunken eye that we all find
   So lovely ends up streaming tears and blind.
The brave one viewed as lion-like we'll see
   Subdued by a small mouse eventually.
The sharp, far-sighted artisan, my friend,
   Appears like an old donkey in the end.
The fine locks that spread musk which you inhale
   Will end up like a donkey's ugly tail.
Existence pleases us in the first place, 1610
   But ends up with corruption and disgrace.
It brought the trap to everybody's view,
   Then fooled a simpleton in front of you,
So don't claim, 'Oh, the world has tricked me there,
   Or else my brain would have escaped the snare.'
The necklace and the sword-belt made of gold

Become the shackles that entrap and hold.
Think of each particle like this, my friend:
  As well as its beginning see its end.
See the end and you'll end up more elated.   1615
  See just this ass-stall world and get deflated.
At first sight, faces all shine like the moon,
  But see the way they'll all end up too soon,
So you won't be one-eyed like Satan, brother:
  That blind one saw one half, but not the other.
He saw no inner faith, just Adam's body;*
  He saw no link beyond, just what is worldly.
And men surpassing women isn't due
  To having more strength than the women do.
Lions and elephants would be superior   1620
  If strength and force should be the real criteria.
Men are superior over women, friends,
  When they remain more focused on the ends.
The crooked one falls short by his own actions,
  Like women, from the final outcome's visions.

From the world come two cries which are opponents,
  So be alert to which one's heard these moments.
The first kind will revive the godly, while
  The second will deceive the mean and vile:
'Once flowers drop, it is the thorn that stays.'   1625
  'I'm really blossom, you with such kind ways!'
The blossom cries, 'Here is the flower seller!'
  The thorn cries, 'Don't approach me any further!'
Accept the blossom's you won't heed the other
  For lovers only hear their loved one, brother.
'Here, I am ready now!' the blossom said,
  The thorn said: 'See my outcome first instead.
My being ready is a false seduction—
  Look for the ending in the start's reflection.'
Of the two sacks, once you have entered one   1630
  You're then unfit to reach the other one.
Happy is he who from the first start hears
  What wise men hear through their own minds and ears.

Corruption settled in those who were empty—
    All else appeared corrupt then consequently.
When a new bowl draws urine inside it,
    Water can never take the filth from it.
Everything draws another thing on earth,
    Unbelief infidels, truth those of worth.
There is both amber and a magnet there: 1635
    Iron or straw, you'll end up in a snare.
If iron, then the magnet pulls you near;
    If straw, you'll move to amber. It's that clear.
When one is not a friend of the good people,
    One will keep company with those who're evil.
To the Egyptians, Moses was the worst;
    To Israelites Haman was truly cursed.
Haman's soul drew Egyptians, who would lose,
    While Moses's soul drew his fellow Jews.
Straw is for donkeys' stomachs, meanwhile wheat   1640
    Is suitable for human beings to eat—
If due to darkness you can't tell, it's easier
    To look at who he's taken as his leader,

Explanation that the mystic has nourishment from the Light of God, for Mohammad said, 'I spend the night with my Lord who gives me food and drink,' And his saying, 'Hunger is God's food through which He revives the bodies of His special saints,' which means that God's food reaches them while in a state of hunger.

For all the foals will follow their own mothers,
    Which shows what is their species to the others.*
The human's milk is what the breasts bestow,
    The donkey's from the udder down below.
It is the justice of God's distribution—
    The wonder is there's no force or compulsion.
If there's compulsion there can't be contrition;   1645
    There's no defence against enforced oppression.
The lesson is tomorrow, for today
    Has ended—mysteries overwhelm one day.

You who depend and trust in the hot air
   And flattery from a wretch should take more care.
You've raised a tent from bubbles, which is wrong
   Because its ropes are weak and won't last long.
Falsehood is like a lightning flash so bright
   The traveller on the way will lose his sight.
This world and worldly men are valueless;   1650
   Both match when it comes to unfaithfulness.
They're both unfaithful, so when facing you
   It is the back of their necks that you view.
The spiritual, like that world, are eternally
   Faithful to their oaths due to their true piety.
When did two Prophets ever come to blows
   Or claim each other's miracles as foes?
Fruit from that world will not turn bad tomorrow;
   The joy from wisdom never turns to sorrow.
The low self should be killed for it lacks promise.   1655
   That self is low and prays towards vile baseness.
The low self matches perfectly the worldly
   Just as the shroud and grave fit the dead body.

The self is clever, sees flaws everywhere.
   It's dead while facing this world deep in prayer.
But when God's inspiration's flow arrives
   Like water, then a living thing revives.
Until that comes, do not be duped—take colour
   Only from Him whose rouge will last forever.
Seek fame that never fades and choose the ray   1660
   Of sunshine that won't set each passing day.
Refined skills and fine speech are Pharaoh's soldiers,
   While death's appointed hour is the Nile's waters:
Although their splendour, pomp, and sorcery
   Draw men to crane their necks so they can see,
Deem them all the magician's tricks that break,
   While death's the wood that turns into a snake:
It turned all of that magic to one bite;
   The day arrived and it consumed the night,
But that consumption didn't add one ray   1665

To light—that stayed exactly the same way.
The light's effect, not essence, grew on shining;
    Essences aren't increasing or declining—
Through His creating, God did not grow more;
    He isn't now what He was not before.
But the effects grew more through His creation;
    Between these two types there's a clear distinction.
Growth of effects is God's own self-display
    Of attributes and how He works away.
But if an essence grows, that's evidence   1670
    Of its being prone to change and transience.

Exegesis of 'Moses sensed a fear in his soul and We said: "Don't feel
fear for you are superior!"'*

Moses said, 'Sorcery as well can stun—
    What should I do when this lot can't discern?'
God said, 'I shall bring forth discernment's light
    And make the brains that lack it now gain sight.
Though they raise up foam like the ocean here,
    Moses, you shall prevail, so have no fear.'

Sorcery had prestige back in his day—
    Staff turned to snake and they lost straight away.
Beauty and grace are both claimed by all men,   1675
    But death's their touchstone, so just wait till then.
Magic went, Moses's miracles as well;
    Toppled from being's rooftop, all bowls fell.
Curses are the sole sound from magic's bowl;
    Faith's bowl's high rank lasts due to its good role.
The touchstone has been hidden long from most,
    So come fake coin among the real and boast:
It's time to brag now that the touchstone's absent—
    They'll pass you hand to hand like a prized present.
The counterfeit will say through haughtiness: 1680
    'Pure gold, I'm like you—how should I be less?'
Real gold says, 'Fellow servant, now we've shared,

But soon the touchstone comes, so be prepared.'
To mystics bodily death's a gift. They're bold
   Because what harm can scissors do to gold?
If false coin saw within on the first day
   Its end, it would have turned black straight away;
If it had been black at the first encounter,
   It wouldn't have been such a false pretender.
It could have sought pure grace's alchemy;   1685
   Wisdom would have removed hypocrisy.
It would have then been broken and not later;
   It would have then discovered the repairer.
Becoming broken after seeing its end,
   It would have passed then to one who can mend.
Grace drives the copper to the alchemy;
   Gold-plated coin's denied contrastingly.
Gold-plated coin, don't make claims. Keep in mind
   That customers will not remain so blind:
The Last Day's light will give sight to their eyes,   1690
   Exposing all your hoodwinking and lies.
Those who have seen the outcome make souls sigh
   In longing; they're the envy of each eye.
To those who see just what's immediate
   And are corrupt within, the doors are shut.
Between dawn and false dawn no difference
   Is noticed by those plagued by ignorance.
False dawn has driven every caravan
   Towards destruction's howling winds, young man.
For every coin a false coin can be shown,   1695
   So pity souls with no tools or touchstone.

Prohibiting the false claimant from pretence and commanding him to follow guidance.

'I am Mohammad,' Bu Mosaylem* said,
   'I've ruined his religion with my head.'
'Don't brag, deluded by the start!' you tell him.
   'Look at the final outcome, Bu Mosaylem.'
Don't act as guide to gain wealth out of greed.

Follow behind and let the candle lead.
Just like the moon, it shows the destination,
    And if there's bait or snare at each location.
In any case it's only with the lanterns   1700
    That you can tell a crow's form from a falcon's,
Seeing as these crows began the fraud and lies—
    They even imitate white falcon cries.
If someone learns the hoopoe's cry, what damage
    Will harm the secrets passed in Sheba's message?
Discern the natural from the false cry, tell
    The kings' crowns from the hoopoe's crown as well.
Shameless people have stolen adages
    And sayings from the mystic dervishes.
Those ancient nations* were destroyed for good,   1705
    For thinking timber was prized sandalwood.
They had discernment, but they lost their mind,
    For greed and lust makes people deaf and blind.
The physically blind still deserve God's mercy,
    Greed's blindness though does not deserve our pity.
The hangman of the king's forgivable,
    But jealous killers are too terrible.
Observe the ending; watch out for the hook.
    Greed won't let your far-sighted eye now look.
With two eyes see what's last and what comes first.   1710
    Don't be one-eyed like Satan, who was cursed.*
One-eyed men see what is immediate only,
    Clueless like beasts about what follows shortly:
A cow's two eyes are worth one human eye
    In the religious laws, which nullify
Their value—they're worth half since they both need
    One of their human rider's eyes to lead.
Destroy a human eye and laws dictate
    Half of his life's blood-price to compensate,
For human eyes are independent, free   1715
    From need for others' eyes and company.
The donkey's eyes see just the start, my friend;
    They're deemed one-eyed for they don't see the end.
This talk could go on, but that feeble weakling
    Out of desire for food has started scribbling:

Remainder of the story about that young man writing a letter to request a wage.

That poet met the kitchen head to say
   'Miser of the king's kitchen, it's some way
Beneath him for this matter that I mention
   About my wage to have reached his attention.'
The kitchen head: 'It's his decree no less,   1720
   And not from miserly tight-fistedness.'
He said, 'By God, this is just tale-spinning—
   Even rare gold has dust's worth to this king.'
The kitchen head showed proofs so he'd take heed,
   But he rejected them all due to greed,
And when that afternoon his pay was cut,
   He cursed to no avail, disconsolate.
'You're doing this on purpose!' he then cried.
   'No, by the king's command our hands are tied.
This comes straight from the source, so understand   1725
   The arrow is released by his own hand.'
'*You did not throw when you threw*'* is a test;
   Don't blame the Prophet. God did it. It's blessed.
Enraged one, from the source the water's murky—
   Open your eyes, look at the water closely!
Due to his grief and rage that servant went
   To write a letter in which he could vent,
But in this letter he expressed much praise
   For the king, threading pearls in skilful ways:
'Your hand is greater than the clouds and sea   1730
   In meeting needs and solving poverty;
The cloud gives just while weeping, but for free
   Your hands lay feasts with smiles continually.'
It was praise on the surface, but his rage
   Came through like a bad smell from every page.

Your actions are devoid of light and ugly,
   For you have lost all your innate light sadly.
Just as fresh fruit rots in a week or less

The good acts of vile men turn valueless.
The splendour of the world, too, fades away,   1735
    For it's from this corrupt world of decay.
When the one praising feels much spite inside
    His praise won't fill a breast with joy and pride.
Heart, cleanse yourself of spite and hatred! Say:
    'Praise be to God!' Get busy straight away.
Your tongue is uttering just pretence and fraud
    If hatred hides within while you praise God.
God has said, 'I don't look at the outside
    Appearance, but instead at what's inside.'

Story about the praiser who thanked his object of praise to keep his
reputation, but the whiff of his inward grief and sorrow and the
raggedness of his outward garb showed that those thanks were lies
and pretence.

Wearing a rough cloak once a man came back   1740
    And friends asked of his time spent in Iraq.
He said, 'Yes, exile was so tough, but it
    Helped me gain blessings and much benefit.
The caliph gave me robes of honour there—
    May praises follow that man everywhere!'
He kept repeating thanks and praise this way,
    So they believed he'd gone too far that day
And said, 'Your awful state before our eyes
    Is proof to us that all your words are lies.
Bareheaded, almost naked and so broken,   1745
    These thanks are either memorized or stolen.
Where is the proof that all your praise is fair
    On your head and your feet, which are now bare?
Your tongue may praise that king without restraint,
    But all your body parts express complaint.
In that king's generosity to you
    Was there no pair of trousers or a shoe?'
'I passed to others what he gave,' he claimed,
    'For falling short that ruler can't be blamed.
I took all of that ruler's generous presents   1750

And gave them to the orphans and poor peasants.
I gained long life by giving wealth away,
    Rewarded for I gambled all away.'
They said, 'Congratulations now seem due.
    The wealth has gone, but what's this stench in you?
There is inside you so much thorn-like hating—
    How can grief be the sign of celebrating?
Where are the signs of love and charity
    If what you now claim is reality?
The wealth has gone, but where's the new strong ardour?   1755
    If a flood passed, where are the signs of water?
Your eyes were dark and soul-expanding too,
    But now they're not—why are they deathly blue?
Where is the sign you gambled self away?
    Shut up! We sniff false claims in what you say.
Charity shows a hundred signs in fact
    And they are also shown by each good act.
If you give wealth in charity, it's true
    That in return come rebirths inside you.
Who's cultivated God's land with good deeds   1760
    And not gained profit, left with obvious needs?
For if God's gardens don't grow one corn ear
    How can *God's earth be vast?** We want to hear.
The transient world does not lack crops that sprout—
    How can God's vaster earth then be without?
The latter's crops will last for evermore;
    Each seed produces seven hundred more.
You praised, but where's the praiser's sign to view?
    There's no trace outside and none inside you.'

The mystic's praise of God is true, for his   1765
    Hands and feet even act as witnesses.
It raised him from the body's pit, and bail
    Arrived to free him from this earthly gaol.
Praise's sign's on his shoulders visibly,
    Intimacy's light, silk of piety.
Having escaped the transient world, he's living
    In the rose garden with *the spring that's gushing.**

This lofty mystic's ranking, seat, and station
　　Are all the throne of souls with aspiration,
Fidelity's seat where God's Friends are placed,　　1770
　　Where all are blooming, joyful, and fresh-faced.
Like the rose garden's praise of spring, their praise
　　Shows up in numerous signs and other ways:
The proofs are rose beds, herbs, springs, and palm trees,
　　And lovely scenery each person sees,
Thousands of witnesses in each direction
　　Like the pearl in the shell deep in the ocean.
Through your foul breath one smells your bad soul's trace
　　And your grief, boaster, shines across your face.
Those sensitive to such smells recognize,　　1775
　　So stop pretending with ecstatic cries.
Don't boast of musk when your breath's onion smell
　　Reveals the secret truth so all can tell.
You claim, 'I've had rose candy', but that stink
　　Of garlic says, 'That's nonsense, don't you think?'

The heart is like a house; despite its size
　　Surrounding houses hide it from our eyes.
A few men see the secrets, and not all,
　　Through window slits and cracks within the wall,
Despite the fact the owner's not aware　　1780
　　Of them and in this knowledge lacks a share.
The scripture says, 'The Devil and his evil
　　Followers smelt the hidden state of people
Through means about which most have been oblivious,
　　Since it's not part of this world of the senses.'*
Don't try fraud near detectives seeking it.
　　Don't boast to touchstones, O base counterfeit.
This touchstone has a way to tell apart
　　True from false; God made him chief of the heart.
The devils with their kinds of thuggishness　　1785
　　Can read our thoughts and secrets nonetheless
And have a route inside for robbery:
　　We are thrown headlong by them tragically.
Each moment they cause damage and mishaps,

For they have tunnels and small window gaps—
Why then should the enlightened souls not see
    Men's hidden states as well so easily?
Have spirits who have pitched their tents in heaven
    Less power than devils have in penetration?
The Devil heads to heaven like a robber   1790
    And he becomes speared by a burning meteor.
He falls headlong from heaven the same way
    A wretch is speared in war from far away.
Possessiveness of spirits whom all love
    Throws down the devils headlong from above.
If you are paralysed, lame, deaf, and blind,
    Don't think less of the spirits of this kind.
Stop bragging, feel ashamed, and realize
    Beyond the body there are many spies.

How divine physicians detect diseases of the heart and faith from the
faces of followers or strangers, and their voice and the colour of their
eyes, and even without any of these through the heart, for the
Prophet said: 'They are spies of the heart and so be sincere when
sitting with them.'

Physicians have much knowledge obviously: 1795
    They know more than you of your malady;
They can tell from your urine how your health is,
    Though you can't through that means detect the illness.
From your pulse, pallor, and your breath as well
    They see diseases in you and will tell.
How should the world's own spiritual physicians
    Not know though you don't tell them your conditions?
A hundred ailments they'll identify
    From your pulse, your complexion, and your eye.
Only novice physicians really need   1800
    Such signs in you that they can clearly read,
Since the perfected ones know who you are
    And enter in your being's depths from afar.
In fact some years before your birth they see
    You and all of your life's course easily.

How Abu Yazid predicted the birth of Abo 'l-Hasan Kharaqani*
years ahead of time as well as signs of his appearance and
behaviour, one by one, and how the historians wrote about it for the
purpose of observation.

About great Bayazid here's a narration
    On what he saw of Abo 'l-Hasan's station:
That mystic king went to a barren plain
    With students following behind in train.
A sweet scent suddenly arrived his way   1805
    From Kharaqan to where he stood near Rayy.
Then he let out right there an ardent cry,
    Inhaling that scent as the wind blew by:
He lovingly breathed in that sweetest scent;
    His spirit tasted wine in what was sent.
When condensation forms on the outside
    Of a pot that contains much ice inside,
This is because of coldness in the air—
    Moisture has not escaped from ice in there.
Scent-filled air turned to water similarly;   1810
    Water then turned to pure wine mystically.

Due to effects of his intoxication,
    A student asked about that inhalation:
'These lovely ecstasies seen in your person
    Which all transcend the physical dimension—
Your face turns red, then yellow, and then white—
    What is this? What's the message of this sight?
You breathe in scent, but flowers can't be seen—
    No doubt it's God's rose garden that's unseen.
You are what every soul aspires to be;   1815
    God's messages reach you continuously.
Each moment, as with Jacob, remedies
    From Joseph reach your nose, so share one please.*
Pour from that pitcher one drop over us;
    Share one scent from that garden far from us.
It's strange for us, O beauty who ranks high,

That you should drink and let our lips stay dry.
Swift climber up to heaven, won't you share
  A swig of what you drank from over there?
There is no prince of any gathering   1820
  As great as you—look at your following!
How can one drink this wine and hide the action?
  Wine powerfully exposes every human.
Though one might find a way to hide the smell,
  How can one hide one's drunken eyes as well?
Even a million veils can't cover up
  This most distinctive smell—one should give up.
This smell can fill the desert and the plain,
  Even heaven's nine spheres, so it's in vain.
The naked can't be clothed—learning from that,   1825
  Don't plaster up the opening of this vat.
You know all mysteries, so be kind today.
  Show what your falcon has made its new prey.'

Bayazid said, 'A wondrous scent came close,
  Like what from Yemen reached the Prophet's nose
When he said, "On a breeze God's scent somehow
  Reached me from distant Yemen's lands just now.
Ramin's scent travelled from the soul of Vays;*
  The scent of God arrives now from Ovays."'*
A scent from Qarani that is so marvellous   1830
  Had made the Prophet drunkenly feel rapturous.
Ovays had been effaced, so the terrestrial,
  Once self-annihilated, turned celestial.
Myrobalan that's been conserved in sugar
  Will then no longer taste extremely bitter.
Myrobalan that has been self-effaced
  Looks like myrobalan, but lacks that taste.
We could go on and on with this discussion,
  So let's hear his words on God's revelation.

*The words of the Prophet, 'I perceive the breath of the Merciful
from the direction of Yemen.'*

Bayazid said, 'From that way comes a scent   1835
　　Which says that there a monarch will be sent:
A king will be born after many years
　　Who'll pitch his tent above the heavens' spheres.
His face so rosy from the Lord's rose garden,
　　He will traverse beyond my mystic station.'

'What is his name?' 'Abo 'l-Hasan,' he said,
　　And then from brow to chin described his head,
Then his hair, his fine stature, and his figure
　　In so much detail, then his face and pallor.
He also showed his spiritual description,   . 1840
　　From attributes to methods and high station.
Bodily descriptions are just there to borrow—
　　Don't set your heart on them! They're gone tomorrow.
The natural spirit's features also die—
　　Seek the soul that is far above the sky.
Though bodies are on earth like lamps, their light
　　Reaches beyond the heavens, far from sight:
The sun's rays come inside each person's home,
　　Its orb though is above the sky's high dome.
If roses' forms touch your nose, it's in vain,   1845
　　Because their scent can't reach up to your brain.
A sleeping man has dreamt of something gory;
　　It will appear as sweat now on his body.
The shirt was kept in Egypt in safe hands,
　　But nonetheless its scent filled Canaan's lands.*

The followers wrote down the time and date,
　　Like skewering kebabs prepared for fate.
The king was born on that date with precision
　　Starting the game of monarchy's backgammon.
Years later, Bo 'l-Hasan came there one day   1850

After great Bayazid had passed away,
And this man's every single quality
    Appeared just as that monarch said they'd be.
The Tablet that's preserved* was his director;
    From what is that preserved? From any error,
Not through stars, sorcery, or dreams at night,
    But God's own words, and *He knows best what's right.*
Sufis sometimes call this 'heart inspiration',
    To hide it from the general population—
Accept this other 'heart' term seeing as He   1855
    Is manifested there; it's error-free.*
You can as well *see by God's light*, believer—
    The Prophet said this; then you're free from error.

The reduction of the allowance of God's food for the heart and soul of the Sufi.

Poverty shouldn't worry dervishes;
    Its essence is their food and wet-nurses,
For heaven grew out of misfortune, while
    Mercy comes from the broken under trial.
God and His creatures' mercy don't come near
    The one who smashes others' heads down here.

This talk has no end, and that poet's lost   1860
    All strength through lack of food, a heavy cost.
Happy the Sufi with a food reduction:
    His bead becomes a pearl, and he an ocean.
He who learns of that special salary
    Merits that pay's source's proximity.
His soul will start to tremble, though, all over
    If his own mystic wages are made lower,
For he'll know he's earned that with an infringement,
    Ruffling the jasmine bed of God's contentment,
Just like that person who wrote to the owner   1865
    About why his crop share had been made lower:
They took his note to the top judge to read;
    He chose not to reply or to take heed:

'Loss of fine food is all he's had to suffer—
   For stupid people silence is the answer.'
He lacks the pain of being apart from Oneness;
   He doesn't seek the root, but worships branches.
He's vile and he has died in selfishness,
   Grieving the branch; the root's not what he'll miss.

Heaven and earth are apples that you see,   1870
   Which are made manifest by God's power's tree.
You're like a worm inside and unaware
   About the tree and how it was grown there.
A worm is in the apple, deep inside,
   And its soul waves a flag on the outside;
Its movements split the apple from within—
   The apple cannot hold that pressure in.
Its movement tears the veils, so it must be
   Worm in form, dragon in reality.
The spark that darts from iron initially   1875
   Places its feet outside so gingerly;
Cotton keeps it alive at first with care,
   Then watches as its flame soars in the air—
Humans at first must eat and sleep, but they
   Can soar beyond the angels' reach one day;
Cotton and matches nurture that one's light,
   But his flame soars beyond stars, far from sight.
He can light up the dark world and dismantle
   Strong iron fetters with a tiny needle.

Though fire is also something physical,   1880
   Isn't its origin still spiritual?
Body has no share in the mystic glory;
   Body is a mere drop next to the soul's sea.
The soul's what makes the body's days increase:
   When the soul leaves, the body's life will cease.
The limit of your body is so small;
   Your soul soars to the sky above us all.
The journey to Baghdad and Samarkand

For spirits is one step across the land.
    Your eyeballs weigh the same as two coins though   1885
        Their spirit's light sees heaven from below.
Without the eyes, through dreams this light can see;
        Without this light, eyes are blind totally.
The spirit's separate from beards and moustaches;
        Without the spirit, bodies are just corpses.
I've talked about the animal type of spirit;
        The human spirit goes beyond its limit.
Transcend the human, Moses, and discussion,
        To reach the shore of Gabriel's spirit's ocean!
Mohammad's soul beyond then kisses you   1890
        And Gabriel will crawl back, so scared of you,
Saying: 'If by one bow-length I come near
        To you, at once I'll be consumed right here.'*

The young man becomes agitated because no reply comes from the king to his letter.

This desert has no top or bottom either.
        That young man found he didn't get an answer:
'How strange the king chose not to answer me!
        Maybe it is the courier's trickery,
Hiding the note I wrote from the king's eyes,
        Like water shifting under straw, through lies?
To test this out I'll write another letter   1895
        And use a different courier who is better.'
The courier, kitchen head, and king: all three
        Were blamed by this fool through stupidity.
He didn't once look at himself to say:
        'I'm being perverse like those whose faith's astray.'

The wind blew improperly on Solomon because of his error.

Wind blew improperly on Solomon's throne.
        'Don't creep improperly,' that king would moan.
The wind said, 'Stop behaving so perversely.
        If you persist you can't complain about me.
God set up weighing scales at the beginning,   1900

So justice is received by all. You're wishing
To give short measure, so that's what I'll do—
    Be straight with me and I'll be straight with you.'
Likewise Solomon's crown once blocked his sight
    When it slid down—it made his day like night.
'Don't slide lopsided, crown, while on my head!
    Sun, don't set on my east!' that king then said.
He repositioned the lopsided crown,
    However, it would keep on sliding down.
He did this eight times; it slid stubbornly.   1905
    He said, 'What's up? Don't creep improperly!'
It said, 'Though often by you I'm corrected,
    I will stay crooked, king, while you are crooked.'
Solomon straightened then his inner being;
    He drew his heart back from what he'd been dreaming
To win, and it returned to its first state
    Just as he'd wanted it—his crown was straight.
He made it crooked then deliberately—
    It sought itself to rest as meant to be.
He made it crooked eight times, but instead   1910
    Each time that crown would straighten on his head.
The crown spoke, 'King, be proud that you today
    Have freed your wings from clay and fly away.'

To say more now is not allowed for me,
    Nor to unveil this matter's mystery.
Cover my mouth when your hand is in reach
    To stop it uttering this unwelcome speech.
Whatever grief befalls you, please admit
    It's your fault—don't blame others now for it.
Don't be suspicious and resort to hating,   1915
    Don't do what that young man was contemplating,
Fighting the kitchen head first, then the courier,
    Directing all his anger at the ruler.
Pharaoh-like, you'll chop every baby's head,
    Though he let the young Moses stay instead
In his own house: that one with a blind heart
    Chopped others' necks and could not tell apart.

You, too, treat badly others who're outside,
  While treating well the harmful self inside.
It is your foe, but you give it a sweet,   1920
  Instead accusing everyone you meet,
Like Pharaoh blind and so blind-hearted too,
  Mean to the blameless, nice to who harms you.
For how long, Pharaoh, will you choose to kill
  The blameless, pampering your body still.
This one excelled all kings with his sharp mind,
  But God's will made him ignorant and blind.
God's seal on wisdom's eyes and ears can turn
  To beasts men who're like Plato, though they learn.
Etched on the Tablet is the Lord's decision   1925
  About what comes, like Bayazid's prediction.

*Shaikh Abo 'l-Hasan hears Bayazid's announcement
informing about his coming to existence and his
circumstances.*

It happened as he'd said it would turn out
  And from his people Bo 'l-Hasan found out
That Bayazid, before he had been born,
  Had said, 'He'll study at my tomb each dawn.'
Bo 'l-Hasan said, 'In dreams I've had a view
  Of him and heard the shaikh's soul say it too.'
He'd set off for his grave each dawn and wait
  Until the sunrise. There he'd meditate.
Bayazid's image either then appeared   1930
  Or wordlessly his problems disappeared,
Until one day he came auspiciously
  When snow had covered all graves recently:
Snow piled as high as standards far and wide
  With mounds on top. He felt much pain inside.
A shout came from the shaikh's tomb suddenly:
  '*I call you so that you might run to me,*
So rush towards my voice—approach this way,
  The world's snow-filled. Seek me, don't turn away.'
His inner state was good from then, and he   1935
  Saw wonders he'd just heard of previously.

That young man writes another note to the king since he did not get a reply to the first one.

That young, suspicious one wrote one more letter
    Full of complaints, blame, and appalling matter.
He wrote, 'I've written this once previously,
    But did it reach the king successfully?'
That handsome king received and read this letter,
    But chose not to reply to this one either,
Maintaining silent treatment as before—
    That young man wrote again and sent five more.
'He works for you,' the chamberlain then said,   1940
    'So there's no fault in answering instead.
How will it harm you if you drop your stance
    And cast upon this servant just one glance?'
'That would be simple,' then the king objected,
    'But he's a wretch whom even God rejected.
If I forgive his sin and his transgression,
    I might catch his disease from his infection.'
From just one scab a hundred quickly spread,
    Especially the kind that all men dread.
May infidels be spared scabs of the brainless   1045
    Whose bad luck even makes the clouds all rainless,
Such that a single drop will not rain down;
    That bad luck also ruins every town.
Those fools' scabs brought in Noah's Flood that razed
    A whole world just so they would be disgraced.
'Whoever is a fool', the Prophet said,
    'Is my foe, the waylaying ghoul men dread.
One who's intelligent is our soul and
    His breeze is like our basil in this land.'
If intellect reproach me, I'm content.   1950
    It brings grace and from grace's source it's sent.
Such a reproach has so much benefit:
    That host's fine table has much food on it.
But if a wretch brings to my lips some halva
    That makes me sick and I soon get a fever.
You should know, if enlightened and with favour,

That kissing donkey's asses has no savour.
He pulls out the moustaches of your manhood;
   His pot makes clothes black, but it is without food.

The table's spread is wisdom, not just meat,   1955
   The light of wisdom, food for souls to eat.
Man has no food apart from light at all.
   There's no alternative to feed the soul.
Cut yourself off from plain food gradually—
   That's donkey feed next to food of the free.
This way you'll gain original food one night
   And you'll consume the morsels of pure light.
That light's reflection made these things food; grace
   From that Soul made our souls in the first place.
Once you take one bite of this food of light,   1960
   You'll bury thoughts of oven bread from sight.
There are two kinds of knowledge and the former
   Is what you learn at school as a young scholar
From your books, teachers, thinking, and your memory,
   Concepts and interesting new fields of study.
You will surpass men with the knowledge gained,
   Yet you'll be burdened by what you've retained,
For in your search you're a retaining tablet—
   One who transcends is the Protected Tablet.
This other knowledge comes from God's bestowal   1965
   And this true wisdom's found inside your soul.
When wisdom's water gushes in your breast
   It never stagnates; it's forever blest.
Why feel concerned if its path's blocked outside
   When it keeps gushing constantly inside?
The knowledge that's acquired though is a river
   That runs through streams to homes to give men water;
If their path's blocked the home's supply will end—
   Seek the fount deep within yourself, my friend!

The story about someone who was consulting another man who then said, 'Consult someone else because I am your enemy.'

A man went to consult another person   1970
  To be delivered from his own confusion.
That man said, 'Go, find someone else instead
  And tell him of what fills you now with dread.
I am a foe, so do not turn to me;
  No one is helped by their own enemy.
Go, find a friend of yours, for friends help out
  And always wish you well, so there's no doubt.
I am a foe, and so inevitably
  Self-interest makes me act with enmity.
Who'd ask a wolf to guard his sheep? Tell me.   1975
  To seek from the wrong place is idiocy.
I am your enemy without a doubt;
  I waylay you; how could I help you out?'

Whoever sits with friends is in a park
  Even if in a furnace, hot and dark.
Whoever sits with foes is in a furnace
  Even if sitting in a park or palace.
Don't hurt your friend by acting selfishly
  In case he should become your enemy.
For God's sake and your own soul's peace, do good   1980
  To other people, treat them as you should,
So they appear as friends always to you
  And your heart blocks out ugly hate's thoughts, too.
Since you've shown enmity, now pay attention—
  Consult a friend who can inspire affection!
He said, 'I know you, Bo 'l-Hasan,* to be
  Someone who's viewed me as an enemy,
But you're so rational and so spiritual;
  Reason stops you from being corrupt at all.'

Our nature wishes us to hate our foe;   1985
    Reason's a chain that keeps the self in tow.
It comes, restrains, and keeps the self at bay
    Like a chief of police in a good way.
Faith's reason is a just chief of police,
    Guarding and governing the heart with peace.
It is alert like cats, not thieves who stay
    Inside a hole like mice throughout the day.
Wherever mice prevail, be certain that
    There's no cat, or just pictures of a cat.
What is a cat? Faith's reason wears the crown,   1990
    A lion that with ease pins others down.
It governs all the ravenous with its roar;
    Its yelling wards off every herbivore.
This city's filled with every kind of thief
    Even if there's a law-enforcement chief.

The Prophet Mohammad made a young man of the Hozayl tribe the commander of a brigade which included senior soldiers and experienced fighters.

The Prophet once sent out a whole brigade
    To fight each infidel and renegade.
He picked a youth from the Hozayl's tribe's groups
    As chief and the commander of the troops.

The chief is the foundation of an army;   1995
    Without a chief they are a headless body.
The fact you're withering and almost dead
    Is due to your abandoning your head:
From being lazy, selfish, and a miser,
    You've turned away and made yourself commander.
You're like the mule who leaves its load alone
    And wanders to the mountain on its own.
The owner chases it and from behind
    Shouts, 'Giddy one, wolves there devour your kind.

If you should disappear now from my vision, 2000
   A wolf will follow you from each direction
And chew all of your bones as if they're sugar,
   So you can't possibly survive much longer.
Rebel and you will certainly lack food;
   Fire is extinguished by a lack of wood.
Beware not to flee now from my control
   And your own heavy load, for I'm your soul.'
You are a beast, too, for your self's your ruler;
   What dominates rules you, O self-adorer.
God called you horse, not ass, so understand. 2005
   Arabs say, '*Come!*' to horses as command.
Mohammad was God's stable chief, so he
   Helped beasts against their base self's tyranny.
'*Say, "Come!"* '* he said through kindness, 'So I can
   Train you—I am the trainer for each man.
I have trained many carnal souls, and I
   Have felt the kicks that animals let fly.'
When someone tries to train and teach another,
   Inevitably kicks come flying, brother.
The most strike Prophets on their holy mission; 2010
   Training, base one, is in itself affliction.
You're stumbling—at my word, try trotting faster
   And smoothly for the carriage of your master.
God said, '*Say, "Come!" Say, "Come!"* '* we also read,
   'To beasts who have fled discipline.' Take heed!
Prophet, if they don't come, don't feel unhappy
   And don't resent those who won't act steadfastly.
The ears of some are deaf to '*Come!*', unable
   To take heed, since all beasts have their own stable.
This call makes some run, very stimulated; 2015
   In stables horses' stalls are separated.
This story makes some sad and desperate
   Because each bird's cage is kept separate.
The angels aren't considered to be even—
   That's why they are of different ranks in heaven.
Though children may attend the same school class,
   Some will excel, some fail, and some just pass.
All men across the world have sense perception,

But just the eye's perception gives us vision:
Although a hundred ears line up to try,   2020
   They would still need help from a seeing eye.
The lined-up ears have their own special role
   For hearing revelation and the soul.
A million eyes can't do the same for you:
   About the auditory, eyes have no clue.
If you go through the senses, you'll discover
   None can perform the function of another.
There are five outward senses, five inside.
   They're ranked* in ten ranks, standing classified.
Those who turn round from faith's rank you will find   2025
   Falling down to a rank that lags behind.
Do not downplay the word '*Come!*'* for this word
   Is a supreme elixir that you've heard.
Though copper ones reject it when they're told it,
   Regardless you should not try to withhold it.
The sorcerer-like self has them now bound;
   Your words will help them later. They're profound.
Say 'Come!' Say 'Come!',* O young man, without cease
   And be aware that *God invites to peace.**
Come back, good man, from selfish leadership;   2030
   Seek out instead a leader—that's my tip.

An objector protested to the Prophet about his appointment of the man from the Hozayl as commander.

The Prophet made that Hozayli commander
   Of that brigade, with God as his supporter.
Sheer jealousy meant one wretch couldn't take it,
   So he objected and would not embrace it.

Look at how dark the people are today—
   They're self-effaced in objects that decay.
They live in separation due to pride;
   Their souls are dead since all their life they've lied.
It's strange the soul's in gaol when you can see   2035
   That in its hand it holds its own cell's key.

That young man is immersed in dung now wholly,
    Although a flowing river flows so closely.
He can't keep still, but fidgets all the while,
    Though there's a couch where he can rest in style.
The light is hidden, but the search makes plain
    The heart does not seek refuge out in vain.
If there were no way out from this world's prison,
    Hearts wouldn't seek escape and feel aversion.
Aversion to this world drags you as guardian,   2040
    Saying, 'Seek now the path of guidance, lost one!'
There is a way out, but it's hidden deeply;
    To find it you must clutch at straws initially.
All separation secretly seeks union;
    Look at the seeker to see there the sought one.
Dead plants in gardens jump up straight away:
    'Understand the life-giver!' they all say.
Prisoners watch the door that leads outside—
    Why do that if there's no news from that side?
Why would a million soiled ones seek clean water   2045
    If there weren't a supply in the clean river?
The ground's not comfortable now for your back;
    At home you have the mattress you now lack—
Without a resting place, no restless roamer.
    Without relief from headaches, no hangover.

That rebel said, 'Prophet, I disagree;
    A leader should have seniority:
Though this youth be a lion cub or bolder,
    The army's leader should be someone older.
And you have also clearly stated once   2050
    "The leader must be old." That's evidence.
Survey this army now, O Messenger—
    Several are older and superior.'
Its leaves have yellowed, but the tree's not dead;
    Focus on its ripe apples now instead.
Yellow leaves aren't a sign of imperfection;
    This is a sign of ripeness and perfection.
Like yellow leaves, a white beard on the chin

Brings good news that some wisdom lies within.
However, green leaves of the newborn type   2055
  Are a clear sign that fruit will be unripe.
The mystic's sign is food from nothingness;
  The flushing banker loves gold's yellowness.
The beard's first hair is on a flushed one's cheek—
  This one has only learned to write this week;
The handwriting of this one is still crooked;
  His body moves fast, but his brain is crippled.
An old man's legs might not run very fast,
  But his brain has acquired wings and soars past.
Just look at Ja'far if you doubt such things: 2060
  In place of limbs God gave His servant wings.*
Leave gold behind; this speech has been disturbed.
  Like mercury my heart has been perturbed.
One hundred silent, sweet-breathed ones within me
  Put fingers to their lips: 'Enough!' they tell me.
The sea is silence; rivers are palaver:
  The sea pursues you; don't seek out the river.
Don't turn round from the sea's signs. Make this end.
  And *God knows best what is correct*, my friend.

But that irreverent one refused to drop it: 2065
  He droned on with vain words before the Prophet.
Speech gave a helping hand, but he was clueless;
  Compared with sight that knowledge is so useless.
It's secondary to vision: that is clear
  For those who're absent, not for those who're here.
For one who has true vision as his gain
  These kinds of knowledge are absurd and vain.
You've sat next to your sweetheart, so today
  Push all the intermediaries away.
Those who have grown up are no longer keen   2070
  To read books or employ a go-between.
That one reads books just for the needs of teaching;
  Helping men learn is his sole aim in speaking.
It's wrong to speak before those who can see;
  That's negligence and a deficiency.

Silence is best near seers who understand:
  '*Be silent!*'* came down as the Lord's command.
Speak joyfully if he invites you to,
  But don't go on at length. Make your words few.
And if he should request that you speak longer,   2075
  Be modest still as you obey his order.
Just as I do with this most handsome youth,
  Hosamoddin, who is the light of Truth.
When I cut short what I provide of guidance,
  He lures me back there with some new contrivance.
Hosamoddin, you are God's Glory's Light—
  Why do you ask for speech when you have sight?
Is *love for the desired one* causing this?
  Give me some wine and tell me what it is.
His cup is on your lips, but your ears dare   2080
  To ask Him still, 'Where then is the ear's share?'
Your share's the warmth—you're warm and drunk in bliss.
  They answer, 'Our desire is more than this.'

The Prophet Mohammad answers the objector.

While present with our own sweet-natured Prophet
  When that man argued on beyond the limit,
That king of '*By the star*', '*His favour's*' ruler,*
  Bit his lip, said 'Enough!' to that vain babbler.
He blocked that man's mouth with his hand to say:
  'How long before the Unseen's knower this way
Will you continue? You have brought dried shit   2085
  And urged, "Instead of purest musk buy it!"
O stinking brain, you place it to your nose
  And say, "How lovely!" though it's not a rose.
Wretch, you've said, "Ah!" to a most noxious smell,
  So that your rotten goods will quickly sell,
So you can trick the holy sense perception,
  The one that grazes in the heavenly garden.'

That giant's forbearance has misled the fickle,
  But one must recognize oneself a little;

The pot was left uncovered through the night,   2090
   But cats should feel ashamed to eat in sight.
That glorious one pretends to sleep—beware:
   Don't try to snatch his turban. He's aware.
O stubborn wretch, for how long will you say
   Those bad spells to the Prophet of the day?
Such men have much forbearance, by the millions,
   And each of these is like a hundred mountains.
Each one, too, makes fools of the watchful spies
   And misleads even men with scores of eyes.
And this forbearance is like lovely wine   2095
   Reaching up to one's brain in ways so fine.
Observe one drunk on marvellous wine—now he
   Moves like a queen in chess, diagonally.
Through the fast-acting wine, that man has rolled
   Onto the street as if he's very old,
That wine especially from the vat of '*Yes!*',*
   Not wine that gives just one night's drunkenness.
That wine which to the seven sleepers gave
   Three hundred and nine years inside the cave.*
Egyptian women drank one cup of it,   2100
   Then cut their hands with knives not meant for it.*
Sorcerers had Moses's intoxication
   And deemed the gallows their beloved station.
Flying Ja'far* got drunk with that wine and
   Selflessly pawned away both leg and hand.

*Story about Abu Yazid's saying 'Glory be to me! How
magnificent my rank is!', the opposition of disciples,
and his response to this through visions rather than through
saying words.*

The noble Sufi Bayazid once told
   His own disciples, 'I am God, behold!'
While drunk that master said explicitly:
   '*There is no god but I, so worship me!*'
When that state left him on the following day,   2105
   They said, 'You spoke in an improper way.'

He said, 'The next time I act similarly
  Then strike at me with knives immediately.
I am with body, that which God transcends.
  When I speak that way you must kill me, friends.'
This sound advice from one so liberated
  Meant each disciple fetched a knife and waited.
Again he got drunk from that awesome flagon
  And he forgot all the advice he'd given.
Sweets came and intellect could not be traced;   2110
  Dawn came and then his candle was effaced.

Reasoning is the chief of police, so when
  The sultan comes it creeps away again.
Reason's shadow, God's sunlight, and not one
  Shadow has ever stood up to the sun.
If just one sprite controls a man, the cost
  Is that his attributes are quickly lost.
What he says is in fact what that sprite said:
  He speaks the absent one's words here instead.
When a mere sprite can be a dominator,   2115
  Imagine then the power of the Creator:
His self has gone—that man's become the sprite;
  The Turk speaks Arabic without the light.
He doesn't know a word when he comes to—
  That sprite's possessed his traits and essence too.
How can the Lord of Man and sprites then be
  Inferior to the sprite? Please answer me.
If someone drunk should kill a lion, you'd say
  'The wine did it, not him!' And if one day
He says words precious as rare gold, then you   2120
  Will say, 'It is the drink that's talking through.'
Some wine can cause a stunning transformation—
  Is God's light too weak for such domination
Which empties yourself from you totally,
  So you're brought low and He speaks loftily?
The Prophet's mouth spoke the Qur'an as well—
  Claim 'They're not God's words,' you're an infidel.

When selflessness's bird flew out of reach
    Great Bayazid then started baffling speech.
Bewilderment's flood stole away his reason;   2125
    He spoke more strongly than he had first spoken:
'There's nothing in my cloak but God,' he said,
    'Why seek on earth and heaven now instead?'
All his disciples fell into a frenzy
    And stuck their knives into his holy body.
Like the Assassins,* each one plunged his blade
    Into his master and none felt afraid.
Whoever stabbed with his knife was reversely
    In fact just splitting open his own body.
On that great master's body wounds weren't found   2130
    But on their bodies which in blood soon drowned.
Whoever had attacked his throat could witness
    His own throat slit, and died abased and helpless,
While he who stabbed him in the chest instead
    Saw his own chest split open and fell dead.
But he who was acquainted with that sultan
    Did not feel right to strike him with his weapon:
His partial knowledge bound his hands—his life
    Was saved and he was just cut by his knife.
Their numbers were depleted by the dawn   2135
    And in their houses men began to mourn.
Thousands of people came to Bayazid,
    Saying: 'Two worlds within one shirt indeed:
If yours were really just a human body
    By daggers you'd have been destroyed now totally.'

A man with self fought someone who was selfless:
    He stabbed with thorns his own eye in the process.
You who stab selfless ones with swords should know
    You only stab yourself with every blow.
The selfless ones live in security;   2140
    Effaced they stay safe for eternity.
His form has gone and he's become a mirror;
    There's naught there but the image of another.
If you spit at it, it falls on your head;

If you strike it, you strike yourself instead.
You see an ugly face there? That is you.
   Jesus and Mary? That view is you, too:
He's neither this nor that; He is transparent.
   It is your own face that He makes apparent.
Lips sealed up when the speech reached this last part;   2145
   Once the pen reached these words, it split apart.
Close your lips, though fine eloquence today
   Is at your service. *God knows the best way.*
You're on the roof's edge, drunkard, so take care.
   Sit down or you will fall off from up there.
Regard each moment of success that's sweet
   As being on the roof edge at some feet.
Fear losing that sweet moment and conceal it
   Like precious treasure, and do not reveal it.
Go to that ambush hideout with much caution   2150
   So you don't suffer there all of a sudden.
At joy's time your soul's fear of loss will mean
   Escape then from the roof edge that's unseen—
Though you don't see the secret roof edge, friend,
   Your soul sees and it fears it's near the end.
Every chastisement that came suddenly
   Has come at joy's own roof edge purposefully.
The roof edge is the sole place where men fall.
   From Noah and Lot's people learn it all.

*Explaining the cause of the eloquence and talkativeness in that
interferer while with the Prophet.*

The Prophet's drunkenness sent out a ray   2155
   Which struck that wretch and made him drunk that day:
His talkativeness was due to euphoria;
   He put aside decorum for hysteria.
Losing your wits does not cause badness always:
   Wine makes ill-mannered ones much worse in their ways;
If one is wise it makes one lovelier,
   But, if bad-tempered, one gets angrier.
They have made wine prohibited to all
   Since most are bad and reprehensible.

*The Prophet's explanation of the reason for his preferring and
choosing the Hozayli man as commander and chief of the army over
the elders and veterans.*

Rulings are based on numbers in these lands: 2160
    Most are bad, so the sword's seized from thieves' hands.
The Prophet said, 'You just see his appearance;
    Don't judge him young and lacking in experience.
With beards still black, some men have wisdom's light;
    Others have black hearts, though their beards are white.
I've tested often his sagacity:
    The youth's work shows his seniority.'
Seniority in wisdom matters there,
    Not a white beard or on one's head white hair.
Who's older than cursed Satan of you men?   2165
    Without intelligence one's worthless then.
A child with Jesus's breath would be free
    From arrogance and craving totally.
Maturity is proven by white hair
    Only to blinkered men who're unaware.
Blind imitators trust such proof alone:
    To them through outward signs the way is known.
We've said for that man's sake, 'When it's some order
    That you desire, then choose one who's maturer,
One free from veils of mere blind imitation   2170
    Who sees the truth through God's illumination.'
His light, without an argument, can split
    The shell so it can deeply enter it.
Form followers can't tell real coin from base—
    How should they know which type they're going to face?
Much gold has turned black due to smoke's trace and
    This has helped it escape the robber's hand.
Much copper has been gilded with real gold,
    So to the gullible it can be sold.
Inward observers like us in each province   2175
    See hearts and disregard the mere appearance.
Judges who see appearances alone
    Make rulings based on them, which is well known.

When someone shows faith and gives testimony,
    These people think he's faithful instantly—
Behind this form pretenders have stayed hidden
    Then secretly killed Muslims by the dozen.

In faith and wisdom try to be most senior
    Like Universal Intellect, see deeper
Within; when it appeared from nothingness,   2180
    God gave it robes of honour as its dress,
And many lovely names, the smallest one
    Of which means that it won't need anyone.
This Intellect shows its face physically—
    Next to its light, day seems dark stunningly.
But if an ugly one is made apparent,
    Next to him suddenly the night seems radiant,
For he is darker than the night. The bat,
    Being wretched, is a customer of that.
Get used to daylight's radiance gradually   2185
    Or you'll lose out like bats eternally.
That one loves problem places and he hates
    Those that have lamps that give one joyful states;
His heart seeks darkness of the sorriest plight
    So his achievements seem great in that light,
So with that plight you'll be preoccupied
    And overlook his ugliness inside.

*The mark of the wise and the half-wise one, the complete
man and the half-complete man, and the worthless wretch.*

The one who has the lamp's the real wise man,
    The guide and leader of the caravan.
That leader follows his own light, lacks self,   2190
    And that's why he can follow just himself.
He has self-confidence, and also you
    Believe in that light which feeds his soul, too.
The second one who only is half-wise
    Uses the fully wise as his own eyes;

Like a blind man he holds on to his guide
　　To see through him and do what's dignified.
The donkey who lacks wisdom totally
　　Ignores the wise through his own idiocy.
He's ignorant of this path and his pride   2195
　　Stops him from following a knowing guide.
He goes into the desert all the same,
　　Sometimes at pace, sometimes as though he's lame.
He has no candle to show the direction,
　　Nor half of one from which to seek instruction.
He lacks full wisdom for a living breath,
　　Or even half, through which to seek sound death:
The half-wise dies before the fully wise,
　　So from his low start he can quickly rise;
If you lack wisdom, then you should choose death,   2200
　　Protected by the wise with living breath.
Others can't breathe like Jesus—not alive yet—
　　And can't receive his pure breath—they've not died yet—
Their blind souls step in every direction,
　　But leap without escaping their location.

Story about the lake, the fishermen, and the three fish— one wise; one half-wise; and one deluded, stupid, heedless, and worthless—and the outcome for all three fish.

This tale about the lake in which were found
　　Three special fish who liked to swim around
Is in Kalila and Dimna* as well,
　　But here's the kernel—that book's is the shell.
Some fishermen passed by the lake one day   2205
　　And noticed deep inside it hidden prey.
They rushed back to their net and brought it there;
　　The fish all noticed and became aware.
The wise one then resolved to move along
　　The path that's difficult and for the strong.
He thought, 'I won't consult them, since they're bound
　　To weaken my resolve which now is sound.

Love of their homeland holds them rigidly;
    Their sloth and ignorance both clash with me.
I need somebody now for consultation   2210
    Who can revive me, but where's his location?'
O traveller, consult one who's the same—
    Consulting weaklings only makes you lame.
Pass from *love of the homeland*; don't stop here—
    The homeland's yonder; souls aren't from this sphere.
You want the homeland? Reach the other side;
    Don't misread this hadith that's verified.*

The mystery of the recitation of specific prayers when one does ablutions.*

For every part while you do your ablution,
    There is a different prayer and recitation:
While rinsing out your nose, you're meant to plead   2215
    For heaven's scent from God, Who's free from need,
So it draws you to paradise at once,
    Since scent is the rose bush's evidence.
When you wipe your arse clean of any shit,
    The prayer is: 'O Lord, please cleanse me of it!
My hand touched there while cleaning—that's its role,
    But it is much too weak to clean the soul.
You who can make a nobody's soul worthy,
    Your grace's hand can reach our spirits easily.
This is my limit—I've done what I can.   2220
    Most generous God, cleanse what's beyond this man.
O God, I cleansed my skin of its pollution—
    Cleanse this friend of the world's events' distraction!'

Someone used to say while cleaning his arse: 'O God, let me smell the scent of paradise!' instead of 'O God, make me a repenter and one of the purified!' which is the proper recitation while cleaning one's arse. He would also say the latter prayer instead when he was rinsing his nose. An esteemed man heard and could not tolerate it.

While cleaning his arse once a man recited:
    'Join me with heaven's scent, so I'm united!'
A man said, 'That's a worthy recitation,

But this is not a fitting situation:
While rinsing out one's nose that prayer is said—
    You've brought the nose prayer to your arse instead.
One gains the scent of heaven through the nose—   2225
    Can it be gained by arses, you suppose?'
You who have made so humble every fool
    And given pride to all the kings who rule,
Disdain towards base men's appropriate—
    You'll just get chained by doing the opposite.
It is for nostrils that we have the rose—
    Its scent, wretch, is intended for the nose:
For our olfactory sense comes rose's scent;
    The dirty hole below is not what's meant.
Through there you can't receive the scent of heaven;   2230
    If you need it, seek scent through the right organ.
Love for the homeland* is right similarly—
    Identify that land initially.

The wise fish thought then, 'I will now depart
    And I'll detach from their advice my heart.'
It's not time to consult now, so just go!
    Like Ali scream it in the well below:*
To find one fit to share that scream is hard,
    Move secretly at night like a skilled guard.
Head from this lake towards the open sea.   2235
    Seek that and leave this maelstrom rapidly.
This wary fish set off in haste that night
    From danger's area to the sea of light.
Like deer being chased by dogs, he will not stop
    But run while his veins still contain one drop.
Dozing while dogs chase is an obvious error—
    How can your eyes feel drowsy while in terror?
That fish departed for the ocean fast,
    Taking the long path through a gulf so vast.
He saw much suffering and eventually   2240
    The path led him to calm security.
He threw himself into the massive ocean
    That looked so limitless then to his vision.

When those same fishermen brought their net later
   The half-wise fish began to feel so bitter:
'I've lost the opportunity!' it cried,
   'How did I fail to leave then with that guide?
Though he went suddenly when he departed
   I should have rushed behind where he had darted.'
Regretting what has passed is error, son;   2245
   It's pointless, for it won't return once gone.

Story about the captive bird which advised: 'Don't regret the past.
Think about it in the present so you won't waste time regretting.'

A man once caught a bird inside a snare.
   The bird said, 'Princely man beyond compare,
You've eaten many cows and sheep, and you
   Have sacrificed so many camels too—
You were not sated once by them and now
   You think my body will suffice somehow?
Release me and I'll give you three wise counsels—
   See if I'm wise or just one of the numbskulls.
I'll tell the first one while perched on your hand,   2250
   The second after I hop off and land
Upon your wall, the third while up a tree,
   Then from these counsels you'll live fortunately.
On your hand: don't accept what you have heard
   From anyone if it should sound absurd.'
Once it had said the first, perched on his hand,
   It hopped off to the wall, freed just as planned.
It gave the second: 'Don't you ever fret
   About the past. It's left you. Quit regret.'
Then 'Hidden in me', that bird chose to state,   2255
   'Is a rare pearl of ten dirhams in weight.
I swear that jewel had always meant to be
   Your fortune and that of your progeny.
But you have lost the pearl of such high worth.
   No other pearl like this exists on earth.'
That man then started wailing like a mother
   About to give birth during painful labour.
The bird continued, 'Didn't I just say

Not to grieve over what passed yesterday?
Since it has passed and gone, why are you grieving?   2260
    Do you not get it? Are you hard of hearing?
The other counsel that I have related
    Is: don't believe when the absurd is stated—
I weigh less than three dirhams, so how can
    Something that weighs ten be in me, brave man?'
The man regained composure and then said,
    'Tell me your third good counsel. Go ahead.'
It said, 'Yeah right, you heeded the first two
    So well that I should tell the third to you!'
Giving the dozy fool advice that's sound   2265
    Is scattering good seeds over barren ground.
Stupidity's rip can't be sewn together—
    Don't ever give it wisdom's seed, good counsellor!

The half-wise fish thinks of a solution and acts dead.

In suffering's hour the half-wise fish then said,
    While cut off from the wise fish's safe shade:
'He's free from grief now he has reached the sea;
    Such a dear comrade has been lost to me.
I'll act myself and not dwell on that now—
    I'll make myself look like I'm dead somehow:
I'll raise my stomach up by rolling over   2270
    With my back upside down while on the water.
Like twigs I'll move across its surface then,
    Floating, not swimming like the living men:
Corpse-like I will surrender to the water;
    The death before death spares you from the torture.'
The death before death is security;
    It's what Mohammad told of helpfully:
'*That all of you should now die is my teaching*
    Before death comes and you die with much grieving.'

The fish played dead with stomach in the air;   2275
    Water then carried that fish here and there.
Each fisherman grew so upset and cried:

'Alas the better of the two fish died!'
The fish rejoiced at the 'Alas!' they said:
   'My trick worked and I have escaped the blade.'
Then a skilled fisherman who'd come around
   Caught it, spat on it, threw it on the ground,
But it rolled in seawater stealthily.
   The third fish stayed in torment stupidly;
That simpleton fish leapt up left, then right,   2280
   To flee through its own effort its sad plight.
They cast their net and caught it easily,
   Flung on the fire by its own idiocy:
Inside a skillet while above the flame,
   Stupidity's bedfellow then became
Completely burned by flames both hot and red—
   '*Didn't a warner reach you?*'* Wisdom said.
While suffering grief and torture, it replied:
   'Yes.' Like the souls of infidels who've died.
Then it continued, 'If on this occasion,   2285
   I can escape this tortuous tribulation,
I'll have no home apart from the huge sea;
   I won't stay in a lake as previously.
I'll be safe in the ocean that is boundless;
   From then on I'll roam safely, free from all stress.'

*Explanation that the vow made by a fool at the time of difficulty
and regret is faithless for 'Though they should be rebutted, they'll
return to what they were prohibited from doing; they are liars.'*
The false dawn is not reliable.*

Wisdom replied, 'You're prone to idiocy
   And that breaks vows you make inevitably.
To keep your vows you need intelligence;
   You lack that, donkey—get away at once!
Intelligence enables your remembering   2290
   Your vow, and tears the veils of all forgetting.
Forgetting rules you, since you are not wise;
   It fights with your control and nullifies.
The wretched moth as well lacked any wisdom,
   Forgetting fire, so burning was its outcome.

Once its wings burn, it will repent, but then
    Lust and forgetfulness rule it again.
Wisdom means noticing and memory,
    For wisdom raised these up originally.
When there's no pearl, how can you have its lustre?   2295
    How can one be contrite without reminder?
Lust is from lack of wisdom similarly,
    For it can't see the facts on idiocy.
And that contrition was just due to terror,
    Not from intelligence that gleams like treasure.
Once torture stops, contrition leaves with it;
    Such false repentance isn't worth a bit.
It was caused by grief's darkness, and they say:
    "What's said at night will be effaced by day."
Pain's darkness left and made that fool so happy;   2300
    Its outcome left that fool's heart just as quickly.
While he repents, the master makes him learn:
    "If they should be rebutted they'll return." '*

Explaining that an imagining is the counterfeit of wisdom and its opposition, and resembles it but is not wisdom, and the story about the replies given to each other by Moses, possessor of wisdom, and Pharaoh, possessor of imaginings.

Wisdom opposes lust like nothing can;
    Don't call what's lustful wisdom then, brave man.
Beggars of lust are just imagining it,
    And that is wisdom's gold coin's counterfeit.
Take them both to a touchstone rapidly
    Or you won't tell the difference tragically.
The touchstone's the Qur'an, the Prophets' ways;   2305
    Like touchstones, each of these two sources says:
'Come, see yourself through being involved with me;
    You can't cope with my path's itinerary.'
If wisdom's sawn into two halves, it will
    Keep smiling through the painful burning still.
Imagining is of Pharaoh, that world-burner,

While wisdom is of Moses, soul-illuminer.
Moses went on the path towards non-being.
    Pharaoh asked, 'Tell me, who are you?' on seeing.
'I'm wisdom, God's own messenger,' he answered,   2310
    'I am God's proof, secure from going wayward.'
'Shut up! Stop this commotion,' Pharaoh said;
    'Tell me your lineage and true name instead.'
'I am one of His dust-pit's own descendants,
    Originally named "the lowest of his servants".
I am the slave of that Lord who is singular,
    With slaves for both my father and my mother.
My lineage comes from water, dust, and clay;
    God gave both heart and soul to these one day.
Back to the earth my body will return,   2315
    The same way that yours will, you nasty one.
Our origin and that of all proud humans
    Is from the earth; the proofs run up to millions,
Since from the earth your body gains help, wretch;
    Food from the earth helps your neck turn and stretch.
When soul leaves, body turns to dust again
    In that grave that is dreaded by all men.
You, I, and those resembling you, one day,
    Will turn to dust and your rank will not stay.'

Pharaoh said, 'You've another name, and it   2320
    Differs from this and is a better fit:
"One of the slaves of Pharaoh, who has many,
    And nurtured first your spirit and your body,"
A rebel enemy who chose desertion,
    Fleeing this realm due to an ill-starred action,
You're false and ignorant while being bloodthirsty;
    From attributes like these you are known easily.
In exile you are threadbare, poor, and low,
    Because you failed to give me thanks you owe.'
Moses said, 'God forbid that one should claim   2325
    Partnership with that King and not feel shame.
In kingship He has no associate;
    His slaves have Him as Master and that's it.

His creatures have no other owner—they
    Who make such false claims will themselves decay.
He has designed me; He is our designer.
    He who claims otherwise is a cruel liar.
You cannot make my eyebrow that you view—
    How could you make my soul then? It's not true.
You're the false rebel in reality,   2330
    For with the Lord you claim duality.
Although I killed a ruffian once in error,
    It wasn't selfish or for my own pleasure.
I punched him and he fell down suddenly.
    He who died lacked a soul originally.
I killed a cur, you children—don't forget
    A million, harmless innocent ones yet:
You've killed those babies and you have the guilt—
    What will come to you from the blood you've spilt?
You murdered most of Jacob's progeny   2335
    In the vain hope of trying to murder me.
In spite of you, God chose me anyway—
    What you concocted was upturned that day.'
Pharaoh said, 'Let that go! Is there a doubt
    That this was my fate's share I've been dealt out,
For you to put me down now in plain sight,
    To darken my day which had shone so bright?'
'Abasement is then on the Final Day
    Much worse if you don't heed the things I say.
A flea's bite is too painful now for you,   2340
    So if a snake should bite what will you do?
It seems I'm spoiling your work outwardly—
    I'm turning it to roses actually.'

Explaining that cultivation lies in destroying, concentration in distraction, soundness in brokenness, attainment in failure, and existence in non-existence, 'and the remainder are opposites and pairs'.

A man once started breaking up the ground.
    An idiot screamed whose anger was unbound:

'Why are you breaking up this earth by digging?
    You're spoiling this good soil now with your tilling.'
The first man said, 'Let me be. Please depart.
    Tell growing and destruction's acts apart.
This can't grow flowers or a field of wheat   2345
    Without disturbance that does not look neat.
How will you see the fruit of a fine orchard
    Until its order first appears haphazard?'

Unless you lance the boil how will it heal,
    And how will you enjoy the way you feel?
How will your health improve unless you try
    The medicines which will detoxify?
The tailor cuts the cloth he sews up later
    To make clothes, but none then attack the tailor,
And asks, 'Why have you cut this satin? What   2350
    Can I do with the pieces you have cut?'
When an old building is replaced, one must
    Demolish it first till what's left is dust.
The ironmongers, carpenters, and butchers
    Will first destroy and then become constructers.
Medicinal herbs are also pulverized,
    So that the body gets revitalized.
Till wheat is ground in mills no one is able
    To put attractive breads on their own table.
That bread and salt appealed I don't forget,   2355
    O fish, to free you from your sad fate's net.
You will escape the endless net of evil
    If you accept now Moses's good counsel.
You've made yourself a slave of base desire;
    You've made a worm a dragon breathing fire.
I've brought another dragon here for that one
    To fix with its breath that of your fierce dragon,
So that it is subdued. Then mine will start
    To tear your fiery dragon's limbs apart.
You can flee both if you accept submission;   2360
    If not your soul will face its demolition.

Pharaoh said, 'You're a sorcerer in fact;
   You've caused division through false ways you act.
You've split a close group into separate factions,
   Just as you've caused splits in the rocks of mountains.'
Moses said, 'I'm immersed in God's decree—
   Who ever mixed God's name with sorcery?
That's based on negligence and unbelief;
   Moses's soul's the bright torch of belief.
Moses resemble sorcerers? You're shameless.   2365
   My breath makes even Jesus feel so jealous.
Resemble sorcerers? Filth, in my station
   My soul gives light to books of revelation!
Since you are flying with desire's base wings
   You doubt me and dream up such hideous things.'

Whoever's actions are so wild and bestial
   Imagines wicked things about great people
Since you are part of this world in its bondage,
   You just see everything in your own image:
If when you turn, your head starts spinning too,   2370
   You'll think the room spins from your point of view.
And if you sail a ship across the ocean,
   You'll think it is the coasts that are in motion.
If after battle you feel crushed with sorrow,
   You'll view the world as being very narrow.
If you feel joy as friends would like you to,
   The world will seem a rose garden to you.
Many have gone as far as to Iraq
   Then told of lies and unbelief once back.
Many have gone on to Herat and India   2375
   And said the trade is all that they remember,
Or on to China and to Turkestan,
   And told just of deceit there from each man.
Since he sees just the colour and the smell,
   Tell him to search in other lands as well.
If a cow comes to Baghdad suddenly
   And wanders here and there so leisurely,
Of all the marvellous pleasures found therein,

She'll notice nothing but a melon skin.
If hay has fallen in the road, or grass,   2380
    It's suitable for that cow or an ass.
Like dried meat hung on hooks from one's base nature,
    One's soul, tied thus to causes, won't grow greater.
That realm where causes are all torn to bits
    Is *God's earth*,* mighty ruler here, and it's
Replaced each moment—souls can actually see
    The world's renewal so explicitly.
Though it be paradise and its famed rivers,
    It would turn ugly with unchanging features.

*Explaining that every human sense perception also has
different objects of perception which the other senses are
unaware of, in the same way that every skilled craftsman
is a stranger to the work of the other skilled craftsmen,
and its lack of awareness about what is not its business
does not prove that those objects of perception don't exist.
Although it denies them due to its condition, here by its
denial we don't mean anything but lack of awareness.*

Your own perception limits your world view;   2385
    Your unclean senses veil the pure from you.
Cleanse them in mystic vision's streams some moments;
    Deem this the Sufis' washing of their garments.
Once you are pure the souls of men who're holy
    Will tear the veil off so they join you fully.
If light and images were everywhere,
    The eyes would certainly then be aware.
You've shut yours and you bring ears in their place
    To show them a fair maiden's curls and face:
'We can't see images,' the ears make clear,   2390
    'But if the image makes noise we can hear.
We're knowledgeable in the field we've chosen,
    Which is when there's a sound or words are spoken.'
If you say, 'Come and see this beauty, nose.'
    It's not the right fit for what you propose.

'If it were musk or roses,' it will say,
  'I'd smell them. All my knowledge comes this way.
How can I see the beauty's face? Don't ask
  Of me such an impossible new task.'
The crooked sense sees everything as flawed,   2395
  Even if you go properly to God.
Cross-eyed eyes never see what's singular—
  My noble friend, of this you should be sure.

Moses said, 'Pharaoh, you're false totally;
  You think you are not different to me.
Do not compare me with yourself, for you
  Perceive one thing as if it's really two.
Just for one moment see me through my seeing,
  To then perceive a realm beyond your being,
And flee from name and honour's narrow well,   2400
  Then see pure love within pure love. Farewell.'

When you've fled body, then you'll realize
  That ear and nose can both change into eyes.
Bayazid's saying's true and not a lie:
  'A mystic's every hair becomes an eye.'
Eyes were not eyes at first, as you should know,
  Inside the womb when in an embryo.
The eye's white fat is not what gives you sight;
  If not, how come you dream with eyes shut tight?
Demons can also see as can the jinn   2405
  Although their eyes don't have white fat within.
There was no link between white fat and vision;*
  The Loving Maker has made that connection.
Man comes from dust, but doesn't look like it;
  Jinn are of fire with naught else mixed with it.
The jinn do not resemble fire, of course,
  However hard you look, though that's their source.
Birds are of air and don't resemble it;
  God linked together things, though they don't fit.
The link between such 'branches' and their 'root'   2410

Is out of reach for reason to compute.
When Man is born of dust originally
   How then are son and father linked? Tell me.
If there's a link, it's veiled from understanding:
   Reason can't know what's outside rationalizing.
If eyeless vision were not gained from God,
   How could the wind have recognized the Aad?
How could it have told faithful one from foe,
   Or wine from cup, if God did not bestow?
If Nimrod's fire did not have eyes to see,   2415
   Could Abraham have been saved specially?
If parting waves did not possess that vision,
   How did it tell a Jew from an Egyptian?
If hills and mountains lacked perception, why
   Did they join David with words from on high?*
And if the ground did not have eyes within,
   How should it then have swallowed Korah in?
The moaning pillar had eyes in its heart
   Knowing the time Mohammad would depart.*
If gravel could not see to understand,   2420
   How then did it bear witness in a hand?*
O intellect, stretch your wings and recite:
   'The earth was made to quake with awesome might.'
How can the earth speak up at Resurrection
   On good and evil if it does lack vision?
She'll share her knowledge and experience, and
   *Reveal her secrets so we understand.**

Moses said, 'His dispatching me to you
   Is proof the sender was aware and knew
That such a medicine fits perfectly   2425
   To remedy this actual malady.
You had yourself foreseen that God would choose
   Me, Moses, for this mission and would use
The rod and light in my hand with success
   To shatter your horn of presumptuousness.
And this is why the Lord of all religions
   Showed you a future through such scary visions

That suit your evil soul's wish to rebel—
    So you'll know He knows what suits you as well,
So you'll know He is wise and knowing; He   2430
    Can heal the sickness with no remedy.
Due to interpreting, you had turned blind
    To them, and thought "It's sleep's tricks on my mind."
Then that astrologer and that physician,
    Though they saw flashes of the truth, kept hidden
Selfishly all the facts: "Anxiety,"
    One said, "Does not suit your great majesty.
Exotic food can lead to strange dreams, too,
    Or food that simply disagrees with you,"
Because he saw you did not seek good counsel,   2435
    Being short-fused, bloodthirsty, far from humble.
Real kings kill for reform, which they must manage,
    Their mercy though is greater than their damage.
The king should have what's like his own Lord's nature:
    His mercy does prevail above His anger.*
Anger should not prevail as with the Devil,
    Such that he sheds blood needlessly through evil.
Neither a mildness that's effete, for then
    His wife and handmaid would choose other men.
You've made your breast the Devil's home today,   2440
    And made spite the direction that you pray.
Your sharp horn has left many with guts torn—
    Behold, my rod can break your shameless horn!'

How worldly people attack other-worldly people and push against them as far as the border of reproduction and generation, which is the frontier of the Unseen, and how the other-worldly are unaware of the ambush, for the infidel makes an assault when the holy warrior is not fighting.

In their attack the worldly people's forces
    Surged at the mystic people's central fortress,
To seize the passes to the Unseen realm,
    So holy ones won't come from there to them.

When holy warriors aren't fighting, then
   The infidels surge—they're contrary men.
When the Unseen's pure warriors, out of kindness,   2445
   Refrain from combat, you men who are hideous
Attack the passes that connect this sphere,
   So men from the Unseen won't come down here.
You wrenched their loins and wombs through wicked ways,
   So you could then control birth's passageways.
How can you seize the route the Glorious One
   Opened for procreation? Stubborn one,
You blocked the frontier passes to end doubt,
   But still a captive managed to get out.
Behold! I am that captain and I'll break   2450
   Your power, name, and honour for His sake.
Come, block the passes tightly and then smile
   At your own honour's moustache for a while—
Fate will tear out your moustache hair by hair:
   '*Fate makes precaution blind*' will be shown there.
Is yours or is the Aad's moustache more scary
   When all lands trembled at their breath, so wary?
Is yours or the Thamud's a fiercer face
   When their like's not found in the human race?
If I give more examples now to you,   2455
   Deaf one, you'll hear but still pretend not to.
I now repent of speech I've used, like sin;
   Without it I've made you some medicine
Which I'll place on your boil that is so tender—
   With your beard it will heal or burn forever,
So that, foe, you'll know He's informed and gives
   What is most fitting to each thing that lives.
When have you ever acted wickedly
   And not seen what fits that eventually?
When have you sent a good deed heavenward   2460
   And not seen its like come back as reward?
If you remain alert and are observant,
   You'll see your action's answer come each moment.
If you're observant and grasp straight away,
   You will not need to wait till Judgement Day.
The one who takes the hint correctly here

Won't need to wait until it's all made clear.
Stupidity is what gives you depression
     When you don't grasp the hint and the allusion.
Your heart turned black due to your evil, so   2465
     Learn that one shouldn't act that way below,
Lest arrow-like that darkness reaches you
     And brings the punishment for evil too.
And if the arrow hasn't come, that's been
     Due to God's mercy. What you did was seen.
So be observant if you are in need
     Of heart—something is born from every deed.
And if you have a loftier aspiration,
     This venture goes beyond close observation.

Explaining that the earthly body of Man, like high-
quality iron, is capable of becoming a mirror, so that even
while in this world, inside it heaven, hell, the
Resurrection, and other things are shown to direct vision
and not just through imagining.

Though you're dark matter, just like iron, you   2470
     Should nonetheless start burnishing well too.
Until your heart completely fills inside
     With lovely images on every side.
Though iron's dark and it lacks any light,
     Burnishing takes its darkness, leaves it bright.
Iron was burnished and this made its face
     So fair that images reflect their trace.
The earthly body's coarse and dark as well—
     Burnish it, for it also shines up well,
To bring the Unseen's forms to our perception,   2475
     Such as the heavenly angels' own reflection.
For burnisher God gave you intellect,
     So your heart's surface might start to reflect.
You've chained the burnisher, you who lack prayer,
     And freed the hands of lust, so be aware
That if lust's put in chains, it's rectified,

For then the burnisher's hands get untied—
All images are sent out to this clean
   Burnished iron that mirrors the Unseen.
You'd made it dark and rusty, so please read: 2480
   *'They work corruption on the earth.'** Take heed.
Till now you have been acting in this way.
   You've made the water dark. Stop for today.
Do not unsettle it—let it stay clear,
   Then watch the moon and stars spin round in here.
Man is like water in the stream, and so
   When it turns dark you cannot see below.
The stream is full of pearls and jewels—make sure
   Not to let it turn murky. It is pure.
Man's spirit's like the air: when dust should rise,   2485
   It veils the spiritual realm then from our eyes;
That blocks the vision of the sun, but then
   Once the dust's gone it's clear and pure again.
Despite your total darkness, God showed you
   Visions so you might take the true path too.

Moses spoke from the Unseen openly about Pharaoh's secrets and his visions, so he might believe.

Moses said, 'Through His power He made so clear
   Visions of things which at the end appear.
So you might stop your evil and oppression,
   But you got worse although you saw each vision.
In dreams He showed you ugly forms to view—   2490
   You fled them, but they're images of you.
A slave saw in the mirror's face reflected
   His ugly face, and so he defecated,
Then screamed, "You're ugly, so this was your due."
   The mirror said, "Wretch, it all comes from you!
You're shitting on your own face, which is ugly,
   Not on me, for I'm radiant and lovely."
Once you saw burned up all the clothes you own,
   Then both your eyes and mouth so tightly sewn,

Then a beast seeking your blood, then your head   2495
   In a wild beast's jaws, filling you with dread.
Then you were in a toilet upside down,
   Then in a bloody torrent where you'd drown.
From the pure heavens you then heard cry out:
   "You're damned, you're damned, you're damned" and then a shout
Came from the mountains, clear to understand:
   "*Begone, you're of the men of the left hand.*"*
From all inanimates then came another:
   "Pharaoh has fallen into hell forever."
There were worse ones that from shame I've not cited   2500
   Just in case your perverse form gets excited.
You who will not accept, I've shown a bit,
   So that you'll know I am informed of it.
You tried to blind and kill yourself back then,
   So you'd not have to see such things again.
It has now come—how long will you try fleeing?
   It came despite your mastery of scheming.'

Explaining that the door of repentance is open

Beware not to continue—take precaution.
   God's kindness keeps repentance's door open.
A door for your repentance in the West   2505
   Is open till the Final Day. Man's blessed.
Till from the West the sun should one day rise*
   That door stays open—don't divert your eyes!
Through mercy, heaven has eight doors, and one
   Of those doors is repentance's door, son.
Other doors sometimes open, sometimes close.
   Repentance's stays open unlike those.
Value this godsend, open constantly.
   Bring your baggage. Shun Satan's jealousy.

Moses tells Pharaoh, 'Accept one piece of advice from me and take in return four benefits.'

Moses said, 'Take one thing from me to learn,   2510
   And gain four new things from me in return.'

'What is that one thing?' Pharaoh then replied,
    'I need to have a bit more clarified.'
'That thing is that you publicly say later
    That there's no God apart from the Creator
Who made the heavens and the stars above,
    People, the Devil, jinn, birds like the dove,
The plain, the hill, the desert, and the sea.
    None bear resemblance. His realm's limit-free.'
Pharaoh asked, 'What are those four things I'll gain   2515
    Which you'll give in exchange? Show them. Explain,
So that this lovely promise's grace might
    Make my own unbelief become more light,
So that my unbelief's lock that's so heavy
    Might open through the promise that's so lovely,
So, through effects of that pure stream of honey,
    Hate's poison might change to that in my body,
So that the pure milk's stream has the effect
    Of nurturing the captive intellect,
So that I get drunk through that stream of wine   2520
    Then start to taste commands that are divine,
So that, through streams of water's grace, my flesh
    That's barren and destroyed might come out fresh,
So verdure might come to my soil that's barren,
    And my thorns turn to shelters up in heaven—
Paradise and its four streams,* through reflection,
    Might help my soul seek God with zeal and passion,
Just as, through hell's reflection, I've been bound
    To turn to fire, and in God's wrath I've drowned;
From the reflection of the snake of hell,   2525
    I poison heaven's people now as well.
From boiling water's image, I start then
    With tyranny to change to bones all men.
From hell's most biting frost, I can start freezing,
    While heat from its hot flames makes me start sizzling.
I'm now hell for those suffering tyranny
    And poverty—woe to those under me!'

Moses explains the four benefits as reward awaiting Pharaoh's embrace of faith.

Moses replied, 'The first one of these four
    Is bodily health for you forevermore.
Diseases written of in medicine   2530
    Will stay far from you, O fine specimen.
You'll have a long life, secondly, for death
    Will hesitate to terminate your breath.
And after such a life, it's not the case
    That you could, discontented, leave this place—
Rather, with zeal for death like babies longing
    For milk, not due to being entrapped in suffering,
You'll seek death—it's not due to suffering's pressure;
    Instead in your home's ruins you'll find treasure.
You'll take the axe with your own hand this way   2535
    And strike the house without fear straight away;
You'll see it as a barrier to the treasure,
    One grain that blocks a harvest none can measure—
You'll fling that one grain into flames and then
    Adopt the practice of the valiant men,
Because of love for one leaf you've lost orchards,
    Like a worm fixed on one leaf losing vineyards—
When grace woke up that worm, it then at once
    Devoured the dragon of its ignorance.
The worm turned to a vineyard straight away,*   2540
    Full of fruit, fortunate and changed this way.'

*Exegesis of 'I was a hidden treasure and I loved to be known'.**

Knock down the house—from Yemen's fine cornelian
    One can erect more houses by the million.
The treasure's underneath, so there's no option—
    Don't fret or hold back from its demolition.
Thousands of houses can be built up later
    From just one treasure, with no toil or labour.

The house itself will in the end decay
   And hidden treasure see the light of day,
But it won't then be yours—the spirit gains   2545
   Rewards for breaking up all the remains:
If you don't do the work, your wage is nothing,
   There's naught for Man but that for which he's struggling.*
You'll bite your hand then and you'll cry aloud:
   'Such a fine moon was there behind the cloud!
I didn't do the good things recommended
   And treasure's gone while I'm left empty-handed.'
You've rented your house—it's not your possession
   For you to buy or sell it through transaction.
The rent term is until your death, so you   2550
   Can work in it until that date is due.
You just sew patches in this store. Two mines
   Are underneath—when will you see the signs?
Hurry now! It is just a rented place—
   Grab an axe and then chop off its firm base,
So you might reach the mine that's down below
   And then need no more patches brought to sew.
What's patching? Bread and water—as you ate,
   You patched a cloak that holds down with its weight.
Your body's cloak gets torn each moment, then   2555
   Through eating you will patch it up again.
You're offspring of the lofty, fortunate king—
   Be your true self. Feel shame at patch-sewing!
Dig up a patch from this store's floor and view
   The two mines that reveal themselves to you,
Before the building's lease expires without
   You trying any of its fine fruit out.
The owner will evict you then and break
   Its structure down, for that more prized mine's sake.
Then, in regret, you'll beat your own head and   2560
   Tear out your silly beard with your own hand.
'This store was mine, but I was blind!' you'll sigh,
   'I never tasted fruit from here, did I?'
The wind has blown my being away. In store
   Is *sorrow for God's slaves** for evermore.

How Man is deluded by the knowledge and imaginings of his base
nature and does not seek knowledge of the Unseen, which is the
knowledge of the Prophets.

I saw in my house countless images
　　And fell in love, smitten with restlessness.
The hidden gold I couldn't understand
　　Or else the axe would have stayed in my hand.
If I had used the axe then properly,　　　　　　　　　　2565
　　I might have now escaped from misery.
I turned my eyes to pictures and then fell
　　In love like children under something's spell.
Sana'i said it in one of his sayings:
　　'You are a child; the house is full of paintings.'
In his *Hadiqat* his advice is true—
　　Raise the dust from your self without ado!

'Moses, enough!' Pharaoh said, 'Now, please tell
　　The third prize! My heart's floundering in this spell.'
'That third's a twofold empire where you'll see　　　　2570
　　Two worlds without a single enemy,
Greater than this realm you possess down here
　　Since there it's peaceful; here there's war each year.
See what in peacetime That One will bestow
　　When during war He gave you this below,
For that bestowal when you were a rebel
　　Gave so much—look what you'll gain when you're loyal.'
'What is the fourth one, Moses? I implore—
　　Be quick! My patience fails as I yearn more.'
'The fourth's that you stay young eternally　　　　　　2575
　　With jet-black hair and rosy cheeks. Trust me.
Colour and scent are worthless to our kind,
　　But I speak at your level, far behind.
Feeling so proud of scents, a home, and colours,
　　Entices only children, not their fathers.'

Explanation of the tradition: 'Speak to people according to their level of intelligence, not in accordance with your own level, so that God and His Messenger do not mislead.'

My work is with a child on this occasion,
 So I must use the language of mere children
And say, 'Attend school, then I'll buy for you
 A bird, or nuts and raisins, if you do.'
You only know about youth and the body— 2580
 Take this youth and take barley then, you donkey!
No wrinkle will appear upon your face,
 Your youthfulness will stay fresh, and no trace
Of ugliness or old age will be visible,
 Nor will your cypress stature get bent double,
Nor will your young man's strength feel a decrease,
 Nor in your teeth will there be cavities,
Nor will your sexual lust's skills see reduction,
 Or women weary of your failed erection—
Youth's glory will then open up to you 2585
 As Okkasha swung heaven's gates thus, too.*

The Prophet's saying: 'Whoever brings me good news about the ending of the month of Safar, I'll give him good news about entry to paradise.'

The passing of Mohammad long ago
 Fell in Rabe' al-awwal, as all know.
When his heart learned the timing of departure,
 Through his own wisdom he experienced rapture.
When Safar* came he felt extremely happy
 And said, 'Next month I will begin my journey.'
Yearning for guidance every night till day,
 'Most High Companion of the path!' he'd pray.
'Whoever's first to let me know about 2590
 When the blessed month of Safar's time runs out,
When Rabe' starts right at the end of Safar,
 I'll give good news and be his intercessor.'
Okkasha rushed to say: 'Safar is over!'
 'Okkasha, heaven will be yours forever.'

'Safar has passed!' another came to state—
   'Okkasha won good news's fruit. Too late!'
Real men rejoice as this world's time has passed,
   While children celebrate if it should last.
Blind birds who've never tasted the clear water   2595
   Imagine brine to be as good as Kawsar.*

Moses told of the gifts of grace, all four:
   'Your fortune's drink will turn to dregs no more.'
Pharaoh said, 'You have spoken well. Now I
   Will first consult a good friend, then reply.'

Pharaoh consulted his wife Asiya about believing in Moses.

He shared these words with Asiya, who said:
   'Black heart, surrender with your soul. Ahead
Good fortune is what this fine speech will bring
   To you, so gain it quickly, virtuous king.
Sowing's hour has arrived; much will be gained.'   2600
   She said this and wept wildly, unrestrained,
Then sprang up and said, 'Now the radiant sun
   Has turned into your crown, bald man. Well done!'
(Hats cover baldness's deficiency,
   When it's the radiant sun especially.)
'When at your meeting you heard what he said,
   Why didn't you scream, "Yes!" and pray instead?
If this great speech had reached the bright sun's ear,
   It would have started chasing it down here.
Don't you know what you have been promised? Learn.   2605
   God is now showing Satan His concern.
When that most kind one called you back, it's strange
   How your heart stayed the same and did not change.
How did it not split open, so you'd gain
   A glance of both worlds? How did it remain?'

The heart that for God's sake at once splits open
   Eats fruit in both worlds like the martyr's own one.

Blindness and heedlessness are good when they
    Help you spend time here—why prolong your stay?
They are both graces since they keep you here   2610
    To build your capital for when you're near.
Too much is sickness with no remedy,
    Poison for souls, haunting minds easily.
About a marketplace which person knows
    Where one can buy a rose bush with one rose?
Where for one seed a hundred groves are sold?
    A hundred mines bought with one scrap of gold?
'*He is for God*' is when with scraps you pay,
    So '*God is for him*'* then comes into play,
Because our own unstable, weak existence   2615
    Emerged through the Eternal Maker's essence,
So when the former dies in Him, it then
    Becomes eternal and won't die again.
It's like a drop which dust and wind both scare
    Because it perishes due to this pair.
When it dives in the sea, which is its source,
    It flees winds, dust, and solar heat of course.
Inside the sea its form is lost from sight,
    Its essence is preserved though, kept upright.
O drop, give up yourself without commotion,   2620
    With no regret, for you will gain an ocean.
Drop, give yourself this fine nobility,
    Become secure from death within the sea.
Who should be now so lucky—from the top
    The ocean is requesting a mere drop!
For God's sake, make this purchase rapidly—
    For one drop you can gain a pearl-filled sea.
By God, you shouldn't wait, but you should race!
    This speech comes from God's Bounteous Ocean's Grace.
All other graces disappear in this one,   2625
    The least of which soars to the seventh heaven.
A falcon has reached you that is so stunning,
    One that will not be found by busily hunting.

'I'll speak with Haman,' Pharaoh said, 'It's clear

A king should ask advice from his vizier.'
She said, 'Don't share this secret with that Haman—
    What would a blind crone know about a falcon?'

*Story about the king's falcon and the decrepit crone.**

If you should give a crone a fine, white falcon,
    From kindness she will try to trim each talon.
It needs its talons so that it can hunt;   2630
    The blind crone trims them, for she's ignorant,
And says, 'Where was your mother? It is wrong
    For talons to be left to grow so long.'
She trims its talons, wings and beak as well—
    This is what wretches do in their love's spell.
The falcon won't eat when she gives it stew,
    So she gets angry, stops her kindness too,
Saying, 'I cooked you stew that tasted lovely,
    But you have shown disdain and acted smugly,
So you deserve your suffering and affliction;   2635
    You don't deserve God's bounty and good fortune.'
She gives it the stew's broth and tells it, 'Eat!
    Maybe you just don't like the balls of wheat?'
The broth does not fit with the falcon's nature,
    So she then frowns and her rage just grows greater.
She pours on it broth hot enough to scald
    And that poor falcon's crown then ends up bald.
The scalding sends tears from its eyes that sting
    And it recalls the kindness of its king;
From those sweet, flirting eyes tears flow at pace,   2640
    Eyes with perfections through the ruler's face,
Eyes that *don't turn round* wounded by a crow's,*
    The good eye suffers from the evil's blows.
That eye has the sea's breadth of vision where
    The two worlds look no more than one thin hair.
Thousands of spheres may enter in its vision,
    But disappear like fountains in the ocean.
This eye's transcended the whole realm of senses;
    Through sight of the Unseen it has won kisses.
I cannot find a single ear that I   2645

Can tell the finer points about this eye.
  If from it glorious water were to trickle,
    Gabriel would try to catch hold of a little,
To rub it on his own wings if that person
  Of truest creed were to give his permission.

The falcon says, 'Though that crone's rage blazed bright,
  It hasn't burned my dignity and light.
My spirit's falcon weaves a hundred forms still.'
  Saleh was not hurt—they just hurt his camel;*
One marvellous breath from Saleh sends the grace   2650
  For mountains to send hundreds in its place.
'Be silent! Pay attention!' says my heart,
  'Or jealousy will tear your frame apart.'
Huge clemencies hide in His jealousy—
  If not He'd burn our world up instantly.

Pharaoh's pride made him choose to turn away
  From her advice; his heart moved from her sway.
'I'll talk with Haman first,' then Pharaoh said,
  'For he's my power's axis and my aide.'
(Bu Bakr was Mohammad's counsellor,   2655
  Bu Lahab was Bu Jahl's—they're similar.)*
Since a deep-rooted likeness drew them near
  And her advice seemed ugly to his ear.
Like goes towards like with a hundred wings
  And breaks chains through its own imaginings.

*Story about that woman whose child crawled onto a waterspout
and was in danger of falling, and how she sought help
from Ali.*

A woman saw Ali and came to shout:
  'My child has gone up to that waterspout!
He won't come near my grasp although I call,
  And if I leave him I'm afraid he'll fall.

He can't yet understand it when I say: 2660
  "Come back to mother, out then of harm's way!"
He doesn't understand hand signals too;
  He acts as if he doesn't have a clue.
For feeding I would show my breast, but he
  Just turned the other way so cluelessly.
You noble ones are those who give support
  In this world and the next to my poor sort—
My heart is trembling. For God's sake, I pray
  You rescue him before he's swept away.'
'Take to the roof another child,' he said,   2665
  'So yours sees one just like himself ahead,
Then he will start to rush to his own kind
  Back from that spout—like's drawn to like, you'll find.'
The woman did this. Once her son had seen
  His own kind, he approached from where he'd been
And reached the safety of the roof. Consider
  Similar things attractors of each other.
He crawled towards the other child, and so
  He managed to avoid a fall below.
Prophets are humans due to this, no doubt—   2670
  So other humans likewise flee the spout.
Mohammad said he's human *just like you*,*
  So you'd approach him and not fall off too.
Homogeneity's a strong attractor;
  There's an attractor drawing every searcher.
Jesus and Edris soared to heaven. They
  Became the same as angels in some way.
Harut and Marut both leaned to what's bodily,
  So they fell from a station that was lofty.

Infidels all belong to Satan's kind;   2675
  Their souls are demons' students and unkind;
They've learnt a million wicked ways and try
  To sew shut their own heart and mind's good eye,
And their least ugly single quality
  Is envy, which struck Satan fatally.
That's where they picked up envy and their spite—

He wants to block men from God's kingdom's light.
When he sees someone perfect is around
   He suffers pain because of what he's found.
Every wretch whose light's snuffed out hates to see   2680
   Others with candles burning gloriously.
Acquire perfection so you won't turn evil,
   Upset at the success of other people.
Beg God to now repel from you this envy,
   So He can liberate you from the body,
Then keep you inwardly preoccupied,
   For you won't be distracted then outside.
God gives to draughts of wine the potency
   To make drunks flee from both worlds totally,
And He has given to hashish the power   2685
   To help flee self-awareness for an hour.
God gives to sleep the power to pull away
   All your attention from the two worlds' sway.
He changed Majnun through love of Layli so
   Love stopped him knowing who was friend from foe.
He has more wines just like this by the millions
   Which He lets dominate your sense perceptions.
And from the self there are wines of damnation
   Which drive the ill-starred from the right location.
The pure mind has wines of felicity   2690
   Which find the place one can stay permanently:
Drunk, it will rip the tent of this world's sky,
   Then the illumined mind soars up on high.
Don't be deceived by every drunkard, heart!
   Tell drunken Jesus and the ass apart.
Seek wine from these vats that give drunkenness
   That can't be matched by those worth so much less.
Each loved thing's like a full vat—they contain
   Pearl-pure wine drops or just dregs that remain.
Wine connoisseur, you have to taste with care   2695
   To find wine not adulterated there.
Both kinds make men drunk, but this drunkenness
   Will take you up to Judgement's Lord, no less,
So you can flee all thoughts, false schemes, and whispering,
   Freed from the mind's chains, like a camel skipping.

Prophets are all from the angelic realm—
    That's how from down here they attracted them.
Wind is like fire and joins it as a friend—
    For both of them their nature's to ascend.
If you seal up a pot though it is empty   2700
    And place it in a river, you will then see
That pot will never sink, but just floats there
    Because inside that pot there's only air,
And since air's nature is to move up, it
    Pulls its container up along with it.
The souls which are like Prophets' similarly
    Are pulled like shadows to them powerfully;
Since their intelligence prevails, no doubt
    That's what the angels share with the devout.
The carnal soul prevails in every foe;   2705
    That soul is base and so they head below.
Egyptians were like Pharaoh, who drew blame;
    The Jews and Moses were one and the same.
Haman was more like Pharaoh with his malice;
    Pharaoh chose him and brought him to his palace—
He dragged him to the bottom of the well,
    Since both were of the denizens of hell.
They both oppose light and are set ablaze
    Like hellfire; they oppose the heart's light rays.
'Believer, pass through quickly!' hell will shout,   2710
    For your light makes its flames all soon go out.
'Move on, believer: when it trails its hem
    Your light extinguishes each one of them.'
That hell-bound one flees light as well, for he
    Has hellfire's nature also tragically.
Hell flees from the believers and their light
    Just as they flee from it with all their might,
For their light lacks compatibility;
    Seekers of light oppose fire actually.
The Prophet said, 'When the believers pray   2715
    For God to keep them far from hell, that way
Hell seeks protection from those persons too,
    Praying, "O God, keep him far, I beg you!"'
Attractions found with congeneity—

Are you with faith or infidelity?
You're Haman's kind if to him you incline,
   But if you lean to Moses, that's divine.
And if you lean to both of them, my brother,
   You have both self and wisdom mixed together.
They are at war. You must strive through its storms   2720
   So spiritual things dominate mere forms.
To feel joy in the world of war, what's needed
   Is witnessing your enemy defeated.

That one who always argued finally
   Consulted Haman on this mystery.
He told what Moses promised on that day
   And took as confidant one far astray.

Pharaoh consults his vizier Haman about believing in Moses.

Pharaoh told Haman when he saw him there;
   Haman ripped his own shirt, jumped in the air—
That cursed one's screams were heard from all around   2725
   As he threw his own headgear on the ground:
'How dare he speak like that to Pharaoh's face,
   Brazenly with vain words? He's a disgrace!
You have subdued the whole world, truth be told.
   Through fortune all your work has turned to gold.
Rulers bring tribute to you from each nation
   Without resistance, with no contestation.
Kings kiss your threshold's dust so happily,
   O Kayqobad-like king with majesty!*
And when our horse is seen by those of foes,   2730
   They gallop off without the need for blows.
You have been worshipped in this world till now—
   Will you turn to the least of slaves somehow?
To walk in flames is a much better thing
   Than to turn to a slave when you're a king.
O king of China even, first kill me
   So my eyes won't see such a tragedy.
Chop off my head first, Khosrow of our nation,*

So my eyes don't see that humiliation.
Nothing like this has happened. I don't lie.   2735
  It is like sky becoming land, land sky,
Or slaves becoming equals suddenly,
  Or cowards starting to fight fearlessly,
Or foes seeing well while friends don't see a bit,
  Or for our garden to become a pit.'

Showing the falseness of Haman's speech.

He couldn't tell his friend from enemy;
  He played this backgammon pathetically.
You were your own foe, cursed one, so don't name
  The innocent as foes. They're not to blame.
Wickedness to you is 'good fortune', 'luck'——   2740
  It starts with gallops, ends with being struck.
If you don't leave this fortune straight away,
  Autumn will soon move spring out of the way.
The East and West have witnessed far too many
  Just like you with head severed from their body.
How could the East and West, which are both transient,
  Cause anybody to become more permanent.
You take pride in the fact that out of fear
  And bondage people flatter you now here.
When people should prostrate in front of someone,   2745
  They stuff inside that person's soul some poison.
And when that one prostrating turns away,
  The poison's seen while he is on his way.
Happy the one whose self *has been brought low*;
  The one pride made feel huge must suffer woe;
This arrogance is poison that is deadly——
  The fool gets drunk on poisonous wine too readily.
When he drinks it for just a little while
  He'll swing his head with joy and start to smile,
But then the poison enters in his soul   2750
  And it begins to take complete control.
If you don't think it's poisonous, or debate
  What poison is, heed the Aad people's fate.
When two kings fight, the one that should prevail

Will kill the other or throw him in gaol,
But if he finds a fallen enemy,
   He bandages him and gives liberally.
If this pride isn't a most poisonous thing,
   Why kill the innocent, you murderous king,
And why treat one well who's no one to you—   2755
   You can detect the poison through these two.
The highwayman will never rob a beggar;
   The wolf won't bite into a dead wolf either.
Khezr damaged that boat, so it could be saved
   From hands of people who were so depraved.
The broken flee—get broken straight away!
   Safety's in poverty, so head that way!
The mountain that held precious mines in it
   Shattered to bits when axes finally hit.
The sword's for necks; it is so useless though   2760
   For shadows they cast which can't feel a blow.
O lost one, grandeur's fire and oil, so why
   Do you walk into flames with nose raised high?
Arrows won't target someone lying flat
   Upon the ground, so please reflect on that.
But if he lifts his head up, he'll be slain
   Like targets—his wounds won't be healed again
The vulgar's ladder's egotism, friend,
   But that is where they fall from in the end.
Those who climb higher have less understanding—   2765
   Their bones will break much more on their hard landing.
And this derived flaw's rooted in the fact
   You're trying to partner God by your proud act.
You haven't died then been revived again
   Through Him—you're seeking equal lordship then.
But if revived through Him, since that is Him,
   It's purest union, not polytheism.
Seek explanations in good action's mirror
   For you won't understand it through mere chatter.
If I share what I've written, then each heart   2770
   Immediately will bleed and split apart.
I'll stop, for wise men this much will suffice;
   To check if someone's home I've shouted twice.

To sum up, through the wicked things he'd say
   Haman waylaid his Pharaoh in this way.
Good fortune's morsel reached his lips, but he
   Opted to slit his own throat suddenly.
Haman gave Pharaoh's harvest-stack away—
   May no kings have such friends who act this way!

*Moses despaired of Pharaoh's accepting the faith because of the
effect of Haman's words on Pharaoh's heart.*

Moses said, 'We've shown kindness and much grace.   2775
   It wasn't something fate let you embrace.
Consider lordship that is not upright
   As having no real power and no real might.
Lordship that has been stolen is a lie,
   Because it doesn't have heart, soul, or eye.
Lordship given by ordinary men,
   Like loans, will be one day called in again.
Give God the lordship that you got on loan,
   So He gives a full contract of His own.'

*The dispute of the Arab leaders with Mohammad when
they said, 'Divide the kingdom up with us to avoid
dispute,' to which the chosen one responded: 'I have been
put in charge regarding this realm,' and their arguments
from both sides.*

One day the Arab tribal chiefs had gathered   2780
   And started arguing before Mohammad:
'You are a chief, but so are we,' they said,
   'Take your share and divide this realm instead.
Through our own share we each want just what's fair.
   Wash your hands clear of what's another's share.'
'God gave to me the leadership you crave;
   The absolute command is what He gave.
"It is Mohammad's epoch now," God said,
   "Accept his order or *fear God with dread!*" '*
'We, too, are leaders due to destiny;   2785

God gave us leadership's role similarly.'
Mohammad said, 'But my one was bestowed,
  While yours were loaned as food while on the road.
Mine lasts until the end of time. A loan
  Like your rule will one day be overthrown.'
They said, 'Please don't continue like a bore.
  What evidence supports your seeking more?'
Immediately a cloud came on command
  And a wild torrent filled up all the land.
They headed for the populated city   2790
  Where terrified men wailed and begged for pity.
Mohammad said, 'The time has come for action,
  So certainty is born from supposition.'
Each tribal chief threw his spear as a test,
  To block the flood if they were truly blessed.
Mohammad threw his rod in the same way,
  That rod which gave no choice but to obey.
The torrent raged on and would not subside,
  Sweeping like straw the spears they'd thrown inside.
Their spears all disappeared; his rod on entry   2795
  Had stayed upright as if it was a sentry,
And it gave that wild torrent such concern
  That it withdrew then, never to return.
On witnessing that he was truly blessed
  With power, the chiefs grew frightened and confessed,
Apart from three with such strong enmity
  That in denial they called this sorcery.
Kingship that has been grafted on is feeble,
  But that which grows organically is noble.
Though you've not seen the spears and rod, you can   2800
  Compare their names with his names, my good man.
Death's rapid torrent swept their names away;
  His fortune and his name will always stay.
For his sake each day they will beat the drums
  Five times until the very last day comes.

He said, 'If you've brains, you'll see I've been kind;
  If you're an ass, my rod's for your behind.

I'll force you from the stable in a way
   That makes your head and ears bleed. You can't stay.
Inside this stable, no man and no donkey   2805
   Is finding a safe haven from your cruelty.
My rod is to reform and see improved;
   It is for donkeys who are not approved.
It will be serpent-like as it subdues,
   For you've become one in the way you choose
To act—you're of the serpents from the mountains,
   But look up at the serpent of the heavens.
This rod has come to give a taste of hell:
   "Hey, scarper to the light!" the rod will yell,
"Or you'll remain in my teeth permanently   2810
   And you will not be able then to flee."
It's then a serpent, though it was a rod,
   So you won't ask, "Where is the hell of God?"' '

Explaining why someone who knows the power of God will not ask: 'Where are heaven and hell?'

Wheresoever God wishes He makes there
   His hell—He makes the zenith a bird's snare.
He makes your teeth begin to ache as well,
   So you might say, 'It's dragon-like. It's hell!'
Or He makes your saliva honey-sweet,
   So you say, 'This is heaven and a treat.'
From your teeth's roots He can make sugar grow—   2815
   The power of God's decree you then will know.
So don't bite with your teeth the innocent.
   Remember that strike which you can't prevent.
As blood for the Egyptians, God selected
   The Nile, yet He kept Israelites protected,
So you'll know God discriminates between
   The sober and the drunk who're clearly seen.
God's grace had taught the Nile to tell apart:
   They closed to foes, for friends the waves would part;
His grace had made those waves intelligent;   2820
   His wrath made Cain a fool who's ignorant.
His grace gave what's inert intelligence;

His wrath took it from learned men at once.
His grace has made it show inside the former;
   As punishment it fled from every scholar.
It poured down like the rain due to His order,
   And likewise it escaped on seeing God's anger.
The sun, moon, stars, and clouds all come and go
   In a planned order witnessed from below;
They come at their appointed time, not late,   2825
   Nor early. There's no rushing and no wait.
You're blind to what God's Prophets have all shown—
   They put this knowledge into wood and stone,
To show inert things by analogy
   Can be like rods and stones through His decree.
Through rod and stone, obedience makes things clear
   About the rest of the inert things here:
'We're well aware of God and we obey.
   We're not haphazard, useless things,' they say,
Just like the waves which then could tell apart   2830
   The two groups, when to drown and when to part.
Just like the earth, which showed you what it knows,
   Sinking Korah, whom God subdued with blows,
Just like the moon, which heard the order and
   Split into two halves quickly on command,*
Just like the rocks and trees which audibly
   Greeted Mohammad in proximity.

*The response to the materialist who denies God's existence and
considers the world eternal.*

'The world is transient,' yesterday one said,
   'God is still there when all the skies are dead.'
Then a philosopher said, 'You can't know;   2835
   Rain can't tell that a cloud's about to go.
You're not a spinning mote now even to
   Know the sun's temporality, are you?
How can a worm in dung now comprehend
   The earth's beginning and when it will end?
You've taken all this blindly from your father;
   Through foolishness you've got entangled further.

What is the proof for temporality?
    Explain or shut up. Don't talk endlessly!'
He said, 'I heard two groups the other day   2840
    Arguing in this deep sea, and their fray
Drew a large number to each one's position,
    All fighting, arguing in opposition.
I went towards the crowd that gathered there
    And listened to learn more of their affair.
"The heavens are just transient," one was saying,
    "No doubt there was a builder for this building."
"It is eternal," then another said,
    "No builders here; it built itself instead."
The first said, "You've denied our own Creator   2845
    Who night and day feeds us as our Provider."
The second answered, "When no evidence
    Is given, I won't heed fools' ignorance.
So bring some proofs, for I won't give my ear
    Unless you bring some evidence that's clear."
"The proof is in my soul. It is concealed
    Inside me. It's not easily revealed.
You cannot see the new moon, though I see
    Because your eye's weak. Don't get mad at me!"

'Then the debate continued and those near   2850
    Grew dizzy thinking of the turning sphere.
The latter said, "The proof's in me, so I
    Have proof about the transience of the sky.
I've certainty; the sign for this is plain:
    I can walk into fire and not feel pain.
Words can't explain this proof; it is above
    Their limit like the lover's state of love.
The inner side of my view leaves no trace
    Other than my most gaunt and sickly face.
Blood and tears both roll down my cheeks at once,   2855
    Becoming thus His beauty's evidence."
"I don't consider them proofs that could be
    Clear evidence to the generality."
"When real and false coins fight," the other argued,

"Saying: 'You're fake while I am highly valued,'
The final test is fire: when they're both thrown
  Into the flames the truth will then be known.
Everyone will know their reality,
  Move from suspicion's doubts to certainty.
Water and fire are tests that must be taken   2860
  For real and false coins not to be mistaken—
Let's both walk into flames and thus be used
  As proof for all the rest, who are confused,
Or else jump in the sea from a high roof,
  So that for them all we can serve as proof."
They chose to enter flames as their dared feat
  And cast themselves into its scorching heat.
That man who spoke of God was saved that day,
  While that vile bastard was just burned away.
Listen to what muezzins all convey   2865
  Despite what the transgressors have to say.
Death hasn't burned this name out totally
  Because its bearer had such majesty.
For centuries those wagers that they play
  Have torn the veils of the deniers away.
Once they both pledged, what's true gained victory
  Regarding miracles, eternity.
I came to see that he who spoke about
  The sky's temporality indeed won out.'

Deniers' proofs are always left undone;   2870
  Where is one sign of their truth? Find me one.
Where can you find a single minaret
  Praising deniers? I've not found one yet.
Where can you find a pulpit where a preacher
  Recounts the life of a vile unbeliever?
Coin faces serve as proof as well, my friend,
  By bearing their names up until the end:
The coins of kings keep being changed, but see
  Mohammad's coin last an eternity.
Show me the name of any vile denier   2875
  Etched on a gold coin or a coin of silver.

Here is a sun-like miracle, so look:
   Men's tongues call it '*The mother of the book*'.*
None dares steal one word from inside its cover
   And no one dares to add to it another.
Befriend the conqueror so that you today
   Prevail. Don't join the conquered, wandering stray!
Deniers argue this way: 'I don't see
   Another homeland near externally.'
He doesn't know that each thing that's apparent   2880
   Serves as deep hidden wisdom's own informant;
The point of each external thing's within
   Just like the benefit of medicine.

Exegesis of the Qur'anic verse: 'We did not create the heavens
and the earth and what is between them other than with
reality,* meaning that we did not create them for the sake of
what you see, but for the inner meaning and eternal wisdom
which you don't see.

Does any painter paint without an aim
   To see fulfilled? Would he paint all the same?
It's for the guests' and youngsters' benefit—
   They can escape anxiety through it.
From that one's painting comes such pleasure to
   The youth, memories of long-lost friendships too.
Is any pot made by a skilful potter   2885
   For its own sake and not to carry water?
Do bowl-makers make bowls for their own sake
   And not for food when they wish to partake?
And do calligraphers write beautifully
   For their art or for readers all to see?
The outward form is for the Unseen's, friend,
   And for another that form will transcend—
Count the third, fourth to tenth, increasingly
   Of higher worth, to your capacity.
And like the skilful move good chess players make,   2890
   The benefit's in the next step they'll take:
They placed it here for that next, hidden one,
   And that move's for the next one, and so on.

Continue till checkmate when you're the winner,
　　Having seen one face hidden in another.
The first is for the second's sake; it's similar
　　To climbing up the rungs of any ladder.
The second's for the third's sake, and the proof
　　Is after all those rungs you'll reach the roof.
Desire to eat is to make semen, so　　　　　　　　　　2895
　　You'll procreate and consequently glow.
One with poor vision sees naught else around;
　　His mind can't travel, like plants in the ground.
Whether the plant is called or not, that will
　　Not matter for it's stuck in firm soil still.
If its head moves with wind, don't be misled
　　Simply because it has a moving head.
'*We heard, O breeze!*' its head is heard to say,
　　But its foot says, '*Leave us. We won't obey.*'
Since he can't travel that man has to act　　　　　　2900
　　Like others, but it's from blind trust in fact,
Fighting like that, going with what will happen,
　　As if obeying dice throws in backgammon.

Those visions that aren't in a frozen state
　　Are piercers of the veils and penetrate.
To vision like that something now appears
　　Though it won't happen until ten more years;
According to men's sight's capacity
　　The future and Unseen's seen similarly.
When there is nowhere in the way a screen,　　　　2905
　　Eyes penetrate the Tablet that's unseen.
When looking back to Being's origin,
　　One then sees clearly how things did begin:
The angels arguing with God when He
　　Made our forefather His own deputy.*
When looking forward one will have clear vision
　　Of all that happens in the Resurrection,
The origin of origins behind,
　　Ahead the Final Day for all Mankind.
To his heart's light's capacity each seeker　　　　　2910

Sees the Unseen if he has cleaned his mirror—
    Whoever's polished more sees more, and all
    The forms will be for him more visible.
You say serenity is from God's grace—
    Success in polishing's from the same place.
Striving and prayer match with your aspiration:
    Man has naught more than that for which he's striven.*
Your aspiration comes from God alone;
    No base one will aspire to a king's throne.
If God assigns work to a man, he still   2915
    Can show obedience, choice, and his free will.
But when He brings ill-fated ones much grief,
    They run away from Him to disbelief.
When God gives grief to someone truly fortunate,
    He draws much closer to God and more intimate.
Through mortal fear, the cowards in the fight
    Have opted for the means for rapid flight.
Through mortal fear as well, the ones with bravery
    Have battled ever closer to the enemy:
Fear and grief made the brave hearts charge ahead;   2920
    Through fear the cowards die within instead.
Such mortal fear and grief are touchstones—you
    Can tell the cowards from the valiant few.

God communicated to Moses, 'O Moses, I who am the Exalted Creator love you.'

God said to Moses through heart inspiration:
    'I'm God. I love you, Moses, whom I've chosen.'
Moses asked, 'What did I do to deserve it,
    O Generous One? Tell me and I'll augment it.'
'You're like a little child with his own mother—
    When she is angry he'll still reach to hug her.
He knows no other friend to reach out to,   2925
    Both drunken and hung-over from her, too.
And if his mother should give him a slap,
    He'll still come for a hug perched on her lap.
He won't seek help from any other people;
    She's all the good he knows and all the evil.

You don't turn to alternative directions
  Whether in good or troubling situations.
The others are like rocks or bricks to you,
  Young boys, grown men, and those in dotage too.'

Just as *it's You we worship** with full passion,   2930
  We don't *seek help** elsewhere in tribulation;
'*It's You we worship*'* means exclusively;
  Its function's to remove hypocrisy.
'*It's You we seek help from*'* is similar,
  Making appeals for help much narrower;
'We worship just for Your sake' it makes known,
  'We also yearn for help from You alone.'

A king gets angry with his boon companion and an intercessor intercedes on behalf of the object of his anger, begging the king to be forgiving. The king accepts his intercession, but the boon companion is annoyed with the intercessor and asks, 'Why did you intercede?'

A king got angry with his boon companion
  And was about to make him food for carrion:
He drew his sword out to make this man pay,   2935
  To strike him since he dared to disobey.
No one there had the nerve to intervene
  By interceding, all except one keen
To try, one called Emad al-Molk, who mattered,
  Privileged with intercession like Mohammad.
He sprang up and prostrated hurriedly;
  The king put down his sword immediately:
'If he's the Devil, I'll forgive,' he said,
  'If he's done evil, I'll conceal instead.
I'm satisfied now that you have stepped in,   2940
  Even if he's caused damage with his sin.
I'd end a million rages all at once
  For you have that much worth and excellence.
I never will reject your intercession,

Since your appeal is mine as well for certain.
Even if he'd made earth and sky collide,
   I would have spared him since you're on his side.
If every atom had appealed instead,
   But not you, that would not have saved his head.
And we don't place on you an obligation,   2945
   Rather we show you glory, boon companion.
You didn't do this; it was really me.
   Your attributes are inside me, you see.
And in this action you are not the actor,
   For you are born through me and not the mother.'
It's like '*when you just threw you did not throw*';*
   Like foam you give yourself to the wave's flow.
You've turned to '*no*'; settle next to '*except*'.*
   You're both prince and the prisoner that is kept.
You didn't give it; that King did of course.   2950
   Only He is. *God knows best the right course.*

That boon companion who fled anger's blow
   Was angry with the intercessor though.
He ended then his friendship; on the street
   He'd turn to face a wall so they'd not meet.
He left his intercessor, cut all ties.
   People began to gossip in surprise,
Saying, 'If he's not mad, why did he end
   All contact with his saviour and good friend?
He saved him. He would then have been beheaded.   2955
   He should be humble now and feel indebted.
He's done the opposite and got so mad,
   Resenting the best friend he's ever had.'
Someone reproached him, saying: 'Why do you
   Treat badly one you should feel grateful to?
That special friend has saved your life—his crime
   Is sparing your beheading at that time.
If he'd done evil, you still shouldn't leave him;
   He actually was good to you—believe him.'
He said, 'For the king's sake life's easily given—   2960
   Why should he intercede and be so driven?

Mohammad said, "*I had with God* time others
    Could not have too, though also Prophet brothers."
Apart from that King's blows I want no mercy,
    And I do not seek any other sanctuary.
I have negated others, for at stake
    Is serving that King, one chance I must take.
If the King should behead me now in anger,
    He will then give me sixty more lives after.
My work's to gamble with my head, be selfless;   2965
    My King's work's to bestow life on the headless.'

Kudos to heads chopped off by the king's hand;
    Shame on those who give others head and hand.
The night the king has made pitch-black displays
    Disdain for thousands of the bright Eid days.
Seers of the king have circumambulation
    Beyond grace, unbelief, wrath, and religion.
It is beyond words, so it can't be written,
    For it is hidden more than all things hidden.
Those names and words, despite being praised, have all   2970
    Been made through human beings visible.
'*He taught the names*'* led Adam to the light,
    But not through words and letters that we write.
The moment Adam turned terrestrial,
    It lowered names that were celestial,
For they donned veils of letters and sounds spoken,
    So in this world their meanings could be open.
Although from one view speech is a revealer,
    From others it's a veil and a concealer.

Abraham replies to Gabriel when he asks him, 'Do you have any needs?' by saying, 'Needs from you? No.'

    'I'm Abraham in this age and he's Gabriel;   2975
        I don't want him as guide when I'm in trouble.'
He didn't learn from Gabriel due respect,
    The latter had asked Abraham's request:

'Do you want something? Can I help some way?
   If not, then I will quickly rush away.'
Abraham said, 'No, go away now, please.
   I've vision; I loathe intermediaries.'
Linking believers, that emissary
   Is in this world as intermediary.
If all could hear divine communication,   2980
   Why would we have words, sounds, and revelation?
Although he is effaced in God and selfless,
   My case is more refined, so don't neglect this.
His action is the same as the king's action,
   But good appears bad in my rare affliction:
What to most men is the most perfect grace,
   Is wrath to those in a much higher place.
The former must endure much pain and anguish,
   So that they can perceive this and distinguish,
For intervening words, O Cave Companion,*   2985
   Are thorns to somebody who has reached union.
Pain, grief, and patience are all prerequisites
   To go beyond all words, for purest spirits.
But some have just grown deafer and don't hear,
   While others soared up to a higher sphere.
This grief is like the water of the Nile:
   Water to blessed ones, bloodbath for the vile.

You're more blessed if you see the destination:
   If more crop's seen that sparks more cultivation,
For sowing in this world will lead the way   2990
   To bigger harvests on the Final Day.
No contract was made for its own sake, was it?
   Contracts are for being placed to make a profit.
There's no denier, if you should look closely,
   Who was denying for denial's sake only—
It was to conquer foes in jealousy
   Or self-display or for supremacy.
Supremacism has its own desire:
   Forms that lack meaning never can inspire.
You ask, 'Why are you doing this? Shed light.'   2995

Because the form is oil, the meaning light.
Why ask: 'What is the point?' Why's that unknown
    If forms are for their own form's sake alone?
Asking about the point is a good question;
    'Why?' is wrong though for any other reason.
If it is only for its own sake, then
    Why do you wish to know its point, good men?
It therefore isn't wise, but a mistake
    To think all things are here for their own sake.
If there's no God, why are things ordered clearly?   3000
    If there is one, then can His acts be empty?
No one draws on the bathhouse walls for mere fun:
    Rightly or wrongly there must be a reason.

Moses asks God, 'Why did You create creatures and destroy them' and the arrival of the answer.

Moses once asked God, 'Master of the Reckoning,
    You made these forms, so why are You now wrecking?
You made the male and female pairs so gorgeous,
    So why do you destroy them? For what purpose?'
'I know your question's not from heedlessness,
    Or unbelief or lust and greediness,
Otherwise I'd chastise you straight away   3005
    And make sure that for this you'll later pay.
What you seek rather is for comprehension
    Of secrets of subsistence through my action,
So you can teach the everyday men and
    Make them less raw once they all understand.
Intentionally you asked so you can show
    To those who don't know, though you clearly know.'
Questioning is half of knowledge—this is true
    But it's not something all outsiders do.
From knowledge, question and response arose—   3010
    From soil and water grow both thorn and rose.
From knowledge, guidance and perdition grew:
    Bitter and sweet fruit both need moisture, too.
Acquaintance leads to love and hate as well;

Rich food gives strength, but makes some men unwell.
Moses became a foreigner who seeks it,
    So he could tell those unaware the secret:
Let's make ourselves seem like outsiders, too,
    And draw the answers as the strangers do.
Ass sellers turn to rivals and start fighting   3015
    When they seek the same contract sealed in writing.

God carried on, 'O wisdom's own possessor,
    Since you asked you can hear from Me the answer.
Now cultivate seeds in the soil, O Moses,
    So you as well might truly do this justice.'
Once Moses had completed all his sowing
    And the corn ears completed all their growing,
He grabbed a scythe to cut them down, and then
    A voice from the Unseen reached him again:
'Why do you reap what you yourself have sown?   3020
    You cut it down once it has fully grown.'
'I raze it once it's finished all its growth,
    For there are grains and straw: this corn has both.
The grain does not belong in barns, and I know
    That straw is not appropriate for the silo;
It is unwise to mix them carelessly:
    Winnowing's therefore a necessity.'
'From whom did you acquire this knowledge to
    Prepare a threshing floor the way you do?'
'You gave me the discernment,' Moses said.   3025
    'So how can I, your God, lack this, instead?
While pure souls are found in creation, there
    Are muddy souls too that are far from fair.'
Shells are not all the same grade; it is known
    While some hold pearls, others hold just a stone.
To manifest both good and bad's a must
    Just as with wheat and straw, as we've discussed.
The world's creation's is so truth's revealed,
    So that our wisdom's gold won't stay concealed.
'*I was a hidden treasure*'* shows it best: 3030
    Don't lose your essence, but be manifest.

Explanation that the animal soul and particular intellect and imaginings and fancies are like buttermilk while the everlasting spirit is like the butter hidden in it.

In falsehood your pure essence has been placed;
　Hidden in buttermilk is butter's taste—
Falsehood's your body, which will rot away;
　The truth is your pure soul, which should hold sway.
For years the body's buttermilk's revealed,
　While the soul's butter stays within, concealed,
Until God sends a Prophet—he's the one
　Who shakes the buttermilk inside the churn,
All so that it gets shaken properly,　　　　　　　　　3035
　So I might learn 'I' was concealed from 'me',
Or till one of His slave's communications
　Enters the ears which seek God's inspirations.
God's speech is kept by *the believer's ear*,
　For theirs are linked to the inviter here,
Just as the children's ears keep what their mothers
　Tell them before they learn to speak to others;
If the child doesn't have a working ear,
　It will be mute because it cannot hear.
The deaf have always been mute like this, brother;　　3040
　The children talk if they can hear their mother.
Deafness and dumbness are deficiencies,
　Blocking knowledge from entering in with ease.
God speaks without being taught thus previously;
　His attributes have no deficiency.
And one like Adam, for whom God was tutor
　Without a medium like a nurse or mother.
And Jesus, who spoke all that God was teaching—
　As soon as he was born he started speaking,*
To rebuff all the whispers of suspicion　　　　　　　3045
　That maybe he was born from fornication.
Shaking was needed for this to set in,
　To find the butter hidden deep within—
In buttermilk it seemed that none remained;
　Buttermilk's label claims that it's contained:

The shell appears like it exists to you;
  The root seems to decay from your own view.
The buttermilk's not formed the butter yet—
  Don't use it till it does. Avoid regret.
Shake it between your hands methodically   3050
  Until it shows the content you can't see.
The Eternal's proof is in the form that dies;
  The cupbearer is known by drunkards' cries.

Another parable on this matter.

The banner's lion's playful movements show
  The ways in which the winds behind it blow:
If those winds moving it weren't really there,
  How could drawn lions leap up in the air?
You can detect the east wind through its motion
  From the west wind; thus it tells of what's hidden.
The body's like the lion on the banner: 3055
  Thought moves it at each moment in some manner.
Thought from the East is like the eastern breeze,
  Thought from the West the west wind with disease.
Thought from the East is different to the West's,
  Though both are winds the body manifests.
The moon's inert as is its eastern side;
  The heart's East is the soul of souls inside.
The East of that sun which shines deep inside
  Has as its shell the sun you see outside,
For when the body dies, it then is clear   3060
  That for it day and night will not appear,
Yet when the inner sun is perfect, night
  And day aren't needed for it to see light.
In dreams the sun and moon come to your vision
  Without them being seen on the horizon.
Learn to discern, since our sleep is *death's brother*,
  The difference between one and the other.
If some say that is just a branch of this one,
  Blind and uncertain followers, don't listen:
In sleep the image of a state appears,   3065
  Which won't if you're awake for twenty years.

You seek interpretations endlessly,
   Rushing towards the wise ones desperately:
'Tell me this dream's true meaning!' you appeal.
   It's base to say it's just derived, unreal.
This is a plain man's sleep while the elect ones'
   Is the root of all privilege and selections.
Just elephants when sleep bears them away
   Will dream of India, seeing as by day;
Donkeys won't dream of India, since they've never   3070
   Felt exiled living far away from India.
One needs an elephant-like soul that's strong
   To go through dreams to India before long;
Through yearning, that strong elephant remembers,
   At night its recollection then forms pictures.
'*Remember God!*'* is not for all and sundry.
   '*Return!*'* is not meant for just anybody.
Don't lose hope! Be an elephant—if you
   Are not one, change to one without ado.

Behold all of the alchemists who're found   3075
   In heaven, hear each moment their work's sound.
In the celestial realm they all design;
   They're busy working for your sake and mine.
If you don't see such ones of the elect,
   Night-blind one, feel instead now their effect
On your perception as you live below:
   Observe how from your own soil new plants grow.
Ebrahim-e Adham was of their number;
   In sleep he could see spread before him India.
He broke apart his chains and then demolished   3080
   His kingdom naturally, before he vanished.
A sign of seeing India is that one
   Leaps up from sleep as if insane, undone,
And buries any plans that still remain,
   And bursts apart each link of one's own chain.
The Prophet said of God's light: 'In one's breast
   The sign of God's light that is manifest
Is turning from *delusion's realm* so firmly

And also shunning joy's realm resolutely.'
O my pure friend, listen to this narration;   3085
It gives Mohammad's saying's explanation.

*Story about the prince to whom the true kingdom showed
itself and then 'on the day when a man shall flee from his
brother, father, and mother'* became the reality of his
experience: he saw the kingdom of the dust pile of the
childlike, from the game of 'castle-taking', where the child
that is victorious climbs the dust pile and boasts, 'The
castle is mine!' The other children envy him: 'Dust is the
pastime of youths.' When that prince escaped the bondage
of colours, he said, 'I call these coloured earthly pieces the
same as that worthless dust, not gold, satin, and brocade.
I have escaped from the brocade and have attained the
Oneness.' God said: 'We gave judgement when he was a
youth.'* God's guidance does not require seniority in age.
None can have an opinion on the capacity to receive in the
face of 'Be! And it is.'**

A king once had a young son who possessed
    Inside and outside virtues deemed the best.
He dreamt that suddenly that son fell dead;
    For him pure wine became dark dregs instead.
Due to fire's heat his water-sack eye drained;
    In that intense heat no tears soon remained.
The king became so filled with pain entirely
    That soon sighs couldn't find a point of entry.
His body lifeless and about to break,   3090
    Yet there was life left when he stirred awake.
He felt such joy on waking up once more
    Unlike what he'd experienced before.
He nearly died of joy so unrestrained:
    Body and soul are captives that are chained;
This lamp is snuffed out by the breath of grief
    But also from joy—it's beyond belief.
Man lives between these two deaths like a yoke;
    This shackled-looking one is such a joke.
The king said to himself, 'By God's decree,   3095

Joy was the cause of sorrow tragically.
How wondrous that it is death from one angle,
  Yet from the other nurturing and revival.'
One circumstance makes it become destruction,
  Another turns the same thing to protection.
In this world, bodily joy seems like perfection,
  But it's a failing flaw at Resurrection.
Dream-readers say that laughter means tomorrow
  Will bring regret, much weeping, and deep sorrow,
While weeping in a dream means happiness   3100
  Will come, my cheerful friend, and not distress.

'This grief has passed,' the king was pondering,
  'But still my soul fears such an awful thing,
And if my foot gets thorn-pricked suddenly,
  Meaning the rose dies, where's my legacy?'
Death has so many causes—to pre-empt
  It now, which should we block as first attempt?
A hundred doors face death's most poisonous bite;
  They creak when opened, which gives such a fright.
Death's door's creaks are not heard by slaves of greed;   3105
  Since their ears can't perceive, they don't take heed.
Doors creaking means pain from the body's view;
  From the foe's view it means their torture too.
Read what's in books of medicine and learn
  From that how all the flames of ailments burn.
Through all those ruptures there's an entry way;
  A scorpion's pit is never far away.
The king said, 'My lamp's weak and wind is blowing;
  I'll light another lamp until that's glowing,
So if, due to the wind, the first one dies   3110
  I'll have one left still. This would be most wise.'
The mystic lights the candle of the heart,
  So from the body's lamp he can depart,
And when eventually the body dies
  He holds the spirit's candle near his eyes.
The king did not perceive this, and instead
  He gave the dying candle to one dead.

The king brings a bride for his son out of fear that his
bloodline will end.

'A bride must now be sought,' the king deduced,
   'So that my offspring will be soon produced.
So if this falcon starts to fade and wither,   3115
   His child can then become his true successor,
For, if this falcon's form should disappear,
   Inside his son his meaning will stay here.'
Among the Prophet's sayings is this one:
   '*The inside of his father is his son.*'
And every loving person for this reason
   Will pass on craft and trade skills to their children,
So that the meaning stays in this world when
   Their earthly body disappears again.
'God in His wisdom has bestowed strong yearning   3120
   To guide small ones who're capable of learning—
I, too, for the continuance of my line,
   See for my son a wife whose traits are fine,
The offspring of those upright and good-natured
   And not the child of kings who are bad-natured.'

The upright one's a king, for he's been freed,
   No longer captive to his lust and greed.
Some have called a mere prisoner 'the king'—
   Naming slaves 'Kaafoor'* is a similar thing.
The desert is a 'safe place', isn't it?   3125
   Some people call the leper 'fortunate'.*
They called the prisoner of base desire
   'Prince' or 'most generous ruler who ranks higher'.
They called those prisoners of destiny
   'Most glorious princes in this territory'.
Beasts in the shoeing-line they call high-ranking:
   Though they have rank and wealth, their souls are lacking.
The king chose an ascetic for his family;
   His women heard of this and took it badly.

The king chooses the daughter of a poor ascetic for his son, and the
women of the harem object and feel ashamed of forming relations
with the poor.

The prince's mother tried an intervention: 3130
   'Spouses should match, says reason and convention.
You're being mean and greedy and not clever,
   Trying to join our son with a mere beggar.'
'Calling a great man "beggar" is so wrong—
   Through God's bestowal his heart is rich and strong.
He goes without, content through piety,
   Not, like a wretched beggar, lazily.
Living with less through piety is blameless,
   It's not the poverty of men who're shameless:
If they find gold scraps, they make a prostration,   3135
   While he shuns treasures through high aspiration.
Noble ones say real beggars are those kings
   Whose greed makes them seek all forbidden things.'
'Where are his palaces for her trousseau?
   Does he have coins and jewels that he can throw?'
'Begone! God's taken such concerns away
   From those who suffer for the higher way.'

The king prevailed, gave the upright man's daughter
   To his own son because of how he saw her:
Her loveliness was rivalled by no one,   3140
   Her face more radiant than the morning sun.
Her beauty and her manners were so fine
   That words can't do them justice, friends of mine.
If you hunt inner goals you will soon find
   Wealth, beauty, rank, and fortune trail behind.
The next world's a wealth-bearing caravan;
   This world trails it like dung and hair, good man:
If you choose hair, the camel's not with you—
   Select the camel, then the hair comes too.

When the king's wish for this unusual wedding   3145
　　With those good ones was sealed with no rebelling,
An old decrepit witch by destiny
　　Fell in love with that fine prince suddenly.
He grew bewitched by that decrepit gypsy
　　And Babylon's famed witchcraft felt some envy:
That young prince fell in love with that vile crone,
　　Abandoning his own bride on her own.
A gypsy of the dark arts who was ugly
　　Had waylaid that young, beautiful prince suddenly.
That ninety-year-old fetid, stinking cunt   3150
　　Left him with lack of wisdom, ignorant.
For a whole year he was infatuated;
　　He'd kiss the soles of her feet as she waited.
And that crone's company left him bereft
　　Till half a soul was all that he had left.
Due to his weakness, others suffered too.
　　Magic had made him drunk; he had no clue.
The king now felt imprisoned. That prince kept
　　Laughing at all the tears his father wept.
It was checkmate when he'd smelled victory.   3155
　　Desperate, he'd give all day to charity.
Whatever remedy the king then tried
　　His son's love for the hag intensified.
He grew sure it was God's mysterious way;
　　The only cure in this case is to pray.
'Your order shall prevail,' he prayed, prostrate.
　　'Apart from You, God, who else can dictate?
This wretch burns now like aloes—help him, please,
　　Merciful, Loving One!' He didn't cease
Until, due to his groaning and petition,   3160
　　There soon appeared on the road a magician.

The answering of the king's prayer for his son to be delivered from the gypsy witch.

That man was far off, but had heard related
　　That a crone left a good boy captivated,
　　That in her sorcery she had no peer,

Without a rival sorcerer who'd come near.
O youth, there is one hand above another
  Up to God's essence in both skill and power,
And all these hands reach God's hand finally:
  The end of all the torrents is the sea.
All clouds above are formed from that, its source   3165
  As well as where the torrent runs its course.

The king told him, 'He's lost control. Help, please!'
  He said, 'I'm one of the best remedies.
No sorcerer is equal to that crone;
  Because I'm from the Unseen, I alone,
Like Moses's hand, at the Lord's decree,
  Can now destroy her horrid sorcery!
This knowledge reached me from beyond this sphere,
  Not study of weak sorcery found here.
I came here to undo her witchcraft trick   3170
  So that the prince of yours will not stay sick.
Go to the graveyard at the dawn's first light;
  Next to the wall you'll find a tomb that's white.
Dig open that one in Mecca's direction,
  To see the power of God's work there in action.'

This story's very long and you are weary;
  I'll boil it down to what is necessary.*
He opened up those tight knots which delivered
  The prince from the ordeal that he had suffered.
The youth came to himself and ran away   3175
  To the king's throne despite trials on the way.
He then fell down prostrate before his father;
  With sword and his own shroud he made the offer.
The king decreed the town be decorated,
  Then all, his bride included, celebrated.
The world revived and seemed so radiant—
  In just one day things were so different.
The king held such a lavish wedding there
  That dogs were fed rose candy with no care.

The old witch died of grief and to the Maker   3180
    She gave back her vile face and ugly nature.
The prince then asked himself in sheer amazement:
    'How did she rob my reason, sight, and judgement?'
He saw his bride moon-like in radiant beauty,
    Surpassing all the others who were pretty—
He lost his wits and fell for her then fully,
    His heart for three days vanished from his body.
He stayed unconscious for this time, throughout;
    There was commotion at his passing out.
Through rose water and treatments, little by little   3185
    He came around and could tell good from evil.
The king spoke to him after one year passed:
    'O son, remember your friend from the past:
That old bedfellow on that bed, so then
    You won't be so disloyally harsh again.'
'No way, I've found the realm of purest rapture
    And fled the pit of that realm of bad error.'
It's like that when believers find the way:
    To God's light from the dark they turn away.

Explaining that the prince is Man, God's deputy's son, his father is Adam, God's deputy to whom the angels prostrated, and that old gypsy is the world who separated father and son through sorcery, and the Prophets and Friends of God are the physician who fixed the situation.

O brother, you should know the prince is you—   3190
    Into this world you can be born anew.
The gypsy witch is this world which has meant
    Men falling captive to its hues and scent.
Since she has flung you in pollution there,
    Make '*Say: "I now take refuge!"*'* now your prayer.
To flee this witchcraft and not feel forlorn,
    Seek refuge with *The Lord of Every Dawn*.*
The Prophet called this world a witch as well,
    Since men fall in the pit due to its spell.
That putrid hag's spells have such powers, beware!   3195
    They've even turned kings into captives there.

She's of *the blowing witches** inside you;
  She tightens witchcraft's knots inside you too.
The sorceress world is wily, and it's tragic
  The masses cannot cope with her black magic.
If men's brains could untie her knots, why then
  Should God have sent the Prophets down to men?
Seek the sweet-breathed knot-loosener who is privy
  To '*God does what He should will*'* and its mystery.
She trapped you in her net like fish so simply: 3200
  That prince stayed for a year; you'd stay for sixty!
You'll stay in her net for that long duration,
  Not happy, not pursuing good tradition.
A wretched scoundrel, your world's neither good
  Nor rescued from sins. You've not understood.
Her breathing's tightened these knots, so now seek
  The breathing of the Maker, who's unique.
'*I breathed in him My spirit*'* saves you from
  This fate and says: 'Ascend now higher. Come!'
Just God's breath can consume breath of the sorcerer;   3205
  The latter's wrath, while love's breath is the former.
His mercy's prior to His wrath,* so you
  Should seek what's prior to be prior too,
So you may reach *the wedded souls** one day,
  For, smitten prince, this is your route away.
There's no knot-loosening with that hag in place,
  With you still in that flirt's net and embrace.
Hasn't Mohammad said, "This world and that one
  Are like *two fellow wives* as a comparison?
You cannot simultaneously unite   3210
  With both: the body's health means spirit's plight.

Is parting hard from this realm that is transient?
  Think how hard it is from the realm that's permanent.
To leave the form is hard for you, so ponder
  How severance from the Lord is that much harder.
Parting this world's too hard for you today—
  How will you cope when God is far away?
You miss so much the water that is black—

How much you'll miss clear fountains that you lack.
If you're without this world's drink you can't rest,   3215
     How then without *the ones who drink*,* the blessed.
If you could see His beauty for one instant
     You'd fling your soul and being in flames, insistent.
Afterwards you will see this world as carrion,
     Once you have seen the glory of His union.
You'll reach your loved one like the prince, then you
     Will take the thorn of self from your foot too.
Strive now for selflessness with all your might;
     Be faster, for *the Lord knows best what's right*.
Do not stay wedded with yourself perpetually.   3220
     Don't always fall in dirt just like a donkey.
Short-sightedness makes people stumble here.
     Like blind men they can't see the slopes appear.
On Joseph's shirt's scent you should now rely,*
     Because its scent gives vision to the eye.
The hidden form and radiance from that forehead
     Have made the eyes of Prophets be far-sighted.
That face's light will save you from the fire.
     Don't be content with borrowed light—aim higher.
The borrowed light makes eyes see what is temporary,   3225
     And it makes body, mind, and spirit scabby.
It's really fire, though it's light in appearance.
     Keep your hands off it if you want real radiance.
The eyes and soul that only see what's transient
     Fall everywhere flat on their face each instant.
Far-sighted men may see more than a scholar
     Just as in dreams unschooled men may see further.
You sleep with parched lips now beside a river,
     Yet run to a mirage to find some water;
You notice a mirage and start to chase—   3230
     You fall in love with your own sight, disgrace!
While dreaming you boast vainly to a friend:
     'With my heart's vision all veils I can rend.
Look, I've seen water over there. Let's go!'
     But that's just a mirage and you don't know.
The further that unreal mirage lures you,
     The further from the water you'll reach too.

Your own resolve veils you from what's right here:
    Water that you can drink extremely near.
Many resolve to make a distant journey   3235
    From that place where their goal is found already.
The sleeper's boast and vision are both nonsense;
    It's just a fantasy, so keep your distance.
You're sleepy, but sleep as you travel there
    While on the path to God, not anywhere,
In case a mystic on the path meets you
    And frees you from vain dreams as he can do.
Though thoughts in sleep be finer that a hair,
    The sleeper won't discover the way there,
And even if that thought is multilayered   3240
    It's error upon error that's been layered.
Sea waves keep striking him without relenting,
    And yet he dreams he's thirsty and keeps panting,
As though he's in a desert with no water—
    In fact real water's *closer than his jugular*!*

Story about that ascetic who was happy and laughing in a year of drought, despite being penniless with a large family, while people were dying of hunger. They said to him, 'What a time to rejoice! This is the time for a hundred laments.' He responded, 'For me it isn't a burden.'

It's like that strange ascetic who would smile
    In drought when other men wept all the while.
They asked, 'What are you smiling now about?
    Good people have been ruined by this drought.
God's mercy's closed its eyes to us; the sun   3245
    Is so strong that our meadows all now burn.
Orchards, vineyards, and farms have all turned black.
    No moisture in the soil, a total lack.
People are dying due to drought and torture
    Now by the hundreds like fish out of water.
Don't you feel for your own community,
    One body with deep family unity?
And if a single body part should suffer
    In peace and war that pain is shared together.'

'To your eyes this is a harsh drought,' he said,   3250
    'To mine this land's like paradise instead:
I see in every place I look upon,
    Reaching up to my waist, abundant corn.
Wind blows those ears—by me it's clearly seen—
    This fills the desert and makes it so green.
To test, I reach and touch them—how can I
    Withdraw from all of this my hand and eye?'

Base people, you're the Pharaoh-body's friend—
    That's why you see the waves as blood. Ascend!
Be Moses of true wisdom's friend. Move faster   3255
    For blood to leave so you can see the water.*
Fall badly out with your own father and
    He'll seem to you a cur, but understand
He's not a cur—That's due to your rebellion:
    That mercy seems a cur to your warped vision.
His brothers saw as wolf-like due to envy
    Sweet Joseph, for they had become so angry.*
Make peace now with your father! Rage will end
    And he won't seem a cur, but your best friend.

*Explaining that the whole world is the form of the Universal
Intellect. If you treat Universal Intellect unjustly by your
corrupt action, the form of the world increases your grief in
most situations, just as when you have fallen out with your
father—his form increases your grief and you can't look at
his face even though before he would have been the light of
your eye and the comfort of your soul.*

The world's the Universal Intellect's form, father   3260
    To human beings who heed God's '*Say!*'* as follower.
When someone shows ingratitude to it,
    All forms look at him just like curs to hit.
Make peace now with the father, end rebellion,
    So this world seems a gold rug to your vision.
The Resurrection will be felt by you;

Heaven and earth will both transform then, too.
Since I'm at peace with him, to my own eyes
    The world appears a wondrous paradise.
A new form and new beauty will appear   3265
    Each moment; weariness will disappear.
I see the world as something full of bounty,
    With springs that keep on gushing water strongly;
Their waters' noises reach my ear—I find
    Myself a drunk and lose my wits and mind:
Like worshippers the branches are all dancing;
    Like minstrels all the leaves on them are clapping.
A flash now shines from inside its felt cover—
    Imagine then when you see the full mirror!
It's not one-thousandth of it I've set out: 3270
    It's less, but all these ears are stuffed with doubt.
To their imaginings it shows future days,
    But 'Here's my cash in hand now,' reason says.

*The story about the sons of Ozayr who were asking after
their father from their father himself without knowing. He
answered, 'Yes, I've seen him. He is coming.' Some
recognized him and became unconscious. Others didn't and
said, 'He only gave news about the future, so why fall
unconscious?'*

It's like the case of the sons of Ozayr
    Who'd ask for news about him everywhere.
While he was made young they had all grown old;
    Their father came once, as it has been told:
Not recognizing him, they asked him, 'Traveller,
    Do you have news about Ozayr, our father,
For just today we all were finally told   3275
    Despair has gone; he'll come back to the fold?'
He said, 'Yes, he's behind me on the way.'
    A son rejoiced at what he heard him say:
'May this kind bearer of good news feel joyous!'
    Another recognized him, fell unconscious,
Saying: 'It's not the time for forecasts, brother,
    For we have fallen in a mine of sugar.'

The wise experience; forecasts aren't direct:
   The forecast's eye is veiled by a defect.
It's pain to infidels, while to believers   3280
   It's good news. But experience can sate seers:
Since lovers get drunk when they taste directly,
   Beyond both faith and unbelief, they're lofty.
The latter pair are doorkeepers, outside
   Like shells that hold the kernels deep inside;
The dried shell's unbelief; it looks away.
   The inner skin's faith—some taste spreads its way.
Dry shells belong in hell, while skins that meet
   With kernels held within will all turn sweet.
Kernels transcend this sweetness nonetheless;   3285
   They grant this sweetness from their own largesse.
This talk could go on till infinity—
   Return, so Moses can transform the sea.
This discourse so far suits the average brains;
   Concealed things follow in what now remains.
Your intellect's gold is like grains and filings—
   How can I mint a coin with those small triflings.
Dealing with crucial things divides your brain,
   Numerous desires and matters strange or plain—
Love joins the separate bits with its own hand   3290
   So you'll become as fine as Samarqand.
Once, grain by grain, you have become united,
   The King's coin can through you be freshly minted.
And if you're larger than a coin's size too,
   The King will make a golden cup from you,
With His name, royal title, and his face,
   Seeker of union, all etched in their place.
So your Beloved can be bread and water,
   Lamp, witness, wine, and almonds wrapped in sugar,
Make yourself one! Union's a merciful grace.   3295
   I'll tell you what is real then to your face,
For speaking's aim is that it be accepted;
   Polytheism's soul heard, but rejected.
The soul is scattered by things in the heavens
   And shared among some sixty different passions—
Silence is therefore best, for it gives permanence:

The answer to the stupid wretch is silence.
I know this; bodily drunkenness though still
   Opens again my mouth against my will,
Just as in sneezing and in yawning too,   3300
   Your mouth will open, though not willed by you.

Commentary on the Prophet's saying: 'I ask God for forgiveness
seventy times every day.'

Like our dear Prophet, I repent each day
   Seventy times for things I loosely say,
But drunkenness breaks my repentance vow,
   Makes me forget and rend clothes anyhow.
The wisdom of revealing all past history
   Gave drunkenness to knowers of the mystery.
With drum and banner, hidden mysteries
   Have gushed out from '*the pen's dry*',* which decrees.
The Boundless Mercy's in a constant flow,   3305
   But you who are asleep still cannot know.
Sleepers' clothes draw in water from the streams
   While they seek a mirage out in their dreams,
Saying: 'There's sign of water miles away.'
   Their thinking blocks themselves from the right way
The sleepers said, 'Away', from fantasy,
   So they divorced thus from reality;
Their souls sleep while they search so far away—
   Feel sorry for those travellers today!
I've not seen true thirst cause sleep, no, not once;   3310
   Sleep comes from thirst in those with ignorance.
True wisdom's that which God Himself has fed,
   Not that which Mercury has brought instead.*

Explaining that the particular intellect does not see beyond the grave.
Regarding such things it is dependent on the Prophets and Friends of God.

This knowledge sees up to the grave, not past;
   The mystic sees till Resurrection's blast.
This knowledge doesn't pass graves any further;
   The foot does not step in the realm of wonder—
Leave both this foot and intellect behind.

Seek eyes for the Unseen. Much gain you'll find.
How can one who needs teachers, books they write,   3315
   Shine from his breast, like Moses, purest light.*
Opinion's knowledge gives just vertigo—
   Instead choose waiting for what He'll bestow.
Do not expect to rise up through your speaking;
   Superior to your speaking is your hearing.
Teaching posts are craved after by fierce rivals;
   Mere thoughts of cravings on this path are idols.
If every fool could find paths to His grace.
   Why did God send the Prophets to this place?
Particular intellect's a lightning flash—   3320
   In just one evening how can one reach Vakhsh?*
Lightning's light's not to lead us just like sheep
   But a command to clouds that they must weep.
Our intellect is meant for tears: for instance
   When non-existence weeps to gain existence.
The child's brain tells him, 'Go to school!' But it
   Can't on its own learn; clearly it's unfit.
The sick one's intellect leads to a healer,
   But it can't on its own cure sickness either.
Devils went to the heavens once to spy,   3325
   Listening to secrets that were shared on high:
They first stole a few little scraps away,
   But then the shooting stars drove them away:
'Begone! A Prophet's gone to earth to speak;
   You can acquire from him the things you seek.
If you seek priceless pearls, the scripture states:
   "*Enter their houses through their proper gates!*"*
Knock and stay waiting at the door, for there
   Is no way for you to alone soar there.
The long route to here wasn't necessary;   3330
   We've shown to humans every mystery.
If you're not heedless, go to him! Take heed.
   Be sugar cane soon, though now a plain reed.'

The guide will make grass grow on dust as proof;
   He isn't less than Gabriel's horse's hoof.*

You too will soon be fresh and green, of course,
    If you become the dust of Gabriel's horse.
That verdure that gives life which Sameri
    Put in the calf to have efficacy,*
That verdure gave it life, so it then roared   3335
    In such a way that its foe then was floored.
Come to the secret's knowers truthfully
    And, like the hooded falcon, you'll break free—
The hood blocks ears from hearing, eyes from vision,
    And it has made downtrodden that poor falcon.
It blinds that falcon's eyes since they're inclined
    Always towards the birds of their own kind—
It joins the king once severed from its own;
    The falconer opens its eyes then alone.
God drove the devils far from His watchtower   3340
    And the particular intellect from power,
Saying, 'Don't domineer; you aren't a ruler,
    But the heart's pupil—that is what you're good for.'
Go to the heart—you're part of that heart's whole,
    A servant of the Just King is your role.
Being His slave's better than being a sultan,
    For '*I am better*' were the words of Satan.*
Choose, captive, once you've seen the difference,
    Adam's slavehood not Satan's arrogance.
'May he whose carnal soul has been undone   3345
    Be blessed!' said His path's special mystic sun.
Go to the Tuba tree's shade and sleep well;
    Rest your head in that shade and don't rebel.
The shade of one whose self has been effaced
    Is where those seeking pureness will be graced.
If you leave this shade for your selfishness,
    You'll lose the path through sheer rebelliousness.

Explaining the Qur'anic verse: 'You who believe, don't put yourself before God and His messenger.'* Since you are not a prophet, be a member of his community; since you are not a sultan, be a subject; be silent and don't bring arrogance and opinion from yourself!

So go, be silent in sincere surrender,

In the shade of commands made by the mentor,
Or, though you're able and have the potential,   3350
    Boasting perfection will become your downfall.
You'll even lose potential for the future
    If you rebel against the mystic tutor:
Be patient, cobbler, with your own position,
    Or you'll be a rag-mender through demotion.
The rag-mender through patience and forbearance
    Learns to become a tailor soon, for instance –
So strive on, and from weariness declare:
    '*The intellect's a fetter.*' Let's compare
With the philosophers who at the Hour   3355
    Saw their intelligence did not have power,
Admitting, though they didn't want to ever,
    'We rode our horse in vain through being clever,
Rebelling then against the true men, we
    Swam in a sea that was imaginary.'
To swim inside the spiritual sea's delusion;
    Other than Noah's ark there's no solution.
Mohammad, King of Prophets shared this notion:
    'I'm the ship in the Universal Ocean,
Or one who is a visionary like me,   3360
    Becoming my successor spiritually.'
We're Noah's ark in seas now—that's the truth.
    Don't turn your face away from this ark, youth.
Don't head, like Canaan, to each soaring mountain:
    '*Today there's no protection*'*—you should listen.
With blinkers on, the ark looks low; it's not.
    You view as high the mountain of mere thought.
Don't deem low what is really lowliness;
    It's linked to grace sent from His Holiness.
Don't be impressed the mountain of thought's tall   3365
    When just one wave can make that mountain fall.
If you're like Canaan, you will not believe me,
    Though you hear hundreds of such counsels from me.
Canaan's ears won't accept these words I share
    When God has put on them His seals to wear:
Sermons can't pass through God's seals, so how can
    A transient thing change what's ordained, good man?

But I am telling news about good fortune,
    All in the hope that you are not a Canaan,
So in the end you can sincerely say   3370
    That from the first you see the final day:
You now can see the end. Do not make blind
    Your eyes which see the end from far behind.
One who is blessed to be a visionary
    Won't trip up on this true itinerary.
If you don't want your stumbling to repeat,
    Give your eyes vision from the mystic's feet.
Make his feet's dust kohl for your eyes instead,
    So you can strike at every hoodlum's head.
Through being a student who is spiritually needy,   3375
    From needle-thin you'll be the sword of Ali.
So make your kohl from dust of those who're pure
    And, though at first it burns eyes, it will cure.
The camel's pair of eyes is very good
    Because for their sake it seeks thorns for food.

*Story about the mule's complaint to the camel: 'I fall on my face
often while moving, but you don't—why is that?' The camel
answers it.*

One day a mule saw that he had retired
    Next to a camel, so he then enquired:
'I fall so frequently flat on my face
    On the hills, roads, and in the marketplace,
But from the mountain top especially—   3380
    I topple down head-first there dangerously.
But you don't fall on your face—why is it?
    Perhaps your pure soul is more fortunate?
I fall down on my head and bang my knees;
    Like my soft snout they start to bleed with ease—
My load and saddle then fall on my head
    And riders on me strike although I've bled.'

It's like those who have weak intelligence,
    Who break their vows with further sins at once—

Satan mocks joyfully all weak-willed men					3385
   Who break their vows so quickly once again.
Like a lame horse that often falls on roads
   Because they're rocky and it bears huge loads,
For breaking vows that man's deprived of luck
   And then from the Unseen he's often struck.
With weak resolve he makes the same vow, then
   The Devil spits once and he falls again.
Although extremely weak, he shows disdain
   Through arrogance to seekers who attain.

The mule said, 'Camel, you are one of those					3390
   Believers who don't fall or raise their nose.
What do you have that you don't fall like me
   Or stumble and fall face-down constantly?'
'We both rely on God, but differences
   Are clear, O mule, between the two of us:
I have a high head and my eyes are lofty;
   Such vision gives security from injury:
From every mountain top, if I should look
   I see each plain and hollow, every nook,
Just as those glorious rulers saw ahead					3395
   All their affairs until when they'd be dead.'
To someone of good essence now appears
   The things that will occur in twenty years,
And, in addition to his own fate, he
   Sees East and West, all people's destiny.
The light makes its home in his heart and eye
   Due to love of its homeland: that is why.
He is like Joseph, who dreamed that the sun
   And moon bowed down to him in unison.
What Joseph saw, once more than ten years passed,					3400
   Raised up its head and was fulfilled at last.*
The Prophet said, '*By God's light he can view*';
   God's light can split the sky above in two.
Begone, for in your eyes this light's not found;
   By bestial senses you remain still bound.

'You see just what's in front,' the camel said,
    'Due to weak eyes; your guide is weak instead:
The eye serves as the guide to legs and hands;
    For where to go or run from in these lands.
Another factor is my eyes are clearer   3405
    And also my creation is much cleaner:
I'm a legitimate child anyway,
    Not born of fornication and astray.
No doubt, you're one of those, as men relate:
    "When the bow's bent, the arrow can't fly straight."'

The mule confirmed the truth of the camel's answer and admitted
the camel's superiority over himself. Then he asked for the camel's
help and sincerely took refuge in him. The camel was kind to him
and showed the way with his support in a fatherly and regal fashion.

The mule said, 'Camel, all your words are true.'
    And after this its eyes grew tearful too.
The mule wept at the camel's feet, subservient,
    Said, 'Chosen by *the Lord of every servant*,
Through blessedness perhaps you can afford   3410
    To now accept me as your slave, my lord?'
The camel said, 'Since now in front of me
    You have confessed, you're free from transiency.
You're spared grief, since you were fair in the end.
    You were a foe, but soar now as God's friend.
It wasn't in your essence in the end
    For a bad essence gives denial, friend;
That only was a surface-grafted badness—
    It makes confession and seeks out forgiveness,
Like Adam's, for his slip was temporary   3415
    And he repented for it urgently.
Since Satan's sin instead was from his essence,
    He couldn't find the way towards repentance.
You've been released from self and your bad flaws,
    The tongues of flames and the wild beasts' huge jaws.
You've now grasped fortune, so continue passing;
    You've dived in fortune that is everlasting.
"*Enter among my servants*" is your own;

"*Enter my garden*"* also you have sewn.
You've made a path to join his servants too,   3420
    And by that hidden way you've entered through.
"*Guide us to the straight path!*"* you have read out;
    He led you to that bliss which you sought out.
My dear, from fire you've turned to light—once sour,
    You've changed to grapes and raisins through His power.
Once a mere star, you now shine much more light—
    O sun, be happy! *God knows best what's right.*'

O Light of God, Hosam, please come and pour
    Into this milk some honey from your store,
So that milk's savour won't change needlessly,   3425
    But rather gain from savour's boundless sea.
When it unites with the sea of Alast,*
    Becoming ocean, free from change at last,
Inside that honey ocean it will find
    An entry, safe from harm of any kind.
Lion of God, give out a lion-like roar
    To reach the seventh heaven to which we soar.
What does the weary soul know of our soaring?
    What does the mouse know of the lion's roaring?
Write all about your mystic states with gold   3430
    For ocean-hearted ones wish to be told.
This soul-expanding talk is the Nile's water—
    Make it blood to Egyptians, Lord, Transformer!

The Egyptian begs the Israelite: fill a jug from the Nile intending it for yourself, then place it to my lips through the right of friendship and brotherhood, for the jug which you Israelites fill from the Nile for yourselves is pure water and that which we Egyptians fill is pure blood.

I heard that an Egyptian went inside
    A Jew's house, since from thirst he'd nearly died,
To beg, 'I am your friend and kinsman, too.
    Today I need a helping hand from you.
Since Moses used his spells and awful magic

To turn the Nile to blood, our fate's been tragic.
You Jews can drink pure water from it, while   3435
   Closed-eyed Egyptians find blood fills the Nile—
See dying now from thirst Egyptian people,
   Due to ill fortune or traits that are evil.
Fill for yourself a cup of water now,
   So this old friend can drink from yours somehow.
When you fill for yourself that cup, I'm sure
   It won't be blood but water that is pure.
I'll drink the water in your situation.
   Parasites flee pain through such imitation.'

'O precious, dear friend, I'll come to your aid;   3440
   I'll handle it,' his Jewish friend then said,
'I'll carry out what you wish happily;
   I'll be your slave in bondage, then act free.'
He filled the cup then from the Nile, put it
   To his own lips and drank down half of it,
Then passed it to his friend: 'You drink some too!'
   But it became dark blood then in full view.
It changed to water when he pulled the cup
   Back to his own lips, so his friend blew up,
Enraged, then sat awhile once he'd calmed down: 3445
   'Brother, whose firm resolve has earned renown,
What can untie this knot that's shackling me?'
   'It's only drunk by men with piety:
The pious one is he who's shunned the way
   Of Pharaoh, and is Moses-like today.
Join Moses's men, then drink all this soon.
   Make peace with and behold light from the moon.
You've so much drunkenness your eyes can't see,
   Due to your rage at every devotee
Of God—put out rage, open eyes, and learn   3450
   From friends, then you can teach when it's your turn.'

You can't drink with me water you so prize
   When your vile unbelief has Mount Qaf's size.

How can a mountain fit a needle's eye
  Unless it turns to one thread? You must try
To make it straw by begging for forgiveness,
  Then from cups for forgiven ones drink in bliss.
It has been banned for faithless men by God,
  So how can you succeed to drink through fraud?
God made all fraud—He won't be fooled, O fraudster,   3455
  By lies that you make up and your imposture.
Become a follower of Moses now.
  Tricks will fail trying to catch the wind somehow.
Does water have the gall to disobey
  God's order and quench infidels today?
Do you think you can drink from your own bowl
  When it's snake poison and destroys your soul?
How can food make the soul start feeling stronger
  When it has turned your heart against God's order?
Do you think when you read this *Masnavi*   3460
  That you can listen to it now for free,
That words of wisdom and deep mysteries
  Reach everybody's mouth and ears with ease?
It's just a tale in that scenario;
  The shell and not the kernel's what will show,
Like sweethearts who veil that face you adore
  From your eyes as they put on a chador.*
You see as the same thing, you wicked man,
  Kalila and Dimna and the Qur'an.
Falsehood and truth are different as can be.   3465
  When your eyes open through God's grace you'll see.
Otherwise musk and dung are one as well
  To someone whose nose can no longer smell.
His aim's to save himself from weariness
  By reading out the words of God, no less,
Hoping those words will cure him and snuff out
  The fire inside of suffering and doubt.
To put out this much fire you easily could
  Use dirty urine, for it's just as good:
Urine and water both put out doubt's fire,   3470
  The way they do in sleep when you retire.
But if you get to know pure water, which

Is God's speech and is spiritually rich,
Doubts in your soul will all be cleared away
  And then your heart takes the rose garden's way,
For he who breathes a whiff of God's great book
  Soars in an orchard with a pleasant brook.
Or do you think that in reality
  Faces of God's Friends' are like what we see?

The Prophet marvelled at this and asked, 'Why   3475
  Is my face not seen by the faithful eye?
Why can't the people see my face's light
  Which has surpassed the sun's since it's so bright?
And, if they do see, why is there confusion
  Till revelation states: "That face is hidden."'
A moon to you, but people see a cloud.
  For infidels free viewing's not allowed.
To you it's bait, to them traps that confine,
  So vulgar men can't drink exclusive wine.
God said, '*They're looking*' to you, didn't He?   3480
  Yet, like the bathhouse paintings, *they can't see;**
It's just a form, though it may now appear
  As if its lifeless eyes see what is here,
Form worshipper—you show before its eyes
  Respect and say: 'What sadness and surprise
That this nice painting won't respond at all
  Though "Peace be unto you!" I loudly call.
With head and moustache it won't indicate
  Approval for the times that I prostrate.'
Though God does not nod outwardly His head,   3485
  His answer's favour's felt inside instead,
And that's worth hundreds of such nods—do soul
  And mind in answer ever nod at all?
If you should strive in serving intellect
  It gives more guidance, earned by your respect.
God doesn't outwardly nod at you either
  But He makes you among the chiefs their leader.
He gives you something very secret too
  That makes all people here prostrate to you,

The way He gave such virtue to mere stone　　　　　　3490
　　That it became loved and as 'gold' is known;
A drop of water gains God's kindest grace,
　　Becomes a pearl and then takes up gold's place.
The body's dust—when God gave it His light
　　It grew just like the moon with conquering might.
This world is a dead sketch and talisman;
　　Its eye lures off the path the stupid man;
It looks as if it's winking when it's seen;
　　Fools choose it as the prop on which they lean.

The Egyptian requests a prayer for blessing and guidance from the Israelite. The Israelite prays for blessing for the Egyptian and receives a reply from the Most Generous and Merciful God.

Next the Egyptian asked, 'Pray for my heart—　　　　3495
　　Its darkness means my mouth is kept apart—
Then maybe my heart's lock will be released
　　And this vile one join beauties at their feast.'
You can make the deformed turn beautiful,
　　Turn Satan back to being celestial,
Or give a dry branch freshness and musk's scent
　　And fruit through Mary's power that's heaven-sent.*
The Israelite fell right then in prostration:
　　'O God who knows both manifest and hidden,
Who else should any servant now pray to?　　　　　3500
　　Both answer and petition come from you.
You also gave desire to pray initially,
　　As You give the response as well eventually.
You are the First and Last, while we are nothing
　　Here in the middle and now not worth mentioning.'
He said such things till his mind grew delirious
　　And his heart then completely fell unconscious,
Then, while in prayer, he came back to again—
　　*Other than what they strive for, naught for men.**
A scream and roar came while he was still praying　　3505
　　From that Egyptian's heart, and it was saying:
'Hurry, accept this faith, no longer dawdle,
　　So I can quickly cut my old faith's girdle.

A fire's been cast into my soul, you see—
    They've treated well one Satan-like as me.
Thank God, your friendship finally led the way
    Because I now can't bear to be away.
Time spent with you was alchemy—may your
    Feet never step outside my heart's front door!
You use a branch from paradise's tree—   3510
    I grasped and was borne there amazingly.
Swept from my body by a flood, this motion
    Carried me to His Kindness's huge ocean.
I headed for the flood so I could drink,
    But gained pearls when I reached the ocean's brink.'

The Israelite brought his cup: 'Drink!' he said.
    'Begone! Water is loathsome now instead—
I've drunk a draught from *"God has bought"*,* my friend,
    So I'll not thirst again until the end.
He who gave water to the stream and fountain   3515
    Has sent to me a fountain like an ocean.
My heart was fond of water in the past,
    But my desire for water now comes last.
For His slaves He becomes *kaf* simply to
    Make *kaf ha ya ayn sad*'s big promise true.*
"I give you every good thing," God told me,
    "Without cause or an intermediary.
I'm All-Sufficing. I feed with no bread.
    Without an army, I make you the head.
Without spring I give flowers, if you look.   3520
    I teach without a teacher or a book.
I cure you without medicine—My grace
    Can make the pit and grave an open space.
I give to Moses with one rod a heart,
    So with swords he can slash a world apart.
I give to Moses's hand light with brightness
    That can outshine the sun yet show it kindness.
I make mere wood a seven-headed serpent,
    A kind not seen being born from one that's pregnant.
I don't let blood mix with Nile's water, rather   3525

I make blood water's essence, for I'm clever.
Like the Nile's waves I turn your joy to sorrow,
   Such that you can't find joy again tomorrow.
When you want to renew your faith again
   But next to Pharaoh you feel helpless, then
You'll see come Mercy's Moses from before
   And the Nile's blood turn back to waves once more.
If you keep safe the end of your faith's thread,
   Your savour's Nile won't change to blood instead."
I thought I would change faiths in place of blood   3530
   To drink some water from this awful flood—
How could I then have known that all the while
   He'd change my nature and make me a Nile?'

I am a flowing Nile to my own eye,
   Though I look motionless to passers-by,
And to the Prophet this world is continuous
   In praising God yet to us it looks heedless:
To him this world is full of love and justice;
   To ordinary men it's dead and lifeless.
He sees the hills and valleys moving round;   3535
   He hears wise words from bricks and from the ground:
They are all dead and limited to most;
   I've never seen a stranger veil exposed.
To our eyes graves are all alike as well—
   God's friends see gardens next to pits of hell.
Vulgar men say, 'Why has the Prophet now
   Become a killjoy and so sour somehow?'
Elite men say, 'He only looks so sour,
   O people, since your sight is lacking power—
For once, come into our eyes for a while   3540
   To see "*Has there once come?*"* raise a huge smile.
For on the pear tree there it will appear
   Topsy-turvy, young man, so come down here.
That pear tree is existence's tree, so
   While up there new things look so old below:
Once up there you'll see bushes full of thorns
   And lots of snakes and angry scorpions.

You'll see for free when back on solid ground
A world with rose-cheeked beauties all around.

*Story about that filthy-acting woman who said to her
husband: 'Those illusions appear to you from the top of the
pear tree, for it shows such things to the human eye. Come
down from the top of the pear tree so those illusions go away.'
And if anyone says that what that man saw was not an
illusion, the answer is that it is a parable not an analogy.
For a parable this amount is enough, for if he had not gone
to the top of the pear tree he would never have seen those
things, whether real or imaginary.*

A woman sought her lover's warm embrace   3545
    Before her cuckold husband's foolish face.
She told her husband, 'Lucky man, I'll be
    In search of fruit to pick upon that tree.'
Once she'd climbed up, she wept and kept her stare
    Fixed on her husband from her perch up there,
Screaming: 'Are you a male whore? Tell me who
    Is that vile queer who has just mounted you?
Beneath you're like a woman who is swooning.
    Have you been always queer? What are you doing?'
Her husband said, 'Your head's afflicted! No,   3550
    There's no one else in this whole field below.'
The woman asked, 'Hiding beneath that hat,
    Who is that stretched on top of you like that?'
'Wife, come down from the tree!' her husband said,
    'You're acting senile and you've lost your head.'
Once she came down, her husband went up there.
    She grabbed her lover in the open air
For an embrace. Her husband shouted, 'Who
    Is that ape-like man, whore, who's mounting you?'
'There's no one else down here near to my presence.   3555
    Your head has been afflicted. Don't talk nonsense!'
He then repeated to her what he'd said.
    She claimed, 'It must be that pear tree instead—
While I was perched on it, I similarly

Saw such things, cuckold, so mistakenly.
Come down to see that there is nothing here.
That pear tree makes illusions all appear.'

Joking is teaching, so pay close attention—
Don't look at just the joke's form of expression.
To jesters every serious thing's hilarious,   3560
But to the wise hilarious jokes are serious.
Lazy men seek the pear tree that is near;
The other pear tree's a long way from here.
Get off the pear tree that has made you dizzy
And left your vision spinning fast and giddy.
The tree here's self-existence's big 'I,'
So it distorts the vision of each eye.
Descend the pear tree, then your speech and sight
Your thought, too, will flee its distortion's plight.
You'll see this has become a tree of fortune,   3565
With its branch reaching to the seventh heaven.
Once you descend and thus abandon it,
God, through His mercy, starts transforming it—
You've come down with humility, and so
True vision is what God will now bestow.
(If vision were so easy to acquire,
Why did the blest Mohammad once desire
This gift from God: 'Show me how parts appear
To You, all parts found high and low down here'?)
Then afterwards return to that pear tree   3570
Now it's been changed, made verdant by his '*Be!*'*
You've moved your load to Moses with this push,
So that tree's similar to his burning bush.
The fire makes it become so green and lovely;
Each of its branches says, '*I am God*' loudly.
In its shade all your needs are met for free;
This is the working of God's alchemy.
Your self and being are now permissible,
Since there God's attributes are visible.
That crooked tree's now straight and not awry;   3575
It's God-revealing, *roots firm, branch to sky.**

The remainder of the story about Moses.

Through revelation a new message said:
   'Abandon crookedness, *be straight** instead!'
The body's Moses's rod—the command
   Came down to him: 'Throw it down from your hand,
To see its merit and its mystery,
   Then pick it up again by His decree.'
Before being thrown it was mere wood, and when
   He picked it up it was mere wood again.
For lambs' sakes it shook down leaves previously,   3580
   Then it made helpless those who wouldn't see.
Now ruler over Pharaoh's men instead,
   It made their water blood and beat each head.
Famine and death were all their fields produced,
   Due to the locusts that were introduced,
Till Moses selflessly was moved to prayer
   Once he had seen the end of their affair:
'Why all this strife? Why make them impotent?
   These men will not want their own betterment.'
'Follow Noah!' was the Great Lord's reply,   3585
   'Don't look just at the ends shown to your eye.
Ignore that! You're a summoner to the way.
   *Deliver!** This is not in vain. Obey!'
The least good in this is that your persistence
   Will show their stubborn evil and resistance;
God's guidance and His leading some astray
   Will be made clear to all the sects this way.
Existence's aim's that it's manifested;
   By guidance and misleading, it gets tested.'
The Devil keeps misleading you and hiding;   3590
   The master of the path persists in guiding.
When that command for harsh ends went ahead
   The Nile turned into blood, from blue to red.
The Pharaoh came himself, appearing humble,
   Pleading to Moses while he was bent double:
'Don't do what we did, sultan! Not the same.
   We won't give an excuse. We've too much shame.

With every fibre I'll accept your order.
    Don't be too hard on me; I'm used to honour.
Move your lips, trusted one, now in your mercy,   3595
    So they will shut my mouth which was so fiery.'

Moses said, 'Lord, he is deceiving me,
    Though I am Your deceiver actually.
Shall I heed him or give deception too,
    So that branch-puller learns the root's with you?
The root of each deception after all
    Is here: all things' roots are celestial.'
God said, 'That cur's not worth it. You can throw
    A bone to him from distance: let him know
By shaking your rod, so the earth gives back   3600
    What locusts had removed and men now lack—
Those locusts will turn black immediately;
    God's power to change will then be clear to see.
For I've no need for means to exercise
    My power; those means' role is just to disguise,
So that the drug absorbs minds of physicians
    And so astrologers look to the heavens,
And so false traders moved by greed, those who
    Start trade at dawn, scared buyers might be few,
Without a wash—they don't obey as well—   3605
    Craving food they become the fuel for hell.
The vulgar souls are eaten as they eat
    Like lambs that graze on hay and happily bleat—
While that lamb grazes, butchers gleefully say:
    "For us it grazes where it wants today":
When you consume you do the work of hell,
    Fattening yourself up for its sake so well.
Do your own work—eat wisdom's daily bread,
    So your majestic heart expands instead.
Bodily eating blocks this eating, men.   3610
    Soul are the merchants, bodies highwaymen.
The merchant's candle lights up when the robber
    Is burned like firewood and no more a bother.
You are that wisdom, but the rest restrain

And hide. Don't lose yourself. Don't strive in vain.
All lust is like hashish and wine inside,
   Veiling wisdom, leaving men stupefied.
Wine's stupor's not the sole one of the wise;
   Whatever's lustful closes ears and eyes.
Satan did not drink wine, yet he was vile,   3615
   Intoxicated on pride and on denial.
The drunk is he who sees what isn't here—
   As if pure gold, copper, and iron appear.
O Moses, this talk never will dry up.
   Move your lips so the plants will all rise up.'
He did this and that moment all the ground
   Turned green with crops and flowers all around.
Those people then jumped on the food, for they
   Had all seen famine, starving till that day.
For several days they ate till full from feasts,   3620
   Those close, the other humans and their beasts.
But once they'd eaten their fill, then those men,
   No longer feeling need, rebelled again.
The self's like Pharaoh—don't give it relief
   Or it will then recall its unbelief.
The self will not improve without fire's heat:
   Only once iron's red do blacksmiths beat.
The body won't move if not hungry, friend;
   You're beating iron that's cold, so in the end
Its weeping and its wailing desperately   3625
   Do not mean it takes faith's vow earnestly.
Like Pharaoh, during famine it has needs;
   It bows its head to Moses and it pleads,
But when its needs are met, it then rebels—
   The donkey shakes its load off, kicks and yells.
It soon forgets, once its condition's better,
   Its previous sighs and pleas. It won't remember.

A man lives many years in the same town.
   His eyes close once his eyelids both slide down
In sleep—he dreams about another place,   3630
   Forgetting his own home town's every trace,

Though he should think, 'I'm from here. This new city
    Is not my home town, so my stay's just temporary.'
He thinks he's always been right there instead
    As if it's where he had been born and bred.
If the soul won't recall its home, where it
    Was born and lived, don't be surprised one bit.
Since, just like sleep, this world will cover up,
    As clouds will cover stars when you look up.
It's stepped in many cities we could mention   3635
    And their dust hasn't left from its perception,
And it's not striven hard to fully see
    What happened, for the heart's own purity,
So that heart might stick up in view its head
    To see the start and ending up ahead.

The modes and stages of the creation of Man from the beginning.

First he came to the mineral realm, and then
    Moved onwards to the plant's stage, and again
Lived at that stage till many years had passed
    And he could not recall his mineral past.
Then he left that to be an animal   3640
    Without recalling being a plant at all,
Besides this pull towards them he can feel
    In spring when herbs smell sweet, which hints it's real,
Like what pulls babies to their mothers' chests,
    Though they don't know why they're drawn to those breasts,
Like what disciples feel fill up inside
    Drawing them to the Sufi Master's side.
The Universal Intellect's the source
    Of this: the shadow trails its source of course.
The shadow fades in him eventually   3645
    And he attains the strong pull's mystery.
How can another branch's shadow shake
    If this tree doesn't move. That's a mistake.
Then the Creator leads him gradually

From animal rank to humanity.
He moves from realm to realm thus, state to state;
   Now he's intelligent, informed, and great.
His previous intellects he can't remember
   And from his present one he'll transform further,
So he'll escape this one that's full of greed,   3650
   See many other marvellous ones, once freed.
Though, like the sleeper, he forgets his past,
   That self-forgetfulness can't surely last.
He'll be led back to wakefulness again
   And he will mock his present standing then:
'Why did I feel great while asleep—how could
   I have forgotten those states that are good?
How did I not know such grief and afflictions
   Are due to sleep's effects, its false perceptions?'

The world is like the sleeper's dream for sure;   3655
   The sleeper thinks it's real and will endure
Till death's hour should approach him suddenly
   And he's freed from the dark and trickery.
He'll laugh aloud at his past sorrows once
   He sees his everlasting residence.
What you see while asleep, the good and wicked,
   Will be made clear when you are resurrected.
What you did in this world's sleep will be shown
   At your awakening's time, when all is known,
So you won't reckon that the bad deed once,   3660
   While sleeping, won't have any consequence.
On that day, it will turn to tears instead,
   Oppressor of the captives, so feel dread!
And count as happiness when you awake
   The tears and sorrow now and every ache:
You who've torn Joseph's cloak will rise from sleep
   As a wolf, though your slumber is now deep.
Your dispositions have turned wolf-like and
   In anger they tear off your leg and hand.
After death, blood still seeks retaliation—   3665
   Don't think: 'Once dead, I'll flee all tribulation.'

Retaliation we see here's not serious;
    Next to the one there it's a game that's frivolous.
God called this world 'a game' for these same reasons:
    Its retribution's game-like next to that one's.
This one is used to stop war and dissension;
    That one's castration, this one's circumcision.

Explaining that the people in hell are hungry and moan to God: 'Make our daily portions bigger and quickly send provisions to us for we cannot endure any more.'

This discourse could continue in this way:
    'Moses, just let those donkeys graze on hay,
So they get fattened by that, then remember   3670
    That we have howling wolves who feel much anger:
We're certain of our own wolves' howls, and we
    Will make those donkeys their food easily.
Your sweet-breathed alchemy desired to make
    These donkeys human—that was a mistake.
You tried hard with a generous invitation,
    But it was not these donkeys' destined ration.
Let them be covered by the quilt of bounty,
    So heedless sleep will carry them off quickly,
And when they rise from sleep another day   3675
    The cupbearer will then have gone away.
Their disobedience kept you in confusion,
    So they'll taste sorrow during retribution.
Our justice will in this way come to view
    And give each vile and hideous thing its due,
Since that king whom they couldn't clearly see
    Was with them in their lives, though secretly.'

Wisdom oversees your own body too,
    Although it's something that you cannot view:
To its perception you are manifest;   3680
    It sees you still, then move, and it will test.

If the Creator of that intellect
   Is also with you, why should you reject
This fact? A man acts badly, leaving wisdom
   And afterwards his intellect will blame him—
You're heedless of your intellect, but it
   Did not forget you: when it blames you, it
Is present; if it were away instead,
   Could it have blamed and slapped you on the head?
And if your self had really not been heedless,   3685
   How should you have displayed such fervent madness?
Your astrolabe's your intellect and you:
   Being's sun's nearness is traced by these two.
Your intellect's too close for me to write;
   It's not in front, nor left, nor to the right.
How should the king not be near just the same,
   Though mental search can't find ways to this aim.
The movement in the finger's not the kind
   That comes from left, right, from front or behind.
In sleep and death it leaves the finger, then   3690
   At waking's hour it joins with it again.
How does it reach your finger? You are clueless,
   Although without it then your finger's useless.
The pupil of your eye and light for visions—
   Where is their source beyond the six directions?
Creation's world has measurable directions;
   The world of God's command has no dimensions.
When His command's world has no sides or border,
   Then think how far beyond is the Commander!
The Knower and the wisdom were beyond it,   3695
   Wider than minds, more spiritual than spirit.
With Him all creatures have a real connection
   And that connection is beyond description.
The spirit has no joining or dividing,
   But thoughts need both division and uniting.

Pursue what is beyond division now
   Through guides, though it won't quench thirsts anyhow.
Pursue from distance to the origin,

Till manhood's vein leads you to union.
How could mere reason find that great connection   3700
  When it is bound by joining and division?
Mohammad counselled us with his insistence:
  'Do not investigate into God's essence!'
The essence that can be investigated
  Is not His essence if the truth is stated.
That's an imagining, for on this way
  To God a million veils stand in the way.
Each man's attached to one although he reckons
  That this veil is in actual fact God's essence.
The Prophet rebuffed this imagining then,   3705
  So crazy thinking wouldn't mislead men.
Such thinking leads some to lack reverence—
  God made such men fall headlong then at once.
This means he falls down, but he might still reckon
  He has become a most important person.
The drunkard's situation is unsound
  And similar: he can't tell sky from ground.
Go, contemplate His wonders carefully,
  Lose yourself in His awesome majesty.
Seeing His craftsmanship can make you humble,   3710
  So you won't talk about Him and be casual:
Ahmad's '*I can't do justice*' is your answer,
  'For that's beyond all limits one can measure.'

Zo 'l-Qarnayn went to Mount Qaf and asked, 'O Mount Qaf, tell me about the majesty of God's attributes.' Mount Qaf said, 'His description is beyond words, for perceptions become annihilated before it.' Zo 'l-Qarnayn begged, 'Tell of His craftsmanship which you can perceive and can more easily speak about.'

Zo 'l-Qarnayn went to Mount Qaf and saw there
  That it was made of emerald so rare.
Ringing the world, it formed a massive circle—
  He was left stunned by that enormous marvel

And asked, 'You are a mountain, but inform me
    What are the others standing near your glory?'
'These other mountains are my veins, but they   3715
    Don't have my power and beauty the same way.
In every town I have a hidden vein;
    All regions are tied to them like a chain.
When God wants earthquakes somewhere, he tells me
    And I make my veins throb immediately;
With wrath I move the vein for that direction,
    The one to which that place has its connection.
When God says, "Stop!" my vein stops at His will;
    I also rest though I'm in motion still.'
At rest like salve that acts invisibly   3720
    And the still mind while we speak rapidly.
Earthquakes, to those whose brains can't understand
    Are only due to vapours in the land.

*An ant walking on paper saw the pen writing and praised
the pen. Another ant with sharper vision said, 'Praise the
fingers, for I see the skill coming from them.' A third ant
with even sharper vision than the previous two said,
'I praise the arm for fingers are an extension of the arm,'
and so on . . .*

A small ant saw a pen write on some paper
    And told another ant about this later:
'Such marvellous drawings that fine pen composes
    Like basil, beds of lilies, and fine roses.'
'The finger is the artist here instead
    Because it leads the pen,' the other said.
A third ant said, 'It is the arm in fact;   3725
    Those fingers draw strength from it first to act.'
This argument continued in this way
    Until a royal ant began to say:
'The forms do not compose that art seen there,
    Since sleep and death both make them unaware.
Form is like clothing or a staff, you'll find.

Pictures are drawn just by the soul or mind.'
It didn't know the heart and mind without
    God's changing them would be inert throughout;
If He withdrew His grace for just one moment   3730
    The wise mind would do stupid things that instant.

When Zo 'l-Qarnayn found Qaf endowed with speech
    He asked it, 'Would you kindly start to teach,
O mystery-knowing, speaking one, and show
    To me God's attributes, so I can know.'
The mountain said, 'Begone, for that description
    Is too enormous for an exposition,
And for the pen to dare to write down data
    About it with its nib on scraps of paper.'
He said, 'So tell a story that is smaller,   3735
    O lovely, knowing one, about a wonder.'
'Look in the distance scores of miles away:
    With snowy mountains He's filled that long way
Entirely, mountain after mountain, countless;
    The snow's supply is one that is continuous.
One mountain joins the next one that is found
    And snow brings frosty coldness to the ground.
More snowy mountains stretching out for miles;
    Each moment from the storehouse come more piles.
King, if this valley had not been thus placed,   3740
    The heat of hell would have left me effaced.'
View heedless ones as snowy mountains who
    Ensure the wise ones' veils aren't burned up too.
If not for that snow-forming ignorance,
    Mount Qaf would burn from longing's fire at once.
Fire is an atom of God's wrath, in place
    As scourge to threaten harshly all the base.
Despite such wrath that overpowers, you'll see
    His mercy's coolness has priority—
Mystic priority beyond description: 3745
    Have you seen prior and subsequent in union?
If not, that's due to weakness of your brain—
    Next to that huge mine, brains are just one grain.

So blame yourself and not that higher dimension
    And its signs—how could clay birds reach their heaven?
The bird flies in the air and can't rise higher,
    For it was nurtured from lust and desire.
Without a 'yes' or 'no', be stunned today
    Until God's mercy carries you away.
Since you're not capable of comprehending   3750
    If you say, 'Yes!' you'll only be pretending.
Say, 'No!' and by this 'No!' your neck gets cut;
    And wrath will slam your window tightly shut.
But if you swoon and fall down on the ground
    Then God's help will arrive from all around.
Once you feel mesmerized and fall unconscious,
    You'll then say with your mystic tongue, '*Please guide us!*'*
It's mighty, but when you begin to shake
    It may turn soft and moderate for your sake.
The mighty form is for deniers—behind this   3755
    Once you submit, you will receive His kindness.

*The Angel Gabriel showed himself to Prophet Mohammad
in his own shape, and when one of his seven hundred wings
appeared it covered the horizon, and the sun was covered
despite all its radiance.*

Mohammad once asked Gabriel, 'Let me see
    The way your form is in reality—
Show me that clearly, so I look at you
    The way a spectator would like to view.'
Gabriel said, 'You can't bear that spectacle;
    For your weak senses it's impossible.'
'Show me so that this body witnesses
    Our senses' frailty and sheer helplessness.'

Man's bodily senses are weak and infirm;   3760
    Within him, though, his nature's strong and firm.

The body is like flint and steel—inside
    Its attributes can spark fires far and wide.
Fire is produced by flint and steel ingredients,
    But then their child, fire, dominates its parents.
The fire inside rules bodies just the same;
    It rules the body and can light a flame.
The Abraham-like flame within has power*
    With which to overcome a fiery tower.
The Prophet once said enigmatically   3765
    'We're last and first, both simultaneously.'
This pair's form's weak on anvils, yet its store
    Of attributes is greater than iron ore.
Man springs from this world in his form, but in
    His attributes he is its origin:
A gnat can cause his outward form to spin,*
    His inner holds the seven heavens within.

Mohammad asked till Gabriel showed a bit
    Of that might which can make huge mountains split.
A single wing spanned East to West—in awe   3770
    Mohammad swooned due to what he then saw.
Once Gabriel saw him witless due to fear,
    He came to hug him like one very dear.
That awe is only the outsider's ration,
    While friends receive for free this kind affection.
When kings are on their thrones before the hordes
    Near them are scary guards who hold huge swords—
The combination of guard, sword, and spear,
    Which would make even lions shake with fear,
And yells of sergeants with their clubs aloft   3775
    From fear of which the people's souls turn soft—
This is all just in order to make known
    To passers-by their king's there on his throne;
The pomp is for the vulgar people's sake,
    So they're not arrogant then by mistake,
To bring down selfishness in all those people
    And stop conceit from scheming up much evil.
The kingdom's safe from that when there's a king

Who has the wrath to punish such a thing:
Then those lusts die in souls—awe felt when near   3780
   The king prevents bad things from happening here.
Yet in the private banquet he'll go to,
   How could there be awe and reprisal too?
There's mercy and much clemency, not fear;
   Other than harp and flute there's naught to hear.
In war, men bang the drums to drive away;
   In leisure with the chosen harps will play.
The masses face account books for failed actions;
   Companions of the wine-jug fair attractions.
In wartime helmet and chain mail are best,   3785
   While silk and music fit one's peacetime rest.
This discourse could continue out of sight—
   Stop now, *God knows best guidance that is right.*

Mohammad's senses that were transient sleep;
   Under Medina's soil they're buried deep,
But wondrous qualities of his that conquer
   Are on serenity's seat and don't alter.
Bodily attributes are what decline;
   The soul's eternal, that sun will still shine.
It isn't of the East; it is unchanging.   3790
   It isn't of the West;* it isn't fading.
How can one atom mesmerize the sun,
   Or moths make candles witless and undone.
Mohammad's body did decay, so know
   That is what bodies have to undergo,
And sickness, pain, and sleep; the soul is free
   From any similar kind of quality.
I can't describe the soul—if I were able
   An earthquake would make this entire realm tremble.
Senses seemed shaken temporarily?   3795
   Its soul's lion was then sleeping probably.
The lion that's free from sleep was sleeping then;
   It was a meek and scared lion seen by men—
The lion was acting sleepy then instead,
   So that the curs thought that he's virtually dead.

Otherwise who on earth would have the gall
  To steal from weaklings even something small?

Mohammad's body was moved by that vision
  And love of Gabriel's form stirred up his ocean.
The moon's a giving hand with vision's light;   3800
  If it has no hand, that too is all right.
And if Mohammad had spread out his huge wing,
  Gabriel would have been left forever swooning.
Mohammad passed the lote tree's high location*
  And broke the limit too of Gabriel's station.
He said to Gabriel, 'Follow me and fly!'
  'You go ahead. I can't,' was his reply.
Mohammad said, 'Burner of veils, come here.
  I've still not reached my zenith in this sphere.'
Gabriel replied, 'My noble and good friend,   3805
  My wings will burn beyond my limit's end.'
This fainting of the favoured in the chosen
  Brings such amazement, records are all broken.
Mere fainting in this realm is simply play—
  Why won't you rush to give your soul away?
O Gabriel, though you're noble and you're dear,
  You're neither moth nor candle. This is clear:
Once it is lit the candle will invite
  And moth-like souls don't fear being set alight.
Bury this topsy-turvy talk you've said—   3810
  Make lions prey of onagers instead.
Stop up this water-skin of piss you've bottled.
  Don't open up the gibberish you've prattled.
It's idle talk and nonsense with no worth
  For those whose limbs have never left this earth.
Deal with them; don't oppose them now, my dear,
  Stranger, staying in their home now right here.
Give them what they want; try to satisfy them,
  Traveller who's residing now in their realm.
Until you reach the king and joy one day,   3815
  Get on with men from Merv, O man from Rayy!*
Moses, you must speak softly now to teach

This era's pharaoh—speak *with gentle speech.**
Pour water over oil that's boiling hot
    And you'll destroy your trivet and your pot.
Speak softly, but don't say what isn't true:
    Don't be false with soft speech whatever you do.

It's afternoon so cut short this discussing,
    You who enlighten men with your juice-pressing.
Tell the clay-eater sugar is much better. 3820
    Don't be soft; don't give clay to harm its eater.
The soul's speech would have been a mystic garden
    If sounds and words were not what it depends on.
Among the sugar canes, the donkey's head
    Leads many to get thorn-pricked where they tread:
From far away they thought that's what they saw—
    Only a head—like bruised rams that withdraw:
The word's form is that donkey's head you're seeing
    Within the vines of paradise and meaning.
Hosam, O Light of Truth, bring here instead 3825
    Inside the mystic melon field that head,
So after it has been skinned by the butcher,
    This place might let it grow back in the future.
I make the form and you give that a soul—
    No, that's wrong. You make both parts of the whole.
O sun, in heaven they all praise your name—
    Be praised on earth forever just the same,
So that in heart and focus the terrestrials,
    And in their nature too, join the celestials.
Dualism, polytheism, disunion 3830
    Will leave—in real existence there's just union.
When my soul recognizes yours, at last
    It brings back that fine union from the past:
Moses and Aaron may be comprehended
    Like milk and honey, sweet and nicely blended.
But when it recognizes yet denies,
    Denial forms a veil that blocks its eyes.
Many did this and turned from what they'd viewed,
    Angering the moon by this ingratitude.

That's why the bad soul couldn't recognize   3835
   The Prophet's soul and walked off from the prize.
You've read all this. Read '*They would not leave off.*'*
   View stubbornness from infidels who'd scoff:
Before Mohammad's form's manifestation
   Infidels used as their charm his description:
They said, 'Someone like this will soon appear.'
   Their hearts raced thinking of his face with cheer.
They bowed down, praying, 'Lord of all mankind,
   As soon as you can, show him to our kind!'
So they could *ask God for a victory**   3840
   In his name, and defeat their enemy.
Whenever frightening wars were started, they
   Turned to Mohammad's help when they could pray.
And when there was a fatal malady,
   Mohammad's name was used as remedy.
On their path his form entered deep inside
   Their hearts, their ears, their mouths, all open wide.
His form can't be what a mere jackal sees—
   That was derived from it, like fantasies.
If his form should appear on a wall's face,   3845
   Blood would seep from the wall's heart at that space;
His form's appearance would leave it so graced
   That this wall would be spared from being two-faced.
Two-facedness is its flaw that all can see
   Next to pure men's one-faced sincerity.
As soon as they saw him, wind blew away
   Respect and love that they'd shown till that day.
The false coin met with fire and changed in colour
   To black. The heart's one place false coin can't enter.
False coin would boast of yearning for the touchstone   3850
   To throw disciples into doubt when still prone:
The worthless wretch falls in their falsehood's snare;
   This doubt plagues wretched, base men everywhere.
'If this were not real gold,' some would enquire,
   'How come the touchstone was its main desire?'
It wants a touchstone, but another sort
   That won't expose its falseness and comes short.
Touchstones that hide such attributes from sight

Aren't real for they lack mystic wisdom's light.
The mirror that hides flaws on a man's face   3855
    For a mere cuckold's sake here has no place;
It's not a real one—it's a hypocrite.
    Don't seek that mirror, but abandon it!

EXPLANATORY NOTES

PROSE INTRODUCTION
[written in Arabic, numbered by page and line]

4:6 *'God is the best protector ... those who show mercy'*: Qur'an 12: 64, where it represents part of Jacob's speech.

TEXT
[numbered by verse, or couplet]

7 *who belongs to God—Now 'God is for Him'*: from a saying of the Prophet Mohammad.

11 *'Prostrate and draw near!'*: Qur'an 96: 19, in encouragement of those keen to get closer to God through worship.

18 *Find this in the Qur'an now and recite*: the next few verses allude to Qur'an 10: 5, which states that God created and arranged the light of the sun and the moon.

24 *'A mercy to the worlds'*: Qur'an 21: 107, a verse usually understood to refer to the Prophet Mohammad.

33 *The Nile was made of blood ... Moses's saved nation*: a reference to the story about the parting of the waves.

71 *Zayd*: the Arabic equivalent of 'Mr X', a name used to represent a random individual.

109 *'Kill me, O trusty friend!'*: this is a variant of part of a verse attributed to the Sufi poet Hallaj, who was executed in 922 CE.

119 *gushing water*: Qur'an 67: 30, where it is part of a question to deniers of God about the source for water.

133 *Sarsar*: the name given to the wind that destroyed the Aad (see Glossary).

wind to Aad ... For Hud: Hud is the Prophet who had been sent to the Aad (see Glossary).

134 *Simoom*: a devastatingly strong desert wind.

185 *'There's no unevenness found in that space'*: Qur'an 20: 107, an eschatological verse that describes God's razing of mountains and flattening of the earth at the end of time.

186 Heading   *chador*: a one-piece veil worn by women to cover both body and most of the face.

Heading   *'The wiles of you women are tremendous'*: Qur'an 12: 28, as part of Zulaikha's husband's reaction to seeing that Joseph's shirt had been torn from the back.

219 *'Kaafoor' can sometimes be a mere slave's name*: it was common in Rumi's time to call African slaves by names of then precious items, such as 'diamond' or in this case 'Kaafoor', one of the Qur'anic (76: 5) springs in paradise from which the righteous drink.

226 *'I always knew', the sought one clarified*: this is a resumption of the story about the lover whose love was not true, which carried over from Book Three to the start of Book Four.

261 *Praying, 'God's strength!'*: an abbreviated version of the invocation *'There is no strength or power except through God'*, which is recommended in many of the sayings of the Prophet Mohammad, especially when one is faced with extreme difficulties.

281 *'The wicked women for the wicked men'*: Qur'an 24: 26, where it is asserted that the wicked are meant for each other just as the good are meant for each other.

284 *'We see you as bad luck'*: Qur'an 36: 18, where it represents the reaction of unbelievers who reject prophets.

302 *'His sweetheart said…'*: this is another resumption of the story about the lover whose love was not true, which originally carried over from Book Three to the start of Book Four.

328 *'We've sinned, Lord'*: Qur'an 7: 23, the response of Adam and Eve to God after they are blamed for eating from the forbidden tree.

348 *"We have done wrong!"*: Qur'an 7:23, see note to v. 328.

389 Heading   *'The Furthest Place of Worship in Jersualem'*: literally the furthest mosque, or place of prostration, but since it is set in the time of Solomon, 'place of worship', 'worship house', and variants are used. See 'The Furthest Mosque/Place of Worship' in the Glossary.

407 Heading   *'the Believers are brothers'*: Qur'an 49: 10, as part of a passage emphasizing the need for unity among Muslims.

Heading   *'We do not distinguish between any of them'*: Qur'an 3: 84, which stresses the unity between Prophets and their revelations.

445 *'They'll be brought to Our presence'*: Qur'an 36: 32, where it refers to the return of all people to God in the afterlife.

468 *Mina-like perfection*: Mina is the small settlement to the east of Mecca which pilgrims visit during the last stage of the Hajj pilgrimage and stay overnight in tents.

505 *You're drunk Bo 'l-Hasan*: this name is used by Rumi on a number of occasions to refer to a random individual. It does not refer to Bo 'l-Hasan Kharaqani or any other specific individual here.

552 *The way Mohammad smelt that scent from Yemen*: this alludes to a saying of the Prophet Mohammad in which he refers to divine communication with Ovays al-Qarani, who became a follower of his in the Yemen without having ever met him.

607 *Maghrebi a 'Mashreqi' ... sunset sunrise-bright, you see*: the name 'Maghrebi' is based on the Arabic word for place of sunset, while 'Mashreqi' is based on the Arabic word for place of sunrise.

612 *He won't see Prophets ... the light*: Qur'an 66: 8, where it is part of a description of the afterlife.

658 *God turns earth silver for the Resurrection*: this seems to allude to eschatological traditions that God will transform the earth to silver.

675 *'Goodness—this youth is for me!'*: Qur'an 12: 19, where it represents the reaction of the traveller who draws Joseph up from the well where his brothers had hidden him.

724 *God invites to peace*: Qur'an 10: 25, where it is stated among a list of God's bounties to creation.

743 *Sama' is food ... union's ecstasies*: see *sama'* in the Glossary.

764 *'You did not throw when you just threw'*: Qur'an 8: 17, in a passage describing the Prophet Mohammad's actions in battle as being in reality God's actions. This is one of the most frequently cited Qur'anic verses in Sufi discussions of annihilation and subsistence in God.

766 *'God's strength!'*: see note to v. 261.

781 *'Guide my folk! They don't understand'*: a prayer of the Prophet Mohammad, which he made after his teeth were broken by an enemy from among his own Qoraysh tribe.

787 *And what mere birds did to that elephant*: an allusion to the Qur'anic story (105: 3) in which God sends birds to throw down stones at a huge army attacking the Prophet Mohammad's tribe and intent on destroying the Kaaba. This defeat of the army from South Arabia, which even boasted an elephant, is traditionally believed to have taken place shortly before Mohammad's birth in the very same year, and thus serves as a sign that God provided help to pave the way for His Prophet's future success.

825 *That's what accursed Satan did that day*: a reference to the Qur'anic story (e.g. 2: 34) about Satan's refusal to bow before Adam when commanded to do so by God.

851 *Joseph's scent, so inhale it and feel bliss*: an allusion to Qur'an 12: 93–6, which describes the restoration of Jacob's sight by the placing of his son Joseph's shirt over his face as a sign (presumably through its smell) that he was still alive.

869 *'There is no God but He'*: Qur'an 3: 18, as part of a theological statement.

873 *'One ant said'*: Qur'an 27: 18, where Solomon perceives an ant tell others to go indoors in order not to be trampled by him and his army.

888 *As Ayaz used his old cloak and old boots*: a reference to a story about Ayaz, the celebrated favourite slave of Shah Mahmud, who kept hold of his old belongings to remind himself of his humble origins.

901 *'has there come a time?'*: Qur'an 76: 1, the start of a chapter of the Qur'an in the form of a question about whether Man has ever been not remembered.

960 *Water rules out ablution using sand*: according to Islamic law, Muslims may perform their ablutions using sand, but only when water is unavailable.

972 *whose wings are green*: a reference to angels in the Islamic tradition.

1036 *Qoraysh*: the name of the tribe into which the Prophet Mohammad was born in Mecca about 570. The leaders of the tribe rejected Mohammad and forced him out of Mecca, after which they waged war against him and his followers in Medina.

1046 Heading   *'If only my people would know!'*: Qur'an 36: 26, where it is uttered by a prophet in reference to his disbelieving community and the knowledge of the honour and pardon he had received from God.

1047 *We're telling a fine tale we've shared before*: the same story is found in Book Two of the *Masnavi*, vv. 2362 ff.

1057 *'The heart's between two fingers'*: this alludes to a saying of the Prophet Mohammad about the hearts of all men being held 'between two fingers of the Merciful God'.

1089 *'God's earth is vast'*: Qur'an 4: 97, where it is stated to make the point that there is plenty of room on earth for everybody.

1114 Heading   *the Furthest Worship House in Jerusalem*: see note to v. 389 and 'The Furthest Mosque/Place of Worship' in the Glossary.

1120 *'A cord of palms on her neck'*: Qur'an 111: 5, in reference to the wife of Abu Lahab (see 'Bu Lahab' in the Glossary).

1121 *Upon their necks we've placed the cord*: Qur'an 36: 8, in reference to people heedless of God's message to whom He sends His Prophet.

1122 *Whose neck is spared reports on what they've done*: the original refers to birds on shoulders, an Islamic image for the retelling of one's deeds in life on Judgement Day.

1139 *Due to what Abraham did long before*: a reference to the Muslim belief that Abraham and his son Ishmael built the Kaaba.

1170 *'The meaning of "Allah"', Sebawayh said, '...to him instead'*: a reference to the much celebrated grammarian Sebawayh, and the etymological discussion of the unusual word for 'God' in Arabic, 'Allah'.

1179 *Folded inside Your hands*: Qur'an 39: 67, where it describes the heavens on the Day of Resurrection.

1182 *'Through prayer and patience seek out help from me!'*: Qur'an 2: 153, where God instructs the believers.

1252 *'Light upon light'*: Qur'an 24: 35, the famous 'Light Verse' of the Qur'an.

1270 *Ahriman*: demon and force of evil in Zoroastrianism.

1310 *'The sight did not swerve'*: Qur'an 53: 17, where it is understood to refer to the Prophet Mohammad's single-mindedness during his ascension.

1336 *from east to furthest west*: Qur'an 43: 38, where those blind to the remembrance of God express their wish to be as far as possible from the demon accompanying them.

1362 *"Look!"*: Qur'an 30: 50, where it is part of an instruction to witness the way God can revive the earth.

1390 *'Lord, we've done wrong!'*: Qur'an 7: 23, the response of Adam and Eve to God after they are blamed for eating from the forbidden tree.

1394 *'Since, Lord, You led me astray'*: Qur'an 7: 16, where it represents Satan's response to God regarding his own misdeeds.

1419 *dry ablution while streams are abundant*: a reference to the fact that Islamic law permits dry ablution but only when water is unavailable. See also note to. v. 960.

1424 *Like women cutting... Joseph's face*: a reference to Qur'an 12: 30–1, which describes Egyptian women cutting their own hands by mistake after being mesmerized by Joseph's handsomeness.

1454 Heading   *'O you who wrap yourself in your garment'*: Qur'an 73: 1, which is usually interpreted as a reference to Mohammad while receiving his first revelations.

1457 *Stay up at night*: Qur'an 73: 2. See note to v. 1454 on the Qur'anic verse immediately preceding this one.

1467 *"Keep silent!"*: Qur'an 7: 204, where God commands that when the Qur'an is recited it should be listened to with concentration and by keeping silent.

1491 Heading   *A demonstration... is in the story which will be related*: this is an instance when the story the heading promises is not actually related to it.

1523 *cattle-like*: Qur'an 7: 179, where the heedless among Mankind are compared with cattle.

1527 *the lowest of the lows*: Qur'an 95: 5, where it is part of a statement explaining that humans had been debased after originally being created in the highest form.

      do not love the ones that set: Qur'an 6: 76, where it represents Abraham's response to the idea that he might worship a star once he sees it set.

1528 Heading   *'As for those... their disgrace'*: Qur'an 9: 125, where it refers to those who respond negatively to hearing a chapter of the Qur'an rather than becoming followers.

      Heading   *'He leads many astray... also guiding many by it'*: Qur'an 2: 26, where it refers to those who respond negatively to the use of similitudes in the Qur'an.

      Since he had the potential... lost it in the end: this is an example of a heading interrupting a statement, since this verse is a continuation of verse 1529 and would not be correct without it.

1617–18 *So you won't be one-eyed like Satan... Adam's body*: this is a reference to the Qur'anic story about Satan's refusal to bow down to Adam despite being commanded to do so by God (Qur'an 2: 30–6).

1642 *For all the foals... to the others*: this is an example of a heading interrupt-
      ing a statement, since this verse is a continuation of verse 1641 and would
      not be correct without it.

1671 Heading   *'Moses sensed a fear... "Don't feel... superior!"'*: Qur'an 20:
      67–8, in the story about Moses and the magicians at the point when
      Moses doubts he can meet the challenge.

1696 *Bu Mosaylem*: one of the false claimants to Prophethood among the
      contemporaries of the Prophet Mohammad. He is reviled in the Muslim
      tradition.

1705 *Those ancient nations*: a reference to the various ancient communities,
      such as the Aad (see Glossary) which were destroyed by God for failing
      to heed the Prophets sent to them.

1710 *Don't be one-eyed like Satan, who was cursed*: see note to vv. 1617–18.

1726 *'You did not throw when you threw'*: Qur'an 8: 17, which is traditionally
      associated with the Prophet Mohammad's action of throwing dust towards
      the enemy army before a battle which Muslims ended up winning against
      all odds.

1761 *God's earth be vast*: Qur'an 4: 97. See note to v. 1089.

1768 *the spring that's gushing*: Qur'an 88: 12, where it is part of the description
      of the garden of paradise.

1781–2 *The scripture says, 'The Devil... world of the senses'*: this seem to be an
      allusion to Qur'an 7: 27, which describes the Devil and his friends being
      able to see humans without being seen by them.

1803 Heading   *How Abu Yazid predicted the birth of Abo 'l-Hasan Kharaqani*:
      in Sufi lineage chains, Abu Yazid is the Master of Abo 'l-Hasan Kharaqani
      even though their lives never overlapped, since the former died before
      the latter was born. This provides the basis of this story about the pre-
      diction of Kharaqani's birth. Such a connection beyond the grave is
      termed an 'Ovaysi' connection among Sufis, in reference to the story
      about Ovays al-Qarani's resolve in distant Yemen to follow the Prophet
      Mohammad without having ever met him, a story which is also incorp-
      orated by Rumi here.

1816 *Each moment... From Joseph reach your nose, so share one please*: see note
      to v. 851.

1829 *Ramin's scent travelled from the soul of Vays*: 'Vays and Ramin', often
      known as 'Vis and Ramin', is a famous Persian love story. Rumi clearly
      vocalizes the first name as transcribed in the text, rather than as Vis.

      The scent of God arrives now from Ovays: see note to v. 1803, Heading.

1847 *The shirt was kept in Egypt... Canaan's lands*: see note to v. 851.

1852 *The Tablet that's preserved*: see 'Tablet' in the Glossary.

1854–5 *'heart inspiration'... error-free*: an allusion to the sacred tradition in
      which God says that only the human heart can contain Him.

1890–1 *And Gabriel will . . . consumed right here*: in the story about the Prophet Mohammad's ascension, Gabriel expresses this sentiment, acknowledging his limitations as an angel in relation to the perfected human, Mohammad, who can rise as high as just 'two bow's length away from God'.

1983 *Bo 'l-Hasan*: see note to v. 505. It does not refer to Bo 'l-Hasan Kharaqani here, nor the vizier in the previous story. Rather, it is the equivalent of 'Joe Bloggs'.

2007 *'Say, "Come!"'*: Qur'an 6: 151, where God instructs Mohammad to summon his followers and instruct them about what is prohibited to them.

2012 *God said, 'Say, "Come!" Say, "Come!"'*: see note to v. 2007. Rumi repeats the Qur'anic citation here to fill the line.

2024 *They're ranked*: Qur'an 37: 165, where it forms part of the angels' self-description.

2026 *'Come!'*: see note to v. 2007.

2029 *Say 'Come!' Say 'Come!'*: Qur'an 6:151, see note to v. 2007. Here Rumi appropriates God's speech by himself commanding 'Say!'

God invites to peace: Qur'an 10:25, see note to v. 724.

2060 *Just look at Ja'far . . . wings*: a reference to 'Ja'far the Flyer', who was the brother of Ali, and the Prophet Mohammad's cousin. He was martyred fighting bravely for the Prophet's army, for which he was rewarded with the ability to fly in paradise.

2073 *'Be silent!'*: Qur'an 7: 204, see note to v. 1467.

2083 *That king of 'By the star', 'His favour's' ruler*: the phrases in quotes are from Qur'an 53 and Qur'an 80 respectively, both of which are chapters traditionally understood to refer to the Prophet Mohammad. Hence, he is their 'ruler' or 'king'.

2098 *'Yes!'*: Qur'an 7: 172, the much-celebrated passage about the primordial covenant, where Mankind answers 'Yes!' to God's question: 'Am I not your Lord?'

2099 *the seven sleepers . . . inside the cave*: a reference to the story about the seven companions who, together with their dog, are described in the Qur'an (18: 9–26) as hiding in a cave during the reign of the Roman tyrant Decius, and praying to God for protection.

2100 *Egyptian women . . . knives not meant for it*: see note to v. 1424.

2102 *Flying Ja'far*: see note to v. 2060.

2128 *Like the Assassins*: a reference to the followers of Hasan Sabbah (d. 1124) among the Nizari Ismailis, who are commonly referred to as 'the Assassins' due to their tactical use of assassination, often by stabbing as implied here. Rumi refers here specifically to their major fort in Gerdkuh, near Damghan in Iran.

2204 *Kalila and Dimna*: the main characters (two jackals) in the famous Sanskrit book *The Panchatantra*. This presents, in the form of accessible animal fables, practical advice for princes. The Arabic translation, which was named after these two characters, was popular in Rumi's time.

2212–13 *love of the homeland … verified*: a quote from the saying of the Prophet Mohammad: 'Love of the homeland is part of faith.'

2214 Heading   *The mystery of the recitation of specific prayers … ablutions*: while performing their ablutions Muslims traditionally recite specific prayers at each stage of cleansing.

2231 *Love for the homeland*: see note to vv. 2212–13.

2233 *Like Ali scream it in the well below*: this is an allusion to the story about the Prophet Mohammad telling his disciple Ali mystical truths that the latter found so difficult to withhold that he resorted to screaming down the well to avoid divulging it to others.

2283 *'Didn't a warner reach you?'*: Qur'an 67: 8, where it represents a question asked of the people in hellfire to which they respond by admitting that they rejected those who had been sent.

2288 Heading   *'Though they should be rebutted … liars'*: Qur'an 6: 28, where it refers to people once they are before the flames of hell and beg for a second chance back in the world.

2301 *"If they should be rebutted … return"*: see note to v. 2288, Heading.

2382 *God's earth*: Qur'an 4: 97, where the angels ask wrongdoers whether God's earth was not vast enough for them after they explain that they had been oppressed in their lands.

2405–6 *their eyes … white fat … vision*: a reference to the ancient belief that the white of the eyeball is the means of human vision.

2417 *If hills and mountains … from on high?*: this alludes to Qur'an 34: 10, where hills and birds are ordered by God to echo David's psalms.

2419 *The moaning pillar … would depart*: an allusion to the story about the moaning pillar in the Prophet Mohammad's biography, which is also retold by Rumi in Book One (vv. 2124–30).

2420 *If gravel … witness in a hand?*: an allusion to the story about the gravel testifying to Mohammad's Prophethood, which is also retold by Rumi in Book One (vv. 2165–71).

2421 *'The earth was made to quake with awesome might'*: Qur'an 99: 1, from a short eschatological chapter of the Qur'an that describes how the earth will reveal her secrets about what good and bad people have done in their lives.

2423 *She'll share her knowledge … understand*: see note to v. 2421.

2437 *His mercy does prevail above His anger*: a Persian rendering of the well-known sacred tradition in which God says that His mercy prevails over His wrath.

2480 *'They work corruption on the earth'*: Qur'an 5: 33, where it describes wrongdoers who will be punished unless they repent.

2498 *men of the left hand*: Qur'an 56: 41, where it refers to the people destined for hell.

2506 *Till from the West the sun should one day rise*: the sun rising from the West is traditionally believed to be one of the signs that the end of time is imminent.

2523 *Paradise and its four streams*: streams of water, milk, wine, and honey are part of the Qur'anic (47: 15) description of paradise.

2540 *The worm turned to a vineyard straight away*: the Persian words for vineyard and worm are very similar, so wordplay is the reason for this statement.

2541 Heading   *'I was a hidden treasure and I loved to be known'*: part of the well-known sacred tradition in which God gives this statement as a response to the question from the Prophet David, 'Why did you make creation?'

2546 *There's naught for Man but that for which he's struggling*: Qur'an 53: 39, where it appears as part of a theological passage assuring recompense for one's actions.

2562 *sorrow for God's slaves*: Qur'an 36: 30, where it refers to those who rejected the Prophets sent to them.

2585 *As Okkasha swung heaven's gates thus, too*: this alludes to the story presented in the following section of the poem, vv. 2586–97.

2586–8 *Rabe' al-awwal...Safar*: two months of the Arabic calendar, with Rabe' al-awwal following immediately after Safar, as the story indicates.

2595 *Kawsar*: literally meaning 'abundance', this term is used in the first verse of the 108th chapter of the Qur'an, so entitled. Kawsar is also the name for the heavenly fount of grace, which is what Rumi is referring to in this instance.

2614 *'He is for God'...'God is for him'*: see note to v. 7.

2629 Heading   *Story about the king's falcon and the decrepit crone*: a variant of this story is already given in Book Two, vv. 325–78.

2641 *Eyes that don't turn round wounded by a crow's*: this hemistich includes the Qur'anic (53: 17) phrase 'don't turn round', which is traditionally understood to refer to the Prophet Mohammad's sight not turning aside from its focus during his ascension. 'Crow' is introduced here because in Persian it is the same as the Arabic verb for 'turn round/aside' in the Qur'anic phrase.

2649 *Saleh was not hurt—they just hurt his camel*: an allusion to the Qur'anic story about Saleh (e.g. 7: 73–9), the Prophet sent to the Thamud (see Glossary) who hamstrung his she-camel mercilessly.

2655 *(Bu Bakr was Mohammad's...they're similar)*: a reference to the Prophet Mohammad's companion and first political successor, Abu Bakr, as well as his pair of enemies in Mecca, Abu Lahab and Abu Jahl.

2671 *just like you*: Qur'an 18: 110, where Mohammad is told to tell people he is only a human and that God has no partners.

2729 *O Kayqobad-like king with majesty!*: Kayqobad is a legendary ancient Persian king in Ferdowsi's *Book of Kings*.

2734 *Khosrow of our nation*: Khosrow is a legendary ancient Persian king in Ferdowsi's *Book of Kings*.

2784 *fear God with dread!*: this is a frequent command in the Qur'an (e.g. 2: 189).

2832 *Just like the moon... on command*: a reference to the miracle story about the moon splitting at the Prophet's command, which is associated with the 'Moon' chapter of the Qur'an (54).

2876 *'The mother of the book'*: Qur'an 43: 4, where it is used to describe the Qur'an itself.

2882 Heading   *'We did not create... with reality'*: Qur'an 46: 3, a theological statement about God as the Creator.

2907 *Made our forefather His own deputy*: an allusion to Qur'an 2: 30 where God presents Adam to the angels as His deputy on earth, which they argued against.

2913 *Man has naught more... striven*: Qur'an 53:39, see note to v. 2546.

2931–2 *'It's You we worship'* ... *'It's You we seek help from'*: Qur'an 1: 5, from the famous opening chapter of the Qur'an which is repeated in daily prayers and on other important religious occasions.

2948 *'when you just threw you did not throw'*: Qur'an 8: 17. See note to v. 764.

2949 *You've turned to 'no'; settle next to 'except'*: here 'no' and 'except' are the Arabic particles used in the Muslim declaration of faith: 'There is no deity except God.'

2971 *'He taught the names'*: Qur'an 2: 31 in the narrative where God presents Adam to the angels as His deputy on earth. The knowledge of 'the names' is used as a proof of Man's superiority to the angels.

2985 *Cave Companion*: a Persian title of Abu Bakr (see Glossary), the disciple who accompanied the Prophet Mohammad in the cave during the flight from Mecca to Medina.

3030 *'I was a hidden treasure'*: see note to v. 2541.

3044 *And Jesus... started speaking*: an allusion to Qur'an 19: 30–3, where Jesus speaks at birth.

3073 *'Remember God!'*: Qur'an 33: 41, where it is an instruction to believers.

'Return!': Qur'an 89: 28, as part of the verses (89: 27–8) used frequently by Sufis in which God tells the tranquil soul to return to Him.

3086 Heading   *'on the day when... his brother, father, and mother'*: Qur'an 80: 34–5, from an eschatological passage describing the moment after the final trumpet blast.

Heading   *'We gave judgement when he was a youth'*: Qur'an 19: 12, where the youth referred to is John the Baptist.

Heading   '*Be! And it is*': the divine fiat; the way in which God is repeatedly described as granting created things existence, before which they are described as non-existents in a storehouse. See Qur'an 36: 82.

3124 '*Kaafoor*': see note to v. 219.

3125 *The desert… 'fortunate*': references to the inappropriate literal meaning of names used for the desert and lepers respectively.

3172–3 *Dig open… what is necessary*: this could be a part of the poem that may not have been fully edited, because Rumi extends the narrative with reference to a graveyard, but abandons it. However, he effectively warns the reader that he is going to omit anything that is not necessary in what follows, which may arguably explain why it was left in.

3192 '*Say: "I now take refuge!"*': Qur'an 113: 1, the start of one of the shortest chapters of the Qur'an, which takes the form of a prayer for protection.

3193 *The Lord of Every Dawn*: Qur'an 113: 1. See note to v. 3192.

3196 *the blowing witches*: Qur'an 113: 4. See note to v. 3192.

3199 '*God does what He should will*': Qur'an 14: 27, where it is stressed that God will guide or lead astray whomever He should choose.

3204 '*I breathed in him My spirit*': Qur'an 15: 29, as part of one of the variants of the story about God's presentation of Adam to the angels for them to prostrate themselves before.

3206 *His mercy's prior to His wrath*: see note to v. 2437.

3207 *the wedded souls*: Qur'an 81: 7, as part of an eschatological passage best known for its reference to daughters who had been buried alive.

3215 *the ones who drink*: Qur'an 76: 5, where it refers to those in paradise in the afterlife.

3222 *On Joseph's shirt's scent you should now rely*: see note to v. 851.

3242 *closer than his jugular*: Qur'an 50: 16, where it is the proximity of God that is described so emphatically.

3254–5 *Base people… the water*: an allusion to the story of the parting of the waves, which is also referred to in the Qur'an (26: 63).

3258 *His brothers… so angry*: a reference to the story about Joseph and his brothers to which the twelfth chapter of the Qur'an is almost entirely devoted.

3260 '*Say!*': each of the last three chapters of the Qur'an (112–14) are prayers introduced by the command '*Say!*'

3304 '*the pen's dry*': part of a saying of the Prophet Mohammad emphasizing the absoluteness of God's decree.

3311 *True wisdom… Mercury has brought instead*: according to ancient beliefs the planet Mercury delivered wisdom.

3315 *Shine from his breast, like Moses, purest light*: an allusion to the miraculous transformation of Moses' hand mentioned in the Qur'an (20: 22; 28: 132). God causes this transformation in order to strengthen Moses' belief.

3320 *how can one reach Vakhsh?*: Vakhsh, which is currently located in Tajikistan and was traditionally part of the greater Balkh region, is likely to have been the birthplace and/or first home of Rumi.

3328 *"Enter their houses through their proper gates!"*: Qur'an 2: 189, a verse that is often cited as a proverb to mean that one should do things in the proper way.

3332 *He isn't less than Gabriel's horse's hoof*: an allusion to the story about Gabriel's horse causing grass to sprout wherever it stepped.

3334 *That verdure...which Sameri | Put in the calf to have efficacy*: an allusion to the story about the golden calf. Qur'an 20: 96 has been interpreted as meaning Sameri put dust from the hoof of the Angel Gabriel's horse into the calf.

3343 *For 'I am better' were the words of Satan*: Qur'an 7: 12, where Satan argues that he is superior to Adam because he is made of fire rather than clay.

3349 Heading   *'You who believe... God and His messenger'*: Qur'an 49: 1, where believers are told to behave with respect towards the Prophet Mohammad.

3362 *'Today there's no protection'*: Qur'an 11: 43, where it represents Noah's speech regarding the day of the Flood.

3400 *What Joseph saw...was fulfilled at last*: a reference to Joseph's dream about the sun, moon, and eleven stars bowing to him in Qur'an 12: 4–6.

3419 *"Enter among my servants"..."Enter my garden"*: Qur'an 89: 29–30, which immediately follows the oft-cited verses (89: 27–8) in which God tells the tranquil soul to return to Him.

3421 *"Guide us to the straight path!"*: Qur'an 1: 6, part of al-Fateha, the opening prayer of the Qur'an.

3426 *Alast*: the Qur'anic 'Covenant of Alast' (7: 172) is when Mankind testified that God is the Lord by saying 'Yes!' in response to his question 'Am I not [*alasto*] your Lord?' This is understood to have taken place when Mankind was pure spirit in the presence of God, before entering the world.

3463 *chador*: see note to v. 186.

3480 *'They're looking'...they can't see*: Qur'an 7: 198, where it refers to unbelievers, who do not see when they look at those offering them guidance.

3498 *And fruit through Mary's power that's heaven-sent*: an allusion to Qur'an 19: 24–5, where Mary is directed by God to shake a palm tree in order for fruit to come down for her to eat.

3504 *Other than what...naught for men*: Qur'an 53:39, see note to v. 2546.

3514 *"God has bought"*: Qur'an 9: 111, where it is said that God has bought the believers' lives with heaven, in return for their complete devotion to him, even if that means being killed while fighting for His cause.

3517 *kaf simply to | Make kaf ha ya ayn sad's big promise true*: kaf ha ya ayn sad are the group of the so-called 'mysterious letters' with which the nineteenth chapter of the Qur'an, 'Mary', begins. Initially in this chapter the promise is to Zechariah regarding the future birth of John the Baptist despite his old age and his wife's barrenness.

3540 *"Has there once come?"*: Qur'an 76:1, see note to v. 901.

3570 *'Be!'*: the divine fiat; the way in which God is repeatedly described as granting created things existence, before which they are described as non-existents in a storehouse. See Qur'an 36: 82.

3575 *roots firm, branch to sky*: Qur'an 14: 24, where the form of trees and their production of fruit is mentioned as a sign of God's power.

3576 *be straight*: Qur'an 11: 112, where God tells the Prophet to be steadfast as commanded.

3586 *Deliver!*: Qur'an 5: 67, where God tells Mohammad to announce what He has revealed or else he will have not delivered His message.

3753 *'Please guide us!'*: Qur'an 1:6, see note to v. 3421.

3764 *The Abraham-like flame within has power*: this refers to the popular story that Nimrod had Abraham thrown into a massive bonfire. Abraham was miraculously protected by God, who turned the fire into a comfortable rose garden for his sake.

3768 *A gnat can cause his outward form to spin*: this alludes to the story about Nimrod being killed by an army of flesh eating and bloodsucking gnats sent by God.

3790 *It isn't of the East… It isn't of the West*: Qur'an 24: 35, the celebrated 'Light Verse' of the Qur'an.

3802 *the lote tree's high location*: Qur'an 53: 13–18, where, in a passage about Prophet Mohammad's ascension to heaven, it refers to a lote tree marking the utmost reach of heaven and the limits of human understanding.

3815 *Get on with men from Merv, O man from Rayy!*: Rayy is south of modern Tehran and Merv is in Turkmenistan. They are therefore paired to stress their distance apart.

3816 *with gentle speech*: Qur'an 20: 44, where Moses and Aaron are instructed to speak to Pharaoh in this way initially.

3836 *'They would not leave off'*: Qur'an 98: 1, where it refers to disbelievers remaining stubborn until the arrival of clear proofs.

3840 *ask God for a victory*: Qur'an 2: 89, where it refers to Christians seeking God's help before the Prophet Mohammad was sent, but then not believing in the message he brought.

GLOSSARY

Aad one of the vanquished nations referred to in the Qur'an (e.g. 7: 69). They lived just after Noah's time and became proud because of their prosperity, which led them to reject the prophet Hud who had been sent to them. They were destroyed in the end by a roaring wind.

Abd al-Mottaleb grandfather of the Prophet Mohammad.

Abdollah Maghrebi Abu Abdollah Maghrebi was an early Sufi known especially for seeing in darkness miraculously.

Abu Bakr the first successor of the Prophet Mohammad as caliph, and thus considered by Sunni Muslims to have been the first of the four Rightly Guided Caliphs.

Abu Jahl (lit. 'Father of Ignorance') the name traditionally given by Muslims to a mortal enemy of the Prophet Mohammad in Mecca.

Ali Ali ebn Abi Taleb, cousin and son-in-law of the Prophet Mohammad. He is presented in Sufi literature as the first Sufi Friend of God, on account of being Mohammad's disciple. In Sunni Islam he is revered as the fourth Rightly Guided Caliph, while in Shi'i Islam he is the first Imam, or religious and political successor of the Prophet.

Anqa a phoenix-like mythical bird which is believed to reside in the range of mountains known as QAF.

Asaf Asaf ebn Barkhiya, the minister of Solomon identified by exegetes to be the individual who miraculously transports Sheba's throne in the Qur'anic narrative (27: 38–40).

Azrael the Angel of Death, who appears in many stories to signal to individuals the imminence of their death. This is represented memorably in one of the shorter stories in Book One of the *Masnavi* (I, vv. 960–74).

Bayazid Abu Yazid al-Bastami (d. 874), an eminent Sufi from what is now north-central Iran. He is a highly popular figure in Persian Sufi literature, in particular because of the many bold and controversial statements he is reported to have made, such as 'Glory be to me! How magnificent my rank is.'

Belqis the monarch of Sheba mentioned several times in the Bible as well as the Qur'an (27: 22–44), but left unnamed in both these sources. It is in the Islamic exegetical tradition where she is named 'Belqis'.

Boraq the name traditionally given to the Prophet's fabulous mount during his Night Journey from Mecca to Jerusalem, followed by his ascension to heaven.

Bu Lahab (lit. 'Father of Flame') an uncle of the Prophet who was his mortal enemy. He and his wife are condemned in the 111th chapter of the Qur'an, which has also been named *lahab*.

Canaan son (or grandson) of Noah according to various traditions, who is cursed and does not escape the flood on the ark.

Ebrahim ebn-e Adham see EBN-E ADHAM.

Ebn-e Adham Ebrahim ebn-e Adham (d. *c.*777), a much-celebrated ascetic precursor to the Sufis from Rumi's native Balkh. He is portrayed in hagiographies as a prince of Balkh who gave up his life of luxury for poverty and extreme asceticism.

Edris a Qur'anic prophet (19: 56–7), who is traditionally believed to have ascended to a high station in heaven, where the Prophet Mohammad encountered him during his own ascension.

The Furthest Mosque/Place of Worship mentioned in Qur'an 17: 1 as the destination of the Prophet Mohammad's Night Journey, its location is traditionally identified as the Temple Mount in Jerusalem, where Muslims soon built a mosque with this very name in Arabic, 'al-Masjid al-aqsa'. Its mention in the Qur'an has made it one of the holiest sites for Muslims. Also referred to in the text as Furthest Prayer-House, Furthest Worship Place.

Halima Halima as-Sa'diya, the wet-nurse of the Prophet Mohammad during his period spent in the desert as a young boy.

Haman Pharaoh's vizier who is mentioned several times in the Qur'an (e.g. 28: 6–8).

Harut and Marut a pair of fallen angels referred to in the Qur'an (2: 102). According to the exegetical tradition, they looked down on Man for his sinful nature, but when put to the test on earth themselves, they became prone to lust and tried to seduce a beautiful woman; that woman became Venus, while Harut and Marut were imprisoned in a well in Babylon forever as punishment.

Homa a mythical bird comparable with the phoenix, but particularly associated with soaring at the highest levels of the heavens and bestowing kingship.

Jinn supernatural creatures living in a parallel universe to humans and sometimes interacting, according to pre-Islamic Arabian tradition and also in later Islamic tradition.

Kharaqani Abo 'l-Hasan Kharaqani (d. 1033) was a major Sufi from Kharaqan, in the vicinity of Bastam. He is listed as successor to Bayazid Bastami in many Sufi lineage chains, even though he was born after the latter had already passed away, as Rumi's story in this volume illustrates.

Khezr a figure usually identified with Enoch (Elias), and described in the Qur'an (18: 65) as someone who has been taught knowledge from God's presence. He is the archetypal spiritual guide in the Sufi tradition. The Qur'anic story about Khezr (18: 65–82) describes Moses as seeking to become his disciple in order to learn some of his special knowledge. Moses is warned that he does not have the patience required, but is finally accepted on the condition that he should not question Khezr about anything.

Korah a biblical figure (Num. 16) who is also mentioned in the Qur'an (28: 76–82; 29: 39; and 40: 24). As a punishment for behaving arrogantly towards Moses and hoarding his wealth, he gets swallowed up by the earth.

Nimrod a powerful ruler mentioned briefly in the Bible, concerning whom numerous popular stories developed. One of these stories related that he had Abraham thrown into a massive bonfire. Abraham was miraculously protected by God, who turned the fire into a comfortable rose garden for his sake, while He had Nimrod killed by an army of flesh-eating and bloodsucking gnats, including one which entered his brain through his nostrils.

Omar Omar ebn al-Khattab, the second successor of the Prophet Mohammad as caliph, and one of the four Rightly Guided Caliphs. Although his career as caliph was highly successful militarily, he is nonetheless portrayed as a pious ruler who lived simply and ruled compassionately, even introducing a moratorium on the corporal punishment for theft during a famine.

Osman Osman ebn Affan, the third political successor of the Prophet Mohammad and thus one of the four Rightly-guided caliphs of Sunni Islam.

Ozayr Ozayr is usually identified with the biblical Ezra. However, the Qur'anic reference to him (Qur'an 9: 30) makes the claim that he was worshipped by Jews as 'a son of God'.

Ozza the name of an idol worshipped by the contemporaries of Mohammad at the Kaaba in Mecca.

Qaf in medieval Islamic cosmology, Qaf represents a range of mountains that surround the world and mark the border with the spiritual realm.

Qotb literally the 'Pole' or 'axis', this is the title for the supreme Sufi saint of each age, who is the *axis mundi*, the central pivot of the universe and all its interests, towards whom all mystics are drawn.

Resurrection this refers to the end of time when the dead are resurrected and the truth is revealed. Rumi uses this Qur'anic image frequently to represent the experience of mystical enlightenment, through which reality can be witnessed in this life.

sama' the technical term for the practice of meditative listening to music, it literally means 'hearing'. The *sema* of the Whirling Dervishes is among the forms of *sama'* that involve choreographed movements as well as meditative listening.

Sana'i Hakim Sana'i (d. 1131), the author of *Hadiqat al-Haqiqat* ('The Garden of Truth'), which is the oldest work of the mystical *masnavi* genre and a major influence on Rumi's *Masnavi*.

The Tablet in Muslim theology, the Preserved Tablet is where all knowledge is recorded and the source of all revelation, of which the Qur'an is one part.

Thamud an ancient nation referred to on several occasions in the Qur'an (e.g. 7: 73–9; 4: 23–31; 11: 61–8). They hamstrung the she-camel of the Prophet Saleh, which had been sent miraculously by God out of a mountain to test their willingness to share water and pasture. They were destroyed as a result either by an earthquake (7: 78) or a mighty blast of noise (4: 31; 11: 67), or perhaps a combination of the two. More elaborate versions of this story describe Saleh as suggesting that they might be forgiven if they catch her foal, but it escapes and disappears into the mountain.

Tuba tree the tree of paradise is called 'Tuba' in the Islamic tradition.

zekr (lit. remembrance) the remembrance of God by means of the repetition of His names or short religious formulae about Him. This repetition, which is at the heart of Sufi practice in all its diverse schools, can be performed silently, under one's breath, or loudly in an assembly. It is also often performed in combination with *sama'*. Sufis are instructed to give total and uncompromising attention to God during *zekr*, losing awareness even of themselves performing the repetition.

Zo 'l-Qarnayn (lit. 'Possessor of two horns'), a Qur'anic figure (18: 83 101), who is usually identified as Alexander the Great.

The Oxford World's Classics Website

www.worldsclassics.co.uk

- Browse the full range of Oxford World's Classics online

- Sign up for our monthly e-alert to receive information on new titles

- Read extracts from the Introductions

- Listen to our editors and translators talk about the world's greatest literature with our Oxford World's Classics audio guides

- Join the conversation, follow us on Twitter at OWC_Oxford

- Teachers and lecturers can order inspection copies quickly and simply via our website

www.worldsclassics.co.uk

A complete list of Oxford World's Classics, including Authors in Context, Oxford English Drama, and the Oxford Shakespeare, is available in the UK from the Marketing Services Department, Oxford University Press, Great Clarendon Street, Oxford OX2 6DP, or visit the website at www.oup.com/uk/worldsclassics.

In the USA, visit www.oup.com/us/owc for a complete title list.

Oxford World's Classics are available from all good bookshops. In case of difficulty, customers in the UK should contact Oxford University Press Bookshop, 116 High Street, Oxford OX1 4BR.

THOMAS AQUINAS	**Selected Philosophical Writings**
FRANCIS BACON	**The Major Works**
WALTER BAGEHOT	**The English Constitution**
GEORGE BERKELEY	**Principles of Human Knowledge and Three Dialogues**
EDMUND BURKE	**A Philosophical Enquiry into the Sublime and Beautiful**
	Reflections on the Revolution in France
CONFUCIUS	**The Analects**
RENÉ DESCARTES	**A Discourse on the Method**
	Meditations on First Philosophy
ÉMILE DURKHEIM	**The Elementary Forms of Religious Life**
FRIEDRICH ENGELS	**The Condition of the Working Class in England**
JAMES GEORGE FRAZER	**The Golden Bough**
SIGMUND FREUD	**The Interpretation of Dreams**
G. W. E. HEGEL	**Outlines of the Philosophy of Right**
THOMAS HOBBES	**Human Nature and De Corpore Politico**
	Leviathan
DAVID HUME	**An Enquiry concerning Human Understanding**
	Selected Essays
IMMANUEL KANT	**Critique of Judgement**
SØREN KIERKEGAARD	**Repetition and Philosophical Crumbs**
JOHN LOCKE	**An Essay concerning Human Understanding**

	Late Victorian Gothic Tales
	Literature and Science in the
	Nineteenth Century
JANE AUSTEN	**Emma**
	Mansfield Park
	Persuasion
	Pride and Prejudice
	Selected Letters
	Sense and Sensibility
MRS BEETON	**Book of Household Management**
MARY ELIZABETH BRADDON	**Lady Audley's Secret**
ANNE BRONTË	**The Tenant of Wildfell Hall**
CHARLOTTE BRONTË	**Jane Eyre**
	Shirley
	Villette
EMILY BRONTË	**Wuthering Heights**
ROBERT BROWNING	**The Major Works**
JOHN CLARE	**The Major Works**
SAMUEL TAYLOR COLERIDGE	**The Major Works**
WILKIE COLLINS	**The Moonstone**
	No Name
	The Woman in White
CHARLES DARWIN	**The Origin of Species**
THOMAS DE QUINCEY	**The Confessions of an English**
	Opium-Eater
	On Murder
CHARLES DICKENS	**The Adventures of Oliver Twist**
	Barnaby Rudge
	Bleak House
	David Copperfield
	Great Expectations
	Nicholas Nickleby